Time's Legacy

An historian by training, Barbara Erskine is the author of three collections of short stories, and eleven bestselling novels that demonstrate her interest in both history and the supernatural. *Lady of Hay*, her first novel, has now sold over two million copies worldwide. She lives with her family in an ancient manor house near Colchester, and a cottage near Hay-on-Wye.

For more information, visit her website, www.barbara-erskine.com.

BARBARA ERSKINE

Time's Legacy

HarperCollins*Publishers*

HarperCollins*Publishers*
77–85 Fulham Palace Road,
Hammersmith, London W6 8JB

www.harpercollins.co.uk

Published by HarperCollins*Publishers* 2010
1

A catalogue record for this book
is available from the British Library

ISBN: 978 0 00 730228 4

This novel is entirely a work of fiction.
The names, characters and incidents portrayed in it are
the work of the author's imagination. Any resemblance to
actual persons, living or dead, events or localities is
entirely coincidental.

Set in Meridien by Palimpsest Book Production Limited,
Grangemouth, Stirlingshire

Printed and bound in Great Britain by
Clays Ltd, St Ives plc

Mixed Sources
Product group from well-managed
forests and other controlled sources
www.fsc.org Cert no. SW-COC-001806
© 1996 Forest Stewardship Council

FSC is a non-profit international organisation established
to promote the responsible management of the world's forests.
Products carrying the FSC label are independently certified
to assure consumers that they come from forests that are managed
to meet the social, economic and ecological needs
of present and future generations.

Find out more about HarperCollins and the environment at
www.harpercollins.co.uk/green

For Daphne and Tony, with love

And did those feet in ancient time
Walk upon England's mountains green?
And was the holy Lamb of God
On England's pleasant pastures seen?

'Jerusalem', William Blake

As Sure as Our Lord came to Priddy

Local Saying

Be ye therefore wise as serpents

Matthew 10.16

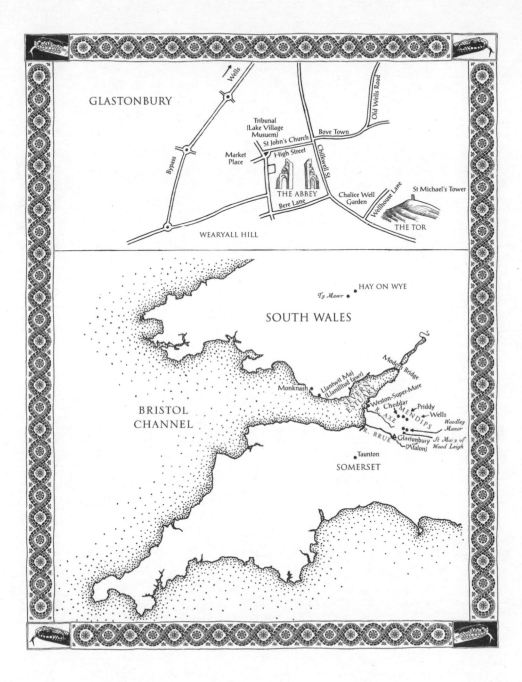

GLASTONBURY

Wells

Tribunal
(Lake Village
Musuem)

Bove Town

Old Wells Road

St John's Church

Market
Place

High Street

Bypass

THE ABBEY

Bere Lane

Chalice Well
Garden

Chillkwell St

Wellhouse Lane

St Michael's Tower

THE TOR

WEARYALL HILL

SOUTH WALES

Hay on Wye

Ty Mawr

Modern Bridge

Monknash

Llantwit Maj
(Llanilltud fawr)

SEVERN
ESTUARY

Weston-Super-Mare

Cheddar

Priddy

Wells

BRISTOL
CHANNEL

R. AXE

MENDIPS

Woodley
Manor

R. BRUE

Glastonbury
(Avalon)

St Mary's of
Wood Leigh

Taunton

SOMERSET

Prologue

An icy wind whipped in across the shallow water bringing with it the first breath of autumn. Pulling her cloak around her, the woman shivered as she gazed out across the troubled cats' paws which raced amongst the reeds around the scattering of small islands. In the sunlight the distant Tor stood out, a rich green cone of a hill, against the sky. From here you couldn't see the terraces, the ancient stones, but you could still feel the power; the sanctity. Her son was out there somewhere and he was in danger. She glanced up. A chevron of swans circled in, the beat and hiss of their wings deafening as they swept in low over her head. They were a sign. But of what? She already knew there was danger. Again she shivered. The message had arrived too late to stop him. Her husband had not returned from Axiom. Her daughter lay tossing and turning with fever in the house behind her. She didn't know what to do. She was alone. She had to act and act quickly.

The birds landed into the wind on a patch of clear water and folded their wings, almost at once breaking formation and calmly starting to feed, their beaks gently sifting through the weed. They had thought they were safe. Here at the ends of the earth they had thought they could hide, but it was too late. He was here. Somewhere amongst the lakes and fens and rivers her husband's twin brother was already heading towards their home, bent on the destruction of everything and everyone she loved.

The wind was blowing, dragging his hair back from his face, shredding the cloud, fretting it into wisps like sea-spume, playing with the tree branches, tossing and shaking the leaves below him on the hillside. Turning slowly he could see the faint shadows race across the surface of the water far below, here shading it to leaden grey, here torn asunder to allow the sunlight through, striking glittering reflections into gold and silver shards.

1

'If I stay I will probably kill him next time he tries to touch me!'
The Reverend Abi Rutherford put down her cup on the small side
table.

'Ah.' David Paxman, Suffragan Bishop of Cambridge, leaned
forwards and set his own cup down beside hers, the action
somehow conveying a sympathy and a collusion which contra-
dicted the anxious frown which had appeared between his eyes.

When she arrived she had seen at once and with relief that
they were not going to sit one on either side of his desk; that
would have smacked too much of headmaster and naughty pupil.
Instead the bishop had waved her to a small sofa near the French
windows which opened onto the terrace. She could smell the roses
on the wall around the door of the beautiful stone-built Regency
house which served as palace to this relatively new bishopric,
created to help cater for the ever-expanding population of Eastern
England. He had poured their coffee himself before sitting down
across from her, from which position he could watch her, she
acknowledged wryly, without seeming to be too intrusive. Fair
enough. After all, it wasn't as though he had summoned her. This
meeting was at her request and he needed to know what it was
about.

'It's all gone terribly wrong. I have to resign.' Her gaze, when
she looked up at him, was first pleading, then defiant.

For a moment she thought he hadn't heard. He picked up his
teaspoon and thoughtfully he began to stir his coffee. It was several
seconds before he responded. 'Are you going to tell me the whole
story?'

'It's complicated.'

'All life is complicated, Abi. That is its challenge.' He glanced
up at last and smiled as he met her gaze. His eyes, she noticed,
were inestimably weary. They were hazel, flecked with green and

very kind and they missed nothing. 'I am sure that you have thought this through with great care, and wouldn't have come to see me without a good deal of heartache, Abi, but I think you are going to have to start at the beginning.'

She sighed. Of course she was. She hadn't expected anything else.

She was an attractive woman; she could hardly deny it, though her looks did not actually interest her much. She was thirty-two years old, tall and willowy, with long, naturally wavy dark hair and clear grey eyes. Confident and with, so she had been told, a great deal of charm, she had arrived in the parish of St Hugh's Juxta Mure to take up the position of curate in a large bustling suburb of north Cambridge, full of quiet anticipation. But, in this day and age, when Anglican priests were in such short supply, she had been not a little disappointed when she found that she was to be given a second curacy instead of her own parish. She had served two years of what amounted to apprenticeship in a rural parish near Huntingdon when she was abruptly called in and told that she was being moved elsewhere. Why? Of course, it was obvious it would be easier to move her as an unmarried woman without the complications of a family already settled into an area, but even so, she was a bit upset. She was after all a mature woman with some experience of the world under her belt – she had spent time both as a history lecturer and a journalist before her ordination – but she curbed her impatience, after she was told that her new posting was in a large, complex community that required the services of at least two full-time priests, that the previous curate had been taken ill and the need for a replacement was urgent. She was mollified to find that there were in fact two churches in the parish. One, St John's, was a large Victorian building in an urban area of run-down streets, seventies developments and building sites which existed cheek by jowl with neat residential pockets and sprawling areas of student flats and bedsits. The other, St Hugh's, from which the whole parish took its name, was a small medieval church on the very edge of the countryside, an area, if the plans were to be believed, soon to be covered in its turn with new developments. For now, though, it retained its quiet rural presence. Abi loved this little church from the first time she visited it and secretly, longingly, almost guiltily, thought of it as, at least potentially, her own.

Kieran Scott, the resident rector and in a sense her new boss, was based at the larger church of St John's. At their first meeting she had liked him immediately. He was a stocky, good-looking man in his early forties, hugely charming, his reddish hair cut to flop attractively across his forehead, his eyes bright and inquisitive, his taste in clothes conservative without being dowdy. He was, she guessed almost at once, a superb administrator, clearly destined for promotion to the upper hierarchy of the church and probably wildly attractive to his female parishioners. He was even attractive, she had to admit, to his new curate, who happened at the moment to be without a man.

On her first day she was greeted at the front door of the Rectory, a three-storey, detached Victorian house next to St John's, by a youngish woman with short fair hair, her slimness accentuated by her close-fitting jeans and a pink floral blouse. 'Hi, Abi. I'm Sandra. Sandra Lang. Kier asked me to be here when you arrived and see you in.' She smiled at Abi with genuine warmth as she helped her up the front steps with her suitcases.

Abandoning the cases in the front hall after tucking away her car, as instructed, in a narrow cul-de-sac round the corner, Abi followed Sandra inside and stared round. The hall was large, lit by an oval skylight high above the well of a wide ornate staircase. A faded floral rug lay in the centre of the floor.

'My goodness, Kieran didn't tell us his new curate was such a stunner!' Sandra said over her shoulder as she closed the front door behind Abi and led her into the spotlessly clean kitchen. She gave her no time to respond to her artless compliment. 'Your flat as you know, is upstairs, but Kieran said to be sure and give you a cup of tea before we go up. He is so sorry not to be here to welcome you himself.'

It wasn't obviously a bachelor's kitchen. On the other hand, how did one know what a bachelor's kitchen would look like? Abi pondered on how to ask Sandra how she fitted into the parish and/or Kieran's life as she pulled up a stool and hauled herself onto it, leaning on her elbows as her hostess produced a plate, arranged biscuits and poured the tea. The woman was obviously very at home in this kitchen and she had, it seemed, been well primed as to what questions to ask. 'We've been so eager to meet you and find out all about you.' Who was 'we', Abi wondered. 'This is your second curacy, I gather?'

Abi nodded. Before she had a chance to elaborate Sandra had rushed on. 'It must be very scary, and a bit odd too, switching parishes like this, mid-term as it were. It's a huge responsibility, isn't it, looking after other people's lives. Why aren't you wearing a dog collar?'

The non sequitur almost caught Abi out. She was in fact dressed very similarly to Sandra, wearing jeans and in her own case an open-necked shirt, navy blue but with a pattern of discreet little grey and white flowers to alleviate the formality. She was rather relieved that the small gold cross she wore around her neck was probably on full view. Her hair, which she had to admit had a tendency to a life of its own, was today firmly tied back with a dark blue scarf. She grinned and shrugged. 'I don't very often. Especially not when I'm off duty and moving house – I prefer mufti. You don't mind, do you?' She met Sandra's gaze and held it firmly.

'Oh God, no. Of course not!' Sandra had the grace to look a little self-conscious. 'And nor will Kieran. He is all for informality.' She paused and cleared her throat. 'How well do you know Kieran?'

Abi grimaced. 'Not at all, really.' Her selection interview had been odd. She had felt as if she were being parachuted in from the quiet countryside to the front line. 'We've met a few times, obviously,' she went on cautiously, 'and I've met most of the PCC – or I thought I had. You weren't there, were you?' She glanced up at the other woman. She had a good memory for faces and she thought she would have remembered this one. The wistful pallor, the large intense eyes, the slight air of something like anxiety. But anxiety about what? Was Sandra just shy or was there something else there? Resentment of another woman on her patch perhaps. It was something she must be ready to recognise and deal with.

As if reading her thoughts, Sandra smiled. 'You must be wondering about me. I've been acting as a sort of parish secretary, coming in a couple of days a week to try and help Kieran keep his head above water. That was why they thought he needed another curate at once. This is a large parish.' She was still smiling. 'Good place for curates to launch their careers.'

8

Abi nodded. The bishop had warned her she would find it tough. He had warned her it was a busy parish, and had there been a hint of something else? If there had, it hadn't been spelled out for her. She had pushed the thought aside. 'Kieran's not married, is he,' she went on after a minute. 'I suspect wives usually end up doing a lot of the stuff that curates do. Not the getting trained part, obviously, but helping with all the other duties. The vicars' wives I know work terribly hard.'

Sandra nodded. 'They call clergy wives unpaid curates, don't they.' She gave a curiously cynical laugh. 'Well, if Kieran marries his current squeeze I think he will be unlucky in that department.'

Abi waited for a further comment. It did not come. Instead Sandra pushed back her cup and stood up. 'Let me help you haul your cases up to the flat. It's a bit of a climb, I'm afraid. Then I will have to leave you to settle in. I have somewhere to be and Kieran will be back soon.'

Running down the stairs a little later, Sandra let herself out of the Rectory, fished in her pocket for her car keys as she paused on the front steps and, almost without realising she had done it, turned to look up at the top window. There was no sign of Abi. She shook her head sadly. Poor woman. She was going to find it very tough here. Not only was there a hard core of the anti-women-priest brigade in the parish, but she was going to have to work closely with Kieran. She took in a deep breath and exhaled sharply. Well, presumably she had been forewarned why the last curate had left so suddenly. The poor man hadn't been able to cope at all with Kieran's – she hesitated, trying to think of the right word – demons, that was it. Abi certainly looked competent, if a little bit – Sandra paused as she ran down the steps and bent to insert her key into the door of the spotlessly clean black Punto parked at the kerb. Wild. That seemed to cover it. She climbed into the car and sat for a moment, staring ahead of her through the windscreen before she inserted the key into the ignition. Kieran could have cleared his diary to be here this afternoon. Instead he had chosen to go to the far side of the parish and attend a meeting which he would normally have gone to great lengths to avoid. She frowned thoughtfully. Why had he asked her to come in to welcome Abi instead of being here to do it himself? Was it to reassure his new curate in some way that everything at the Rectory was as it should be?

Turning on the engine she pulled away from the kerb, shot up the street and turned into the main road. In the course of the next day or so she would have to come back and go through all the paperwork with Abi. Now there was someone else to help with organising the parish she was going to hand it over with as much speed as possible and good riddance. She glanced in the mirror and flicked her indicator. Why had Kieran chosen someone like that to work with him? As far as she knew there had been three other candidates for the curacy. At least two, according to Bill Friar, one of the church wardens, had been far more suitable than this woman. For a start they had all been men. She pulled the car into a side street and slowly drove towards the far end, searching for a parking space. Kier knew there was going to be a lot of resistance to a female priest in the parish. He should have told the bishop. Surely he hadn't chosen her because she looked as though she would make a good secretary?

Abi was nothing like she had expected. If she had been an older, less good-looking woman, someone with a good dollop of experience under her belt, she might have been acceptable in the parish, but she was young, modern and, Sandra sucked in her cheeks, she gave the impression that she was pretty uninhibited. She was not going to be easily intimidated. She saw a space, slammed on her brakes, put up a finger to the driver behind her who had hooted wildly having spotted the same place, and shot in backwards, parking neatly with only inches to spare either end of the car. 'There wouldn't have been room for you anyway,' she muttered under her breath as the other driver yelled something rude at her, luckily muffled by his closed window as he accelerated up the street. She hoped he wouldn't come back for revenge if he didn't find somewhere else to park.

Climbing out, she locked the car and headed across the road towards her house. She would give a very great deal to know what Kier's girlfriend, Sue, would say about it when she first clapped eyes on the new curate. Especially if Abi was wearing those jeans when they first met.

*   *   *

10

Once upstairs, Sandra gone and her own front door safely closed behind her, Abi stood still, looking round with a sense of enormous pleasure. Her domain consisted of a small bedroom, slightly masculine in its furnishings, but neat and still smelling faintly of carpet shampoo, a fairly modern bathroom, a kitchenette and an attractive little sitting room with a view across and between the roofs towards the distant spires of the centre of Cambridge itself. There was a comfortable two-seater sofa, Ikea, she suspected, a small easy chair and a desk which she immediately dragged up to the window so she could stare out at the rooftops of the city as she sat in front of her laptop. It probably wasn't a good idea to have such built-in distraction in her work space but the thought of sitting there gave her a huge amount of pleasure. There was only one problem that she could immediately identify: the flat felt melancholy. She paused and looked round. Yes, it was overwhelmingly sad. A definite presence seemed to hang about the rooms. She sighed. Being sensitive to atmosphere was not always a blessing, but at least she knew what to do about it.

She focused on it for a moment and shook her head. Not a ghost. A residue. Someone had spent a lot of time here filling the room with unhappy thoughts. She could sense misery, loneliness and resignation and maybe, fear. She sent up a quick prayer of comfort for her predecessor, if it was indeed him, resolving to hold a healing ceremony that very evening to cleanse and bless the place, then over the coming weeks and months, to fill the flat with flowers and music and, hopefully, laughter.

Kieran arrived about an hour later full of apologies for not being there to meet her. He was formally dressed, including the dog collar, and looked exhausted as, having shaken hands and welcomed her again, he followed her into the sitting room and threw himself down on the sofa. 'This is the trouble with a twenty-four hour job,' he said wearily. He smiled. 'So, Sandra looked after you?'

Abi nodded.

'And you are ready to start work tomorrow?'

Abi sat down opposite him. 'I'm looking forward to meeting everyone.'

'And they are all looking forward to meeting you.' The easy warmth which she had remembered from their first meeting was immediately reassuring. 'If you shadow me for a few days, just to find out who is who and what is what, then we can decide what part of the load you can take over.' He leaned forward, his elbows on his knees and held her gaze for a moment. 'I'm going to throw you in at the deep end, Abi.'

Walking into his study on the ground floor of the Rectory half an hour later, Kier sighed, throwing himself down at his desk. He glanced at the answerphone, saw the number six flashing reproachfully and reluctantly he reached forward to press the play button.

'Kier? Where are you?' The woman's voice, exaggeratedly patient, was punctuated with a theatrical sigh. 'Why don't you answer my calls?'

Sue.

She knew why. He had been out all day, that was why.

Two calls from parishioners followed, both distressed, both needy, then a second from Sue. The last two were silent.

He put his head in his hands, running his fingers through his hair. For a moment he was tempted to ignore her. Let it go for tonight. She knew what he did, she knew the pressures, the hours, the battles he was fighting with work, the two parishes, the mess left behind by Luke. But looking on the bright side, that was about to change. His thoughts strayed to his new curate, upstairs in her flat, the smile of welcome she had given him, the suitcases and boxes and bags strewn around the room, as yet unpacked. The glass of wine she had offered him, the way she had thrown herself down on the chair, crossing her legs in the slim-fitting jeans, and casually pulled off the scarf, shaking the long wild hair free on her shoulders.

He frowned. She was new to the job and obviously still a bit of a free spirit. Time and hard work would cure both character traits and put her on track to being a useful member of the team. He thought back to the interviews before they offered her the position. Enquiries about partners, children, commitments. She was an only child; parents alive and active, so not needing extra help. No partner, no children. One fairly long-term relationship, with a man – he remembered her mischievous smile as she recognised their delicate probing as to her sexuality – no girlfriends in the wings, then, though one glance at her could have told anyone who was interested she was no closet lesbian. It appeared that she

12

had had just the one long and loving relationship which had been brought with mutual agreement to an end when the guy had been offered a job in Australia which he found he couldn't, hadn't wanted to, refuse. If she had gone with him it would have put an end to her plans and dreams. They had talked endlessly apparently, and discovered at last that the relationship wasn't strong enough or deep enough to hold them together. They parted sadly but amicably. Since then, no-one. He pondered the point again and decided that this was probably true, for, as far as he could gather, no-one had accompanied her this afternoon to help her move in. Please God she was as uncomplicated and competent as she seemed.

Slowly his hand strayed to the phone. Parishioners first. Then Sue.

2

The little church of St Hugh's was tucked away on the edge of the sprawling urban parish up a long deserted country lane. Wedging the door open to let in as much light as possible next morning, Kier ushered Abi inside, then found himself as usual tiptoeing up the aisle between the old oak pews as though afraid someone would hear him. Ridiculous. As though there was someone to hear. He paused, listening. The M11 was less than a couple of miles away and with the wind in the right direction one could hear the reassuring roar of traffic, but on days like today, with no wind at all, he could hear nothing. The silence in the old stone building was profound and it disturbed him. He found himself clenching his fists. It was only in this one place out of the entire parish, that his childhood nightmares surfaced, the certainty that from time to time he could see things, people, hazy images around him; images over which he had no control. He hated it.

He ran a finger round the inside of his dog collar, feeling it suddenly uncomfortably tight. Any day now permission would arrive from the diocesan office, allowing him to tear the guts out of the church, burn the pews, open everything up so people could use it for meetings, for a playgroup, for line dancing, for a farmers' market for all he cared. Anything to chase out the ghosts. He glared up at the window over the altar. No chance, sadly, of getting rid of the medieval stained glass and replacing it with something cool and clear, which would let in the light. He sighed. Almost as though someone, somewhere had registered his thoughts he watched a beam of sunlight throw a cold blue wash onto the ancient paving slabs at his feet and he shivered violently.

'So, how do you like it? It's a bit of an old dump I'm afraid.' He grinned at Abi. She had been standing staring round the little church with an expression of bemused delight. He shook his head. Until the glorious day came when he could deal with the place,

Abi could take the services here. That was one thing she could usefully do where hopefully she couldn't do any harm and who knows, perhaps she could do something about the atmosphere of the place. One of the things that had attracted him to her, over the other candidates for the curacy, was the fact that she had some kind of indefinable aura of peace about her. If the nightmares got out of hand, he had felt at once, she would know what to do.

There was a sound behind him in the corner and he spun round, his heart thudding with fear. There was nothing there. It was probably a timber flexing. Wood expanded and contracted. That was one of the problems with old buildings. They made noises all the time. He closed his eyes and breathed a quick prayer. There was no place for superstitious nonsense in his rigid discipline. The structure of his Church did not allow ghosts, spiritualism, mumbo jumbo. His beliefs, carefully honed and pared to a minimum, had been constructed to protect him from those whirling shadows. They kept him safe. And sane.

Unfortunately Abi was completely unaware that her new boss had spotted some kind of peacefulness about her, and that he had not asked her to join the team for her opinions, so almost from the start they argued. A lot. The truth of the matter was that very quickly she began to find his churchmanship sterile and rigid and totally unappealing; it was austere, verging on the puritan. 'Can't you see, Kier, how much the people long for love!' She shoved her unruly hair back and clamped it into its clips. 'The love of Jesus and also a vicar who shows that he or she cares. They want informality these days. Joy.'

Kier shook his head patiently. 'What these people need is discipline. Without that they are lost. You are too emotional, Abi. You must keep all this passion under wraps.'

Was he being the tiniest bit patronising? She thought so. 'What about bringing out the mysticism of the Eucharist? That would appeal to so many people here.'

Once more he shook his head – a habit which was soon driving her wild with fury. 'This is a puritan county, Abi. We don't do mysticism.' He glanced at her and for a moment she thought he was going to say something else. She waited for yet another criticism, but it didn't come. At least not then.

The stresses and strains of the job were a shock, it was so very different from her first curacy. There, the Rev Martin Smith, the training incumbent, had been at pains to help and train her in parish work, to encourage her, and a year into her deaconate, when she was at last made a priest, to stand slowly back, encouraging her to find her feet. Kier was from the start very different. He was, she had seen at once, one of those vicars who saw his training role primarily as a chance to obtain the services of an assistant, while at the same time laying down the law as to the way he felt his curate should behave and what he or she should believe. The churchy bit, to which she had so looked forward, the services, the prayers, were saved for Sundays – Kier said there was no appetite for more at the moment and in church her role was definitely subordinate. She was allocated some of the prayers and allowed to help with Communion. Apart from that there was little she was allowed to do.

Sitting apart from the congregation, in a special chair next to the choir stalls, she was able to watch him. His easy charm made him wildly popular, particularly as she had suspected amongst the female sections of his congregation and St John's was packed for each of the two Sunday services. What the men – about a third of the congregation – thought of him, she wasn't sure. It was the women who adored him. There were few children; no teenagers. Hardly any young people. It was as though he was afraid of anyone or anything getting out of hand.

It was different at St Hugh's. It was a pretty church and she loved it, but at once she had sensed his dislike of it. It puzzled her that he seemed so uneasy there. To her the atmosphere seemed warm and accepting. The congregation was however tiny and to her disappointment after several weeks she had still not managed to make it grow very much although she was beginning to make some inroads. Kier came and listened to her sermons once or twice, sitting at the back near the door, and he took notes. His comments made her furious. He criticised her for her humour and her warmth. This was not what the people of the parish wanted, he said firmly. They needed guidance. Rules. Threats. Her pleas that this was not the Christianity she recognised were met by a look of pained surprise and she had to let the matter go, curbing her frustration. Perhaps he was right. Perhaps they didn't like her. If there was going to be a time and a place for her views they would have to wait until she was given her own parish. She was here to learn. To watch. She knew she was probably being arrogant, that perhaps he was right in his approach, but still she was finding it all very tough. And puzzling. Why was the flamboyant, confident rector of St Hugh's afraid of this little church?

Abi's flat had its own front door and was self-contained, but to reach it at the top of the main staircase she had to let herself in to the front door of the Rectory and walk through the ground floor hall of the house, onto which opened Kieran's study, kitchen and sitting room, then up to the first landing onto which opened his own bedroom, two spare rooms and his bathroom. Only when she reached the next flight of stairs did she begin to feel that she was certain of any privacy. Almost never, when he was working at home, which he often was, did she manage to reach this bit of her domain without him hearing her and popping out for a word.

At first it was reassuring and almost without her noticing it a tentative friendship had begun to develop between them. As long as they kept away from contentious issues they got on well and she was, she realised, not entirely reluctantly, falling more and more under his spell.

Kieran, not content with greeting her and asking after her day, from time to time invited her into the kitchen for a coffee or a glass of wine or sometimes a quick bite of supper when she returned home in the evening. It allowed them to review the parish work and compare notes about some of Abi's outstanding problems of which there were many. It allowed them to become friends and even, a little, to flirt.

Kier kept the weddings, baptisms and funerals, for himself. Abi's share consisted of counselling, confirmation classes, hospital visits and all the secretarial work, to which after half an hour's handover period Sandra had abandoned her. It was as much as she could cope with. Life had become very tiring and stressful.

One aspect of her job, the most important bit that Kier was prepared, in fact almost eager, to hand over, had been the home visits. Over this he was a brilliant delegator and although anxious to prove she could do her share and rise to every challenge he threw at her, she found herself eventually buckling under the load of work.

One wet evening she had returned to the Rectory feeling

unusually low when Kieran put his head round the kitchen door as he heard her key in the lock. He invited her in and she found herself to her surprise pouring out her heart to him. 'Could you take over some more of the home visits for a week or two?' she pleaded as she flopped onto a stool at his kitchen counter. Outside the rain was pouring down and it was growing prematurely dark. Her hair was wet through and she thought she was coming down with a cold. 'I just don't think I can get round to everyone on my list this week,' she added wearily. 'It would give me a chance to catch up on some paperwork and some sleep.' She couldn't remember when she had last had a night in on her own and as for a private life, no chance.

Kieran turned from the sink where he was rinsing a couple of wine glasses under the tap. 'I didn't realise you were so tired.' He frowned. 'I suppose I keep forgetting you are new at the job.' He smiled. 'You are so good with people, Abi, I've been taking advantage of your good nature without realising it.'

She shrugged, fighting the reflex reaction of denying that she couldn't cope. 'I suppose it does take a while to get used to the hours. And the misery and the deprivation and the hostility. No peace for the wicked!' She forced herself to smile at her own feeble attempt at a joke. Her throat was sore and she felt shivery as he put a glass down before her and poured out the wine.

He stood in front of her for a moment, anxiously studying her face then he reached out and put his hands on her shoulders. 'I'm sorry, Abi. I've been selfish. I'll take over the home visits for a bit. Of course I will. I wanted you to experience the realities of this job first hand as soon as possible. I wanted to make sure you understood what the church is all about. I thought if you saw the worst at once, in a sense it could only get better. That was stupid of me. I should have seen it was all too much for you.' He paused. Then he leaned across and dropped a small dry kiss on her forehead. It was avuncular, she told herself firmly, suppressing a quick shiver of pleasure. His action had conveyed nothing more than affectionate sympathy.

Which didn't in the event last long. Within a few days he had gently suggested she resume her duties and she was working as hard as before.

*   *   *

18

Wednesday, Abi had discovered, was the day the curate visited the sick and lonely. As she found herself wearily climbing the stairs of a six-storey concrete low-rise off a shabby noisy street half coned off for repairs, she realised this would be her third visit of the day, her fourth in a month to this particular address. She wrinkled her nose at the unedifying odours coming from the suspiciously damp corners on the landings and turned at last to the final flight.

Ethel Barryman's door was blistered and scarred. She could see from the marks that the lock had been replaced at least twice. There was no bell. She raised her hand and knocked sharply, wincing as her knuckles met the roughened wood. The door opened so quickly she wondered if the old lady had been standing on the other side, waiting for her.

'Come in, dear.' Ethel was small, wizened and frail, her face a transparent white, her hair thin, the remains of an ancient perm snaking through the faded hennaed strands.

In the sparsely furnished living room the table was laid with a white lace cloth on which stood a teapot, a plate of biscuits and two porcelain cups without saucers – those had been smashed by the last pair of thugs who had broken in, seemingly just for the sheer joy of doing it as there had been so little to steal. 'For after.' The old lady smiled.

Abi nodded. 'Is your granddaughter still doing your shopping?' She unslung her bag from her shoulder, in it the tools of her trade: small brass candlestick, candle, little cross on a base. Little box containing the necessities for Communion.

'She's good to me,' Ethel nodded. 'Comes twice a week. Sometimes more. And there's Angela, downstairs. She gives me a hand when the pain is bad.' Her eyes filled with tears and she turned away sharply. 'Silly bugger me! Think I'd be used to it, by now.'

Abi smiled gently. 'No word yet about a place at the hospice?' She didn't need the shaken head to know the answer. 'Shall we pray together?' She could feel her hands heating up. The urge to lay them on the woman was overwhelming. The need to draw away the pain, to replace it with gentle cool healing.

She laid out the little cruet, containers of bread and wine and lit the candle. Then she moved over to rest her hands on the old lady's head.

19

When the short service was over it was Abi who made the tea. She glanced at Ethel with a smile. The old lady had relaxed. The pain had gone from her eyes. 'You're a good girl, Abi,' Ethel said after a while. 'I still can't bring myself to call you vicar!' She looked up at Abi, her face full of lively humour. 'Come and see me again soon.'

'You know I will.' Abi dropped a kiss on her head as she left. From the doorway she turned and raised a hand in blessing.

The next day Kier told her that Ethel Barryman was dead. Her granddaughter had found her in the chair where Abi had left her.

Abi stared at him in shock. 'But she was better! She was cheerful.'

'You gave her Communion?'

Abi nodded.

'Then you did your best. It's part of your job, Abi. You'll get used to it.' He patted her arm before opening a file on his desk, pulling out another address. 'Go and see this woman next. Molly Cathcart. Constantly whingeing. Real fuss pot. Wants attention all the time.' He groaned.

'But Ethel –' Abi was still thinking about the old lady's gentle smile. 'Can I take her funeral, Kier? I'd like to.'

He shrugged. 'I'll see what the family thinks. They may prefer me.'

She didn't argue. What was the point.

Abi met Sandra in town one Monday a couple of weeks later. Mondays were supposed to be Abi's day off and she had promised herself time for a trip to visit Marks & Spencer. They talked casually for a few minutes on the pavement then drifted across Sidney Street, dodging through the crowds to find a coffee shop. Sandra ordered coffee and teacakes for both of them then she sat back and looked at Abi closely. 'So, how are you coping up at Chateau Scott?'

Abi smiled uncomfortably. 'All right, I think. It's hard work.'

'You've lost weight.'

Abi nodded. 'I often don't have time for meals. So this is a special treat. Thank you.'

'I suppose he's making you chase around all the hopeless cases?'

Abi frowned. 'No-one is hopeless,' she said uncertainly.

'You knew he had a curate before, didn't you?'

Abi nodded again. 'Curates move on.'

'Luke had a nervous breakdown. Overwork.'

That had explained the atmosphere in the flat. Abi eyed Sandra thoughtfully.

'He's a bit of a control freak, Kieran,' Sandra went on. 'Things have to be done his way. But I expect you've discovered that. I suspect you are a tougher cookie than poor old Luke.'

Abi sighed. She had prayed for the young man and blessed him, filled the rooms with flowers and the sad echoes had gone. He had gone on to a parish the other end of the country and she had heard through the grapevine that he was happier now that he was no longer working with Kier. She had been told only that they had not been compatible; not why. 'Yes,' she said thoughtfully, 'I expect I am a lot tougher cookie than him.'

'I didn't mean that in a bad way.' Glancing up, Sandra smiled apologetically. 'I just thought I should drop a hint.' She took a deep breath. 'I heard you'd been to visit Molly Cathcart.'

Abi nodded. The coffee arrived and there was a pause as they each took a sip.

'She's much better than she was,' Sandra went on.

Abi nodded. 'I felt so sorry for her. She's in so much pain with her rheumatism, and she's all alone in that small flat.'

'You prayed with her, I hear.'

Abi nodded. 'That's part of the job.' She helped herself to a toasted teacake and reached for the butter.

'And you gave her healing.'

Something in Sandra's tone made Abi look up. Sandra shrugged. 'Be careful, Abi. There are people round here who pretty much equate healing with witchcraft. Kier is one of them.'

Abi stared at her in astonishment. 'But the ministry of healing is part of the job,' she protested.

'Not in Kier's book.'

Of course. She should have guessed. Besides the heavy work-load dumped fairly and squarely on her shoulders, the reality of confronting, time after time, parishioners who felt that a female vicar was something between the short end of the wedge, a witch and Satan's little helper had hit her hard. It just hadn't occurred to her that Kier might be one of them.

The voice of one of her lecturers at college echoed in her head for a moment. 'Abi, remember, although more than half of all the clergy being ordained today are women, there are still a lot of people out there who are suspicious of them, not least a good proportion of the other clergy!' How right he had been! She thought back over the first months of her curacy here and she sighed. It was all so much harder than she had ever imagined it would be.

She confronted Kier that evening. 'Why didn't you tell me that you disapproved of healing?'

He glanced up at her. She had cornered him this time, walking into the study where he was seated before his desk. The room was warm, lit by the last of the sun and its light was catching his hair, turning it a deep coppery red. He looked up at her and laid down his pen, carefully aligning it with his blotter. The computer was on a side table on the far side of the room. Beside it piles of letters and papers were arranged in neat sequences, graded by size. 'It did not occur to me that it would be something you would attempt,' he said carefully. 'When I began to receive reports, I didn't believe it at first. I assumed that people were misinterpreting your zeal for prayer.'

'Has someone complained?'

He nodded. 'I'm afraid so. It has reinforced the natural aversion some parishioners still feel towards a female priest. I'm sorry, Abi. I should have mentioned it. I just hoped you would realise that it was not appropriate.'

'But it is appropriate! It is what Jesus taught us to do. It is what I learned at college. I was encouraged to do it!' She was furious.

'People round here don't like it, Abi.'

'Ethel liked it. So does Molly Cathcart. It has helped her. She was healed. She has been outside for the first time in months.'

'And you take credit for that healing, do you?'

'Yes I do. I'm the only one who has even bothered to go and see her apart from her carer!' Abi paused. 'I mean, no. Of course I don't take credit for it. That was God. But I was the one who made it happen.'

Kier raised an eyebrow. 'Did you use your magic wand?'

There was a moment of silence as Abi registered the cold sarcasm in his voice. 'How dare you!' For a moment she wondered how she would stop herself hitting him.

'I dare, Abi, because it is my job to care.' There was a carefully modified touch of sadness in the wry smile. 'To put you back on course if you stray. You're very new to the life. You find it glamorous and exciting. Of course you do, that's natural. But you have to stay within the accepted parameters. You have to stay in control.' He clenched his fists, then forced himself to relax them again. 'We pray if people are ill. Laying on healing hands is not acceptable in my parish I'm afraid. End of!' He stood up. There was a moment of silence as he looked at her. 'Anger suits you, Abi, if you'll pardon the cliché! It makes you look quite beautiful.' He reached forward and playfully tugged at a lock of her hair. The clips that normally kept it restrained on the nape of her neck had come free and a heavy lock had fallen across her shoulder. 'We are going to have to tame you, I can see.' She jerked back out of his reach. 'That hair is a bit too wild, isn't it. Perhaps it would be better if you cut it.'

She stared at him. 'I will do no such thing!'

'Then keep it under control, Abi. It makes you look far too enticing.'

She thought long and hard that night up in her flat as she stood at the window looking out across the rooftops. So, healing was not acceptable and neither it seemed was her hair. She shivered.

She had first discovered she had what was, for the want of a better term, the power of healing, when a fortune teller at a fairground had told her so when she was sixteen. The old gypsy in a colourful caravan had taken her hands and scrutinised them for several seconds, then she had shaken her head as though puzzled by the wonders she found there and begun to speak with, as it turned out, quite remarkable accuracy. 'You will have a life of service, dear,' the old woman had said. The great black gaping holes between her teeth gave her the expression of a storybook elf as did her mischievously sparkling eyes. 'You are a sensitive and you have healing hands. I can feel their power. You must train yourself to use your powers for good. It is too easy to go to the bad! You will have the potential to do so much for people.' Abi had been a bit miffed at the time. She bet herself that the woman said that to everyone and that was not what she wanted to hear. She wanted to hear about future romance. The old woman, effortlessly reading her thoughts, had sighed. She looked again at

Abi's hand, tracing the lines with a grubby forefinger. 'I see two men here. More than two.' She glanced up disapprovingly. 'But one is special. The trick will be to decide which one he is.' She had cackled with laughter. Abi remembered wondering cynically if she had trained herself to laugh like that or if it was natural.

The remark about her healing hands had however lodged somewhere in her unconscious and years later, after yet another person had told her how good it was after she had massaged a neck or laid a cool authoritative hand on an aching head, she had enrolled for a course with the National Federation of Spiritual Healers. One of the many things she had not told her parents about. The course was fascinating. It showed people how to channel energy. To be aware. To work with the body of the sick person, to remove pain and direct healing. The spiritual side of it was non specific. It did not involve prayer, but even now as a priest Abi still found herself instinctively using the skills she had learned on that course. She prefaced her actions with prayer now of course and gave thanks afterwards. She could not believe that what she did was evil.

She recalled the expression on Kier's face as he had brought up the subject. Sandra had warned her. There was something strange going on here and she did not feel comfortable about it. Any more than she had felt comfortable with him touching her hair. She was finally beginning to wonder if she was really enjoying living that close to him. Her initial attraction to the man was waning. She could never quite put her finger on it, but there was something about him which was increasingly making her uneasy.

From then on she began to notice things; from time to time their hands touched accidentally when they were sitting at his desk, their heads together over parish reports; once or twice they brushed against one another when they were robing in the vestry of the church. She never encouraged him. He was flirting mildly, that was all. It was his manner. Perhaps it was just that she had started to notice it more. She had thought she could cope with it. She acknowledged that at the beginning she had enjoyed it, missing, she had to admit, the company of a man, flattered and rewarded by his attention. Now suddenly she realised that she had been foolish. It had been wrong to encourage him, even if only subconsciously. Quite apart from anything else, he had a girlfriend.

Sue Green was a teacher at a girl's prep school on the far side of the city. She and Kier had been together in an offhand sort of way for three or four years, living apart most if not all the time. Abi wasn't sure how frequently she stayed overnight, but it couldn't be very often, that was for sure. Abi met her very seldom – usually when they passed in the hallway or on the stairs, but the knowledge that she existed was somehow comforting. Another female presence in the house. That was important, because there were never any other women there. She seldom saw Sandra, and although she frequently saw Kier talking to women, and watched their reaction as they melted beneath his smile be they in church or on the street, or when she accompanied him to visit parishioners or sit in on their visits to the Rectory, none actually came and stayed for more than a few minutes save the two cleaning ladies who came together once a week and worked together and left together. Once or twice she found herself wondering if it was because he didn't trust himself with women.

From now on she would keep Kier at arm's length and since he made such a big deal about it she would make sure she kept her irrepressible hair tightly restrained in its clips and pins. Any healing she did she would keep carefully low key. There was no point in antagonising him. But there was no way she was going to stop, either. It was what she did. More and more she began to distance herself from his attentions. More and more often she found herself creeping in at the end of the day, and, almost ludicrously, tiptoeing up the stairs to try and avoid him.

It all came to a head on a hot July evening. She was writing notes for her sermon in her upstairs eyrie. The evening sun was shining on the spires and grey stone roofs in the distance, the roofs of the other Cambridge, the idyllic Cambridge of the tourist brochures and the luckiest students on earth, did they but know it, and she was staring thoughtfully out, thinking how the sight never failed to enchant her. Lost in those thoughts, she almost missed the sound of footsteps running up the stairs to her front door. Standing up, she went to open it. 'You seem to be in a hurry, Kier – She broke off abruptly. It was Sue.

'Sorry to disappoint you! Were you expecting him?' Sue pushed past her and turned to face Abi in the middle of the room. She was a small, intense woman in her mid-thirties, attractive, neat and self-contained. Her hair was usually pinned back into a tidy pleat at the back of her head. This time it was down, swinging shoulder length and newly blonde. It made her look younger and somehow more vulnerable. 'Have you no shame? You're supposed to be a vicar! I hope you rot in hell!' Sue dissolved into angry sobs.

'Sue?' Abi was appalled. 'What's happened? What are you talking about?'

'As if you didn't know!' Her tears dashed away, Sue's large blue eyes were cold. 'I trusted you. It never crossed my mind you were having an affair.'

'I'm not! I'm not having an affair with anyone! Who?' She paused. 'Not Kier? You don't think Kier and I . . . ?' She was suddenly furious.

'Of course Kier and you. Do you think I am naïve? But of course I am. I never suspected. I liked you. I trusted you!' For a moment she stood staring at Abi, her face twisted with misery and hatred, then she turned back to the door. 'Well, you can have him. I don't want the two-timing, loony bastard. But don't think you will get away with this. The whole parish is talking and I'm going to report you. I'm going to make sure you are sacked. You are not fit to enter a church!'

Abi stood completely still in shock as Sue ran back down the stairs. Moments later the sound of the slamming front door echoed up to her.

Kier had been standing below in the front hall. He walked slowly up towards her as she appeared in the doorway and looked down. 'I'm so sorry, Abi.' He looked exhausted. 'I suppose it was inevitable.'

'Why? Why was it inevitable?' She stared at him furiously. 'What on earth gave that poor woman the idea that you and I are having an affair?'

He shrugged. 'I haven't seen her much lately. You and I've been so busy with the parish. I talk about you a lot, I suppose.' He looked away uncomfortably and lapsed into silence. 'She just got the wrong end of the stick.'

Abi pre-empted the situation at once, phoning the bishop's office the same evening in spite of Kieran's protests that it would all blow over, explaining that it was not possible for a female curate to share a house with an unmarried priest and two days later she moved out of the Rectory to a small furnished flat in a terrace of pretty two-storeyed houses several blocks away. Her sitting room there had no view. It opened out into a small courtyard garden, thick with nettles and brambles. In its centre there was an abandoned rusty bicycle, but strangely the atmosphere was fine. It was a cheerful little place; it seemed to welcome her and as soon as the door had closed behind her she felt cherished and safe. The upstairs flat was empty. She liked it that way.

She knew the bishop had spoken to Kieran. She wasn't sure of the outcome. Kieran never mentioned what was said. He took back more of her workload, encouraged her to take more services on her own at St Hugh's and their regular meetings took place more often than not in St John's. It seemed convenient. They would sit in a pew at the back, talking quietly, keeping to business. There were no more glasses of wine. She didn't ask him if he and Sue had made up their quarrel.

3

While Abi was standing in the patch of nettles at the back of her new flat, surveying the scene and wondering if she had time to cut back some of the weeds and plant a few token flowers to give the place a bit of colour, almost exactly 203 miles away by road, in Woodley in Somerset, Cal Cavendish was standing in the gardens behind her somewhat larger, detached house, staring into space, a pair of secateurs in her hand. A basket of cut flowers lay at her feet and she hadn't moved for several minutes, lost in thought. They were in trouble, deep trouble financially, far worse than they had thought. The only income that came in now that her husband, Mat, had retired was from his suddenly rather meagre-seeming pension and her B & B business and it had not been a good summer. She sighed. She and Mat had just come back from one of those interminable meetings with the bank and the trustees in Taunton, which always left them feeling so depressed. Her instinct had been to go into the garden to hide amongst the flowers, Mat's to take the dogs and go out for a long walk.

As the sun set the house threw oblique shadows across the lawn. It was a beautiful place, the kind of house anyone would kill for. She had thought it a dream come true when she realised that she and Mat were going to live here. It was an ancient manor house, built of mellow local stone. Parts of it still reflected its medieval foundations, parts had been remodelled in the eighteenth century to give it, outwardly at least, a Georgian symmetry which was to her mind utterly beautiful. A building had stood on this site for nearly two thousand years – they had Roman remains in the garden to prove it – and it wore its history like an ancient velvet cloak, confident, stately, elegant and distinctly shabby. Her thoughts went back to the bank. You weren't called in to see local managers these days. There were no more lunches with a man who you thought of as your friend or at least as a civilised person to whom you could talk. The loan department was based in Taunton and the young man who had spoken to them had employed an edgy, slightly threatening tone which she could see had grated on Mat as much as it had on her. The house's history, the fact that it had been in Mat's family for hundreds of years, the efforts they were making to repay the various loans Mat's father had cheerfully taken out over the years without bothering to inform his three sons, none of this seemed to engage him in the slightest. All he was interested in was the computer screen in front of him. The screen which he kept swinging to face them, but which never quite seemed to be legible or comprehensible to either of them. She glanced at the house. In this light you couldn't see the crumbling cornices, the rotting wood, the splits in the mullions, the missing slates. In this light it looked like something out of a fairy tale.

A movement in the flowerbed caught her eye. It was the woman in the blue dress. Cal sighed. She watched her with only half her attention, seeing the figure drift seemingly aimlessly amongst the autumn roses. 'I wish you could bloody well help,' she said out loud after a moment. 'What about bringing us some luck for a change.' Wearily she bent to pick up her basket. When she looked again the woman had vanished.

'Can you drive over to see me, darling? I would so love it if you could. Your father is at a conference in New York, so it would be safe to come home!' Laura Rutherford sounded as cheerful and humorous as usual. Abi stared down at the phone thoughtfully as she replaced the receiver. But something was different. Had there been a waver in her mother's voice? If there had it would have been unheard of. Laura was a strong and determined woman. Serenity was her middle name.

The fact that Abi's sudden re-posting had been to a Cambridge parish had in a way been a disappointment, for she had known the city for a large part of her life. Her father had been a professor at the university until his retirement and her parents still lived in the house on the far side of the city where she had been brought up. As it turned out her new job was in an area of a Cambridge she had never known before and one that every day shocked and surprised her more and more, but in many ways she would have preferred to be based somewhere far away because much as she loved her mother, her relationship with her father was uncomfortable to say the least.

The household into which Abi had been born had been aggressively godless. Her father, the world-renowned chemist Professor Harry Rutherford, had drummed a compulsory atheism into his only child from the first. When she had gone up to Lady Margaret Hall in Oxford and chosen to read history he had nearly had apoplexy, but her lack of talent in maths and the sciences at school could neither be overlooked nor sidestepped and he was forced to give in with good grace to the inevitable fact that chemistry would never be her thing. He even understood his daughter's love of sacred music. Music was his own passion, sacred music an illogical but profound side shoot of something that had a comfortable root in mathematical progressions. The areas of her life which involved healing and intuition and irrational spiritual longings she kept very carefully to herself. Had he known that sometimes she lingered in churches and cathedrals to sit, lost in thought which sometimes turned to prayer, he would have disowned her on the spot. As it was, her decision to study theology and later to seek ordination led to a quarrel which had kept them apart for five years in spite of her best efforts to effect some kind of reconciliation. Since her move back to Cambridge she and her mother had met alone, secretly, for furtive lunches in small restaurants in the narrow winding streets of the old city far from the modern science laboratories which were still her father's usual habitat even now he was retired.

Laura Rutherford was a deeply spiritual woman but she had no time at all for the strictures and structures of the church. 'I am afraid you will regret this, sweetheart,' she had said with a sigh, when Abi had told her of her emerging vocation, 'but you have to follow your own star. You will always have my blessing, whatever you do. You know that.' Her own worship was centred on her love of plants, her world famous garden, the time she spent alone in the company of flowers. With her husband she was able to maintain a sufficient level of scientific involvement with horticulture and plant chemistry to keep their marriage stable and happy over its thirty-five years of existence. Her private beliefs, whatever they were, she kept to herself. Neither her husband nor her daughter were a party to them.

Her mother greeted Abi at the front door and they hugged each other with guilty glee. 'It's so lovely to see you!' Laura led the way indoors. 'Darling, Harry! I'm quite glad to be shot of him for a few days. He is such a bigot!' There was a bleak emphasis on the last word which brought Abi up short. She caught her mother's hand and swung her round to face her. 'Mummy? Is everything OK?'

Laura nodded. 'Of course, darling. Now, you tell me what has been happening to you. I was very surprised to hear you had moved. Why the sudden flight from the Rectory? Has that oleaginous man been pawing you?'

Abi let out a snort of laughter. 'He's not oleaginous. He's basically a nice person, but yes, we were getting a bit too close and his fiancee objected. All over now. The bishop had a word. It's strictly business from now on.'

Laura led the way into a garden full of roses. 'You still shouldn't be working with a man like that. How can you concentrate on your job!' her mother retorted.

'It is my job to learn to get on with people. To manage situations. To cope with men like Kier. If I fall at the first fence I might as well give up.' Abi flung herself down on a mossy stone bench. A small fountain trickled gently in the circular pond at their feet.

Her mother sat down next to her. She smiled fondly at the water spout. 'Solar powered. Isn't that clever.' She turned to her daughter. 'You are not talking about your clients here. Your parishioners. Whatever you call them. You are talking about sexual harassment at work.'

Abi shook her head. 'I have to deal with it, Mummy. God must have sent me to St Hugh's for a reason.'

Her mother glanced across at her. 'Perhaps God is trying to show you that you are in the wrong place. In the wrong job.'

Abi looked away. 'I'm not in the wrong job!'

'So, you're enjoying it?' Laura turned back to the fountain, studying the moving rainbows in the water with exaggerated care.

There was a short pause. 'I'm finding it a bit tough, actually,' Abi said at last. 'It's not just Kier. It's the whole pastoral thing. It was so different before, in my last parish. I saw myself as a healer, not a social worker. Now I'm expected to give advice, recite an austere prayer, but keep my distance from people and I hate it.'

31

She bit her lip. It sounded shameful, said out loud like that. 'It must be what God wants for me, and I have dedicated myself to serving him, but –' She paused.

There was so much missing from the reality of being a priest now, compared with her expectations, she didn't know where to start. She had tried again and again to face what was wrong, to pray about it, to ask God what she should do differently, to try and find why so much was missing in her life now that had been there before, even when she was a student. The sense of the numinous. The wonder. The absolute knowing that there was so much there which cannot be seen but which is known absolutely deep inside. It was a certainty which made the whole world shine and that shine had gone. 'I'm not very good at poverty and obedience, I suppose. I didn't sign up to be a nun! Everything I do here presents some kind of conflict. I'm a mystic by nature, but I have to be a realist as well. I have such a sense of duty towards this job, and yet, I long to be free. I know I have a calling but now I want to rebel at every turn. I want to help and heal, but apparently I'm not allowed to. I want beauty and passion and a sense of the sacred in my worship! It's not there. I sense the other world around me, but I don't dare mention it. It is as though Kier is terrified of anything spiritual. There is no Mystery in what I do. With a capital M. At least not when –'

'Not when?' Laura did not look up. Her hands in her lap were clenched.

'Not when Kier is there. It's his way, I suppose. He is a sincere, dedicated man, and he believes in what he is doing, he's passionate, but he bullies the congregation. He talks about sin all the time, never the hope and beauty of God's love. He works to rigid rules as though he's afraid to allow any mysticism to escape. In fact as though he's afraid of everything.'

Laura grimaced. 'It sounds to me as though it's Kier who is your problem, not God! Don't you take services on your own? Can't you do your own thing?'

'Not very often. I take them at the little church in the parish, but even there I am always conscious of being watched. Spied on. Someone is always there to sneak back and tell him I'm doing something wrong.'

'He sounds awful.'

Abi laughed. 'No. It's just a different approach to mine. I have to learn his way of doing things. He's also warm and funny and very charismatic in his own way.'

'He doesn't sound any of those things from what you are saying.'

Abi opened her mouth to deny it, but somehow the words didn't come.

That evening when she walked into her flat there was a message on her phone from Kier asking her to meet him over at St John's. They arrived more or less together and he ushered her in, closing the door behind them. Carefully deliberate in his action he turned the key and taking it out of the lock he put it in his pocket.

'Why did you do that?' She looked at him, startled.

He shrugged. 'I often do in the evenings when I am over here alone. You know as well as I do there are some rough types around. Once or twice they have come in and tried to cause aggro. It can be a bit intimidating.' He walked a few steps away from her, looking troubled. He was dressed more informally than usual, an open-necked shirt under a casual jacket and with a slight sense of surprise she caught sight of a silver cross on a chain around his neck.

She frowned. 'What is it, Kier? Is something wrong?' He had turned on only one light. It shone fitfully in the area at the back of the nave. The rest of the church was shady as the sun began to drop below the neighbouring rooftops; the atmosphere was tense. It was very quiet.

'Yes, something is wrong.' He turned to face her. 'We get on well, don't we, Abi.'

She smiled uneasily. 'Of course we do.'

'And we like each other.'

'We're colleagues. We work well together.' She felt a flicker of apprehension.

'That's what I thought.' He nodded slowly. 'I don't know how to put this, Abi. It seems wrong just to put it baldly, but the way things are at the moment, well, the thing is, I think you're causing some dissension in the parish.' He didn't meet her eyes, staring down instead at the strip of carpet on the flagstone floor. It was designed to bring some vestige of warmth to the often cold church but suddenly it seemed like a barrier between them as they stood

33

awkwardly facing one another. 'Since you moved out I've been able to see things more dispassionately. I've thought about this a lot over the last weeks and I've prayed endlessly about it. You are stirring up difficult and unacceptable emotions in our congregation. And,' he paused, still not looking at her, 'in me.'

Abi laughed. She couldn't stop herself. It was shock rather than amusement and as soon as she had done it she was sorry. 'Kier, I don't understand. What on earth do you mean?' She frowned. 'Is this about Sue . . .' Her voice died away as he looked up at her at last and she saw the burning intensity in his eyes.

'Sue and I were over the day she came up and spoke to you. She knew. She understood how much I need you,' he said quietly. 'She can't help me the way you can.'

Abi took a deep breath. 'Kier, I am still not sure I understand. How could I help you any more than I am? No!' She put out her hand to fend him off as he moved closer. Suddenly she was angry. Was the man actually admitting he fancied her? 'This can't happen, Kier. You are a priest of the church. You are my mentor. I trust you.' She paused. 'I trusted you,' she added softly. He was holding her gaze with frantic intensity. 'You are going to make it impossible for me to work with you if you say another word.'

The church seemed to resound with the silence that followed. She didn't dare move.

'You misunderstand, Abi,' he said at last. His voice was flat. 'I am not propositioning you. I won't deny that I find you attractive, but that is not why I need you.'

She took a careful step backwards, holding his gaze. Until he extricated the key from his pocket she was locked in with him. 'I know you need me, Kier. That is why I am here,' she said robustly. 'As your curate. Nothing more.'

He grimaced. 'It is as my curate, Abi, that I want you there. I have to have you there, on the premises.'

She stared at him, shocked. 'You are asking me to move back to the Rectory?'

He nodded. 'God sent you to look after me.'

'God didn't send me, Kier,' she said sharply. 'The bishop sent me because he felt you needed someone to help you with the parish.'

'And the bishop was instructed by God. He prayed for the right person this time. So did I.'

'The right person for the job, Kier.' Her unease was steadily building inside her. There was something strange about him which was making her nervous. 'Which doesn't include living on the premises. This is a complete nonsense and you know it. And the bishop knows it.' She saw her fear reflected in his eyes for a moment and took another step back. Desperately she made herself remember her training. The situation had to be defused. She had to get out of the church. 'Look, I will think about this,' she added more gently. 'Of course I will. I need to go away and consider what you've said.'

He was shaking his head. 'You need me too, Abi, as much as I need you. More so. Out there, on your own, you are not under proper supervision. People don't like it. They don't trust you. When you are at the Rectory I can tell them I'm keeping an eye on you. I can reassure them that I am overseeing your work. I need your promise, Abi, to come back. You have to be there. If you defy the will of God He will be angry.'

'If it is the will of God, Kier, He will tell me so in my prayers.' She couldn't keep the sharpness out of her voice. Her hands had grown clammy. She took another step back from him. 'I need to go, Kier. I have to pray about this, surely you can see that? Can I have the key, please.' She tried to keep her voice calm.

He hesitated, then he looked up at her and she could see an answering stubbornness in his eyes. 'Are you are defying God, Abi? Are you defying me?'

For a moment she was too shocked at his choice of words to answer. 'I came to this parish to serve God! If God wants me to move back to the Rectory He will make it clear, I am sure. Until that point, I will make my own decisions and at this moment I just want to go home. The key please.' She held out her hand and somehow she kept it steady, waiting for him to produce it, using every ounce of will she had to make him comply. For a moment she thought he was going to turn away but with a shrug he took a deep breath and reaching into his pocket he pulled it out and after a moment's hesitation he dropped it onto her palm.

'Very well. We will leave it for now. I can see the suggestion is a shock for you. I thought you had understood, but I will give you time to come to terms with your duty in this. It is what we both need, Abi. I promise you, it will work.'

Somehow biting back an angry retort she turned away, almost

running to the door. Dragging it open she glanced back over her shoulder. He was walking slowly up the aisle towards the altar. He did not look back.

The sound of the door closing behind her echoed round the church. Kier stood for a while looking at the altar then he moved into the choir stalls and sat down, his head in his hands. How could he explain? How could he tell her?

Since she had left the Rectory his fear, his terrors, his childhood nightmares had returned. The huge empty house had echoed round him. He lay awake staring into the dark, aware of the echoes everywhere and he felt tears trickle slowly down his face. He had rung Sue, but she had not wanted to speak to him. Several times he had gone upstairs and let himself into Abi's empty flat. It felt happy. It was bright and safe. Her bedroom was warm in the evening sun and her bed, even stripped of bedclothes seemed to retain the fragrance of her body. Quietly, embarrassed and ashamed by his own action, he lay down on the bed and hugged her pillow. There he could keep the ghosts at bay.

It took Abi a long time to calm down. The walk home helped, striding fast through the warm streets, ignoring the groups of hoodies clustered at the crossroads, the chattering crowds around the doors of the pubs, cigarette smoke rising into the air, summer students coming out of some sort of meeting in the old Adventist meeting hall. Running up the steps to the door of her flat she let herself in and slammed it behind her. Her heart was thudding in her chest, her mouth dry. It was several minutes before she had composed herself enough to walk through to her bedroom. In the corner was a small table which she used as a prayer desk. The little wooden cross came from Iona, the candlestick from Walsingham. The room was dark, the window shrouded by the heavy lace curtain which prevented people in the street from looking in. At first she had wanted to tear the curtain down, let in the natural daylight, but she soon realised why it was there. Pedestrians strolling down the street could look straight in, only feet from her bed.

'OK, big boss. Tell me what to do.' She slumped on her knees on the cushion in front of the cross. 'I can't cope with this on my own. Something is very wrong with him. He's too needy and too afraid. Surely you don't mean me to go back. You wouldn't serve me up like some sort of sacrifice. You couldn't!' She stared up at the cross. 'Could you?'

Climbing to her feet she walked across to the window and stared through the curtain at the street outside. It was quiet and it was getting dark at last. Somewhere up there in the sky beyond the reflection of the streetlights no doubt the stars were beginning to appear. With a sigh she turned away from the window. 'Tell me what to do? Should I go to the bishop? I don't know if I can handle this myself. Kier was so – scary!' She bit her lip. To fail so soon in her first appointment. To have to ask for help. It was humiliating. She was a grown woman, not a girl. She had fended off dozens of difficult men in her time. So what was different about Kier? She reached across and turned on the bedside lamp. By the dim light she stared at her reflection in the mirror. Her hair had pulled free of its clip again. It framed her face and cascaded down over her shoulders, emphasising the luminous quality of her pale skin, the extraordinary clarity of her eyes. She was wearing a V-necked cotton T-shirt and she stared miserably at the small gold cross at her throat. Bloody Kier! He was putting everything in jeopardy. Her career, her future, even her faith! She was star-tled to see a look of sheer hatred flash across her face. It terrified her.

'I've said no. I've said I don't want to see him any more. I've told him I will apply for a transfer. I had to bolt my front door last night! I woke up to see him peering in through the net curtains. I don't know if he could see me, but it gave me the creeps.' At the first opportunity she had gone back to her parents' house, pouring out the story to her mother. 'I don't know what's wrong with the man! One minute he seems obsessed with me, the next he's a little boy who has lost his mum in the super-market. He's terrified of something. I've had to leave the answer phone on. He keeps ringing. All the time. I don't know what to do!'

'Have you told David?' Laura led the way into the garden.

Abi shook her head. It always shocked her slightly, her mother's casual friendship with the bishop. It wasn't till after her appointment to his diocese that Laura had told her, smiling mischievously, of her lifelong friendship with David Paxman, of their adventures growing up together in the Mendip Hills in Somerset, where their families had been neighbours, of the scrapes they had got into, of the early signs of childhood romance. She had frowned, wondering if strings had been pulled to get her the Cambridge curacy. At the very least it explained the personal interest the bishop had taken in such a lowly newcomer to his diocese.

'You have to tell him. I didn't like that man the only time I met him. I told you not to trust him!' Laura's judgments were always instantaneous and usually right. She leaned forward and broke off a dead rose, crumbling the brown petals between her fingers and letting them fall on the path. 'Abi, you are a beautiful woman. You are kind and thoughtful and loving and strong. A lot of men are going to fall in love with you.' She snorted humorously. 'I know, a lot already have! But when the right one comes along he will support you and cherish you and you will know to give yourself to him forever without hesitation. Until then you have to learn how to deal with this sort of thing, and, yes, I know you think it is probably some sort of test of your faith, but in the situation you are in it will be impossible for you to function properly. Tell David. Tell him you have to leave. Tell him to find you a new parish! One of your own this time!'

Abi bit her lip, staring down into the pond and the circle of small splashes round the water jet. 'I suppose you are right.' She sighed. Was Kier in love with her? He fancied her, she had known that from the beginning, but it was more than that. There was something else there besides the fact that he was used to getting his own way and resentful of anyone who turned him down. Something she was only now beginning to recognise for what it was. A neediness. She thought back to the last time she had seen him. His eyes had been full of something very far from desire. She pictured the flashes of panic in his face. That was it. He was terribly afraid. She shook her head slowly and brought her attention back to her mother's words. They had sounded wistful. Sad. The two women sat in silence for several minutes, then Abi glanced up. She smiled fondly at her mother. 'Is that how it is with Dad? Does he support and cherish you?'

The silence before her mother's reply was just a second too long. 'You know he does, sweetheart.'

There was another long pause. Abi was still watching her mother. She seemed lost in thought. Laura looked ill, Abi realised suddenly. Her face had grown thin and there were shadows around her eyes. She reached across and touched her mother's hand. 'I'm sorry. I shouldn't have brought that up,' she whispered.

Laura smiled. 'We rub along fine, my darling. You know we do.' She sighed. Then abruptly she stood up. 'Come with me. The time has come for me to show you something.'

The Limes was large and square, built of grey stone some time in the 1920s in the centre of an acre of gardens. It was gracious, more restrained than some of its neighbours, but still a little extrovert with the architectural details, built on three storeys with a small rather skittish turret at the eastern corner. The top floor of the house was sparsely furnished. From time to time when the cousins, the children of Laura's two sisters, had descended into Abi's solitary childhood the rooms had echoed with laughter and music but as they all grew older and their jobs took them across the world the family gatherings had grown smaller and more infrequent. Now only one of the top floor rooms was used. It was her mother's den. There was plenty of room downstairs but Laura preferred this low-ceilinged attic with windows on three sides, constantly full of sunshine and, when she opened the windows, the scent of flowers and the songs of birds.

The large table in the centre was strewn with papers and books and sketches of flowerbeds. Three chests of drawers lined the walls, some with their drawers so stuffed full of papers they wouldn't shut properly.

Abi had always suspected Laura loved this room because it was away from her husband's eagle eye. She had never seen her father up here. Not once, in her whole life. Maybe he came, but she suspected he couldn't be bothered. He had no interest in gardens other than as places to sit, or probably in anything his wife did which did not involve or revolve around him.

She followed Laura in and as always succumbed at once to the feeling of security and happiness which filled the room. It took her back to her childhood which had been in some ways idyllic.

39

The room smelled of flowers and paint – her mother often painted and sketched the flowers she loved so much, leaving the paintings stacked in careless heaps on the chests of drawers. She never bothered to frame any of them, laughing off Abi's suggestion that they were worth hanging on the wall.

Abi threw herself down on the chaise longue which stood near the open window looking out across the garden. This piece of furniture, lovingly rescued by her mother from a local house sale, draped with a succession of bright Spanish shawls, had led to the christening of the room as Aunt Laura's Boudoir by one of her cousins. The name had stuck.

Following her inside Laura closed the door behind her. She was pale, Abi noticed again, and she was slightly out of breath after the climb up the stairs. She sat up. 'Are you sure you are all right, Mummy? You look tired.'

Laura smiled at her. 'I'm fine.' She came over to Abi and, stooping, caught Abi's hands in her own. 'Sweetheart, there's something I have to show you and I want you to promise that whatever you think of it, whatever you feel, you will do as I ask.'

Abi frowned. 'That sounds a bit portentous.'

Laura grimaced. As though realising how odd it must seem she released Abi's hands and sat down beside her. 'Promise, darling. I wouldn't ask you to do anything if it wasn't important.'

'Of course I promise.' Abi felt a shiver of apprehension creep down her spine.

'This is something I have kept hidden from your father. He must never know I have told you about it.' Laura stood up again. She hesitated, then she moved across the room to the chest of drawers standing in the alcove which had once been the fireplace before the attic chimney had been sealed. She knelt before it and dragged out the bottom drawer. At the back was a tin box which she extricated with difficulty. Abi sat without moving. She felt suddenly frozen. Outside a breeze rustled through the leaves on the beech hedge far below on the edge of the lawn. Standing up with a grimace at the sudden twinge in her back Laura lifted the box and put it on the table. Prising off the lid she extricated the contents, something heavy wrapped in a white silk scarf. Returning to the chaise longue she sat down again with the bundle on her lap. Her hand rested gently on the scarf. Abi stared down at it. She didn't say a word. The room seemed heavy with foreboding.

Laura took a short, almost painful breath and slowly began to unwrap the scarf. Inside was a smallish round lump of rock.

Abi glanced from it to her mother's face, puzzled. 'What on earth is it?'

Laura gave a hesitant smile. 'Take it. See if you can guess.'

Reluctantly Abi held out her hands. The rock, although only about the size of an apple, was surprisingly heavy and she found she had to grasp it tightly to prevent herself from dropping it as in an identical gesture to her mother's she lowered it onto her knees. Slowly she turned it over, studying every angle. 'There are shiny bits, like windows. Rock crystal. It looks as though it is crystal inside a rock casing.' She paused. 'How weird. It's almost as if my fingers are tingling.' She looked up, startled. 'It's not radioactive, is it?'

Laura shook her head. She was smiling. 'No my darling, it's not radioactive. And it is rock crystal. You are right.'

Abi stared down at it for a few more seconds, then abruptly she gathered it up with both hands and stood up. 'Here, take it!'

'Why? What's wrong?' Laura reached out for it almost tenderly and rewrapped it. Carrying it across the room she laid it reverently back in its box.

'I could feel it moving. As if it were alive.'

Laura laughed. 'Not alive. Just powerful.'

Abi shuddered. 'Mummy! For God's sake, tell me. What is it?'

'I can't explain while you are still a vicar, Abi. I will tell you all about it when you have left the Church.'

'I'm not leaving the Church!' Abi looked up at her, startled. 'At least, only that particular church. Possibly. I will still be a priest.' She stood up and moved slowly across the room to stare out of the window. 'What on earth is there about that stone you can't tell me if I'm a priest? Is it voodoo or something?' She fell silent for a moment. Her mother didn't reply. 'I thought you were OK with me being in the Church,' she said sadly. She stared down into the garden.

There was a long silence. 'I am OK with it, darling,' Laura said at last. 'Of course I am. How could I not be.' She gave short laugh. 'I am proud of you. Very proud. I misunderstood, that's all.'

'So, tell me about the rock. What is it?'

41

'Just that. A piece of rock.'

'No. There is obviously something special about it. Something weird.' Without realising it Abi was wiping the palms of her hands up and down on the seat of her jeans.

Laura slotted the box back into the drawer and pushed it closed. She stood up and faced her daughter. 'I just wanted you to know about it and to know where I keep it. If anything ever happens to me you must take it and keep it somewhere safe. Understand? And one day you must pass it on to your daughter in turn. I will tell you its story. But not now. For now we will leave it alone. And I will tell you why. The story will change your view of the Church forever. It might destroy your faith. That's what it did for me. No!' Her voice was suddenly sharp. 'That is enough. Not another word.' Just for a second Abi caught an expression in her mother's eye she had never seen before. It had gone before she could interpret it. There was anxiety there, and some kind of calculation and something else. Satisfaction. That was it. In spite of her seeming disappointment at Abi's reaction, something had happened that had pleased her mother very much indeed.

St Hugh's Church stood silently in the evening sun at the end of its muddy lane. Leaving her car in the layby near the gate on her way back to her flat that evening, Abi threaded her way through the deserted churchyard past gravestones yet again sprayed with red swastikas. She found herself thinking suddenly about her mother's old piece of crystal as she glanced at the piles of crushed lager cans that had been lobbed at the stones, the broken bottles and empty syringes lying in the grass. Her parents' house might as well be on a different planet. She sighed sadly, glancing up at the windows, heavily wired to stop them being broken, and breathed a quiet prayer. How often had she cleared up the mess in the last couple of months, her hands heavily gloved, a huge binbag beside her? And every time it had happened again. Would changing the use of the church save it from this? Make the people care? Sadly she doubted it.

Unlocking the door, she pushed it open and pocketed the key. Inside she was greeted by an overwhelming, almost audible, silence. It felt more intense than usual, she realised; more profound. Pushing the door closed behind her she listened to the heavy clunk as the latch dropped into place before walking softly up the aisle to stand for a moment in the semi-darkness in front of the altar. The tough walls, the lancet windows with their ancient stained glass, the breath of long-forgotten incense which seemed to hang in the air, all brought an atmosphere of deep peace to the old church. She loved it like this when she was here alone but this would probably be the last time. Her spell as pretend priest-in-charge was over. Tomorrow, if all went according to plan, Kieran was coming up here with a group of supporters from St John's to clear up the churchyard and move all the old pews out of the nave. She shook her head, trying not to feel sad. They were going to change the church into a social-ising space, bringing in toys and drawing things for the small children; coffee and mugs for the mums. That was right. That was how it should be. They hoped it would encourage people to care for the place, to love it and look after it. It would bring in the young mothers, reinforce a community feeling, intro-duce them to each other and to the church. She would prob-ably be the only one to mourn the silence and the sanctity. Another thought struck her and she sighed. Tomorrow, thanks to her avoidance skills, would be the first time she had seen Kieran since his frenetic proposal that she move back into the Rectory. She frowned. It was his last chance to prove he could behave normally towards her. There would be a lot of other people here. She would be safe.

She looked up at the cross on the wall behind the altar below the east window. It was carved and old and didn't look worth stealing so it had been left alone. 'This is what you wanted, isn't it?' she whispered. 'We are doing the right thing here? And it is right for me to try and stay?'

A light came on behind her in the body of the church and she turned round nervously. It was a moment before she realised that it was a last ray of sunlight slanting low through the stained glass window as the sun slipped down behind the trees, throwing gently coloured patterns onto the flags at her feet. She caught her breath, staring at it, mesmerised as near her, suddenly, someone started to sing.

'Love divine, all loves excelling,
Joy of heaven, to earth come down'

Abi peered towards the empty choir stalls, trying to see into the shadows as the pure, breathy voice sang on, the words of the hymn barely audible. She had seen no-one there when she had come in.

'Hello?' Abi moved away from the altar rail and slowly walked down towards the choir stalls. 'Who's there?' She put her hand up, shading her eyes against the sun.

The singing stopped abruptly.

'Please, don't stop,' Abi called out. 'That was beautiful.'

She could sense someone listening. 'Where are you? I can't see you.' As suddenly as it had appeared the ray of sunlight disappeared as the sun slid down behind the trees outside. The church fell into semi-darkness and she sensed she was alone again.

'Come back, please.' Her own voice sounded plaintive and thin. There was no response.

Slowly and methodically she searched the church, unlocking the vestry, peering into corners and under pews. But she knew there was no point. 'It was a ghost,' she whispered to herself. 'An echo from the past.'

The thought didn't frighten her; since she was a child she had been aware of the world beyond the world. Ghosts were part of the wonder of God's creation, but she had never heard anything this clearly before. It made her feel blessed.

Reaching the far end of the church she paused and turned back to look up the aisle. A man was standing at the altar. A vicar, but not Kier. This man was taller, with white hair, dressed in a black cassock. He turned as she watched and looked directly at her. Slowly he raised his hand and she saw him make the sign of the cross and as he did so she realised the church was full of people. Shadowy figures crowded the pews, there were candles alight on the altar and in the distance she could hear it again, the pure voice echoing into the silence.

'Jesus, thou art all compassion,
Pure unbounded love thou art;'

Mesmerised, she watched. She was being shown something so special it took her breath away.

Behind her the latch on the door lifted and the door creaked open. She spun round, shocked at the noise and found herself face to face with Kier. 'I saw your car.' He stepped inside and closed the door behind him. The church was suddenly still and dark and very empty. There were no longer candles on the altar. The singing had stopped abruptly, leaving not even an echo in the vaulted roof. The suddenness of the change of atmosphere left her feeling bereft and strangely empty.

Staring round nervously he reached for the bank of switches, clicking them on one by one until the nave was blazing with light. 'I've come to prepare for tomorrow.' His voice was bleak. 'The sooner this mausoleum is transformed the better.' She saw him glance at her but he made no move towards her. He seemed anxious.

'It's not a mausoleum, it's a beautiful old country church,' she said reproachfully. She was overwhelmed by a wave of sadness. 'Are you sure, Kier? Are you sure this is what God wants us to do here?'

He frowned. 'Of course this is what God wants.' He shivered. 'What use is a church that's used by only a minute ageing congregation? For goodness sake, Abi, we've talked about this.' He sounded thoroughly irritated. 'What I plan will bring in the young mothers, the teenagers. When the new development starts, there will be more families, people who want somewhere as a social centre, maybe a drop in clinic. It will still be a church. We will still hold services here. They will just be different.' He stopped abruptly. 'I can smell candles. Have you been burning candles in here?'

She smiled sadly. 'Would it matter if I had?'

He shook his head. 'Of course not. It's just odd. It smells so strongly.' To her surprise she saw beads of sweat break out on his forehead.

Impulsively she took a step towards him. 'Kier, I saw them. Just now. The congregation that used to worship here. The candles were their candles. The rector was here. I expect his name is one of those on the wall up there. He blessed the church. Someone was singing. I'm surprised you didn't hear her. It was wonderful . . .' Her voice died away.

His face had gone white and he was staring at her in horror. 'No!' he shook his head. 'No. That's all your imagination.' He seemed terrified.

45

She stared at him. 'It was real for you too, Kier. After all, you can still smell their candles.'

'No!' He shook his head again, more violently this time.

'Have you ever seen a ghost?' she asked, suddenly curious. She saw his face tighten in denial but she ploughed on recklessly. 'I've often thought I did, but nothing like this. This was so clear. So real. They weren't frightening. They weren't some sort of echo. It was as if they were still there, in some other dimension, getting on with their thing. And their thing was surrounding this ancient place of prayer with more prayer, with love and blessings. It was beautiful.'

'Do you know what you are saying?' His voice had dropped almost to a whisper. He was staring at her in horror. 'For God's sake, Abi!'

'There's nothing to be scared of,' she said suddenly. 'Look, Kier. Look around. Feel the peace and blessings this place dispenses round it. This is what churches do. They become some kind of powerhouse for the neighbourhood. Prayer radiates out of churches. It doesn't matter how many people do or don't go to the service. The stones themselves exude prayer and it has an effect.'

'No!' Kier shook his head. 'Be quiet! Shut up!' His voice broke. 'My mind is made up. It has all been arranged with the diocese. I can see it's a beautiful place. I am sad it has to change but there are lots of other lovely old churches which will stay the same. Just not this one.' He tightened his lips. 'Trying to scare me is not going to change anyone's mind.'

She shrugged. 'I wasn't trying to scare you. I thought maybe you would see something. Sense something of what there is here.'

'There is nothing here, Abi!' He was almost shouting. 'Just walls!' He took a deep breath, visibly trying to steady himself. 'I tell you what, why don't we lock up and go and have a glass of wine somewhere. There's a good place just up the road.'

She shook her head. 'No thanks, I am tired. I've had a busy day; I went to visit my mother. I'll go home now, and see you tomorrow.' She managed a smile. 'What time are the others coming?' She had to pass him to get to the door. Taking a deep breath she moved towards him, making herself walk steadily down the aisle, realising at once he wasn't going to step out of her way. 'Excuse me. I need to go.'

'Abi, you've been avoiding me and we must talk.' His eyes were wild. 'I need your help. You mustn't go!'

Again she shook her head. 'No, Kier. Now is not a good time. I want to go home.'

She wasn't expecting him to lunge towards her. Before she had a chance to duck out of his way he had grabbed her arms. She struggled frantically but he was far too strong for her as he pulled her towards him. 'Abi, you don't understand. I can't bear it on my own. These people are everywhere –' He let go of her with one hand and gestured round the church. 'You have to help me! I've been fighting it so long. I could just about manage it when Sue was there but when you came I found I could control it. I was safe. You are strong. You know what to do. Women know about these things. You could keep them at bay, but now I'm on my own . . .' He paused, looking into her face. His eyes were full of terror now, darting back and forth. He was like a trapped animal. 'I don't know what to do!' She saw him swallow hard. 'You can save me, Abi. You must.' And suddenly he was pulling her closer, his fingers biting into her arms. His mouth on hers was eager and soft. It repelled her. With a cry of distress she tried to free herself but she could do nothing. The kiss seemed to last forever but finally he released her. 'Darling, Abi –'

His words were cut off short as she pulled back her fist and hit him full in the mouth. 'Don't you dare! Don't you dare touch me again.' The initial wave of compassion which she had felt as he began his plea had vanished and she was overwhelmed with anger. 'Do you hear? Never! I want nothing to do with you, Kier. Nothing.'

'Oh God, Abi, I'm sorry.' He was clutching his face. 'I don't know why I did that. They made me. Someone made me do it –' He reached out for her again. 'Abi, listen!'

'No! You listen. Leave me alone.' She tried to dodge backwards, and came up hard against the end of a pew.

He caught her by the shoulders. Suddenly his voice changed. 'You've hurt me, Abi.' There was blood seeping down his chin.

'And I'll hurt you again.' She could feel the panic mounting as his fingers bit into her flesh. She tried to wriggle free. 'Let me go, you bastard!'

He released her shoulders and with a quick movement of one hand slapped her across the face. 'Don't use that language with

47

me. Don't you dare!' His eyes were still frantic. 'Don't you see, we can help each other. I'm trying to be patient with you! You have to understand.'

'Don't bother!' She managed to duck free of his grasp and lurched past him towards the door. In seconds she had wrenched it open and was outside, running down the path towards the cars.

Kier had waited for everyone else to arrive before he went back into the church next morning. Hovering in the doorway he looked round. The place was bright and full of noise; he could smell coffee, hear laughter, see the dust of centuries rising before the onslaught of brooms as one by one the pews were hauled out of their serried ranks towards the back of the church. There was no sign of Abi.

Kier rang her mobile twice, but it was switched off. Determinedly he put her out of his mind. There were enough people to keep the terrors away.

It was late by the time they had finished and his was the only car left parked in the lane. All he had to do was pull the door to and turn the key. He stood in the doorway and looked inside. The church was very quiet now the others had gone home. Hesitantly he stepped inside and looked around. He waited tensely, afraid for a moment they would still be there, the shadows, but there was nothing. The place felt clean and free. The churchyard had been tidied up, the pews stacked at the back of the nave. Tomorrow a van would collect them and they would go into storage until the diocese decided what to do with them. Pub furniture was a favoured option, he had heard. It would raise some much-needed money. Now the nave of the old building was empty it felt much larger than before. Somehow wrong. He pushed the thought aside, turning to face the altar. It was bare but for a plain blue cloth. No cross, no candlesticks, just that hideous old crucifix on the wall below the east window. He shuddered. That would have to go. The young people would hate it. They should have moved it today. Slowly he began to walk up what had been the aisle, the line of it still marked by the dust left on the old paving slabs where the pews had stood for so many years. Strange, that Abi hadn't liked this idea of clearing the church. As a young new face she ought to represent the young avant-garde wing of the church, against all the ritual and the flummery. He shook his head sadly. How could he have messed up so badly with her? Everything he had said and done she had misunderstood. He shivered. She was strong. Yet she had seen the ghosts. He bit the knuckle of his finger thoughtfully. And she hadn't seemed to mind. She hadn't been afraid.

He shook his head. He was beginning to have serious second thoughts about Abi. He had thought her capable, able to cope with any phenomena which manifested here, in the church, but perhaps he was wrong in thinking that was a good thing. Perhaps she was the cause of the unrest. He stared round, his eyes darting here and there into the shadows. Maybe people were right in having reservations about women in the priesthood.

Could he have been so wrong about her? At the beginning he had thought she was everything a good priest should be. Was it his fault she was veering off the path like this? Surely they would have spotted any problems at college when they were first assessing her suitability for the priesthood. He shook his head. Spiritual healing, voices. Superstition. And now ghosts! She had seen the ghosts in here, in this church! He shuddered. He turned round, forcing himself to stay calm. They had gone. No, they had never been here. After all, he had seen nothing. Not really. It was all imagination. It always had been, since he was a child. A residue of nightmares. In a dark old building it was easy to think one had seen things. Nothing but shadows, that was all. His hands were beginning to sweat. He rubbed his face and winced. The bruise where she had hit him hurt. His tooth still felt wobbly. For a while this morning he had thought it was going to fall out. But he shouldn't have slapped her. That was unforgivable. He had lost his temper and that was not acceptable behaviour. He had prayed for hours last night, trying to see a way through the mess, pleading with God to make her see sense. To make her understand how much he needed her.

The obvious answer of course was that she needed him as much as he needed her. If he could give her the strength to overcome her weaknesses, show her the true path then she would be in a position to help him. Or would she? Would she always be a danger, a threat to his sanity? He had a sudden picture of her clear passionate eyes, her wild hair and he felt another clammy frisson of fear.

There was a sound behind him, a creak from the choir stalls which they had left in place for now. He turned round quickly, listening. Nothing. Then, suddenly, a small rattle as though someone had dropped a coin. He shivered nervously, forcing himself to stand still, trying to pull himself together. Flakes of plaster probably fell now and then from loose patches in the vaulted roof. All their banging and crashing earlier in the day would have shaken the structure a bit. He found himself turning round again, acutely aware of the emptiness around him. It had been fun in here earlier, with the others here. There had been a constant stream of banter and easy conversation and laughter. A couple of people had brought thermoses of coffee. He had forgotten it was a church for a while. It was just a job to be done; a space to be cleared, a re-allocation of resources. When the others had gone he had stayed behind to turn off the lights. Check everything was all right. Lock up. Abi hadn't come to help of course, but he had hardly expected her to do that after last night. He frowned. He still didn't understand why she had reacted the way she had when he had kissed her. Women usually found him attractive. He had thought she found him attractive. She always seemed to like his company. Or she had until recently. He sighed and shook his head. He was offering her an awful lot. A home, a future, support. And she needed no end of support, he saw that now.

Another creak from the stalls made him swing round, straining his eyes into the shadows. 'Hello? Is there anyone there?' He took a deep breath, trying to steady himself. 'Come on out.' Even in full sunlight this was a dark church but he could see there was no-one there. Nowhere to hide.

'Come on! Time to go. I'm about to lock up.'

The silence was almost tangible.

Behind him a light flickered. He swung round to face the altar and gasped. There were two candlesticks on it now, two candles, lit, a lace cloth, a cross. His mouth dry with terror he stared for a long moment, not daring to breathe. Raising his hand at last he reached out and at once the candles vanished. 'Our Father who art in Heaven,' he whispered. This was Abi's doing. She hadn't wanted them to touch this place. He backed away towards the door. 'Hallowed be thy name.' It was her. She had brought evil here with her. That was why she didn't want him to touch

50

her. That was why she had panicked when he had reached out for her.

There was only one word for what was happening here. Witchcraft.

David Paxman looked at Abi quizzically. 'I gather you almost knocked out one of his teeth, Abi. That must have been some punch!'

'He's spoken to you?' She clenched her fists again, trying to speak calmly. 'Did he tell you that he hit me?'

The bishop nodded wearily. 'He more or less corroborates your story, although he does feel you were out to seduce him from the start. He is also worried as to what exactly you were doing in the church that necessitated the lighting of so many candles.'

'Candles?' She felt the colour drain from her face.

'Candles.' The bishop sat back and picked up his cup. He was watching her carefully.

'They weren't real candles.' She met his eye defiantly. 'The church was full of ghosts. There was a choir and a parson and the pews were full and someone was singing the most beautiful solo hymn.' Uneasily she began to pleat the folds of her skirt between her fingers. 'And then Kieran arrived and, just like that,' she clicked her fingers, 'they disappeared. The church was dark when he came in. Dark and cold and empty.'

'There was a mention of witchcraft.' The bishop grinned broadly.

'Oh, please!' Abi stood up. 'I don't believe it. I suppose that's because I rejected his advances.'

'Actually he assumes it helped you lure him against his better judgement.'

'The vindictive bastard! Does he want me burned at the stake!'

'Not good Christian sentiments, Abi, but yes, something along those lines.'

'Well, I'm resigning, remember? So he can take his box of matches somewhere else.' She sat down again, furiously. 'He is right about one thing. I was wrong to take holy orders. I accept that now. I have no vocation!' She stopped abruptly. She hadn't planned to say that. 'It's not just that I am seeing ghosts,' she went on doggedly, deciding she might as well make a clean breast

51

of things. 'I've been practising the ministry of healing. He doesn't like that at all, either.' She paused, then went on. 'He was so afraid. I don't know if he was more afraid of the ghosts or of me or of himself. All three, perhaps.' She shrugged. 'After I saw him, after I left the church, I don't know what happened. Perhaps I was in shock, but I was seeing everything differently suddenly.' She hesitated. 'The ghosts, everything, have always been there, but I couldn't quite see them before. I've sensed them. I knew there was so much going on that I couldn't quite put my finger on. Then suddenly it was as though someone flicked a switch and all the lights came on in my head.'

The bishop said nothing. He waited, his eyes on her face.

'Everything was glowing. People, houses, trees. It was like looking through some kind of prism; shimmering colours. Everywhere. And people in the streets. People who weren't there.' Her voice had dropped to a whisper. It had been incredible, somehow how she imagined it must be the first time or two one got high on drugs. Beyond anything she had ever experienced. She realised the bishop was still watching her closely.

'People?' he prompted at last.

'People in old-fashioned clothes. Ghosts. Like in the church.' To her embarrassment her eyes suddenly filled with tears. 'I could feel their pain. Their loneliness. Their fear.'

For a moment there was complete silence in the room. Outside in the hall, a phone rang and almost immediately stopped. 'What's happened to me?' She looked up at him pleadingly.

'I think in modern parlance, Abi, that you are probably suffering from stress,' he said at last. He rubbed his chin thoughtfully. 'We have been overworking you, that much is clear, and the man who should have been your guide and mentor has betrayed your trust. And mine!' He paused a little grimly. There was another moment of silence. 'Can you see those prisms and lights now?'

She shook her head.

'Any ghosts?' He was very serious.

She shook her head again.

'Good.'

'I spent yesterday praying,' she went on after a moment. 'When you couldn't see me at once, I panicked. I didn't know what to do. I went for a long walk in the country. Up towards Wandlebury

Hill. I should have been helping them clear out St Hugh's but I couldn't bear the thought of seeing Kier again. Up there, I made the lights go away. I wouldn't let them happen. They wanted to. They wanted to show me the past. It's an ancient site up there, but I somehow controlled them. Out there in the fields they seemed all wrong. Unchristian. Pagan. So, you see why I can't go on being a priest. Perhaps he has identified my problem. Perhaps I am a witch! You'll have to accept my resignation. My parents hated me being ordained. My father because he's an atheist, but my mother, well, you know what she thinks.' She shrugged. 'Whatever the reason, they were right.'

He nodded slowly. 'Your mother told me she lost her faith, Abi, but never why.' He shrugged. 'But you are wrong in thinking she didn't want you to be ordained. She told me it was your choice and she only wanted what was best for you.' He looked at her pensively. 'I think, Abi, the best thing would be for you to take a leave of absence for a few weeks while we all calm down and think things over.'

'You needn't expect me to think anything over when it comes to Kieran,' she retorted hotly.

'And I won't. But there are other matters to consider.' The bishop took a deep breath. 'You are too valuable a member of the team, Abi, to lose you. And so is he. He too has offered to resign. He behaved unforgivably and has infringed every rule in the book regarding his relationship to you. He has put himself as well as you in a very vulnerable position. He will be coming to see me later this evening and in the meantime I think we should all take some time out to pray.' He paused.

'I don't want him to lose his job,' she said with unexpected meekness. 'Perhaps he's right and I did attract him in some way – without realising it. I didn't mean to. He misunderstood.'

'Abi, he should have been able to control himself. Put him out of your mind, my dear. I shall deal with him. Now, we must think about you.'

'You haven't said. Do you think I'm mad?'

'Why should I think that?'

'Seeing ghosts.'

'I don't think you're mad.' He stood up and held out his hands to her. Automatically she stood up too and after a second's hesitation put her own into his. 'I'm going to send you away for a while, Abi. Think of it as a retreat. A chance to pray, to think things over in a safe environment, far away from here. Somewhere you can think about your options and talk them over. Will you do that? Let me make some phone calls and I will contact you.'

'And in the meantime I don't have to meet Kieran?'

'No, you don't have to meet Kieran.' He smiled. 'Bless you, my dear. It will all come out all right, I promise you.'

4

The Reverend Ben Cavendish pulled out a chair and sat himself down at the kitchen table in Woodley Manor, looking first at his sister-in-law and then at his brother. There was a strong family likeness, the two men tall, with rugged outdoor complexions and greying pepper and salt hair, Ben some five years older than his brother. 'I know it is a great favour to ask, especially of you, Cal, but I think she could be useful to you both,' he said gently. It was no secret in the family that some catastrophic investments by his advisers had reduced Mat's pension to almost nothing. 'The diocese will pay and as she might be here a while it will work out far more than your average occasional B & B guest who only stays one night. And if she stayed here, rather than with me and Janet, she could do a bit in the garden, maybe help you sort out what you want to do with the designs if you go ahead with this plan to open to the public. Her mother is Laura Rutherford.'

His brother, Mat, looked blank. It was Cal who reacted. '*The* Laura Rutherford? The garden designer?' Petite, with hair a similar colour to that of her husband, if slightly more artfully arranged, and with faded blue eyes, Cal leaned forward, her elbows on the table. Her weather-beaten face was eager.

Ben nodded.

'But the daughter is a vicar, not a garden designer, Ben! It doesn't mean she knows anything about gardening!' Mat protested.

Ben shrugged. 'She must have watched her mother at some point, surely. And even if she didn't, it must be in her genes there somewhere, mustn't it?' He gave a disingenuous smile. 'David wants her to have a complete break. She's had some kind of awful experience with the man she works with. Her first job, she hasn't even had her own parish yet, and the so and so jumped on her. She wants to resign but the bishop says she'll make a good pastor; he doesn't want to lose her so he has decided to send her down to us here to revisit her roots in Somerset. We've got to soothe her and reassure her and I'm to be her spiritual adviser. But David is anxious I shouldn't ram the whole pastoral experience down her throat at the moment, so I thought it might be better to suggest she stay here, based away from the Rectory.'

Cal smiled. 'Reading between the lines, she's obviously a looker and Janet has said, "not in my house thank you very much otherwise she might set her cap at my husband too"!'

Ben grinned. 'Something like that maybe, yes. You know my wife. But to be fair, David did say she looked as though she needed feeding up. That is your department, Cal, as you cook like an angel.'

Cal chose to ignore the compliment. 'I hope that doesn't mean she's anorexic as well as sexy.'

Mat threw back his head and laughed. 'I doubt it. If I remember right, David Paxman likes his women curvy.' He clapped his hand to his mouth in mock horror. 'Sorry, I didn't say that. It's unfair to remember a bishop when he was a boy and the terror of the whole neighbourhood.'

'You're right, though,' Ben put in soberly. 'It does tend to get between one and all the mystique we're supposed to feel! That's why I could never be in his diocese. Quite apart from that, though, you clearly haven't put two and two together! Laura Rutherford was none other than little Lally Purvis from up near Priddy. So we all knew each other in the old days.' He grinned. 'Abi is practically family. And we are far enough away from her tormentor here on the other side of the country for her to feel safe.'

Mat sighed. 'So how can we refuse. When will she arrive?' He glanced at his wife. 'We will have her, right?'

She nodded. 'Of course we'll have her. There is always room for another pair of hands, and if she tries to seduce my husband, she's welcome to him!' She punched him on the shoulder.

'Good, because she'll be here within the week,' Ben said.

In the event it was to be much longer. The next day, Ben took a call from the bishop. When it was over he put down the phone and stared blankly at his wife. 'I can't believe it. Laura Rutherford is dead.'

Janet came over and sat down next to him. 'She can't be. She is a relatively young woman!'

56

Ben glanced at his wife and sighed. Her reaction was typical. He was sure she didn't mean it that way, but as usual her response to unexpected bad news was to be indignant at a perceived inconvenience rather than instantly sympathetic. He frowned. She was looking particularly elegant today. She was on her way to a coffee morning in Wells and had been to the hairdresser only the day before. It was obviously a 'smart casual' affair of the kind his wife spent hours dolling up for, to end up looking so far from casual that it hurt. Well, poor Laura was not going to be an inconvenience to her and neither by the look of things now, was her daughter.

'Laura had a congenital heart defect, apparently.' He shook his head. 'David said she had only found out a few months ago that there was something wrong. They thought she would be OK with the right medication, but . . .' He shrugged. 'Poor Abi. She knew nothing about her mother's condition. It's been the most awful shock. On top of all her other problems.'

The room still smelled the same. Of paint and flowers. Abi sat down on the chaise-longue and lifted a corner of the Spanish shawl, holding it up to her face. The house felt so empty. Downstairs, her father was sitting in his study, staring at the wall. It had been the same every day since the funeral, the horrible, godless funeral he had insisted on at the City Crematorium.

She had offered to stay on for a while and taken his shrug to signal acquiescence. She sighed. She didn't know how to comfort him. She couldn't talk to him about the certainties that shored up her own faith; she couldn't even mention them. She wanted to hug him; even more she wanted him to hug her. When she was a child they had been so close. Her mother's warmth and affection had enveloped them both, filled the whole house. That had made it so much harder when God had entered the frame. Her father's fury, his uncomprehending indignation, his assumption that she had rejected him and everything he stood for out of some perverse need to pursue a personal vendetta, bewildered her. Even now he couldn't bring himself to look at her. When she had made coffee and toast for them both this morning he had taken a cup and a plate without a word and carried them to his study, closing the door behind him.

Abi walked over to the window and pushed it open, resting her elbows on the sill.

'Give him time, darling.' Her mother's voice seemed to come from the room behind her! Abi swung round. 'Mummy?'

The room was empty. Of course it was empty. And yet . . .

'Mummy?' she whispered again. 'Are you there?'

There was no reply.

She stood for a moment longer without moving, then slowly and thoughtfully she went over to the chest of drawers which stood against the opposite wall and kneeling down she dragged open the bottom drawer. The tin box was where her mother had put it, wedged at the back amongst all kinds of boxes and packages and folders of newspaper cuttings. One day it would be up to her to sort through all her mother's possessions. But not now. It was too soon. Too painful. Easing out the box she carried it over to the table and putting it down she stood looking at it for a long time. Had her mother realised that she was going to die? Obviously she had known she was ill, but wouldn't she have said something if she had realised how gravely? Carefully she pulled off the lid. 'You were going to tell me about this,' she said to the empty room. 'Why did you change your mind? What is so special about this lump of rock?' Unfolding the cloth in which it was wrapped she looked down at it. The uppermost opaque crystal face gleamed softly and she ran her finger over it experimentally. It was cold; inert. Cautiously she lifted it out of the box and laid it on the table. Exposed like this she could see it in more detail. It was a roughly spherical lump of pure crystal with some two thirds of the surface exposed, parts of it crazed and cloudy, some of it clear as glass. The rest was hidden by the rock casing from which it had been hewn.

'It is some sort of crystal ball,' she murmured to herself. 'Is that it? An ancient crystal ball?' She glanced into the box. In the bottom, hidden by the crumpled silk was a piece of paper. Unfolding it carefully she squinted at the faded brown ink.

For my little Amelia. When you are grown up the Serpent Stone will tell its story to you if you listen. Treasure it and pass it on to one of your daughters when you in your turn are old. What you do about the story and who you tell is for you to decide. Els

It was signed with a faint scrawl. Her great-grandmother had been called Amelia. Abi squinted at the signature. Elizabeth? Elspeth?

58

Something beginning with E. She refolded the paper and tucked it back into the box. The Serpent Stone. She shivered. 'So, you have a story to tell?' she whispered. 'A dangerous story.' What had her mother said? It had destroyed her faith.

The door opened so suddenly she nearly jumped out of her skin. 'What are you doing up here?' Her father erupted into the room. He was panting heavily from the stairs. He was wearing the same checked shirt he had had on for three days. She could smell the stale aroma of sweat with a faint oily overlay of alcohol. She frowned. He must have been drinking in the privacy of his lonely study. She stood away from the table almost guiltily. 'I just came up to be near her,' she said after a moment.

He glared at her. 'You can't be near her. She's gone. Don't you understand? She's gone!' It was a wild cry of despair.

'I know.' Abi held out her hand towards him. 'I miss her too,' she pleaded.

Her gesture seemed to inflame his rage even further. 'You? You miss her? You moved out! You betrayed us! You turned your back on everything we believed. You broke her heart!' He stepped closer to her and spotted the box on the table with the stone sitting next to it in full view. He stopped in his tracks. 'That thing! I told her to get rid of it.' For a moment he seemed paralysed with shock. 'How could she defy me? How could she lie? After all that happened!'

'What is it, Dad? I don't understand. What happened?' Abi looked down at the stone then back at his face. Her mother's voice echoed in her head suddenly. 'This is something I have kept hidden from your father.'

He took a deep breath, visibly trying to steady himself and sat down heavily on the chaise longue by the window. He was still breathing hard from the stairs. 'When we were first married we were happy. So happy. I had a research post at Bristol University.' He appeared almost to be talking to himself, staring past her, his eyes fixed on some point in space she could not see. Then you came along. It was all so wonderful and then it was ruined.' There was a long silence.

'Ruined? By me?' Abi whispered at last. Her own memories of her childhood were of sunny holidays, fond grandparents, laughing cousins, her parents holding hands, looking into each other's eyes, sharing jokes, unspoken messages of tenderness, or complicity against the world. They had loved her. She was sure they had both loved her. When had it all gone wrong? And why hadn't she noticed?

She moved away from the table and sat down on a wooden chair next to the wall. He didn't seem to register that she had moved. 'I was awarded a research post here at Cambridge,' he went on. His voice was shaking slightly. 'We were thrilled. It was one of the top jobs in the country.'

Abi remembered that. She had thought it was wonderful, so different from the Victorian cottage in Bristol, falling in love with Cambridge even as a small child with the ethereal beauty of the colleges, the Backs, the river, its magical atmosphere, its romantic stories and with the huge, rambling grey house into which they moved. The garden had been an exciting wilderness. It was the challenge of all those brambles, those hidden corners and those rampant nettles which had set her mother on the quest for order and beauty and peace which would lead her to fame and fortune. Well, fame. Abi gave a faint smile at the memory.

'That thing was a farewell present from her mother.' His voice grew hard and cold. 'Some present! I didn't even know about it. She gave it to Lally because we were moving so far away; in case we never saw her again.' His voice trailed into silence.

Abi sat still, waiting. She didn't dare speak. He was staring into space, no longer seeing her, his eyes fixed on some moment in the distant past.

'We didn't, of course. She must have known she was dying.' He heaved another sigh. 'Lally brought it to me one day. "Look at this, Harry," she said, so pleased with herself. "You think you know it all but I bet you can't explain this!" She was laughing, her eyes so bright. Excited. "Touch it!" she said. "Tell me what it is." I could see what it was. Quartz crystal. SiO_2. Silicon dioxide. It can be quite beautiful, but this was a hideous lump of the stuff, still in its rock matrix. I told her to put it on her rockery and grow something over it. "Oh no," she said. "No way. Hold it. Feel the vibes!" She was wearing a long gypsy skirt. She looked like a happy child. You must have been about six then.' So he remembered she was still there. Abi shifted uneasily. 'She put it in my hands.' He paused. 'I felt it grow hot. It was vibrating. The crystal faces appeared to be moving.' He shuddered. 'I told her it wasn't possible. It was a trick. She snatched it away from me. "Women's magic," she said. "Not for you!" She laughed at me. She called me a silly old scientist.' He looked at Abi at last and she saw tears in his eyes. 'Why did she die! She was fifteen years younger than me. I should have been the one to go first!'

Abi bit her lip, trying to hold back her own distress. She knew better than to go to him again. At the crematorium when she had tried to take his arm he had shaken her off, in front of everyone, as though her very touch had polluted him.

As if reading her thoughts he looked up at her. 'Don't you dare try and comfort me with platitudes about your Jesus!' His tone was vicious.

'I wasn't going to. I know better than that.'

He wasn't listening. He moved towards the table and stared down at the lump of crystal. 'She kept it. She hid it from me, but not from you. She told you. That's how you were infected with this Jesus business. It not only stole my beloved wife. It stole my little daughter as well.' His voice rose to a howl of anguish.

'Dad –'

'Don't bother to deny it. Don't even try. It's all too late. I want you to get out. Pack your bags and go. Do you hear? Leave me alone. There is nothing you can do here. Nothing!' Tears were streaming down his face.

'Dad, please.'

'Get out!' The howl turned into a scream of fury. Abi flinched away from him. 'Get out!' He pointed to the door. 'Now! As for this thing.' He grabbed the crystal in both hands. 'It can go and shatter on the rockery where it belongs!' Taking three swift paces towards the window he hurled it out into the sunshine. It fell three storeys and disappeared.

Through the heavy cloud the sun threw splinters of light onto the waters of the mere. It was here he came to pray. He loved it here, outside, on the hill, on the sedge-lined banks, sometimes drifting in a boat, watching the flocks of ducks, the birds, listening to their calls, alien at first but now familiar, listening to the splash of otter and beaver, the cry of the fox and the wolf, the autumnal bellow of a great red stag high in the hills in the distance, a sound which echoed out across the wetlands and spoke of the power of God.

5

Abi pulled up at the side of the road and peered across between the lichen-covered stone pillars of the gateway up the short driveway. Woodley Manor was situated on wooded, rocky outcrop rising out of the Somerset levels, halfway between Wells and Glastonbury, barely seven miles or so from the Mendip village of Priddy where her mother and the bishop had grown up as child-hood neighbours. The house, long and low with a pillared Georgian front door, and covered in deep richly crimson swathes of Virginia Creeper was built of warm honey-coloured stone under a roof of moss-grown slates and lay dreaming in the mellow sunshine. It was the most beautiful place she had seen for a long time. Pulling across the road and in between the gateposts, she drew up again and opening the door she climbed out, stiff after her long journey, to lean for a moment on the car roof. The air smelled glorious, of warm stone and grass and flowers.

'Abi?' The deep voice behind her startled her; she had thought she was quite alone. She turned. A tall middle-aged man in an open-necked shirt and shabby cords was standing a few feet from her. 'Hi. I'm Mat Cavendish.'

She gave a rueful smile. 'You caught me, I'm afraid. This place is so beautiful I couldn't believe it could be real. I just wanted to get out of the car and stare.'

He laughed. 'I feel that way every time I drive in. Can I hop in and hitch a ride up to the front door?'

His wife, Cal, was standing on the steps waiting for them as Abi drew up. 'I saw you coming. The kettle is on. You must be knackered after your long drive, my dear. Come and have some tea, then Mat can help you with your bags. These are Pyramis and Thisby.' She indicated the two portly black Labradors which sat on either side of her, tails wagging. 'Known to their numerous fans as Pym and Thiz. And before you ask,' she shrugged ruefully, 'those names are all that now remains of my misspent student past when there was talk of a thesis about plays within plays and Shakespeare. All now forgotten, thankfully.' She laughed. 'This way. Mind your head, the lintels are low.'

Abi followed her hosts down a long, paved hallway to the back of the house and into a cavernous kitchen. She stared half-appalled, half-enchanted at the huge inglenook fireplace where a fire burned steadily under an enormous black kettle which was suspended by an iron bar which was swung out from the back wall of the chimney. 'You don't cook on that?'

Cal laughed. 'I have been known to cook soup there occasionally, but I'm afraid I have an ordinary cooker for the day to day stuff. Over there, lurking in the shadows, overwhelmed with an inferiority complex because it's electric! Do sit down, my dear. Take the weight off your feet.' She paused and took a deep breath. 'We were so sorry to hear about your mother, Abi. What a terrible shock for you.' She turned away tactfully. When she turned back a few moments later she was carrying a plate with a chocolate cake on it. Both dogs immediately sat down respectfully one on either side of Abi, their eyes huge and imploring.

That first evening Abi found herself confronted by a confusing whirl of facts and names and faces. The house, she learned, had been inherited by the three brothers of whom Mat was the middle. Ben, the eldest, her designated mentor, was rector of a parish some three miles away. The youngest brother wasn't mentioned beyond the fact that 'he was away at the moment'. Mat and Cal had 'drawn the short straw', to actually live in the place and try to stop it falling down. Apart from anything else they were the only ones with children so far. 'Three. All grown up. All out of the nest. Thank God! All possible heirs to the pile.' It didn't seem to have occurred to them that they might sell the place and Abi, hearing the affection for it in their voices, was beginning to understand why. Cal cut a slice of cake for Abi and another for herself. ('My parents christened me Calliope. Can you imagine! I hope you would refuse if anyone asked you to abuse a child by giving God's blessing to a name like that!') Mat had disappeared to do something urgently. The dogs were still gazing at Abi and the cake, dribbling disgustingly. Abi suddenly found herself smiling for the first time in weeks. She was going to enjoy living here.

'The bishop said I'd be able to help,' she said when she could at last get a word in edgeways. 'I want to earn my keep.'

Cal smiled. 'You will. Just keeping ourselves going is a full time job. I want to you rest and do absolutely nothing for a while. Take time. But when you're ready I'm going to suggest you muck in with Mat and me and do anything and everything that we do! Honest hard work.' She raised an eyebrow and gave the deep throaty chuckle which appeared to be her signature. 'Then if you show an incredible talent for something like painting walls or sanding medieval woodwork we'll jump on you. Or gardening.' She looked up cautiously.

Abi smiled. 'I'm afraid I'm not much of a gardener. I did help my mother when I was a child.' She took a deep breath and steadied her voice with an effort. She could and must talk about her. 'I loved doing it, but I haven't had much time or space for gardening in the last few years, to be honest. I can weed with the best, though, and cut down brambles.'

'But not till I've had the blackberries.' Cal poured them both more tea. 'There is a fabulous garden here. Somewhere. We hoped we might one day be able to restore it. Put it to work. Maybe get people to pay to come and see it. Mat took early retirement, which was a huge mistake as it turns out. He doesn't have nearly enough pension to support a house like this.'

Abi wasn't sure what to say. She hesitated. 'While I'm here, I should pay you rent –'

'No! No! No!' Cal looked horrified. 'Oh my dear girl, I'm sorry. I didn't mean that. And anyway you are. Didn't you realise? Dear old David is paying us to look after you, well, his diocese is, so in theory you don't have to lift a finger. Except I think he feels some sort of occupational therapy would be good. Am I being tactless mentioning that? I'm sorry.'

Abi smiled. 'I prefer people who speak out. Then we all know where we stand and it makes life so much easier.' She liked this family. She had immediately felt at ease with them.

Cal nodded. She stood up. 'I'm going to show you your room before I open my mouth and put my foot in it any more than I have already. Make yourself at home. Unpack. Settle in. Explore a bit and show up in here at about seven for a drink before supper. How does that sound? Ben is going to come and claim you tomorrow, I gather, for a bit of praying and retreating and all that, and if you need a church there's one at the end of the garden. You can't miss it and we've got our own gate which is handy. There's only a service once a month, I'm afraid. Ben looks after it. It's part of his parish, but he will explain all that.'

Her bedroom window looked south-west, across flat meadows and lines of pollarded willows towards Glastonbury Tor. She stared at it, mesmerised, as it rose, an iconic cone of a hill in the distance, against the bright blue of the sky. The house seemed to have been built on an island in the flat green landscape; perhaps it had once been a real island. It reminded her of the fens at home with the long straight drainage ditches, the serenity of the landscape. Turning away at last she sat down on her bed and stared round taking stock of the room. Cal's non-stop chatter had left her exhausted, but not so exhausted that she couldn't admire her new abode. It was a good-sized rectangular room with a small double bed, a low, comfortable easy chair, an antique chest of drawers, a dressing table, writing table and a fireplace decorated with dried flowers. The bedspread and curtains were a tasteful, restful, soft blue. It was attractive and welcoming. She found herself smiling with pleasure. She loved it.

Mat had brought up her two heavy suitcases and left them by the door. There was masses of other stuff left in the car, but she could bring it all up later herself. In fact, as she had given up the Cambridge flat, all her wordly goods were there. Luckily she didn't have much, at least, not in her present incarnation. She had a room stuffed full of books and clothes and other possessions at home in The Limes, in the room her mother had insisted was still hers, but she hadn't gone back to collect anything she hadn't packed already after her abrupt departure following the quarrel with her father. David's lay secretary had spoken to her father on the phone and explained that Abi would be away for a while and that he wasn't to worry about her. At Abi's request she hadn't told him where Abi was going and he hadn't asked. Nor, he had said apparently, did he intend to worry one iota.

No more than she intended to worry about Kier, she told herself sternly. She hadn't asked David what had happened to him and David had not once mentioned his name.

Washing her face and hands in the small bathroom across the

corridor which Cal had said was for her use alone she stared at herself in the mirror. She had lost a lot of weight in the last few weeks and her cheekbones stood out, giving her face a gaunt beauty. But there were dark rings under her eyes and her hair was looking lank and uncared for. She reached for her brush. She should cut it all off. Tame it. She shivered. That would be a victory for Kier and that could not be allowed to happen. She sighed. It was harder to put him out of her mind than she had imagined. He still haunted her dreams. His eyes were there all the time, watching her, their wild anger and panic terrifyingly real. Firmly she tried again to put behind her the niggling discomfort and fear which even the thought of him caused. With a sigh she dragged the brush through her long hair and pinned it up in a knot. Tonight she would wash it and comb it into some sort of shape and perhaps let it loose to tangle in the autumn wind. After all she was no longer a priest; she was an odd job woman; a gardener; a recluse. And perhaps she was at last going to find out which of these, if any, was the real Abi.

The house stood in some ten acres of paddocks and orchards, she was told, all sloping, draped around the shoulders of the hill like a cloak and the back garden had been laid out by a friend of Gertrude Jekyll. She wandered out onto the lawn and looked around. It was neatly mowed; the beds were a disaster though, their shape barely visible amongst the nettles and a sturdy thatch of couch grass where only a few more-desirable plants had managed to survive. She walked away from the house, following a path beneath an old pear tree, past a natural pond fringed with reeds, towards a stone arch, hung with yellow, sweet-scented roses. The arch was part of what appeared to be some sort of folly, artfully placed against a background of evergreen shrubs. A wooden bench had been placed near it and she sat down gratefully and took a deep breath of the rose-scented air.

Seconds later she realised she wasn't alone. A woman was standing not twenty feet away staring straight at her. She was tall and slender, her dark hair caught into a knot on the back of her neck. She was wearing a long blue dress hitched up into her belt and on her arm there was a basket. She had been cutting flowers. Abi frowned. The dress looked strangely archaic, draped in a Greek

69

or Roman style – but then round Glastonbury with its quota of hippy types she supposed that was not unusual. Perhaps she was a traveller of some kind. She raised a hand and smiled at the woman. 'Sorry to disturb you. I couldn't resist sitting here for a moment in the evening sun.'

The woman didn't respond. She went on staring, not so much at Abi as straight through her. Abi felt a tremor of unease. She stood up and took a step towards her. 'I'm Abi. I've come to stay for a while.'

The woman turned away. She walked towards the arch and out of sight behind it without a word. Abi followed her and stood staring round. The shrubbery opened out into another area of lawn and more flowerbeds. The woman had vanished. With a shrug Abi went back to the bench. It wasn't compulsory to be friendly. She didn't feel much like talking herself, but it was odd that Cal hadn't mentioned anyone else being there. She shivered. Seconds later she was startled to see a girl standing in almost the same place as the woman had earlier. She too had picked some flowers; a spray of blooms hung from her hand. 'Where are you?' the girl called towards the archway. 'Mama?' She moved away and Abi saw she was limping badly. Her face was pale and even from that distance she could see the child was unwell and in pain. She was about to stand up when a man ran past. He was dressed in rough trousers and a loose tunic. 'Petronilla! Come in at once. You will catch cold! Mora is here. She has brought your medicine.'

'I was looking for Mama!' The girl stopped. She turned to face him and smiled. Abi felt a lump in her throat as she saw the girl hold out her arms to him. 'Let me collect some more flowers, Papa. I'm not cold.' But he swept her off her feet, carrying her as though she was much smaller than she actually was, and infinitely precious, and turning, he walked with her towards the hedge. Abi stared after them, puzzled, watching the girl's head droop on her father's shoulder as another woman appeared. Younger, with coppery hair, she also held a basket over her arm. Her dress too was long. Beside her a boy of about thirteen was gazing up at her adoringly.

'Mora!' The girl had raised her head from her father's shoulder. 'Thank you for coming.' The younger woman smiled. She seemed to radiate kindness as she reached out to the girl and touched her head lightly. And then they had gone, the boy running after them as they disappeared through the hedge.

Where was it they were going? Abi didn't attempt to stand up and go after them this time. The small family group seemed so close, so warm together in their affection and she felt suddenly excluded. Swallowing the wave of loneliness which swept over her as they disappeared she stood up and turned sadly back towards the house. It would soon be seven and she could join the others in the kitchen.

'I don't believe it!' Mat pressed a glass of wine into her hand and urged her towards an old wooden rocking chair beside the fire. 'You've only been here about ten minutes and already you've met our ghosts!'

Apparently Cal had been the first to see them when she had visited the house shortly after she and Mat were married. Mat's grandfather lived there then, an irascible old man, long widowed, whose only condescension when anyone visited was to allow them to cook him a meal. Cal and Ben's wife, Janet, took it in turns, stoically producing a roast and two veg week after week for years. Their prize, their husbands had declared later, was the inheritance of Woodley Manor. Millstone Hall as Mat and Cal's eldest son, Rory, called it. Cal had been in the garden picking mint and parsley and, straightening up with her bowl in her hand, had found herself looking at a slim tall dark-haired woman dressed in a blue floor-length gown standing only yards from her. The woman was looking past her, focusing on something in the distance. Inevitably Cal had turned to see what she was looking at with such concentration. When she turned back the woman had gone. Cal was puzzled, even indignant. As if Grandfather hadn't got enough problems living here alone, spaced out trespassers were visitors he just did not need. A few weeks later she saw the woman again, from the house this time. She was standing staring out of the kitchen window, lost in her own thoughts when she saw the same woman walking – drifting – across the lawn. This time she was not alone. A boy was following her and they looked as though they were arguing. Cal tapped sharply on the glass. They took no notice. She ran to the back door but when she emerged on the grass they were nowhere to be seen.

'There are some gypsies parked down on the other side of

71

Wookey,' Mat said when she told him about it. 'I expect they come from there. They've probably come to nick something from the vegetable garden.'

The next time she had seen them was after she and Mat had moved in and were living here. The family were standing in the ruins which formed the base of the rockery and the archway which she and Mat reckoned was an eighteenth-century folly. They were with a man and when Cal accosted the group they disappeared in front of her eyes, one moment there, the next vanished without trace. When she had got over her shock she had studied the ground where they had been standing, muddy, rain-puddled earth, and there were no foot-prints and it was only then that she realised that though she was wet through as the rain beat down on the garden, the three visitors had been bone dry and she had had the distinct impression that where they were, wherever that was, the sun had been shining.

Mat's younger brother Justin had been staying in the house then and he saw the figures the next day. 'Don't worry, Cal. They are harmless. Just stuck between worlds. They can't see you. I'll see if I can talk to them, find out why they are still here, help them to move on.'

But the next day he had had one of his monumental rows with Mat and packed his gear and left. They had no idea where he had gone. They hadn't heard from him in months. But that was Justin all over. And it meant that no-one had tried to talk to the ghosts. She had seen them again only a few weeks ago. This time she had tiptoed away and told no-one, not even Mat. Better that way.

'The ruins out at the back there are part of a Roman villa,' Mat went on, squatting down opposite Abi to throw a couple of logs onto the fire. 'We thought it was a folly dating from the time when some ancestors of ours had pretensions to grandeur a couple of hundred or so years ago, but apparently not. A local archaeologist came up and showed us how it all worked. There has been a settlement here for a couple of thousand years at least, probably longer – since the Iron Age. We've dug up all sorts of bits of pottery and coins in the flowerbeds, most of them Roman or medieval, but some of the pot-sherds were even older. They match up with stuff found in the Lake Villages out there on the levels.'

He waved an arm vaguely towards Glastonbury. 'Exciting, really.' He grinned. 'I've no idea when our ghosts lived here, but we're pretty sure they were Roman or Romano-British. Their clothes seem to fit into that era, according to Cal.' He glanced up at Abi and she saw his eyes narrow briefly as though he were trying to make up his mind whether to confide in her. 'I've discovered the clergy fall into two more or less distinct groups,' he went on cautiously. 'Those who believe in ghosts and those who don't. Ben does, but doesn't believe in interfering, I'm glad to say. If any exorcisms are needed in his parish he will go and pray with people but if anything more complicated is needed he passes it over to the relevant authorities who have health and safety clearance and follow EU guidelines on spirit disposal and recycling.' He smiled again. 'Do you have strong views on any of this?'

Abi grinned. She thought for a minute. 'Up to a few weeks ago I had never knowingly seen a ghost. I think I have always been aware of them. I've sensed them, maybe glimpsed them, but never enough to be sure. Then I saw a whole church full of them in my last parish.' Her last parish! It made her sound as though she had had dozens of parishes. 'I don't really know what I think, to be honest. None of them looked as though they needed exorcising. And neither did the lady and the little girl here. They just looked as though they were getting on with doing their own thing.'

Cal turned away from the stove on the far side of the room and nodded. 'I think that is exactly what is happening. They mind their own business and we mind ours. They have never done us any harm.'

'Do you see them often?' Abi cupped her glass of wine in her hands and stared down into it thoughtfully.

Cal shook her head. 'Every few months perhaps. When I am busy and concentrating on what I am doing either I don't notice them or perhaps they aren't there, I don't know. When I have seen them it has been when I have been standing with my mind a blank.' She chortled. 'I do that less now. There is so much to get on with all the time.' She turned back to the cooker and lifted off a heavy pan, taking it to the sink to drain. 'Mat has never seen them.'

'Why do I take that as being a criticism?' Mat said mildly.

'It's not meant that way,' Cal called. She had dropped a lump of butter into the pan with some creamy milk and was energetically beginning to mash the potatoes.

73

'They spoke English,' Abi said after a moment. 'It sounded like normal English to me. The little girl with the limp was called Petronilla.'

Mat and Cal stared at her. 'You spoke to them?' Cal said after a minute. Her voice had dropped to an awed whisper.

Abi shook her head. 'No. Or at least I did but they didn't seem to hear me. I just listened to what they were saying. The little girl was calling her mother.'

'I never saw a little girl,' Cal said. She had abandoned her potatoes. She pulled a chair away from the table and dragged it over to Abi. Sitting down she stared at Abi's face with such intense concentration that Abi looked away embarrassed. 'And I never heard them say a word. They spoke English with no accent?'

Abi nodded.

'So much for the Roman theory,' Mat said. He seemed disappointed. 'They must be far more recent.' He didn't seem to doubt that they were ghosts.

Cal stood up and went back to her pan. She ground some pepper over it, then put down the grinder and came back to the fire. 'The little girl was limping, you say?'

Abi nodded. 'She looked very ill.' She was beginning to feel guilty. She seemed to have destroyed some pet theory. 'Have you never seen them in the house?' she asked after a moment's thought.

Cal shook her head.

'And have there never been any reports of other people seeing them? Usually places get a reputation for being haunted, don't they? A reputation which goes back for years.'

Mat sighed. 'There have been lots of stories. But then, as you say, all old houses accrue these legends. There is one particular mention in an old book we've got – where is it Cal, can you remember? – I think that was where we got the idea that they were Roman.'

'It's in the study.' Cal turned back to her pan yet again. 'We'll look for it later. Come on, folks. Let's eat, then we'll see what it says while we have our coffee.'

The book was printed in 1798.

'Well, that takes the legend way back,' Cal said as she turned the pages, looking for the entry. 'Here we are. "The ruins are haunted by the ghosts of generations of Roman men and women who made our country their own. From time to time on moonlit nights they may be espied drifting through the remains of this once great house and their cries may be heard in the mists as melancholy as the call of the owls who haunt, no, hunt, the fields. Who knows, perhaps the great King Arthur himself stayed here on the way back to Avalon."' She looked up and smiled. 'I take it your guy didn't look like King Arthur?'

Abi shook her head. She was leaning back in the chair, cradling a cup of coffee on her knee feeling extremely happy. The dogs were asleep at their feet in front of the fire. 'No, he looked like a harassed family man. Not a knight or a round table in sight.'

'The fact that they talk about generations of Romans, and then King Arthur means they don't actually have a clue who the ghosts are,' Mat put in. He had inserted himself into a high-backed settle against the wall. He held out his hand for the book. Flipping back to the flyleaf he squinted at it. 'There are all sorts of inscriptions here, most of them smudged. The first owner of the book seems to have been an Edward Cavendish, then a Benjamin. Then a Maria.' He smiled. 'A bit like a family Bible. They all stake their claim in turn. I wonder how many of them saw them.' He passed the book over to Abi. She held it for a moment uncomfortably. The leather cover was unexpectedly cold and damp and it smelled musty. Overwhelmed by a sudden wave of unhappiness Abi hastily put it down, resisting the urge to wipe her hands on her jeans as she stared down at it, puzzled.

Cal had been watching her face. 'What's wrong?'

'Nothing. I'm not sure. It's just – I felt strange for a moment. I'm tired. I'm sorry. I suppose the long drive and everything that has been happening are catching up with me a bit. Would you think me very rude if I went up?'

'Of course not,' Cal said sympathetically. 'You must do whatever you like here, Abi. Our home is your home. We'll see you in the morning.'

They waited until she had closed the door behind her, then Mat and Cal exchanged glances. Cal leaned forward and picked up the book. She held it for a few moments thoughtfully. 'What was it she felt?' she said quietly.

Mat shrugged. 'Something pretty horrible. Does it feel strange to you?'

Cal shook her head. She was holding the book in both hands, turning it around. 'She's very psychic, isn't she. Ben did say the bishop was worried.' With a shrug she put the book down. 'Do you think we ought to tell Ben when he comes over tomorrow?'

'It might be good to let it come up in the conversation naturally with her there.' Mat stood up and stretched. Immediately the two dogs rose to their feet, tails wagging. 'I'll take them for a walk up the drive before bed. You go on up.' He reached for the fireguard and hauled it into place in front of the dying embers. 'It looks as though our guest is going to prove quite interesting.' He winked at her as he made his way to the door. 'Perhaps she will be the one finally to unravel the story of those poor, cold souls out there in the garden.'

6

'What is wrong, Mama?' Petra looked up from the fire where she was sitting huddled in a cocoon of sheepskins and woven rugs. It had been a wet summer and now it was a wet autumn, the fens still lakes, the fields puddled. The colours of the dogwoods and maples on the slopes of the hills were already brilliant against the clouds when the sun appeared, but tonight as on so many nights, everything was awash. The summer country had not dried out this year.

Lydia was standing staring down into the hissing logs, her own cloak pulled tightly round her shoulders, her lips set in a hard line as they listened to the rain beating down on the reed thatch above their heads.

'Your father and your brother should be home by now.'

'I thought Papa said he would be gone for several days.' Petra was trying to keep her teeth from chattering.

'And several days have passed.'

Lydia squatted down and held her hands out to the flames. 'And Romanus. He promised me he would be back by nightfall.'

'Perhaps Mora wasn't there. He wouldn't come back without her.' The girl forced a smile. 'He will wait at the college until she returns, you know how much he likes her.'

The scene had been played out so many times before. Romanus, Lydia's son, Petra's young brother, had gone across to the island to fetch the healer, Mora. When she came she brought herbs and amulets, incantations and magic, gentle, confident smiles and warm comforting hands to make his sister more comfortable in the mysterious illness which was reducing her more and more quickly to a small shrunken figure overwhelmed with pain. And while they waited, Lydia's husband, the children's father, would have made his way to the coast to meet the trading vessels, to broker deals between the merchants who came from across the world to the port of Axiom, bringing wine and luxury goods from across the Empire and buying in exchange local lead and tin and copper, slaves and hunting dogs. Above all he went to meet the trading vessels which had come from the Roman provinces of Gaul and Hispania and from the Tyrrhenian Sea itself. He was frustrated in his self-appointed exile, lonely and homesick. It never seemed to occur to him that his wife might be as well. That she too might need to be out of the little primitive house to which he had brought them all, the house in the cold damp country which had crippled his daughter with its icy winds and creeping mists and was turning his British-born son into a rebellious thug.

At the time it had seemed they had no choice. Gaius Atilius Geminus had been born, the elder by several hours, one of a pair of twins. Miraculously both children and their mother had survived, though the younger child, Flavius, had for a long time been sickly and was shorter and markedly less handsome than his brother. The difference had set them apart and in spite of their parents' insistence that both children be treated alike in every way, the younger twin grew up perceiving nuances of favouritism towards his brother at every turn. Childish rivalry grew into teenage jealousy and then into adult resentment. Flavius used his not inconsiderable charm and strength of personality to steal effortlessly and maliciously everything his increasingly reclusive elder brother held dear. Especially his girl-friends. When at last Gaius found the woman he wanted to marry, Flavius set his cap for her at once. She rejected him. Flavius grew angry. He went to a sibyl practising her trade near the Temple of the Vestals and bought charms to win her over. When they didn't work he went back demanding a refund and, when the woman told him spitefully that she had seen in her scrying bowl his doom in a woman's eyes, he thought better of it and produced his purse and bought curses instead. His jealousy of his brother turned to hatred. The young men's parents, well aware of what was happening and blaming themselves, though not knowing what they could have done differently, settled on the idea of buying Flavius a commission in the army to take him away from Rome. He was posted to the Province of Judea, but then, as effortlessly as he accomplished most things Flavius turned the plan around, manoeuvring himself into the exclusive Imperial bodyguard. It would be Gaius who would have to leave. Uncomplaining, he apprenticed himself to a merchant trader and proved himself extremely able, travelling further and further abroad on the ships owned by his wealthy employer, his young and beautiful wife at his side. They travelled to Gaul and Hispania, south into Mauritania and to Leptis Magna, to Egypt and finally north again to Macedonia, and at last to Antioch and Damascus where their first child, Petronilla, was born. The little family were happy and secure and reasonably wealthy. Then they heard that Flavius had managed to obtain a posting back to Caesarea. He was on their trail.

Anxious to avoid him and his never-ending spite they travelled to the edge of the known world, to Britannia, and there they decided to stay. Flavius would never find them in this mist-shrouded isle. The country was mysterious, sacred. It was also the seat of a bustling trading economy and Gaius found himself at once busy and in demand as a negotiator and entrepreneur. At first they settled in Calleva. It was Petra's illness which had pushed them westwards to Ynys yr Afalon, the Isle of Apples, where the college of druids, in one of the most sacred of the great sanctuaries of the Pretannic Isles, boasted, so it was said, the cleverest healers in the known world, and there their son Romanus was born, named for the city from which they hailed and which they both still missed so much. Gaius turned his attention northwards to the ports on the estuary of the great river Sabrina, where the trade in lead and silver was at its most active and lucrative, leaving Lydia at home with the children in a small house in the foothills of the Meyn Dyppa, overlooking the meres and lakes and the island where the buildings of the college clustered around the strange conical hill they called the Tor, which was the centre of its power and sacredness.

The Roman family had been welcomed by their neighbours. They were some distance from the nearest hill fort, the centre of the local branch of the great Dubunni tribe, but the area was safe and free from danger. Their farmstead though not large was comfortable, the main house, round and reed-thatched like those of their neighbours was most of the time warm and dry and well appointed. But it could not keep out the creeping damp of the autumn mists, nor the bone-aching cold of the winter winds. They made friends, they had servants and slaves to work the small patches of ground where they grew beans and peas and in the larger fields barley and oats and to watch over the sheep which grazed on the hills around them. In the summer the countryside was benevolent and beautiful, rich in game and fish and very fertile. The warmth of even this northern sun penetrated Petra's aching body and gave her some relief, but in the winter the girl grew more and more ill until she was crying with pain. The healers from the settlement helped her. They gave her decoctions made from the local willow trees which brought down her fever and let her rest. They were kind and reassuring. She would grow out of it, they said. This ailment was common amongst young girls in this country. Soon she would improve.

Then they met the beautiful and enigmatic Mora and Petra had made a friend and thirteen-year-old Romanus had fallen in love. Mora had come one day with one of the older, most experienced of druid healers. Mora was, he said, the daughter of Fergus Mor, the college father, the most senior druid on the island and she had a gift such as he had not seen in years. He felt that she would build up a rapport with Petra which would benefit them both. He handed over the case to the young woman, scarcely more than a few years older than Petra herself, and from that day the sick girl improved. Until now. A particularly vicious wind had blown from the north for days now, cutting Lydia to the bone. She could not begin to think how Petra must be hurting for the girl to cry so piteously.

Romanus had not been able to bear to see his sister in such pain. 'I'll go and fetch Mora,' he said at last, and Lydia had let him go. What else could she do? She couldn't stop him going to find the object of his infatuation now he had an excuse, and Mora was not due to come for at least a month. Besides, it was not far. It would mean running down through the woods and fields, then he would have to take one of the dugout canoes, and thread his way across the low-lying fens, following the deeper channels between the willow and alder and reeds, to the centre on the island where Mora lived. Easy for a boy of thirteen, but even so for reasons she did not quite understand, she had been filled with misgivings. The weather was bad, and Petra had clung to her brother begging him not to go. 'Wait for Papa to return,' she wailed. 'I can hang on. There is enough of the medicine left.'

Lydia had glanced at the small jar on the shelf and shaken her head. There was barely any left at all.

The letter had come only hours after Romanus had set off, a scroll from one of the traders based on the coast, dropped off at the door by a young man on horseback. It was addressed to Gaius.

I thought you should be aware that there is a man here claiming to be your brother, and he is indeed very like you. He has been asking where you are and several of the traders have told him how to find you. I thought it strange that he did not know where his own brother lived, and I did not like his demeanour. Forgive me if I have misjudged the situation, but I send this missive with good intentions.

Lydia's hands crushed the parchment and she let it fall. She was trembling all over. This could not have happened. For thirteen years they had been free of Flavius. They had thought themselves safe from his malign attentions; thought never to see or hear from him again. How had he tracked them down? Had he gone back to Rome to consult the seer? Why had he come? After all this time surely he did not still harbour the old grudges. She became aware suddenly that Petra was studying her face. 'Mama, what is it?'

Lydia took a deep breath. 'A message for your father, child. It seems the messenger missed him at Axiom.'

Why had he missed him? Her heart missed a beat. Gaius had been there for several days now. Had he left for home before Flavius arrived, and if so why had the messenger not overtaken him on the track? Where was he? A gust of wind battered the house, causing the fire to smoke, stirring the floor coverings and making the lamp flames dip and flare and she suppressed a groan of anguish.

There was no sign of Gaius that day or the next, nor of Flavius. And still Romanus had not returned. On the third morning she decided she must go after her son. The daughter of their neighbour had come to see Petra, bringing a gift from her mother of two freshly tanned sheepskins for her bed and the girl agreed to stay until Lydia came back. She stood for a long while outside the house staring down the track towards the north. There was no sign of anyone coming up the long slope from the woods. She must pray to the gods to protect her daughter and go to find Romanus and bring him home.

She took one of the farm ponies, making good speed on the soft muddy ground, heading west down the track towards the levels. It had stopped raining and a fitful sun was peering between the clouds, reflecting in the puddles. Once at the edge of the mere she would have to find someone to take her across to the island. Normally she would have enjoyed such a journey. The wind had backed into the west and was warmer now and more gentle. Her pony was frisky, pleased to be out of its pen. As she gained the more level ground the going was easier and the trackway through the trees firmer beneath the pony's feet.

She drew up at last at the landing stage and slid from the pony's back. The place was deserted. There were no boats pulled up on the mud. It was then she heard the swans circling overhead, swans which her Celtic neighbours said carried the souls of dead children to the otherworld.

Ben glanced across at Abi as they walked slowly through the garden towards the church. It was a glorious morning, the sunlight catching the turning leaves and changing them to burnished gold and crimson and tawny. They stopped beside the ruins, staring at the remnants of the walls. 'They started to excavate in the late thirties, I believe,' he said after a long silence as they stood looking down at the stones. 'They found quite a lot of stuff from the Roman villa. Then the war came and they hastily covered most of it up. They never quite got round to it again.'

'Mat and Cal told you I thought I saw a ghost or two yesterday?' Abi thought it better to take the bull by the horns.

Ben nodded.

'Have you ever seen them?'

He shook his head. 'Cal is the psychic one amongst us. But there have been lots of stories down the centuries.'

'All my life I've seen things, and suspected I was what for a want of a better term is called psychic,' Abi said thoughtfully,' but I've never really *seen* ghosts in my life before. Then a few weeks ago in Cambridge I saw a whole lot of them. And other strange

82

things. And then there was no doubt in my mind at all as to what they were. It's as though something has switched on this ability –' She stopped in mid-sentence.

Ben waited silently. Listening was something he was good at. A long attentive silence, relaxed, not threatening. He would wait until she was ready to go on. When she did she had changed the subject. Whatever it was she had thought of, she was not ready to talk about it yet. 'Does Kier know where I am?'

Ben shook his head slowly. 'Not unless you have told him yourself. Bishop David was very clear on that point. He told me that you had requested that neither your father nor Kieran Scott should be told where you were going.'

'Kier frightened me. There was something in his eyes. A fanaticism which I have never seen in anyone before.' She shook her head miserably. 'He kept saying God had planned for me to move in to look after him, then in the next breath he said such terrible things about me. He accused me of being a witch!' It was a cry of anguish. 'And who knows, maybe he is right. That's why I can't go on being a priest.'

Ben sighed. It was not for him to question the decision of a bishop, not even David Paxman, but as far as he knew Kieran had been allowed to stay in his parish. Ben could not imagine why if the man was becoming unhinged 'Shall we walk on a little way? You will have the chance to do a lot of thinking while you are here, Abi, and if you need to, you will be able to pray, too. You must not let this man give you cause to doubt yourself. I suggest you take things slowly. Make no irrevocable decisions at this stage. We can discuss the future when you have had a chance to recover. You have had a lot to deal with over the past few weeks. There is no hurry.'

Abi smiled at him. 'You are good at this.'

'Good at what?'

'Consolation. Advice. Spiritual ice packs.'

'I've had a lot of practice over the years.' Ben nodded with a resigned smile. 'Make full use of me, Abi. Use me as a sounding board, a punch bag, an echo chamber. Whatever you like. I can take it. And in the meantime let me show you the way to my favourite church. I want you to go there every day. Several times a day if it helps. It is a place of solace and peace and safety.'

The little church towards which they were heading stood on an outcrop of land very similar to the one on which Woodley was built. Two small islands in the flat green of the fields, side by side, close together. So close that the ancient orchards which surrounded Woodley's gardens, spilling down the side of the hill, were separated from the ancient churchyard on the neighbouring slopes, only by a crumbling wall and a lych-gate roofed in ancient silvered oak.

They never reached it. As if by some unspoken mutual agreement they stopped at the gate at the foot of the little overgrown graveyard, spending several minutes in silent contemplation of the yew trees and the wild flowers growing on the graves, listening to the gentle gossip of the jackdaws on the squat, Norman tower before quietly turning to climb back towards the house. When Abi went there to pray she would go alone.

An hour later Abi was in her bedroom kneeling in front of one of her suitcases. In the bottom, wrapped in a sweater, was the lump of crystal. She had run out into the garden moments after her father had hurled it out of the window, her heart in her mouth in case it had shattered on the paving stones beneath. Looking up she had seen that he was still standing at the attic window, staring out. He did not react as she had walked outside into the sunlight, staring round, looking for it. When she failed to spot it at once she feared she might not find it at all amongst all the flowerbeds and plants and shrubs but she did, almost at once. It was lying on a patch of short grass near the little fountain, the sunlight reflecting off one of its clear glassy faces. She couldn't miss it. It was as though it had called out to her. Pushing the thought aside she had scooped it up, glancing quickly up at the window of her mother's boudoir. There was no sign now of her father. With a sigh of relief she turned back to the French door and through to where her cases were standing in the hall. In minutes she had loaded all her belongings into the car and driven away.

She unwrapped the crystal carefully and put it down on the window sill where the sunlight immediately caught one of the faces, sending prisms flashing round the room. Its power was almost tangible. It felt as if she had been administered a double shot of caffeine. Jumpy. Alert. All her senses suddenly in over-drive, her heart thudding uncomfortably. Spontaneously she stepped back from it and at once felt a diminution of the sensations. The thought that had come to her earlier as she was talking to Ben was resurfacing. It was since she had touched the crystal that first time in her mother's room she had begun to see ghosts so clearly. To experience them in a way which brooked no denial. The shock of her mother's death and the logistics of leaving her job and her flat and parting from her father had distracted her from analysing what had been happening to her. Now, for the first time she concentrated on the stone. It was after she had first held it that she had become aware of people's auras, that she had felt able to communicate in some strange way with the dead, that she had experienced this absolute certainty. She shivered. Was this what her mother had been so pleased about? The fact that her daughter had felt the crystal tingling beneath her fingers. Was this what Laura had been going to tell her about? And if so, why had she thought it would destroy Abi's Christian faith? She reached out and ran her finger over the crystal face experimentally. It gave off a crackle and a spark. She jumped back. But of course that was natural. After all, crystals had power, the piezoelectric effect. That was why modern technology was dependent on them. She groped in her memory for the definition in her science books at school. It had been something to do with the fact that quartz under pressure produces electricity naturally. It was inherent in its structure. There was nothing spooky about it. This was a big one. It had enormous power. The Serpent Stone, her great-great-grandmother had called it in her note. She looked down at it thoughtfully, hesitant about touching it again. Slowly she put her finger out towards it. The crackle came while it was still several inches away. It wasn't like an electric shock. It merely made a sound like a hiss, a presence trying to make itself heard. The hiss of a serpent. Was that where it had got its name? Or of a radio, searching for a station. 'That's it, isn't it,' she whispered. 'You are trying to tune in.' Almost fearfully she laid her finger on the clear face again, touching it lightly and instantly removing her finger. As the contact was made a sound rang out in the room, a split second of speech, too short for her even to catch the words. It was there and in a tenth of a second it was over. She swallowed. Do it again. More slowly this time. This time she laid two fingers side by side on the crystal face and left them there. Nothing. She moved away, astonished to find she was trembling. Taking a deep breath she approached it again and once again touched it, this time just with her index finger. Nothing. 'OK. So I've offended you,' she murmured. 'Last chance.' Picking the crystal up, she turned it round in the sunlight from the window, once more filling the room with dancing lights. And figures. Two figures. For a fraction of a second, standing by the door. Two shadowy shapes, barely recognisable as human. She almost dropped the crystal. Putting it back on the window sill she stared at the place where the figures had been. There was nothing there now. No prisms, no colours flickering against the wall, no figures. Nothing.

'It's a transmitter,' she whispered, awed. 'It really is. It made some kind of hologram.' Exhaling, she sat down on the bed and sat staring at it. Where on earth had it come from, this strange bequest of her mother's? Something so special, and yet so primitive. And what was there about it that had affected her father so strongly? Standing up she went back to the window sill and touched it again.

Nothing happened. Outside a cloud drifted over the sun and the crystal dulled.

I'll find you Abi!

She turned round, startled. The voice had been in the room with her. Only faint, but clearly audible. This time she recognised it. It was Kier's voice. She swallowed hard. 'No, you won't,' she whispered. 'Never in a million years.'

Ben was perched on the edge of the kitchen table watching his sister-in-law peel potatoes. 'I like her, but she's got some pretty big issues with this chap, Kier,' Cal said cautiously. 'He sounds like a complete shit.' She threw down the potato peeler. 'The kind of clergyman guaranteed to turn off people in droves and send them fleeing from the church.'

'Not true, unfortunately.' Ben eased himself further onto the table to get comfortable, one leg swinging gently. 'There are a lot of people out there who like nothing better than a rabid fundamentalist.

It sounds to me as if this poor woman was thrown to him like a sacrificial virgin.'

Cal smiled broadly. She reached for a tea towel and dried her hands. 'I doubt she's any kind of virgin,' she said practically, 'but I get your point. She seems to have a very touching naïveté about what a vicar does. Are you going to be able to save her for the church or is she a goner?'

Ben shook his head. 'We shouldn't be talking about her like this.'

'No, but you are her spiritual adviser and I am her landlady. We have to conspire to make her feel happy and secure.' She paused. 'What do you think about the ghosts?'

'I doubt they would make her feel either happy or secure.'

'She's not imagining them?'

'How can she be if you've seen them too? And if they've been described in loving detail in all sorts of old books for the last God knows how many years?'

'I wish Justin were here.'

Ben exhaled sharply. 'Don't let Mat hear you say that.'

'I won't. But Justin would know what to do.'

'And I don't?'

She put her arms round him and gave him a hug. 'Of course you do, my dear. It's just you are not quite so glamorous!'

That afternoon Abi offered to do some weeding round the back, near the rockery which it now turned out was the remains of a Roman villa. Cal studied her. 'You want to see them again?'

Abi nodded.

'And the thought doesn't frighten you?'

'I don't think so.' Abi glanced at her hostess and shrugged. 'This is all new to me. Like most people I imagined ghosts appeared in the dark in old houses on stormy windy nights wailing and gnashing their teeth. That would be scary.' She shook her head. 'These were outside in the sunshine and they were somehow busy with their own lives. It felt as though they were still there in a world of their own, a world through the looking glass. Like the people in St Hugh's' Church. They didn't feel threatening. I am curious, I'm being nosy, and I want to see what is happening in their world.'

87

Collecting some gardening tools and a wheelbarrow from an outbuilding at the side of the house Abi made her way through the garden. The stone arch had been much restored, she could see that now with the sunlight behind her. The neatly seamed joints between the stones were too solid, too well ordered to be in their original state. The walls, thrusting from the rich earth of the beds were, though; they were little more than piles of rubble with here and there two or three brick-shaped stones cemented with pale crumbling mortar. Picking up the fork she thrust it into the soil and wrestled a thistle out of the ground. The fork came up with a piece of grey pottery stuck between the tines. She smiled, working it free with her fingers. Roman? She wasn't sure. Shaking her head, she let it fall. Whatever it was, this was where it belonged. She dug on for several minutes, keeping her eye open for shadows moving around her. There was nothing. The only movement came from a robin which watched her with beady little eyes from its perch on the lowest branch of a berry-laden cotoneaster nearby.

Sticking the fork into the earth, she stepped back and went to the barrow. With the trowel and the hoe, wrapped in an unbleached cotton shopping bag, was the crystal. Carefully wiping her hands on the seat of her jeans she picked it up and unwrapped it, feeling suddenly a little nervous. Behind her the robin flew to the handle of the fork. It fluffed up its breast and began to sing. Abi smiled, reassured. Surely if something frightening were about to happen the bird would have flown away. She cradled the crystal between her hands and turned back to the archway. 'Come on. Let's see you then,' she whispered. 'Petra? Are you there?' Robin or no robin she was a little scared, she realised suddenly. Scared it would happen. Or was she more scared that it wouldn't? She stepped closer to the flowerbed.

Was the crystal vibrating in her hands? She wasn't sure. Holding it firmly she looked up at the arch. With a sharp call of warning the robin flew back to the tree. The story had begun.

Romanus had pulled his canoe up onto the muddy bank amongst a line of other craft of different shapes and sizes which had been left there, and he headed up towards the cluster of houses, some large, some smaller, which formed the centre of the college. Mora's house was further on, higher up on the slope of one of the lesser hills amongst rows of other small circular huts, cells where each individual student, priest and priestess lived and studied and prayed. He glanced round nervously. He had known the men and women of this college for most of his thirteen years, but the place still filled him with awe when he came across to the island. This was one of the most sacred places in the world, a centre of learning where students came from every corner of the land and even from across the ocean. At its centre on the great Tor was the sanctuary dedicated to the god of the otherworld, Gwyn ap Nudd; beneath the hill was the entrance to his kingdom. Tiptoeing in his efforts not to draw attention to himself, he dodged past the huts of the college servants and between the animal pens to climb the slopes towards the trees. Mora's little house stood there, on its own, in the shelter of an old oak tree. He could see the first golden leaves of autumn had fallen and scattered on the reed roof. There was no smoke filtering up through the reeds to show she was at home. His heart sank. 'Mora?' The boy stood outside and cleared his throat nervously. 'Mora, are you there?'

Silence.

He stepped forward and pulled aside the heavy curtain which hung across the doorway. The interior of the house was dark. It smelled smoky from the fire, but also of something else. Rich herbs. To his intense disappointment he could see that the hearth was empty and cold. He glanced up to where the bunches of herbs she was drying for her medicines hung from the roof beams. They moved slightly in the draught from the doorway as he held the curtain aside, peering in. Above them the roof was stained black from the smoke of her fire.

'Romanus?' A sharp voice behind him made him start. He dropped the curtain and jumped backwards. 'Cynan!'

The young priest smiled at him, his warm green eyes friendly. 'Mora has gone to visit the settlements. She won't be back for several days.' He saw the boy's face fall. 'Is something wrong? Is it Petra?' The men and women of the druid college had come to know the Roman family who lived on the small island in the fen between Ynys yr Afalon and the lowest slopes of the Meyn

Dyppa very well in the thirteen years since they had come to the area. They lived very near a small deserted sacred island where he himself often went to meditate and pray alone at the isolated little temple to the gods of the marsh and waters of the mere. The plight of their beautiful daughter had touched all their hearts. One or two of them had become especial friends, and Cynan, Mora's close companion, training to be a seer and diviner, the man she would probably one day marry, was one of them. He often came with Mora on her visits to their homestead and the whole family had in their turn become fond of him.

Romanus nodded. 'She cries in her sleep with the pain and her joints are swelling again. Mora is the only one who can soothe her. She tries to be brave and she never complains, but Mora is not due to come for several weeks and the medicine is nearly finished.' The boy bit his lip. He adored his big sister; her anguish hurt him as though the pain were his own.

Cynan sighed. 'I wish I could help. I tell you what, we'll go to Addedomaros and ask him. I am sure he can give you some medicine to help until Mora returns. The moment she comes back I will ask her to come across to your house.' He smiled kindly as he saw Romanus's hesitation. The senior healer druid on the island was a formidable man. He could quite understand the boy's reluctance to approach him, though he knew that for Petra he would dare anything.

Romanus squared his shoulders. 'You will come with me to ask him?'

Cynan nodded. 'You know I will.'

The healer's lecture hall was at the centre of the settlement which served the sanctuary. He was standing at a table, lit by several lamps, and round him stood a group of students, their faces shadowed and intense in the flickering light. They were all studying the selection of bowls and jars on the table in front of them, and the heavy mortar in the centre into which one of their number was carefully measuring some dark brown liquid from a bottle. It smelled bitter and corrosive.

Addedomaros glanced up. 'Cynan? We have a visitor I see.' The old man's white hair and beard were neatly trimmed, his well-worn, patched robe freshly laundered. At first sight there was nothing to show that this man was one of the most powerful healers in all the Pretannic Isles.

Romanus was standing a little behind Cynan. He met the man's eyes nervously. 'My sister is ill again, Father Addedomaros.'

The old man nodded. 'I feared as much. And Mora is not here?'

Cynan shook his head.

'She has gone to the mainland with Yeshua?' Addedomaros asked. He gestured sharply at the young man with the bottle, who hastily stopped pouring, put it down and re-stoppered it.

Cynan nodded reluctantly. 'He is keen to see everything she does.'

'He is here to learn as well as teach.' The older man spoke gently but there was a slight note of reproach in his voice. 'It was her father's wish she mentor him, Cynan.'

Cynan looked down at his feet. 'Could you make up something for Romanus to take back with him?' he asked after a moment.

'Of course. Sylvia will make it up.' Addedomaros glanced across at one of the students. The girl looked horrified at being singled out so peremptorily. 'Willow and ash bark in equal quantities. With some birch leaf and burdock,' he commanded. 'And add some elderberries.' He glanced at Cynan. 'Should you be at your studies?'

Cynan nodded.

'Then go. We will see that Romanus has his medicine.'

It did not take long. Clutching the flask to his chest Romanus raced back to his canoe and stowing the precious liquid in the bow he pushed off, the water ice-cold around his ankles, the mud soft between his toes as he hauled the heavy boat off the bank and into the deeper water. Leaping in, he seized his paddle and drove the dugout round threading his way through the reeds back towards the shore of the mainland. A pair of pelicans, landing heavily in the water near him, distracted him for a moment and so he did not notice the tall man waiting for him. Only when he had dragged the vessel up onto the grass and thrown a rope around a tree trunk to make sure it was safe did he look up and see him. 'Papa!' His face lit up. Then, after a second searching glance, he stepped back, puzzled. The man standing looking down at him was at first sight so like his father it was uncanny. But this man was shorter. Where his father had adopted the style of the local people and wore his hair long and sported a fine moustache, this man was clean-shaven and his hair was short-cut, his clothes like those Romanus had seen down at Axiom when the traders had come in from the distant corners of the Empire.

The man smiled. 'So this is Romanus, I presume? What perfect timing. As I came up river from the port with some local fishermen they spotted you and said you were Romanus the son of Gaius. I am your Uncle Flavius, young man. Now you can show me the way to your house. Your mother is going to be so pleased to see me.'

'Abi?' Cal, wandering out into the garden later, found her guest standing transfixed, staring into space. 'Are you all right? Did you see something?'

Abi jumped. For a moment she didn't seem to recognise Cal, then she shook her head. 'I'm sorry. I was miles away.'

Cal noted the fork in the flowerbed. Almost no progress had been made with the weeding. The robin was singing from the top of the cotoneaster now, his breast blending perfectly with the russet of the leaves and berries. 'So, what did you see?'

'It was amazing!' Abi shook her head. 'It was as if I had some sort of day dream. I didn't see the ghosts. At least, not like before. I wasn't looking at them from outside the way I saw them yesterday. I seemed to be dreaming their story. Of course I might have been making it up. Having some sort of weird reverie; a fantasy. Perhaps I was asleep. The scene was set in a round house, not a Roman villa. Petra, the daughter, was ill and her younger brother was trying to fetch some medicine for her. He went to Glastonbury. It seemed to be a real island then and he paddled a dugout canoe across to it. I could see the Tor. He visited some sort of druid village and went to see the senior chap who seemed to be taking a class of students. He gave him some medicine for Petra. Then he came back and his uncle was waiting for him.'

Cal sat down on the bench. 'My God! You make it sound like a film. Then what happened?'

Abi shrugged. 'Nothing. You came.' She shook her head. 'Sorry, that sounded a bit cross. I didn't mean it that way.' She paused thoughtfully. 'I must have been dreaming, but it was all so real!' She paused again. 'Have you heard of a place called Axiom?'

Cal wrinkled her nose. 'Axium was a Roman port on the Bristol Channel. I think it's at Uphill near Weston. The rivers and coastline have all changed so much over the millennia but somewhere like that. Does that help?'

Abi nodded. 'It fits, I think.'

'I've read masses about the area over the years. Glastonbury wasn't – isn't – technically quite an island as I expect you know. It's a peninsula. Now the levels have been drained, it's an island in a flat landscape, but once it was surrounded by water at least in the winter. They think Ponters Ball, which is an earthwork across the neck of land between Glasto and the mainland, was a defensive barrier which effectively turned it into an island. No one knows for sure what was here, as far as I know, in Roman times or before, but if it was a sacred place, a sanctuary under the druids, then that would have been its boundary.' She ran her fingers through her hair. 'I'm trying to remember my local history. If it helps, the names of both our rivers, the Axe and the Brue, meant river in Celtic times. Axe from the same word as Isca and Brue meaning something like fast flowing water. Which it isn't. Not now! So, Axium just meant a place on the river! If your port was called Axiom perhaps it was the pre-Roman name.' Her gaze was resting on the crystal ball in Abi's hands. 'What on earth is that? I've been dying to ask.'

Abi looked down at it almost guiltily. 'Something my mother gave me.' She reached into the wheelbarrow for the cotton bag and carefully inserted the lump of crystal into it, wrapping it gently. 'It's strange, I know, but I have been wondering if this is what helped me make contact with your ghosts. An ancient crystal ball.' She laughed in embarrassment.

'And did it?'

Abi shrugged again. 'Something did.' She laid the bag back in the wheelbarrow. 'Is Ben still around?'

Cal shook her head. 'He went home a while back. If you need to see him again I am sure you could give him a ring and drive over there. It is not far.' She wiggled the fork free of the soil and laid it in the barrow. 'Come in, Abi. You look very cold. If you've been standing out here for hours you must be chilled to the bone in this wind. And we have a problem.' She sighed. 'I've had a phone call from your father.'

93

Abi looked up, startled. 'He's not supposed to know where I am!' she said sharply.

'No, that's what I thought you said. He gave me a number and asked me to get you to ring him. He said you weren't returning his calls on your mobile. He sounded –' She broke off as though uncertain how to put it. 'He sounded a little impatient.'

'My father is always impatient.' Abi stooped to pick up the handles of the barrow. 'I am so sorry if he was rude. That was one of the reasons I didn't want him to know where I was. I hoped my mother's death,' she paused and took a deep breath, 'well, I hoped it might bring us closer together, but it seemed to do just the opposite.' He hadn't rung her mobile. No-one had. All her friends, it appeared, had decided to give her some space.

The number he had given Cal was the home phone. After some hesitation she pressed dial on her mobile as she stood at her bedroom window looking out towards the Tor. Her father answered after two rings. He must be sitting at his desk. She tried to suppress the wave of misery which threatened to overwhelm her as she thought of him alone in the echoing empty house.

'Abigail?' His voice rang in the room. 'Why didn't you tell me that you had been sacked?'

She closed her eyes briefly. 'I haven't been sacked, Daddy. I resigned. As a matter of interest, how did you get this number?'

'The bishop's office. Your boss came to see me,' her father went on without pause. His voice was neutral. She couldn't read his thoughts. 'Kieran Scott.'

'I am sorry.' She gave a wry smile; she thought of Jesus as her boss. She toyed for a second with the thought of her father and what his reactions would be to an encounter with Jesus Christ, wondering who would win the argument.

'We talked. He's an interesting man.'

'He's an ordained priest,' she retorted. Had Kier turned up without the dog collar, knowing her father was an atheist? If so he was a hypocrite – something to add to all his other sins in her eyes.

'He explained he had been your employer. Why did you feel the need to run away from him?' Her father sounded merely curious, his tone level. She still couldn't guess where he was coming from.

'Didn't he tell you?'

'He said he misinterpreted your feelings; he said he might have frightened you. He is extremely sorry that he upset you.'

'And he's asked you to be his spokesman?' She was incredulous.

'Not in so many words. I liked the man.' She detected a note of embarrassment. 'He believes in God which I suppose is his prerogative, but he assured me he would never require anyone else to do the same. We talked about the chemistry of the universe. We talked about definitions. He agreed that a great deal of the received attitude to mysticism is a nonsense which the church as an institution could well do without.'

'I see.' Abi pushed open the window and leaned on the sill, staring out at the garden. So Kier was crawling to her father. Thank goodness she had insisted no-one tell him where she was staying. The thought, as soon as it occurred to her, was dashed. 'He said he hadn't been told where you are,' her father said. 'But I don't see why you don't want him to know. Why not give the man a chance?'

'Because, I don't want to see him ever again. He was violent. Did he tell you that? He was threatening and he has destroyed my career.'

Her father let out a sound which sounded very much like 'Tosh!' 'He said you had over-reacted,' he continued with exaggerated patience. 'He said you leaped to conclusions. Silly girl. You've always done that. I told him given time you would come round.'

'I beg your pardon!' Abi was incandescent with fury. 'How dare you say that! You had no right.'

'I had every right. I'm your father. I know you better than anyone, even you yourself if you would just admit it. If you are going to persist with this stupid God stuff, you would be much better to do it under the firm guidance of a man who knows that the whole thing is a metaphor.'

Her hands were shaking. Somehow she resisted the urge to switch off the phone and cut him off. 'You haven't told him where I am, have you?' she said furiously. 'Please tell me you haven't. Please, don't encourage him to think that I am amenable to persuasion. I don't want to hear from him again. OK?' She paused. There was no answer. He had hung up.

Abi sat down heavily on the settle and stared at Cal in despair. 'My father knows where I am.'

Cal shrugged. 'I don't suppose it was hard to find out. I know Ben wouldn't have said anything, he knows that you wanted your whereabouts kept secret, but he was dealing with the bishop's office. I imagine there are several people there who would know. If your father rang and said he'd lost your number and that it was urgent, there might have been someone who thought it OK to tell him.'

Abi nodded. 'Will he tell Kier, though? Knowing I don't want him to has given him power over me. He liked that. I could hear it in his voice.'

Cal came and sat down opposite her. The fire was still unlit. A bed of grey ash lay in the hearth, illuminated by a patch of sunshine which had strayed down the huge chimney. The dogs had gone out somewhere with Mat. 'Abi, if your father could find out, so could anyone, I'm afraid, but remember, you are safe here. If your father comes, even if Kier comes, they can't drag you away. We will give them a cup of tea, talk to them nicely and then ask them to leave. If they don't go, then you can go and stay somewhere else for a day or a week or a month if necessary until they do.' She grinned broadly. 'I defy anyone to stay here if Mat decides he doesn't like them. You don't know him well enough yet, but the dear old stick can make himself extremely prickly when he wants to. And no-one is going to threaten you or hurt you with the Cavendish brothers on the premises. OK?'

Abi nodded, speechless for a moment. 'Thank you,' she whispered. It was ridiculous, feeling like bursting into tears because someone was being kind to you. Cal had the tact to look away. She stood up. 'Tea before you go out again?'

The small church, dedicated to St Mary of Wood Leigh, was a gem. Like Woodley itself, it rose on an outcrop of rock and sand, one of the many small 'islands' rising from the levels, the churchyard surrounded by a low wall of warm honey-coloured stone, the lych-gate carved from gnarled oak. Letting herself in, panting after the steep climb between the moss-covered gravestones, Abi stared round, feeling the atmosphere wrapping itself around her like a warm blanket, reassuring, calm, steady. Even without glancing at the short history of the church for sale at the entrance for the princely sum of twenty pence, Abi had guessed that it was incredibly ancient and built upon an even more ancient sacred site. She could feel it. Something from the distant past, an older sanctity which predated and somehow transcended its life as a Christian church. Firmly she pushed the feeling aside. She had come here to pray to her own god.

Closing the door softly behind her she walked up the aisle. Instead of pews there were about two dozen rush-seated chairs, grouped roughly into two ranks on either side of a central aisle. She sat down on one about halfway up the nave. She hadn't brought the Serpent Stone with her. It seemed wrong somehow to bring it into a church.

'You're still there then.' She whispered the words into the spaces. Was it really several days since she had prayed? What had happened to her daily prayers, the structure of her faith? 'I'm sorry. I did my best. I really thought I would be good at the job.' She looked up at the east window. The colours in the stained glass were murky, greens and ochres, old colours, natural stains from the hills and fens around the church. The figure of Christ on the cross was primitive. Medieval. In spite of the barbaric pose, the huge nails through his wrists and ankles, the face of the Lord sported a huge grin. She found herself smiling back. 'So you knew it was all going to be OK,' she said quietly. 'Not so easy for the rest of us.'

She loved the smell of old churches. People always said they were redolent of ancient incense, but that wasn't it of course. Just stone. And old hassocks and crumbling hymn books and candles. And prayers. The atmosphere was very still. When she had come in it was sleepy; gentle. Lost in dreams. Now almost imperceptibly, it was changing, something was stirring. She looked round nervously. It was as though someone – or something – was watching her. She glanced back at the window. The smile had gone. What she had taken for a loving grin was a grimace of pain. Scrambling to her feet she turned and made for the door. 'I'm sorry. I shouldn't have come. I thought it would be all right.' Scrabbling for the door handle she let herself out into the wind. The sun had moved. It was low in the sky and the shadows were lengthening. Closing the door firmly behind her she felt the breeze tugging at her hair and she pulled off her hairclip, shaking her head and turning back, retraced her way down between the moss-covered gravestones, towards the orchards at the bottom of the manor's gardens.

7

Lydia stared at her brother-in-law, in shock. 'Why have you come?'

He smiled, the shape of his mouth so like his brother's it caught at her heart. 'You think I've come across the whole world just to find you, Lydia?'

'Yes, that is what I think!' She held his gaze, her eyes sparking defiance.

'Well, I'm sorry to disappoint you. I am on a mission for the Emperor.' The smile had quickly settled into a sneer of disdain. 'Where is Gaius? I seem to have missed him on my way up the river.'

'He's not back.' As soon as she said the words she regretted it. Now he would know she was alone and defenceless. Apart from the children. Romanus was standing behind his uncle, staring at him in awe.

Flavius stepped past her into the house and looked round. The slight flare of his nostrils was enough to make her see it through his eyes. His and Gaius's parents, her parents, all from well-born senatorial families had had large, rich town houses in Rome with costly mosaic floors and elegantly carved furniture, attended by slaves. They were influential and powerful. When she followed Gaius round from country to country they had almost always had comfortable Roman-built houses, or lived in richly appointed quarters on large vessels as they plied their trade across the Tyrrhenian Sea. When they settled in Damascus, that house had been the grandest of all. They had loved it there, until Flavius had arrived to chase them away again. She followed his gaze around this, their home for the last thirteen years. It was large and well appointed for a round house, but, compared to a villa, it was so very small, built of timber and wattle and cob, thatched with reed. Their living quarters around the walls were curtained off with woollen hangings – ornate and beautifully woven, granted, but hardly substantial walls and now in the daytime drawn back.

The central hearth was surrounded with simple stones. Outside in the kitchen hut, their utensils and pans and crockery were of fine workmanship, the imported wine they drank of the best quality, their olive oil and fish sauce for which Gaius had never lost his fondness, stored in elegant amphorae in stands near the cooking table. Their clothes were well made, the table and carved stools sturdy and attractive as were the beautifully woven wicker chairs, but to Flavius it must look as though they lived like peasants. She flushed uncomfortably. 'We plan to build a villa here one day,' she said defensively. His answering smile conveyed derision.

He turned and looked at Petra, who was reclining on a couch near the fire, swathed in rugs. 'And who is this? Surely not the baby you had in Damascus?'

Lydia nodded, biting her lip.

'And this is your son?' He looked Romanus up and down again 'He is much like my brother. Like me, I suppose.' He grinned at her and turning, pulled up a stool, placing it next to Petra. 'So, young lady. Why in bed at this hour? Are you not well?'

Petra shook her head. She appeared to have been struck dumb by the arrival of her uncle.

'Please leave the children alone, Flavius!' Lydia said sharply. Two dogs who had been lying watchfully by the fire rose to their feet. They slunk towards the doorway.

Flavius glanced at her mockingly. 'Why, Lydia? That would be rude. Besides, I have gifts for them. My baggage is following. They hadn't yet unloaded it from the boat when I found to my surprise that I had relatives in the area and decided I must come straight here. It is so strange that the gods should have sent me straight to your door, isn't it. As I said, I come on the Emperor's business, but how delightful that I should be able to settle my own at the same time.' He pointed at another stool and gestured to the boy to bring it and sit next to him. 'Come, Romanus. We need to get acquainted, young man. I shall make you my especial envoy. A young pair of legs and eagle eyes. You shall be my messenger and for your pains you will have a commission from the Emperor Tiberius himself and be paid.'

'Romanus!' Lydia's voice was sharp. In the shock of seeing Flavius she had completely forgotten the reason for her son's trip down to the mere. 'Where is Mora? Did you bring the medicine for your sister?'

Romanus scrambled to his feet. He flushed scarlet. 'Mama! Mora is away, but Cynan says he will tell her to come the moment she returns. And the medicine is in the dugout. I forgot! I'm sorry.' He glanced apologetically at his uncle. 'I will go back and fetch it. I will run all the way.'

'Do so, please.' Lydia walked over to Petra and laid her hand on her daughter's shoulder. 'It will not be long, sweetheart. Your brother can be there and back before dark.'

'I doubt that!' Flavius glanced out of the doorway. 'It is already growing dull out there. It seemed a very long way to me.' He shivered. 'Surely it can wait till morning.' He looked back at Petra. 'What is wrong with the girl?'

Petra shifted uncomfortably in her rugs. 'It can wait, Mama. Don't make Romanus go out again. There is a little of the mixture left, isn't there?'

But Romanus was already at the doorway. 'I'll go. It doesn't matter if it gets dark. I can see by the stars.' Before anyone had time to argue he ducked outside and disappeared. Flavius walked to the door after him and stared out. 'What strange half light.'

'It is dusk. The sun goes down slowly in these islands,' Lydia said at last. 'It is often so beautiful one can only stand and watch.' She gave a rueful smile. Behind them a servant was moving round in the shadows lighting the lamps. She was fair-haired and slender, dressed much like Lydia in a woollen gown with leather boots on her feet. She threw more logs on the fire and gently added another rug to Petra's shoulders. Flavius, after rising to pull the curtain across the doorway and blocking out the windy scene outside with a shudder had turned to watch, a speculative glint in his eye. 'Is this girl a Briton? With a good wash she could be pretty!'

'She is a member of our household, Flavius! And our friend,' Lydia retorted briskly. She spoke to the young woman in an undertone, using her own language and the girl nodded with a glance at Flavius which looked anything but friendly.

Petra giggled. 'Sorcha will bring her brothers up tomorrow if you are not careful, Mama,' she said, using the same tongue. She looked insolently at her uncle. 'Do you want her to send one of them to find Papa?'

Lydia stood for a moment looking down into the fire, torn with indecision. Then she looked up. 'Yes,' she said. 'Please, Sorcha, will you do that? We need him here.'

Sorcha nodded. Grabbing a cloak from a peg on the wall by the door she threw it round her shoulders and ducked outside.

'Sent her for reinforcements?' Flavius sneered.

'I have sent her to find Gaius,' Lydia said crisply. 'Presumably it is your brother you want to see?'

'I'm in no hurry,' he said. 'The years have been kind to you. I admit that girl has young flesh and looks as though she would warm someone's bed very nicely, but it's you I have always loved.'

Petra let out a little gasp. Flavius glanced at her. 'I am sorry, child. But it is best you know. Your mother was mine before ever your father set eyes on her.'

'That is not true, and you know it.' Lydia's eyes were blazing. 'Did I not befriend you first? Was it not me who brought you home to meet my family?'

'I seem to remember, Flavius,' she took, a deep breath, 'that it was my sister you set your cap at. You were never interested in me until Gaius fell in love with me. You always wanted everything he had. The moment he showed an interest in me you dropped my sister and nothing would please you but that you took me away from him. But it didn't work, did it! And it has never worked. I love your brother more than life itself and I always will. And I detest you. You know that. We have moved clean across the world to avoid you!'

'And I have found you at last.' Flavius sat down on a bench on the far side of the fire pit and stuck his feet out towards the embers. 'There is only one person standing between us, my darling, remember that.' He glanced across the fire at Petra who was staring at them open-mouthed. 'So, you don't remember the warm balmy nights in Damascus, child, when your mother and I dallied by the fountains while your father was away? Your birth came between us. It was very inconvenient.'

Petra was staring from Flavius to her mother and back. 'Mama?'

'Take no notice of him, Petra. It's what he does best. Making trouble. Stirring up enmity between people. Lying.' Lydia folded her arms as she stood looking down at him. 'Perhaps you should leave, Flavius. You are not welcome in this house.'

'I'm not going anywhere.' Flavius didn't bother to look up at her. 'You have a duty of hospitality to your brother-in-law, Lydia, and I will stay here as long as I need to. I need a drink. Can you stand up and fetch me one, child, or are you a complete cripple?' His words were deliberately cruel.

Petra flushed scarlet. 'I –'

'Sit still, Petra,' Lydia said sharply. 'I will pour some wine for us all.' She walked across to a side table. Taking three goblets from a shelf she poured wine from a jar, mixing into one the last of the medicine from the flask for Petra.

With her own goblet she went to sit down in a wicker chair as far from her brother-in-law as possible.

He drained his goblet at once. She saw him consider holding it out to her for a refill. He thought better of it and stood up himself, going across to the sideboard and picking up the jar. 'I knew where you all were,' he said over his shoulder. 'That was the irony of being sent here. I've known for five years that Gaius had settled in the Pretannic Islands. I just could not be bothered to trek across the world to find you. I went to see the seer in Rome on my way back and she confirmed it, looking into her scrying bowl.' Refilling his goblet for the third time he resumed his seat. 'I'm still with the elite force of Herod Antipas in Caesarea. One of our jobs is to find people and it would hardly be a good recommendation if I could not find my own brother.'

'So, if you did not come to find us,' Lydia said coldly, 'who did you come to find?'

'A Jewish troublemaker. Tiberius is very insistent that the eastern Empire is strongly held. Where insurrection is seen to be brewing we clamp down on it hard and fast.'

'And what is your Jewish troublemaker doing so far away from home?' Lydia glanced at Petra to make sure she was sipping her wine.

'Good question!' Flavius grinned broadly. 'He is something of a scholar, this young man. And a wanderer. I have followed him all over the place! First to Egypt, where he was too well-guarded to get near him, then he came back to Judea but before I knew it he was off again. This time he followed the silk road east, where I lost him for a couple of years.' He frowned. 'Then I heard he was retracing his steps. He took ship in Antioch, heading for Gaul, then I find he has decided to come across to Britannia to study with the druids here.'

'And you think he has come to Ynys yr Afalon?'

'I know he has.'

'And now you have caught up with him, what do you intend to do? Nothing good, I am sure.'

Flavius smiled. 'The enemies of Rome have to be exterminated, Lydia. For the greater good of all and sometimes in order to keep the peace they have to be exterminated secretly.'

'So, you are nothing more than a hired killer.'

'I am a soldier.' He leaned forward to set his empty goblet on the ground at his feet. 'But you don't have to worry your pretty little head about what I intend to do when I find him. If he is innocent, he will be safe. I need to question him, that is all, and to find out what he is doing on these extensive travels of his. If he is as he claims nothing but a scholar I shall leave him to go on his way. All you need to worry about, my dear, is finding me a comfortable bed and a decent meal. I see no signs of either being prepared and I am hungry.' He paused for several heartbeats, then he smiled at her. 'It will be good to see you and Gaius again.'

'Abi? Are you all right?'

Mat's voice swam up out of the shadows of the round house and a dog's cold nose touched her hand. Abi stared around her, blinking.

They had gone. Lydia and Flavius and Petra, the smoking fire, the smell of warm wine and herbs. She was in the windy orchard with Mat, his hair wildly blowing round his head, and the two dogs, panting at his heels; all three were looking at her in concern. She shook her head slowly. 'Sorry. I was miles away.'

Mat studied her face for a moment. 'I saw you from the foot-path. It's just about time for a drink before supper, so I thought I would collect you on my way past. It's time we initiated you into the local brew. A lethally innocuous-tasting scrumpy!'

With a smile she glanced at her wristwatch. 'I didn't realise.'

'Don't worry.' He whistled the dogs. 'Come on. We'll cut up through the garden.' He took a few steps then he stopped and turned to face her. 'I don't know how safe it is, Abi. Spending so much time in a day dream?' He shrugged. 'Cal mentioned she thought you had been in the garden a long time when she found you. If nothing else you are liable to get very cold if you stand immobile for so long in the wind. Sorry, maybe it's none of my business.'

She laughed uncomfortably. She felt guilty, she realised. This was more than day dreaming; this was messing with the dark arts. Maybe Kier was right.

'Don't worry, I can handle it! But you're right, I mustn't let it become addictive.' She paused, shaking her head thoughtfully. 'It's strange. I've only known of these people's existence for such a short time – if they exist at all, that is – and yet I'm completely fascinated.'

Justin Cavendish pulled his car into the lay-by a few hundred yards from the gates to the manor and glanced at his watch. By now Mat should have been off into Taunton as he always did on the first Tuesday in the month for lunch with his former colleagues, but his car was still parked outside the front door. A preliminary cautious drive past had shown several cars in the driveway. Cal's old battered Volvo; another small runabout – dark green and muddy – and Mat's ancient, seen-better-days Mercedes. Both family cars were on their second time round the clock. Thoroughly un-eco-friendly but who could afford a new car these days? Justin slapped the steering wheel of his own ancient Land Rover affectionately. Living where he did it was four-wheel-drive or nothing. He leaned his head back and closed his eyes. No point in going in until Mat had gone, not after the last row. He sighed. All he wanted was to pick up some books, then he would be away again. If Cal was there he would have some coffee with her, some desultory chat. If she wasn't he would let himself in. He still had his key. Then he would be gone without them even realising he had called in. Mat never went near their grandfather's library. Justin doubted he would notice if every single book disappeared.

Half an hour or so later, glancing in the rear-view mirror, he saw the Mercedes turn out of the gates and head away from the house. There were two people inside. He waited until it was out of sight around the corner, then he leaned forward and turned the ignition key.

The house was quiet; they must have taken the dogs with them. He grimaced; he was fond of those two animals. It took only half an hour to collect the various books he wanted. As a boy he had been the one to come up here to talk to his grandfather for hours, borrowing books, discussing them, arguing late into the night, imbibing the old man's wisdom. His two elder brothers, while fond

105

of the old boy, had been too busy with their own lives to bother much with the past. The history. The topography. The legends. Like their father they were more interested in their own careers. He sighed. Their father had lived here for only ten years in the end. He had died five years before and their mother, broken-hearted, had followed her husband only two years later. Mat and Ben were both more interested in the house now, but in a way it was too late. They hadn't assimilated the background the way he had. He frowned, running his fingers along the bottom of the shelf. There was one book missing. His hand hovered over the gap where it should have been. He sighed. No matter. He could come back another time. He glanced at his watch again. There was somewhere else he had to be.

Opening the door he stepped out into the hall and stopped dead. A strange woman was running down the staircase. Tall, slim, dressed in a dark-blue shirt and jeans, her long hair loose on her shoulders, she looked like some storybook Cathie looking for her Heathcliffe. She paused, mid-stride, and her mouth dropped open. 'Who are you?'

'I might ask the same question.' He lifted his bag of books onto his shoulder. 'I live here. At least I have a pied-à-terre here. Justin Cavendish.'

'Ah.' She nodded. 'The one who doesn't get on with Mat.'

He gave a tight smile. 'Well that knowledge at least betrays the fact that you know something of our family. You are?'

'Abi Rutherford. I'm –' She hesitated for a moment. 'I am staying here for a few weeks. A paying guest.'

'Right. Well, tell Cal I was here. Don't mention it in front of Mat if you want to maintain your vision of him as a sane man. Tell her I've taken some books. That will be OK with her.' He turned towards the front door.

'Do you live near here?' She wasn't sure why she had asked, perhaps to delay him a little. He intrigued her.

'No, I don't,' he replied shortly. He was tall and handsome as were his two brothers, with the same unruly thatch of hair. But whilst Ben's and Mat's was greying, his was fair. He must be a good ten years younger than Mat, she suspected. He reached the door and pulled it open.

'You don't want to have a cup of coffee, I suppose?' she asked quietly.

106

If he heard he chose to ignore the question. Stepping out into the sunshine he pulled the door shut behind him leaving her standing in the passage alone.

From the top of the ancient fir Romanus spotted his father walking his horse up the track while he was still half a mile away. Shinning down the tree, the boy set off at a lope through the rain to meet him.

'He arrived yesterday, Papa, and he brought us all presents. His baggage came this morning on a mule from Axiom. Is he very rich?' Romanus was almost dancing round his father as they headed back towards the farmstead. 'Look what he brought me.' From a sheath on his belt he produced a beautifully polished dagger.

Gaius's face had darkened as he slid from his saddle.

'And for Petra and Mama there was real silk. Enough to make a gown each. It's incredible. Cold like water and it slips through your fingers.' He paused, aware suddenly of his father's silence. 'What is it, Papa? Is something wrong?'

'Is your mother all right?'

Romanus nodded.

'And Petra?'

The boy nodded again and then shrugged to qualify the assurance. 'Petra has been feeling bad again. I went to find Mora but she wasn't there, so I had to bring medicine from Addedomaros.'

'And where did Flavius spend the night?'

'By the fire, Papa.'

His father's face tightened grimly. 'And where is he this morning?'

'He was eating breakfast. Mama and Petra were with him. Papa?' The boy stood still, puzzled, as his father, tossing his horse's rein to him, began to run, splashing through the puddles on the track. It was several seconds before he pulled himself together and followed, dragging the horse behind him.

Flavius was eating a bannock by the fire, a beaker of ale at his side as Gaius pushed his way through the curtain at the doorway and came in, panting. The visitor looked up with a sardonic grin. 'So, you have come home at last. I suspect your wife would have forgotten what you looked like were I not here to remind her!' He threw the bannock down onto the plate on the stool beside him and stood up.

107

'Gaius!' Lydia rose to her feet. She ran to her husband and put her arms around him. 'Where have you been?'

'I was engaged in a business deal which took longer than I expected,' Gaius replied grimly. 'The price of metals is rising. I got the miners from Iscalis a good deal on their lead and silver. So, brother. Why are you here?'

'That doesn't sound very welcoming!' Flavius squatted down to retrieve his ale. 'Don't you have decent side tables, here, Gaius? Solid wooden chairs? Baths? Beds for your visitors? This place is squalid!'

Lydia bit her lip. She was clinging to Gaius's tunic.

Gaius refused to rise to the taunt. 'Then you will be relieved to move on. We have no room for visitors.'

'But Papa,' Romanus put in. He was staring at the three adults in turn in some confusion. 'We have a guest house. With clean beds and beautiful rugs. Mama told Uncle Flavius that.' He looked bewildered. 'And we have silver plates and jugs. He doesn't have to eat off that.' He glared down at the stoneware plate.

'Perhaps as a soldier he felt such luxuries would make him soft,' Gaius said quietly. He reached out to ruffle his son's hair which was as wet as his own from the rain. 'You haven't answered my question, Flavius. Why are you here?' His voice was suddenly very hard.

'I told your family, I am looking for someone. It was coincidence that my quest should have brought me to Britannia and your doorstep.'

'Too great a coincidence for me to believe it,' Gaius said dryly. 'So who is it you are following and why should you think he is here?'

'He is an itinerant student, so I am informed, and he is studying with your druids.'

'And why should you need to find him?' Gaius raised an eyebrow.

'The druids are dangerous.' Flavius walked across the room and picked up a stool. Carrying it back to the fire he set it down and sat himself down next to Petra as he had the night before. 'They threaten the peace of the Empire. Tiberius sees them as a major threat in Gaul. Anyone who spends too much time with them is seen as suspect.'

'Tiberius is not Emperor over these islands,' Gaius said calmly. 'What he thinks is not our concern.'

108

'You are happy to trade with the Empire.'

Gaius shrugged. 'The other way round, I think. We have riches they want.'

'We!' Flavius looked at him incredulously. 'So you identify with the barbarians now.' He chuckled. 'But of course I can see that. Your barber is obviously one of them. And your cloakmaker. Thank the gods our father cannot see you.'

'There is nothing wrong with the druids!' Petra put in suddenly. She looked up defiantly. 'They are clever and kind.'

Romanus nodded. 'I've thought of studying with them. Mora says even though I am not of a druid family, because my parents are from Rome I can go in as a foreign student.'

'You, a healer?' Petra turned her attention to her brother with a crow of derision.

'Why not?' He blushed. 'But they don't only study healing. I could be one of the *vates*, like Cynan. I want to learn about everything.'

Flavius looked up in mock despair. 'What a nest of little rebels you nurture here, brother. Can he even read?'

Gaius nodded. 'They can both read.'

'And what do they read? Your account books? Your druid friends write nothing down so I've heard, to keep their sinister doings secret.'

'Petra can read and write in Greek and Latin; Romanus is learning,' Lydia put in. 'Leave the children alone, Flavius. We do very well here. We can do without your malice.' She felt braver now her husband was there.

Flavius shrugged. 'I will stay as long as I need to. When my job is done, then I will decide what to do about my family.' He smirked at his brother. 'I seem to remember threatening to kill you last time we met.'

Romanus and Petra gasped.

'I think the threat was mutual,' Gaius retorted. 'Keep away from us.'

Flavius shook his head. 'Not a chance. This is where I am staying for now under the sacred law of hospitality. Romanus, my boy, show me this glorious guest house of yours. I will move my bags in there. I will bother you as little as possible, Lydia.' He bowed graciously. 'Just food and fire is all I need. For now.'

Romanus looked from his mother to his father in confusion. 'Shall I show him?'

It was Lydia who nodded. 'Help him with his bags, Romanus.'

They waited in silence until Romanus and Flavius had left the house. Gaius went to the door and watched as they made their way through the heavy rain, across the yard and headed into one of the small buildings on the far side of the granary. It was well thatched and smart and the inside was well appointed. For all his cynical sneering his brother would be very comfortable there.

When he turned back he saw Lydia shaking her head. 'This can't be happening. I was so sure he would never find us.'

'Why do you hate each other so much?' Petra said anxiously. 'Mama? Papa? What is this about? Why is Mama so frightened?' She pulled a rug around her shoulders with a groan, tucking her swollen hands under her armpits for warmth.

Gaius took a deep breath. He sat down on the stool vacated by his brother and reached out to touch her shoulder. 'We have quarrelled all our lives, Petra. Something I'm not proud of. For some reason Flavius has always resented me. I was born first and he saw me as an obstacle to the sole love of our parents. Then I met your mother and fell in love and he,' he paused and took a deep breath, trying to keep his rising anger in check, 'he decided to try and take her off me. He has tried to come between us ever since. We saw no reason to bother you and your brother with this history. We thought we would never see him again.'

'And was he speaking the truth when he said you had sworn to kill each other?' Petra's voice was very faint.

Lydia went over to her. 'Angry words are often meaningless,' she said firmly. 'I am sure he just reminded us of that to make mischief.'

'I think we should go,' Gaius said after a moment. 'We can be packed and gone in less time than it would take for him to go down to the lake village and come back. When he goes down there or over to Ynys yr Afalon and to the villagers on the Glast Mere to enquire after this man he is following I think we should disappear.'

'No.' Lydia shook her head. She straightened her shoulders. 'I am not running any more. I love this place. We have friends here. Our children like it here. And where else is there to go, Gaius? This is where we make a stand. He is only one man, for goodness sake. And he is older now. For all we know he is married himself.'

Gaius bit his lip. 'You think me a coward, to have run away from him?'

'No! Of course I don't. You did what you thought was best. All we wanted was to be together. After all your parents tried to separate you. They understood the problem. They loved you both but they recognised you could not be in the same country. No more though, Gaius. I am not going to move. And he will go back to Caesarea. He is proud of his post there. You heard him. He cannot resist teasing us, but he will go.'

Gazing into the flames she did not see that her husband was shaking his head in despair.

Turning to face the north he imagined he could see the sea, a grey line on the horizon. He could see distant hills, far away, sense their height and their mystery. At their foot the tides roared up and down the estuary with terrifying speed. He pictured the muddy waters, restless, powerful, always watchful, one day gentle beneath a benevolent wind as the grey wavelets drove into the river mouths on the incoming tide to ride the mud flats with their thousands of birds and tease the salt-laden reeds, the next a furious rage of white-topped waves, tearing away greats lumps of mud. On those waves rode the small fishing vessels, the larger traders, the ferries always defying the elements, always brave. He turned away, his face to the wind and raised his hands in prayer for all those souls in peril on the sea.

8

Abi shook herself awake. She had been sitting in the rocking chair in the kitchen where she had gone after Justin left. Making herself a cup of coffee she had sat down for a few minutes, intending to go outside to make a plan of the most urgent gardening jobs which she felt she could put her hand to. His abrupt departure had annoyed her but whatever his problems were with his brother they were none of her business; his rudeness was not personal. She reached for her coffee. It was stone cold. She glanced at her watch. It had happened again. For over an hour she had been lost in dreams about Lydia and Gaius. Levering herself out of the chair she went and switched on the kettle. This was happening too often. And this time she wasn't even holding the stone, if that was indeed the catalyst that was making all this happen. She shivered. These people from the past seemed to be taking her over. Was this some form of possession? Was Kier right? Had he seen something in her she hadn't recognised herself? Some paranormal ability which taken to extremes could be dangerous. She ought to discuss it with Ben. But he would take steps to prevent it happening; insist that she reject whatever it was that was inside her which was allowing her to do this.

Should she reject it? Did she have any choice? She hadn't invited these characters into her head this time. She hadn't gone outside, seeking a front row seat to watch their performance. She had sat down and closed her eyes and at once they had been there, elbowing their way into her brain, and the story had continued. Pouring scalding water into the top of her mug to warm the cold coffee she sipped it slowly. If only her mother had had the chance to tell her more about the crystal. How it worked. What significance it had in her life. Both their lives. She bit her lip sadly. 'Mummy, you've really dropped me in it this time,' she murmured.

Five minutes later she had an idea. She would drive over to Glastonbury and find a crystal shop. Surely someone in that Mecca of New Age knowledge, or as someone she once knew had put it, the wackiest town in Britain, would be able to advise her what was happening to her or provide her with a book on the subject of crystals.

She set off, heading towards the ever-visible Tor, down the road which must, she now realised, have once been a causeway. Perhaps it still was technically. In the past, the past she had been watching, it hadn't been there at all. This was where Romanus had paddled his dugout canoe and cut across the shallow waters of the mere towards the Isle of Avalon. Of course, as Cal had pointed out, in reality Glastonbury had never been a complete island. A neck of land to the south-east had always connected it to the higher ground, but to all intents and purposes it was an island even now, the more so when the mist lay across the levels as a pool of white. A lovely mysterious island steeped in legend and lore.

At first sight it appeared to be the same attractive busy small town she remembered, tucked between its famous landmark hills, the Tor, Wearyall and Chalice Hill. Ignoring the by-pass, she turned into the narrow steeply winding roads which led towards the town centre, making her way down the high street, decorated with its colourful hanging baskets and its intriguing range of shops, most of them glitteringly New Age, although there were, she was glad to see, still some food shops there as well. She drove past St John's Church and the lovely old Tribunal building and the ancient George and Pilgrims pub, swinging round the market place into Magdalene Street where she turned into the car park behind the ruined abbey and pulled up.

She walked slowly back up the noisy, crowded high street, listening with half an ear to a street musician installed outside St John's. There were several crystal shops to choose from. She wandered past a couple and then at random selected a third. The fascia was painted a deep rich green and the sign writing in an ornate gold script announced that it was called *Athena's Attic*. The opening door set off a rippling chime somewhere deep in the shop.

Letting the door close behind her she looked round. The whole place was full of crystals. It seemed to sing with their energy. She made her way in, taking in the cases of exquisite jewellery, the shelves, the tables loaded with dishes of coloured stones,

116

heading towards the counter where a young woman was sitting, reading a novel. She glanced up at Abi then went back to her story. Abi smiled. She obviously didn't look like your average shop-lifter or indeed, perhaps, the average customer either. She walked across and cleared her throat. 'I'm sorry to interrupt.'

The girl set down the book. 'That's OK. Most people just want to look.' She was wearing long amber earrings which matched her eyes and a green blouse embroidered with sequins. It made her look somehow ethereal, like a dryad from some magical woodland.

'I want some advice,' Abi said cautiously. 'About a crystal I have at home.'

The girl shrugged. 'I'm not an expert. We've got books at the back there. What do you want to know about it?'

Abi was floored. She couldn't bring herself to say, well, it seems to be projecting memories and I want to learn how to switch it on and off and change channel. 'I suppose I want to know how you – er, use them,' she said cautiously. 'I've been left this thing. And it seems very powerful.' It seemed all right to say that in a shop like this. 'And I'm not sure what one does . . .' Her voice faded away.

'Have a look at the books.' The girl waved a hand which Abi saw was laden with amber and silver rings. 'If they're no good you could talk to Athena who owns the shop. She will be back later. She knows everything there is to know about crystals.' She smiled amiably. 'Go and have a root about. You'll probably find something to help you.' She had already picked up her book. Abi glanced at the cover wondering what the title was. It was obviously hard to put down. Following the direction of the wafting hand she made her way down some steps and into a second show room at the back of the shop. There were fewer crystals here – they probably didn't like it away from the sunshine, she thought with a wry smile but there were all sorts of other interesting arte-facts. Abi found herself staring in fascination at the statues, the wands, the rows of little bottles of sacred oils and jars of incense. There were shops like this at home of course – in fact in every town in the country, but this one was somehow special. Was that because this was Glastonbury? She wasn't sure. She wove her way between the tables towards a wall of books, the shelves neatly labelled and began to search amongst the volumes dedicated to crystals.

117

The voice behind her some time later made her jump. 'Excuse me? Bella thought you might need some advice about crystals?'

Abi turned and found herself looking at a tall well-built woman with clouds of silver hair. Dressed in a floor-length embroidered skirt and a black sweater Athena, like her assistant, was wearing copious amounts of jewellery, but instead of looking over the top and stereotyped it just seemed glorious. Abi smiled. It was as though the woman's deep grey eyes could look straight into her soul.

'Athena?' she said. 'So, one of your parents was a classicist. Homer, am I right?'

Athena raised her eyebrows. 'Impressive. Not many people recognise the allusion. The grey-eyed goddess, that's me!' She grinned. 'Not my parents, actually. They christened me Elizabeth. No, the name came later.' They smiled at each other. Abi nodded. She took a deep breath. 'Yes, I gather you might be able to help me.' This was no time for embarrassment or prevarication. 'I seem to have been left the most amazing crystal by my mother.'

Before she had got very far with the story Athena had held up her hand. The silver bangles on her wrist jangled. 'I think we need to go somewhere we can sit down,' she said firmly. 'Follow me.' Five minutes later they were settled in the coffee shop next door, Abi in front of a frothy cappuccino, Athena with a cup of green tea. The shop was crowded and warm and cheerful. Strangely enough, even though there was noise all around them they seemed to be sitting in their own oasis of quiet as Abi poured out her tale. When she had finished she sat back, sipping her coffee. The only fact that she had left out was her own calling. She had a feeling that declaring oneself a priest, even a lapsed priest, of the Church of England, might not go down too well in this environment.

Athena seemed lost in thought. At last she raised her eyes to Abi's and smiled. 'When I was a student I trained at the Royal College of Art. Then I decided I wanted to become a jeweller. I designed stuff which went all round the world. Precious stones. Gold. But then I came down here on a visit back in the seventies and I found an alternative man – the one who named me Athena – and,' she smiled, 'I was drawn in to the whole Glastonbury thing. The man moved on, but I didn't. I bought the shop and I began to work with lines of less expensive jewellery – semi-precious stones. Crystals. Working with them I began to

118

open to them without even realising what was happening. Crystals are here to teach us; to heal; to enlighten. All natural stones are, of course. It is part of their nature, but rock crystals are special. Their purity combined with their earthiness makes them very powerful.' She took a sip of tea. 'There are people who have analysed them, categorised them. People who claim to have channelled information which has come from the ancient masters of Atlantis.' She was staring down at the tablecloth, her voice matter of fact.

Abi waited. The woman had an air of serene confidence which she envied deeply. She was, Abi guessed, nearer sixty than the forty she had originally guessed at – she must be if she had come here in the seventies. 'Crystals come into my shop in all sorts of states of,' Athena hesitated, 'I was going to say mind.' She looked up and smiled. Abi found herself smiling back. 'But that is right. That is what it is. Some are traumatised by the way they have been blasted from their rock beds. Some are frightened. Some are angry. Some have been calmed and reassured by wherever it is they have been; most are wise. Wise with natural wisdom. Some contain memories which they have picked up on their travels and others have been programmed.' She held Abi's gaze. 'My guess is that yours is one of those. From what you say yours is a natural crystal ball. Maybe it is a natural crystal from this country. It hasn't come from far away. And it is not telling you its own story. It is telling you the story of this Roman family and that implies that someone in that family had the knowledge and the desire to implant those memories. And there must have been a reason for that. They were not just recording a daily diary. There must be some piece of information there which is important. So important that they wanted it remembered forever.

Abi shook her head. 'I don't know what to say. It's all too extraordinary.'

Athena laughed. 'Heavy, too, I dare say. Don't try and rationalise it. Play with the ideas for a while. See if you think they fit. The thing to bear in mind is that it is you who is the catalyst here. You are making it work. Your mother obviously knew how as well. She seems to have tested you to see what would happen and, satisfied that you could do it, she left it to you to find out whatever it is you need to know.' She paused. 'I don't think she was necessarily going to tell you anything else, Abi. I can see you feel that her death somehow prevented her from letting you into the big secret. Maybe she wanted you to find it out for yourself.' Another sip. 'You are inhibited by your own fear and doubt and incredulity as we all are at first when we come across something like this. The intelligence of our programming; the science we have been taught; the whole atmosphere of disbelief in our culture. It all adds up to make it so hard for us to open ourselves to the unexplained. Let yourself get used to it.'

'And you really think it could switch on my higher powers?' Abi tried to keep the ironical inverted commas out of her voice. 'Would it have told me the same story if I was still in Cambridge? Or would it have picked up something else over there?' She was still trying to rationalise – she couldn't help herself.

'Ask it. But remember to listen for the answer with an open mind.'

'Mummy did come from near here. She was born in Priddy.' Abi was still trying to pursue the rational approach.

'Remember there is no such thing as coincidence. Perhaps the crystal led you here.'

No, it was the bishop. Abi bit the words back in time. But of course, Athena was right. Her mother's mother had given Laura the crystal. And *her* mother's mother before that, judging by the note. The bishop too had been born in the Mendips. She was here because he knew these people; because the Cavendishes too had lived here for generations. It was all wheels within wheels.

Her coffee was finished. Suddenly she realised that they were going to have to leave and she didn't want the conversation to be over. Athena was in some strange way a kindred spirit. She liked her.

'Would it affect the crystal if someone else touched it?'

Athena shrugged. 'You said your father threw it out of the window.'

Abi nodded sadly. 'I was wondering whether I could show it to you.'

'You are looking for someone to make sense of it for you, Abi,' Athena said gently. 'It is better if you do that yourself. You have to have the courage of your own convictions. There may be more to this quest than just looking at a story. You may be drawn in. There may be a job for you to do.'

Abi grimaced. She gave a deep sigh. Athena frowned. 'I'm

always here if you want a chat. Where did you say you were staying?'

'With a family called Cavendish. At Woodley Manor on the Wells Road.'

Athena nodded. 'I know Justin.'

Abi's eyes widened. 'He dropped in this morning.'

'Really?' Athena seemed astonished.

'Mat and Cal were out.' Abi rubbed her forehead. She was feeling her way. She didn't want to gossip but on the other hand perhaps Athena was a friend of the family. She hoped so.

Athena laughed. It was a deep throaty chuckle. 'Justin and Mat have never got on. They come from two different planets.' She hesitated. 'A word to the wise. Be careful of Justin.' She leaned forward on her elbows, cupping her chin in her hands. 'So, Abi, how do you fit in with the family? You didn't say.'

'I was having man problems. A . . .' She hesitated. 'A friend suggested I come down to stay for a few weeks while I got my head together.'

'I see.' Athena glanced up at her face thoughtfully. 'And what did you say you do for a living?'

'I didn't.' Abi bit her lip. She didn't know what to say. She couldn't lie to this woman, but on the other hand if she told her Athena would probably get up and walk out. Almost certainly she was a pagan if she was anything at all and pagans in her experience did not like Christian priests. There were several students who called themselves pagan on her beat in the parish at home. They had made their feelings abundantly clear. Her church was to blame for witch burnings, for the crusades, for the Inquisition, for the persecution of women in general, for every real and perceived iniquity which had been enforced against the feminist cause, for destroying the planet, for burning the rain forest, for exploiting animals. The list went on and on. And most of the accusations, she had to admit, were to some extent based on real attitudes and real stances which from time to time various elements within the Christian church had embraced with so much misguided fervour. Not all, she wanted to say. Not today. Not me. It was not what Jesus wanted. It never mattered. She was tarred with the Christian brush. They never let her go any further with her self-justification. She looked at Athena and shrugged. 'I resigned from my last job. I'm unemployed at the moment.' That at least was

121

true. Athena nodded. Abi had a feeling she knew that this was not the whole story but for now she was prepared to let it lie. 'I hope we meet again. I will come into the shop next time I come to Glastonbury,' she went on quickly. 'I've so much enjoyed our talk.'

Athena smiled. 'Me too.' She stood up, and to Abi's surprise leaned across to give her a warm hug. 'Relax, Abi. Listen to your heart. Stop worrying about what everyone else thinks.' Again she seemed to have read Abi's thoughts. 'Be your own woman!'

The crystal was still there on the window sill. Abi gazed at it for a few minutes, then she picked it up. Carefully rewrapping it in its cotton bag she laid it in a drawer hidden under some jerseys. Then she knelt down by her bed and began to pray.

Mora lay back on her elbows and stared up at the sky. She had fair skin and red-gold hair, bound into a heavy plait which she wore twisted round her head. Her eyes were slate-blue. Wearing a brown woollen cloak, she gave the impression of a slender flower emerging from the dead leaves of winter. 'Was it ever this beautiful in your country?' She threw a glance at her companion.

Yeshua was sitting a few yards away from her, staring down from the hillside across the glittering sunlit waters of the reedy mere spread out beneath them. He smiled. 'Every country I have visited has its own beauty.' He reached for the jug at his feet and drank a few sips of the sweet local cider. 'Some are hot with desert sands; some are green and full of forests or grassy plains. Some have mountains so high you cannot see the top. They have snows all the year round. But here, yes, there is a special beauty. The water is everywhere. Your sunlight is soft, your mists beguiling, the smell of apple blossom enchanting.' His eyes were deep warm brown. She could see he was laughing at her.

'Pass me the jug.'

Standing up, he brought it over. He was a tall, slim man with light olive skin and dark brown wavy hair. Between them lay two woven bags, full of packets of dried herbs, their pharmacopoeia and medicine chest. 'We must get on.' Drinking her fill, Mora rammed the stopper back into the jug. 'We need to be at the

122

fisherman's house before the sun begins to drop. I need good light to examine his wife. She has a canker in her breast.' She shook her head. 'I have tried everything. I'm afraid all I can do is relieve her pain. Maybe you can do something.' She was beginning to have great faith in this young man's powers of healing. He was a student and a teacher, who had travelled far across the seas to study with the druid priests of the Pretannic Islands and on arrival in Afalon had been assigned to her care by her father, Fergus, the archdruid, to watch and help her as she carried out her duties as a healer. More often than not however, their roles had been reversed. She it was who was watching and learning from him. He had not studied medicine. He did not use herbs as she did. He worked through instinct and through prayer. He examined a patient, and considered the nature of the illness, and sometimes he held his hands over the wound, or he ran his fingers across a sore stomach or laid his palms gently on an aching head and bade the illness go. She had tried it secretly. It didn't seem to work for her.

The message from the fishing village had come as they were setting off towards home after several days moving sometimes in rain, sometimes in sunlight, amongst the homesteads and farms in the foothills to the east of their watery home. They would barely make it before dark.

Trefor was waiting for them at the door to his house, his face lined with sorrow. 'It is too late, Mora. She's gone.'

He turned and led the way inside, gesturing towards the bed by the fire. His wife lay there, her eyes closed, her face white as marble.

Mora sighed. 'I'm so sorry.' She had already guessed as much. The lonely call of the curlew across the marshes had signalled a death. She knelt at the bedside and touched the woman's face. It was ice cold. 'At least she is free of pain, now,' she said sadly. 'And she is with the ancestors where there is no fear or anguish. You will see her again.' She looked up at him.

Trefor nodded. He shrugged his great shoulders miserably. 'Who will look after the children?'

'You will find yourself a new wife, my friend.' She rose to her feet and laid a hand on his arm. Behind her Yeshua stepped forward and bent over the cold body. He laid a hand on the woman's forehead for a moment, then he too shook his head sadly.

123

'Who are you?' Trefor had swung round suddenly as he saw the stranger stoop over his wife. 'Don't you touch her.' He looked afraid.

Mora stepped forward. 'Peace, Trefor. This is Yeshua, one of the students at the college. He is a healer like me.' She frowned at Yeshua. 'There is nothing we can do.'

Yeshua nodded and stood away from the woman's body. 'I'm sorry. I had no intention of upsetting you.' He smiled regretfully. 'She was a beautiful woman.' Mora saw the older man frown, hearing the strange accent. But the meaning of his words were clear and he nodded sadly, reassured.

Behind them three small faces had appeared at the doorway. Yeshua turned. He walked over to them and in moments they had come trustingly into his arms. It was a long time before they let him depart. Mora gave an inner smile. Wherever they went he attracted children. They seemed to adore him unreservedly, begging for stories, queuing for the little models of animals and birds he whittled for them with his knife, reassured when they were sad, comforted when they were in pain.

'It makes me so angry when we are too late!' Yeshua shouldered his bag at last and led the way out of the compound. It would soon be dark, but the family in their distress had not thought to ask them to stay. 'If we had been there days ago, perhaps we could have done something. The poverty! The exhaustion on that poor woman's face! It is so wrong. If the children were only old enough to help her! Or her husband did more! If he had gone to the king and begged!' His voice rose in anger. 'I can't bear it when I see so much suffering everywhere I go. Good people, in so much pain and so much misery and grief. How can God allow it?'

'Her spirit was ready to leave,' Mora replied as she ran to keep up with him. 'One cannot always save people, you know that. She wanted to go.'

He stopped and turned to face her. 'How do you know?'

'I saw her.'

'You saw her spirit?'

She nodded. 'She was tired. Sad to leave him and the children, but she was exhausted; beyond life. Beyond recall.'

'So, you are saying I couldn't have saved her?'

Mora nodded. 'You know we couldn't.'

'I get too angry!' He shook his head after a moment.

'Only because you care so much.' There was a long pause. She stood looking down the track ahead of them towards the fen. The sun was setting, leaving a trail of gold in the waters. 'Do your people believe as we do that there is somewhere wonderful that we go when we die?'

He nodded. 'It is called Heaven.'

'And is Heaven full of apple trees?'

He smiled at last, his anger subsiding. 'Ah, there is a garden called Eden. It is a place of everlasting blessings.'

Mora nodded, reassured. 'She will be happy there.' She sighed.

He glanced at her. 'But her spirit is lingering, watching over them all.'

Mora nodded again. 'That house is full of the dead. I sometimes think we should teach people how to speak to their loved ones who linger, and help them on their way.' She shrugged. 'Trefor needs to let the sunlight and the air into that place. It courts illness. Three of his children have died. That is his third wife. The other two also died. One in childbirth, with the baby barely born, the other of an injury which went bad. I could do nothing for any of them, and yet still he asks me to come. He trusts me. He believes I can help him.' Her voice rose in frustration.

Yeshua reached across and laid his hand on her arm. 'Don't punish yourself, Mora. You do what you can. There are many others you do help. I have watched you.'

She gave a sad little smile and shook her head. 'Come. We must set out. It will be full dark soon.' She sighed.

'The nights come earlier and earlier,' he said after a moment. 'You know I am going to have to leave before the winter sets in.'

'Not yet.' She went cold at his words. 'There is so much for us to talk about. So much to study together. There will be time for some more visits before you go?' She heard the plea in her voice and despised herself for it.

'Oh, yes.' He smiled. 'There will be time for a few more yet.'

She reached out her hand as if to touch his, then changed her mind. Already he was striding ahead of her into the trees. He hadn't noticed the gesture.

Abi jerked away from the scene with a start. She had put the stone away. This was ridiculous. She had to take control of herself.

125

She sat down on her bed. So, Mora, the healer, was away visiting her patients whilst the family out here in the garden were looking for her. She was a herbalist, but her skills were limited; a druid healer who was not all-powerful. She didn't use a wand or magic or invoke the druid gods of healing. She did her best with the medicinal herbs she had collected from the countryside around. Like her companion, she was frustrated and angry and miserable because she couldn't help. And her patient had died of what, breast cancer? Abi stood up and walked across to the window and stared out towards the Tor. Two thousand years later and they still hadn't conquered it!

She found Cal in the kitchen. For once she wasn't cooking. She was sitting at the scrubbed oak table surrounded by sheaves of bills. Abi grimaced. 'Oh dear. Is this a bad time?'

Cal looked up. 'It's always a bad time when I have to try and sort this lot out. Come and sit down. Did you have a good day?'

Abi nodded. 'I went into Glastonbury and wandered around. Went into some of the shops. Had coffee with a fascinating woman from a crystal shop. Athena.'

Cal shook her head. 'My God! Boadicea herself! How on earth did you get talking to her?' She shuffled several bills together and fixed them with a paperclip.

Abi shrugged. 'I was in her shop. We talked about this and that. She designs jewellery.' She paused. 'She mentioned Justin.' She hesitated. 'He was here this morning. Did you know?'

Cal looked up. 'Here? In the house?'

Abi nodded. 'He said better not to mention it in front of Mat.'

'Too right!' Cal said fervently. 'What did he want? He obviously knew Mat and I were out.'

'I think he must have waited until he saw you leave. He was indoors – I didn't let him in. He was in the library, looking for some books.'

Cal nodded. 'He always thinks of the books as his own. I think their grandfather promised them to him at some point. It seems only fair as Mat and Ben got all the rest. Not because Justin was diddled out of it, he just didn't want to be part of it. They were supposed to end up with third shares in the house, but it didn't work out that way.'

'Can I ask why they don't get on?'

Cal let out a gusty breath, blowing the pepper and salt fringe up away from her eyes. 'Chalk and cheese. Justin is a good ten years younger than Mat. Mat resented him when he was born, I think. He had been the baby for a long time. But they never had anything in common. Justin is a natural rebel. A bit of a free thinker. I am not surprised Athena knows him.'

A word to the wise . . .

Athena's warning rang in Abi's head for a moment.

Cal pushed back her chair and stood up with a groan. 'Tea? I'm exhausted after a day in town. Too much traffic; too many people; too much noise. I've turned into a country bumpkin. But at least I got some shopping done. I needed a halfway decent coat for the winter.' She paused frowning. 'But at this moment I've got a splitting headache and I feel like death.'

'Would you like me to massage your shoulders?' Abi offered. 'Something I'm quite good at,' she added humbly. She didn't call it healing any more. Not after Kier's comments.

Cal gave a wan smile. 'Thanks. I'd love it.' She subsided back into the chair.

Abi stood behind her and rested her hands gently on Cal's shoulders. She could feel her fingers tingling. Her hands were heating up. Then suddenly the sensation was gone. She stared down, devastated. She couldn't do it. Not any more. She gave Cal's neck a perfunctory massage, then stepped back. 'Is that better?' She could hear the huskiness in her voice.

Cal stood up. 'Much. Thank you.' She glanced at Abi, frowning, sensing that something was wrong, but not quite sure what. 'Shall I make us that tea?'

She was holding the kettle under the tap as the phone rang. 'Can you get that?'

Abi picked it up. 'Hello?'

Silence.

'Hello, Woodley Manor?'

There was a quiet laugh. 'Hello Abi.'

'Kier?' Abi froze.

'Your father gave me the number. How are you?' He paused and when she didn't answer he went on. 'Things are not going well here. I'm not very happy, Abi. I thought you should know. The bishop has suspended me.'

'Because of what you did to me?'

'Of course. He thinks I should take time out to consider my

127

behaviour.' He gave a weak laugh. 'So, what did you tell him about me, exactly?'

'Only the truth, Kier. That I couldn't work with you any more. That I wanted to leave. It wasn't all your fault, and he knows that. I realised that I no longer had a calling to the priesthood. Perhaps I never did.'

Hearing Abi's tone Cal turned off the tap and put down the kettle. She ran her finger across her throat. Hang up!

Abi shrugged and shook her head. 'Kier, I am truly sorry, but the bishop knows best. If he thinks you should take a break –'

'They've brought in someone else to look after the parish. They have told them I'm not well. Sandra thought I must have cancer.' He gave a strange, humourless laugh. 'You have ruined my career, Abi. Did you set out to do that? To seduce me? To use magical powers to draw me in?' His voice was tight and oddly expressionless.

Abi opened her mouth to retort and found no words came. She was literally speechless.

'I suspected as much when I heard what you were doing in the parish,' he went on. 'I tried to understand, to give you leeway, but you just used the time to condemn yourself more. I have told him about all that. Your healing powers, your magical passes, your spells and potions.'

'What spells and potions?' Abi stammered at last. 'What on earth are you talking about!'

'Don't pretend not to know,' Kier went on. 'That was how you drew me in, didn't you. You probably put something in my drink. And The Bishop knows it. After all, he hasn't moved you to another parish, has he. He's suspended you too. You will go before a consistory court to explain what you've been doing, I shall see to that. I'm afraid you will be unfrocked, Abi. You may even go to prison, but I will support you. You know I will –'

Abi slammed down the phone. She was shaking. 'OK.' Cal came over to her. 'Sit down. I got the gist of that, the man was speaking so loudly. This is your ex-colleague, Kieran, I gather, and he thinks you're a witch?' Suddenly Cal's face creased with laughter. 'I'm sorry, Abi, but this is ludicrous. This is the twenty-first century, for goodness sake!' She broke off, seeing Abi's expression. 'Oh no, I'm sorry. I shouldn't have laughed. Of course I shouldn't. This is your career, but truly, he sounded completely off his rocker!'

'My career doesn't matter any more.' Abi had sat down at the table. Her hands were shaking. 'I have tried to give in my resignation. I expect now it will be accepted with alacrity.' She gave a small bitter laugh. 'It's just so damn wrong! A bigoted, sexist man shouldn't have the power to ruin someone's life. I might have been a good priest but I never got the chance to find out. We were warned there were a lot of people out there who would try and bring us down just because we were women, we were even warned from time to time people would mention witchcraft, but we all laughed; we thought it was a joke. That happened at the beginning, not now there have been women priests for ages. I never expected this.'

'Why did David send you to that parish in the first place?' Cal asked. She switched on the kettle and then came and sat down opposite Abi. 'He must have known what Kieran was like.'

Abi shrugged. 'I suppose the matter hadn't arisen before. His last curate was a man.' She paused. 'He had a nervous breakdown, I gather, but that was due to overwork.' Hesitating, she sniffed and groped for a tissue. 'You know, this started because I was a healer. I trained before I went into the ministry and I went on using the skills I had developed. That's where the idea that I was practising witchcraft came from. Stupid, stupid man!'

Cal shook her head. 'My dear, he won't be the first man to claim a woman has used magical arts to lure him in against his will. It's a way of saving face. "She used witchcraft to get her wicked way with me, my lord, but when I saw her for what she was I backed off and came to my senses,". For that read: "She couldn't stand me pawing at her and she rejected me and I can't believe that anyone would say no to me as I'm such a gorgeous specimen, so she's either mad or bad!"' She smiled.

Abi laughed. 'Thanks. You've made me feel a lot better.'

She looked up sadly and frowned suddenly. There was someone else in the room with them. A figure, swathed in a brown cloak, was standing watching her, halfway between the door and the window, her eyes fixed on Abi's.

'Mora!' Abi leaped up, pushing her chair back so hard it fell over.

'Abi, what is it?' Cal stood up too, alarmed.

The figure had gone.

'Did you see her?' Abi's voice was shaking. She pointed. 'There. Did you see?'

Cal stared round anxiously. 'I couldn't see anything. Not one of the Romans? Not in here?' She backed towards the window.

'The healer from the college. One of the druids.' Abi's mouth had gone dry.

For a moment Cal said nothing. She was glancing round the room. There was nothing there. 'Tea,' she said firmly at last. She reached for the caddy from a shelf. 'Sit down again, Abi. You are overwrought and I'm not surprised.'

'She must have heard me. Perhaps she understood.'

'You mean she's come with the sympathy vote?' Cal smiled tentatively. 'Poor old Abi. Look, don't answer the phone again. Leave it for one of us or the answer machine. The last thing you want is that vile man threatening you.' She poured water into the teapot. 'Shall I call Ben? He should know about this.'

'About Mora?'

'About Kieran.'

'You don't believe I saw her, do you.'

'I know you think you did. It's just –' Cal hesitated. 'No-one has ever seen them indoors before, Abi. But that doesn't mean they can't come in. I believe you. Of course I do. You appear to be very psychic. Far more so than I am.'

'I wasn't making it up.' Abi bit her lip. 'But on the other hand, she was only there for a fraction of a second. It could have been a trick of the light, I suppose. I don't know. I'm just so confused.' She put her head in her hands.

'Drink this.' Cal pushed a cup and saucer over towards her. 'And try to stop worrying.'

'Did Bishop David tell Ben I had lost it?' Abi raised her head and looked up at Cal. 'Was Kier right? Is that why I'm here?'

'No.' Cal took a deep breath. 'Look, I don't know if I'm supposed to tell you this, I thought perhaps you knew it anyway, but the reason you've been sent here to us, and to Ben, is to try and keep you in the church. The bishop thinks you are too valuable as a priest to lose.'

Abi gave a little snort. 'Somehow I don't believe that.'

Cal shrugged. 'Up to you. I can't believe that after one call from that odious man you've been reduced to a quivering jelly!'

Abi smiled. 'My mother called him oleaginous.'

'Good for your mother! Come on, Abi. Where's your backbone! You don't strike me as the type to cave in at the first fence!'

There was a moment's silence. Abi took a deep breath. 'You're right. I'm sorry. I have to stand up for myself. It just shows, doesn't it, what men do to us women if we're not careful.'

Cal sat down opposite Abi again, studying her face with care. 'Talk to Ben about all this. He is a genuinely good man. He's very experienced in counselling people. I know it's trendy to denounce counsellors but some of them do an awful lot of good.'

Abi nodded. 'I will. I'll ring him now.'

Mora was standing lost in thought. It had happened before, this strange feeling that she had slipped somehow into another world. Lost in her own meditations, alone as she walked the fields and hills, or sat beside the waters of the fen, listening to the soft whisperings of the reed beds she would suddenly be aware of other people nearby. Other people in another world; not nature spirits, not gods, not souls of the ancestors, people just like her, going about their own business, unaware of her. Until now. Now there was another woman there in that world. A woman who had looked up and seen her. She was half afraid, half intrigued. This was a special place, a place where physical worlds conjoined, the territories of three tribes, all neighbours, all respectfully standing back from this sacred place; a place where past, present and future too overlapped and interlocked and the border between them was thin. That was why there was a college here; that was why the waters and the hills and the islands were sacred. That was why the high Tor itself was entrance to the otherworld. She shook her head, looking round. The moment had lasted only a second and then it was over. She had thought of telling Cynan about it, but somehow the right moment hadn't come. He had been more distant lately, spending more time alone in meditation on his little island across the water near the mainland. Their easy affectionate friendship had wavered and she knew why. He was jealous of all the time she was spending with Yeshua. But then her father had put Yeshua under her supervision, as a healer like her, whilst Cynan was a studying to be a seer. She shrugged. She might be destined to marry Cynan, but that did not make her his exclusive property. She liked Yeshua. She liked him very much, they had grown closer as the months passed. Perhaps she could talk to him about it. In fact she could always talk to him; he was wise and gentle

131

and very learned, even if from time to time he, like her, exploded with rage and frustration at the iniquities of the world around them.

She always knew where to find him. He was sitting in his accustomed place beneath the ancient yew tree which overhung the spring. He was often there, praying. He prayed more than anyone she knew. For a moment she studied his face. In repose like this, eyes closed, he radiated a serenity she found strangely disturbing. It excluded her so completely.

'Were you looking for me?' His eyes were still full of that other-worldliness as he registered her presence.

'I wanted to talk to you about someone I've just seen.'

He raised an eyebrow, patting the ground beside him. She subsided onto the grass and sat cross-legged. 'Someone special?'

She nodded. She never needed to explain with him. 'I don't know if she is a spirit or a ghost. There is something strange about her. I see her as if through clear water, in the distance. But today she was closer and our eyes met and I felt her reach out to me.'

He sat in silence for a while, staring out across the slopes of the hill below them. Two women were collecting late apples in baskets in the sunlight; she could hear their voices in the silence.

'If she is reaching out to you, you should go to meet her,' he said at last.

She nodded and waited in case he was going to say anything else. He too was watching the women with their baskets of fruit. 'I need to go across to see Petronilla,' she said at last, letting the subject drop. 'I wondered if you would like to come and meet her and her family? Her brother was here. He left a message for me.'

'Of course.' He rose to his feet.

'Where were you just now?' She hadn't moved.

He smiled. 'Sometimes, when I pray for my family, I feel I can see them all there, at home. I like to check up on them. My mother and father; my brothers and sisters; touch each one on the hand.'

'You are homesick.' She smiled sadly.

'A little, perhaps. I have been away a long time.'

'You said you had to go back soon?' She rose to her feet, clutching her cloak around her as the wind rose and snatched back her hood.

He shrugged, then nodded. 'I had thought maybe I could take another year for my studies, but now suddenly I can feel –' He paused, looking up at her. 'I can feel the appointed time for me to go drawing near.'

Her heart sank. She was still studying his face. 'And that frightens you, doesn't it?'

He sighed. 'God thinks I am ready.'

'You talk about your god with my father.'

He nodded again and this time she saw the humour she loved so much surface in his eyes. 'Your father is a learned man. That is why I came here, to study with him. His reputation has spread far across the continents. I enjoy my discussions with him. He tells me the legends of your peoples and your gods, and I tell him about the Torah, the written law and teaching of my people, the Jews. It was he who suggested that I come out here to pray alone in the sacred places of your tribe.'

'But you do not pray to our gods.'

He shook his head. 'My God doesn't allow us to pray to other gods; but your father sees aspects of my great God everywhere and in everything around him. In this sacred spring; in this tree; in birds of the air; in the mountains and the hills in the storm. Where he sees gods, I see angels, caring for my father's world. So we can talk.' Rising to his feet, he smiled again. 'Come, let's go and see Petronilla. This is the child you mentioned, with the swollen joints? You have tried willow bark, of course?'

Mora punched him affectionately on the arm. 'Of course I have tried willow bark. My medicines are the best for miles around and they work for her, that was why Romanus came to fetch me. Medicine was sent back with him, and Addedomaros promised I would go and see her as soon as I could, but I thought, maybe . . .' She hesitated. 'Maybe if you came with me, you could ask your God to heal her?'

He folded his arms. 'Yours don't help, then?' He raised an eyebrow humorously.

She shrugged, refusing to rise to the bait. 'Don't or won't. Who can understand why they heal one person and not another? But it occurred to me that Petra's parents come from Rome. Maybe your God would help them.'

He gave a snort. 'Rome is not considered a friend in my country.'

'But Lydia and Gaius have chosen to settle with us; they have the protection of my people. You will like this family, I promise.'

'I'm sure I will.' He reassured her. 'And I will do what I can,

133

Mora. I always do, no matter from where they come or what their beliefs –' He broke off as Cynan appeared, climbing the hillside, through the blowing leaves, the patterns of sunlight reflecting on his woollen robe.

He paused and looked at them. 'Am I interrupting?'

'Of course not!' Mora could feel herself blushing as she stepped away from Yeshua. Why did Cynan always make her feel guilty when he caught them alone together?

'I heard you might be going across to see Petra's family. If so I was going to offer to come with you. I can distract young Romanus from making sheep's eyes at you while you talk to her.'

Mora hesitated. It was Yeshua who stepped back. 'I think it would actually be better if you two went. I have work to do on my hut. It needs substantial repairs before the storms you have warned me about begin. Even if I am no longer here, someone will want my house and I wouldn't want to leave them a ruin.' He smiled.

'But you were going to help me with Petra!' Mora couldn't keep the disappointment out of her voice.

'I will pray for her. And there will be other times when I can come and see her. I have arranged for one of the wattle men to show me how you weave your walls. It fascinates me and my house is full of holes!' He laughed. 'I know. But I enjoy working with my hands. I used to watch the builders working near our home when I was a boy; my father is a master mason and wood-worker.' He was already moving away from them. He raised his hand in blessing and began to stride down the hillside.

Mora turned away from Cynan with a frown. 'You just can't resist it, can you!'

'What?'

'You hear I am going out to visit patients with Yeshua and you have to interfere! Are you jealous or something?'

Cynan looked at the ground. His face had turned puce. He shook his head. 'Of course not. I'm sorry. I didn't realise he would change his mind if I came too. I'll go after him if you like and say I'm not coming.'

'No!' She shook her head. 'No, don't bother.'

'Is he really leaving soon?' He looked at her anxiously.

She nodded. Taking a deep breath she made herself smile. 'As it happens he looked as though he was quite pleased to stay behind. I'll go and fetch my bag of medicines then you can paddle the dugout for me.' Relenting, she caught his arm. 'You're right. Romanus is beginning to be a bit of a pain. He's growing up and noticing women for the first time. I just wish it wasn't me! Take him away and teach him to fish or something.'

Cynan laughed. 'I think it would be a case of him teaching me. But I will do my best.'

Janet Cavendish opened the front door to Abi next morning and smiled warmly. 'Come in, my dear. Ben is expecting you. Through there.' She waved towards an open door before turning away and disappearing herself in the opposite direction. Abi gave a tentative knock on the door and pushed it open. 'Ben?'

He was sitting at an untidy desk, staring out of the window, but he climbed wearily to his feet as she came in. 'Come and sit by the fire, Abi.' Sweet scented logs were roaring happily in the hearth, obviously newly lit and still fed by firelighters, she noted as she took one of the squashy armchairs. They were upholstered in blue patterned chintz which seemed somewhat incongruous in the distinctly masculine surroundings of Ben's study. Very comfortable though. She noticed the discreet box of Kleenex on the small table at her elbow. The window looked out over the front drive where she had left her battered green car parked under a field maple. The leaves were turning the most stunning shades of scarlet and ochre.

'I'm seeing ghosts, Ben.' She hadn't even waited for him to sit down opposite her as she blurted out her confession.

Deciding to remain standing, he arranged himself comfortably with his back to the fire. 'Tell me about them.'

'Aren't you shocked?'

He shook his head. 'David told me all about your experiences in Cambridge and Mat and Cal said you'd already seen our own domestic crew.' He smiled.

'It doesn't worry you?'

'Not if it doesn't worry you.'

She paused, thinking about that one. She was worried, obviously, otherwise why would she have come to see him. But about what? She had prayed for a long time the night before and this morning, in the cold light of dawn as the sun rose over the Mendips

135

she realised what it was that had alarmed her so much. Mora had followed her inside, had appeared while she was talking about being a healer and then, and this was what had scared her, had made eye contact. This was not like a film, watching a bunch of people in another dimension somehow going about their daily lives and allowing her to watch. Or being completely unaware that she was watching. Nor was it some kind of eternally playing record, etched onto the Woodley atmosphere. This was one of their number, a druid priestess, by all accounts, trying to contact her.

Ben listened to her halting description of what had happened. 'And Cal didn't see her too?'

Abi shook her head.

'Or the dogs. Dogs often see ghosts in my experience.' He smiled.

'The dogs were out with Mat.'

Abandoning the fire he threw himself down in the armchair facing hers, steepling his fingers over his knees thoughtfully as he stared down at the carpet between them. 'You have prayed, of course.'

She nodded. 'Kier rang me yesterday, Ben,' she went on suddenly. 'David has suspended him.'

Ben waited for her to say something else. When she lapsed into silence he glanced up. 'I can see this has upset you,' he said cautiously.

'He had the phone number of the house. He knows where I am. He is still accusing me of witchcraft.' She gave a shrill laugh. 'I know it's stupid, Ben, but it frightened me. He sounded so vicious.' She bit her lip. 'And what if he's right? What if I am possessed in some way? What if seeing Mora, contacting her, is exactly that. Witchcraft.'

'Abi, you have not contacted this,' he hesitated, seeking the right word, 'this entity, this woman, deliberately. You have not performed rites or spells or conjured her intentionally. You have prayed for help. And you have come to me for advice, so get the idea of your being a witch right out of your head. Kieran Scott is at the moment a disturbed and angry man with his own problems. He is not thinking rationally and he is looking for excuses for his own bad behaviour. Leave him to David. He is not your concern.' He paused for a moment, deep in thought.

Abi watched him. He had a gentle, intelligent face, not unlike his two brothers, but older, more lined, his hair already white. There was wisdom and reassurance in this man. Instinctively she liked and trusted him. 'I did contact her deliberately,' she said softly. She glanced up at him. His eyes were fixed on the tips of his fingers, on his knees. 'Not at first, of course, but once I discovered how easy it was, I couldn't resist trying to do it again.'

He said nothing. She hesitated, then went on. 'It was the crystal ball my mother gave me. Not a round shiny thing, like you see in jokes about fortune tellers. No, this is a lump of unpolished rock crystal, dredged out of a mountain or a river somewhere. It is a wild crystal, still encased in its bedrock.' She smiled at this description. Athena would approve. 'Somehow it acts as a key. It has switched me on to see and hear and know things I didn't know before. I only have to think about them and I seem to be there. It is an heirloom. It seems to have been passed down my mother's family and it has enabled the women in the family to tune in to the unseen.' She stood up and took a short turn round the room, moving in short agitated steps towards the fireplace and then back to her chair. Throwing herself down again she shook her head. 'I don't believe it's evil. It's not witchcraft, is it! It sounds as though it is, but I am not conjuring spirits. I can't be. Those spirits have always been there. They are your family's ghosts, not mine!' The words came out as a wail of despair. 'Ben, my mother left it to me as a sacred trust. I mustn't get rid of it; I can't drop it into a lake. I can't lose it or give it away except to my own daughter.' She rubbed her hands down her face and looked up again in despair. 'My mother told me it would destroy my Christian faith.'

Ben didn't move, still intent on studying his fingertips. When at last he spoke, it was without looking up at her. 'This must terrify you, Abi.'

For a moment she considered. Then she shook her head. 'No, I don't think so. Not terrify. That's not the right word. What is happening is odd and disconcerting. Unsettling. But not terrifying.'

He thought for a moment. 'Do you still believe in the power of prayer?'

'Of course I do.' She stood up again, pushing her hair back off her face. 'This hasn't destroyed my faith in God, just in myself as a priest.'

'Then why don't we pray together.' He looked up at last. 'Sit

137

down and take a moment to compose yourself. Push away your doubts and fears. Still your mind.'

Behind him a log shifted in the fire. She reached into her pocket for a tissue and sat miserably twisting it between her fingers as she stared down at the carpet. Ben stood up. Stepping forward he removed it gently from her hands and turning, threw it on the fire. Then he went back to his chair. After a moment he began to say the Lord's Prayer. Abi closed her eyes. When he had finished they both sat quietly for several minutes.

'"My daughter, in time of illness do not be remiss,
but pray to the Lord and he will heal you.
Keep clear of wrong-doing, amend your ways,
And cleanse your heart from all sin."'

Ben raised his eyes and looked at her. 'You know the passage from Ecclesiasticus?'

She nodded dumbly. 'Am I committing a sin?'

'Only God can know that. You aren't happy about what is happening or you wouldn't have come to me about it, would you. You feel uncomfortable. You are uncertain. I can only suggest you pray. Surround yourself with the love of God. If you feel you shouldn't be doing this, Abi, stop.' He fixed his gaze on her. 'Recite the Breastplate. "Christ in quiet, Christ in danger, Christ in mouth of friend and stranger", remember? If the crystal frightens you, hide it. Put it away. Give it to someone to look after it for you. Don't think about it. Don't let it have power over you. The fact that it came from your mother is inci-dental. Don't allow your loyalty or your grief to sway you into doing something you wouldn't do normally.'

Abi was thoughtful. 'It has passed through generations of women in my family,' she said after another silence. 'I wondered if Lydia or Petronilla might be my ancestor.' As soon as she said the words her eyes flew up to meet his. 'Oh, my God, Ben! I don't know why I said that. And it's ludicrous. Woodley is your family home, not mine.'

'Though your mother came from not far away.' He smiled. 'It might be true but I doubt if you can ever prove it.'

'What if the crystal was Mora's? What if she knows it is telling

138

her story? What if it has come down through her descendents from mother to daughter all those generations?'

Ben looked sceptical. 'I hardly think that is likely or even possible. If these people are Romans and druids, you are talking about nearly a couple of thousand years, Abi!'

'But it makes sense of what is happening to me.' Suddenly she was excited.

'Does it?' He held her gaze. 'Are you sure?'

She looked away, deflated, and shrugged. 'I still don't know what to do.'

He grinned affably. 'So, you're not going to stop?'

'I'm not sure I can. Not because I'm not capable of saying no, but because I'm not always sure when it is going to happen or how or why.' She stood up. 'I don't have to be holding the stone. It has happened more often without it than with! Spontaneously. Without me doing anything to initiate it.'

'Then, whoever she is for now, we must hope she means you well.'

'So, taking all that into account, do you think Kieran is right and I'm some sort of witch?'

Ben laughed. 'Is that what is really worrying you? Not that what you are doing might be in some way wrong, but that it might be seen as witchcraft? What is witchcraft, Abi? How do you see witches?'

'Isn't it more about how he sees them? For him I am the impersonation of the female half of the evil zeitgeist.'

Ben raised an eyebrow. 'And do you feel this describes you at all?'

'No, of course not.'

'Then forget witchcraft.' He stepped forward and took her hand. 'Go home, Abi. Relax. Rest. Pray. Spend time in St Mary's. That is what you are here for. Try to resist the urge to conjure spirits. If they come anyway, watch, but stay uninvolved. We will talk again in a day or two.'

As Abi's car disappeared out of the gate Janet came into the room. She went over to the log basket and threw a couple of logs onto the fire. 'Glamorous lady. You didn't tell me she was beautiful.'

Ben smiled. 'I can't pretend I hadn't noticed.'

'Is she much troubled?'

He nodded. 'Oh yes. I need to pray about this.'

'Be careful, Ben.'

He glanced across at her with a rueful smile. 'You know, I think this is one for brother Justin if I only knew where to find him.'

9

Gaius watched as his brother rode off down the track. Flavius was heading towards the fishing village on the edge of the winter fens to interview one of the men there. A passing trapper, delivering a load of furs, had passed on word that a foreign-looking young man had gone out there to try and cure the old man's wife. He had failed. Flavius had smiled when he heard the story. 'Not such a miracle worker, then. But I must follow this up. There can't be many men of foreign complexion working as healers in this part of the world.' He had taken Gaius's best horse, swinging onto the saddle with ease and eyeing the animal's harness. The bridle was of tooled leather and the bronze bit and headpiece were of the finest workmanship. He smiled grimly, then kicked the animal into a canter.

Once he was out of sight Gaius turned back inside. 'Let us hope this poor man he is after has already put many miles between himself and the village!' he said grimly to his wife. 'I wouldn't wish the most vicious criminal a run in with my brother, never mind an innocent healer!'

Lydia glanced at Petra, who was lying on her couch, her eyes closed. She went over to Gaius and put her hand on his arm. 'What are we going to do?' she said softly.

'We are not going to let him chase us out of our home again,' he said robustly. 'You are right. This time we make a stand.' But how? The words remained unspoken between them. Flavius's ability to cause trouble had always been subtle. There was no knowing which way his attack would come. 'Never be alone with him,' he whispered into her hair as he put his arms around her. 'And never turn your back. Don't let the children be alone with him either. Tell the servants and the herdsmen. I would rather they stay close to the compound while he is here. Sorcha knows. I could see she had the measure of him.' He paused and looked round. 'Where is Romanus?'

Lydia pulled away from him, suddenly worried. 'He is obsessed by Flavius. He was watching him mount up this morning, taking in every detail of his clothes and baggage. Surely he wouldn't have followed him?' She turned towards the doorway. 'Sorcha? Where is Romanus?'

Sorcha appeared. She had been sitting outside with the quern. Her clothes were covered with a large apron, but there was still flour in her hair and on her hands. 'He went off early. He had a bow with him.'

'Thank the gods!' Lydia sighed with relief. 'I was so afraid he might have followed my husband's brother.'

Sorcha raised an eyebrow. 'He will, if not today, then tomorrow. Your man's brother is already drawing the boy in with his tales and stories of travelling in distant countries. Romanus is fascinated. Life here is dull for him.' She shrugged. 'And he's not made to be a druid, if you forgive me for saying so!'

Lydia glanced at her husband who was bending over Petra, feeling her forehead with his hand. 'We hoped he would follow his father into some form of trade, but he is so taken with Mora and Cynan. He sees their way of life as glamorous and serving the gods.'

'And so it is, for those who are born to it!' Sorcha's mouth turned down. Lydia hid a sympathetic smile. Everyone for miles knew that the girl had set her cap at a handsome young bard from the college, but his parents had ordered him to turn her down because she did not come from the druid caste. A shame because the girl was intelligent and attractive and would make some man a good wife. She deserved better than being tied to a trapper or a shepherd and there were few farmers around who were not already married.

Mora arrived with Cynan as the sun stood high in the sky. Romanus still hadn't returned and Cynan waited outside, watching Sorcha at her tasks while Mora went in to talk to Petra. The two young women sat by the smoky fire watching Lydia at her loom for a few minutes, then Mora took Petra's hands in hers and began to examine the swollen joints. 'These are no better?'

Petra shook her head. She was biting her lips with pain as Mora gently straightened the fingers. 'I have brought you a new medicine. I am trying a slightly different combination of herbs, and I have brought you some ointment to rub into your hands and wrists and to put on your aching legs.' She was talking softly. 'I had hoped to bring a colleague with me. A young healer from the far side of the Roman Empire who has come here to study and teach. He has worked miracles with some of our patients.' She looked up and smiled. 'He is praying for you.' Her smile faded. 'What is wrong?'

Petra shook her head. 'Nothing.' Her face was full of anxiety. 'It's just, my uncle has come from Caesarea and he is hunting down a young man whom he wants to question. He says he might be a traitor to the Emperor. Caesarea is on the far side of the Empire. It couldn't be the same man. Could it?'

Mora shook her head. 'I hardly think so. Yeshua is a gentle, kind man. I told you, he's a healer and a teacher. Besides he has been travelling the world. It is a long time since he was in his own country.' She pulled a small pottery jar of ointment out of her bag, unstoppered it and began to work it gently into Petra's hands.

Petra groaned with pleasure. 'It gives me so much relief.'

Mora nodded. 'The medicines are blessed by our own mother goddess and I have used water brought from the sacred hot spring of the goddess Sul to blend the ingredients. You must keep your hands warm. Do you still wear your fur mittens?'

Petra nodded.

'Go out on dry days in the sunshine, just for a few minutes if you can. The air will bless you and make you feel better. But on wet cold days stay in by the fire.' She frowned. 'Do you eat well?'

Petra smiled. 'I have little appetite.' She looked up as her mother tucked her shuttle into the weft and web of her weaving, making the loom weights rattle, and walked towards them. 'How is she, Mora?'

Mora looked up. 'She will be better. In my experience this aching of the bones often gets less as girls grow older. I am hoping it will start to ease soon. If it doesn't, I have another medicine I could try. It is very strong, though. I'd rather not use it if possible.' She laid her hand on Petra's forehead.

Behind them Cynan ducked in through the door. 'Sorcha is making some bannocks. She asked me to find out how many we would like. We are to have them with honey and blackberries.' He smiled at Mora, then sat down next to Petra. 'How are you?'

'Better.' She looked at him wanly. 'You promised one day you

143

would take me out in your canoe. I will hold you to that one nice sunny day. Mora thinks the air will do me good.'

'Any time.' The young man smiled at her kindly. 'So, who's hungry?'

When they left, Lydia looked at her daughter. 'We will not mention this friend of Mora's to anyone. I doubt if he is the same man, but if he is, I don't feel inclined to help your uncle in his search.'

Petra nodded. 'He brings such anger and cruelty with him. I can see it in his eyes. I want him to go away, Mama, if he makes you unhappy.'

Lydia sighed. 'He will go soon.' She wasn't sure how, but one way or another she was going to have to make sure Flavius moved on otherwise he would destroy their family. But she was not going to help him by sacrificing some innocent stranger to him. Her mouth set with determination. On several occasions Flavius had come very near to ruining her life. It was not going to happen again.

Abi sat staring down at the rock crystal ball which lay in her lap. She was sitting on the bench near the ruins, feeling the warm autumnal sun on her face, her hair stirring slightly in the gentle wind. Her vision gone, she was staring out across the garden towards the orchards. From here she couldn't see the Tor. Her stomach was churning; her brain was making connections which filled her with dismay.

'Caesarea. The Roman province of Judea. A wandering healer. A teacher. A man with gentle eyes. A Jew. It couldn't be him. It just couldn't!'

She was frowning with concentration, thinking back to her studies when she was at theological college and before that, to her history degree. As far as she could remember they had been told that there had been numbers of itinerant teachers and healers and miracle workers wandering around the Holy Land at the time of Jesus. He had in a sense at first been one of many. One of the great unsolved mysteries of his story was what had he done and where had he been in the 'missing years' between his childhood and the start of his ministry. Of course she had heard the legends. Who hadn't? The story that Joseph of Arimathaea had come to the West Country and that maybe he had brought the boy Jesus

144

with him. There were other stories too. Some of these claimed that Jesus had travelled elsewhere in those hidden years, when no-one knows where he was. She remembered her tutor's smile as he had recounted some of the most outrageous claims. The legends that he had gone to India or Tibet. And come back to the Glastonbury he had visited as a child, to study with the druids.

As if!

Nonsense!

She found she was holding the ball so tightly that her fingers had gone white; her hands were sweating. Her mother's voice echoed in her ears for a moment: *This will destroy your faith. That's what it did for me.*

Why? Even if this was – Jesus – her mind balked at even framing the word, why had this story destroyed her faith?

Because it would prove that he was just an ordinary young man travelling in his gap year? That he wasn't the son of God? Because the Serpent Stone had lifted him off the altar and put him on a windy hillside and given him muddy feet and all too human emotions?

But he had to have been somewhere. Why not here?

She shook her head slowly.

No, this was ridiculous. She was inventing the whole thing. She had allowed herself to be overwhelmed with all that had been happening to her and now, being here in Glastonbury, her brain was working overtime to slot everything into a convenient mould. The stone. Her mother. Her mother's death. Her faith and the strange things that had happened in Cambridge. It all had to be part of some brain fever. She didn't need counselling so much as hospitalisation and some hefty doses of anti-psychotic drugs.

She put the stone down beside her on the wooden slats of the bench and rubbed her hands up and down on her jeans with a shiver. She had to stop this. Now. It had gone far enough. Cal was making lunch. In ten minutes she would come to the kitchen door and call her. She must stand up, go back in and that would be that. No more. Put away the stone. Hide it. Bury it. Throw it into the pond. Go back to Ben and ask him – ask him what? She stood up and leaving the stone on the bench walked over to the ruins, pushing her hands deep into the pockets of her jacket. She should pray. But how could she pray now when that young man's face would come to her, between her prayers and Jesus Christ?

This will destroy your faith.

She stared down the garden towards the orchard. The old apple trees, lichen-covered and bent, their branches knotted and thickened like arthritic limbs, were starting to shed their leaves, but there were still apples on them, small knobbly apples of some ancient species. She watched a blackbird pecking at one. It stopped as she spotted it and flew off startled to perch on the top of the tree. A movement at the corner of her eye caught her attention and she turned. Mora was standing near her, watching her.

'No!' She stepped back. 'No! This is not happening!'

The blackbird flew squawking its alarm and disappeared over the hedge. Mora had gone.

'Abi!' Cal's voice echoed down the garden. 'Lunch!'

It wasn't until she was sitting opposite Cal at the kitchen table that she realised she had left the Serpent Stone on the bench.

Mat looked at his brother and raised an eyebrow. 'So, how do you think Abi is getting on?' They were sitting at a corner table in the Black Lion, each with a pint and a ploughman's before them.

'OK.' Ben's reply was guarded.

'Can't talk about her?'

Ben shook his head. 'Not much. Anyway, she has to work a lot of this stuff out for herself.'

'With God's help?'

Ben nodded. 'Exactly.'

'It's just, all this ghost stuff. It's weird how she's stirred it up.'

Ben nodded again.

Mat grinned. 'Apparently one of the ghosts came into the kitchen while she and Cal were talking. Did she tell you?'

Ben reached for his glass and took a sip. 'She did mention it, yes.' He wiped froth off his upper lip.

'Cal was stunned. She didn't see anything, but she said Abi's reaction was interesting!'

'Ah.' Ben pulled his plate towards him. 'This whole business is interesting!'

The little church was shadowy and very quiet. Abi let herself in and walked thoughtfully to a chair about halfway along the aisle.

Sitting down she stared up at the east window. Her mind was a blank. She hadn't been able to eat much lunch and her conversation had been non-existent when Cal tried to chat to her, glancing every now and then at her in concern.

In the end Abi gave up pretending. 'I'm sorry. I'm not very good company. I think I need to go and think about things on my own for an hour or two. I might go over to the church.'

Cal had smiled and moved the plates without comment. 'Take your time,' she said as Abi walked out into the sunshine.

Old churches always had an atmosphere. A combination of worship and prayer, pain and sorrow, alternated with long periods of quiet and emptiness as the stone absorbed the emotions of the men and women who had come there with their supplications. Old churches like this one and St Hugh's, medieval churches, had been built, she had once read, incorporating special long-forgotten mystical techniques to ensure the processing of pain and the constant gentle broadcasting of peace and love and prayer. They were, in effect, prayer machines. She gave a wistful smile remembering how she had tried to tell Kier as much. Maybe it was rubbish, but it was alluring rubbish and it was working now. The place was gently radiating peace and reassurance. She was, she realised, avoiding looking at the east window with its ancient depiction of the man on the cross. Her Lord. Jesus.

Could he really be Yeshua? A living, breathing young man with intense brown eyes, with all the compassion and gentleness which she would expect and yet a young man who was wandering round this countryside with a druid priestess, who clearly fancied her, who had doubts and worries and –

She stood up abruptly and walked up to the altar, staring up at the window. 'What am I thinking?' she asked out loud. 'What on earth is going on? It can't be you. It just can't. This is nonsense. Nobody believes you came here. Nobody! The thought makes historians fall about laughing, theologians become apoplectic and mutter about the New Age and atheists take it as proof that everyone is mad!' Her voice rang out in the silence and was absorbed by the limestone walls. 'Well? Say something! Come on. Explain what is going on!' She rested her hands on the altar, frowning up at the window. On the great slab of carved wood beneath her fingers were two brass candlesticks and a wooden cross. The slab was cold to the touch. Above her the glass in its soft lead framing was rippled and flawed, the colours gently muddy, throwing a warm wash of insipid light across the chancel as she stared into the face of the man on the cross. His skin was pasty, almost green, his loin cloth the colour of raw linen, his head streaked with blood from the enormous thorns on the woven twigs wedged down on his brow. His eyes were closed, his face serene. She shook her head. 'This is not happening to me!' Turning on her heel she walked swiftly back to the door and let herself out, closing it behind her with a bang before diving out into the sunshine. Almost running, she headed down through the church-yard into the orchard and stood there panting, trying to push the image of the man on the cross out of her mind.

Flavius returned at dusk. Throwing the reins of his horse to one of the boys working in the granary with a barked order to rub him down and feed him, he ducked into the round house and stared down at Lydia and Petra who were seated in their usual places by the fire. Cooking for the household was usually done in the separate kitchen, but tonight Sorcha had brought in a caul-dron of bean and mutton soup and hung it from a tripod over their fire. She was feeding twigs into the flames to warm it, her face reflecting the flickering light as she concentrated on her task.

'So!' Flavius stood, hands on hips looking down at them. 'The woman, Mora. Is she not the one who comes here with medicine for you, Petra?'

Petra looked up at him, her face white. 'Why?'

'Why?' His face was tight with anger. 'Because I have just ridden across the countryside to find out that the man I am looking for is one of her companions. He has been here months. He goes everywhere with her. He has probably been to this very house!'

Lydia stood up, her fists clenched in the folds of her skirts. 'Do not dare to shout at my daughter, Flavius,' she said, her voice tight with anger. 'I can assure you no-one has come to this house with Mora except sometimes her betrothed, Cynan, who is as local as Sorcha here.'

'What if I say I don't believe you?' Flavius pushed his face aggressively towards hers, his eyes as hard as flint.

'What you believe, Flavius, is of no consequence to anyone here,' Lydia said. Somehow she managed to keep her voice steady.

She moved away from him around the fire and went to stand in front of her loom. As the flames under the cauldron rose, licking at the metal, the large room was full of leaping shadows. Lydia was studying the length of woven material hanging before her with exaggerated concentration, noting how the dancing light emphasised the russets and greens of her checked patterns. She reached out for the shuttle and weaving comb.

'Leave it!' Flavius was behind her in two long strides. He seized them out of her hand and threw them to the floor. 'Look at me, Lydia!' He grasped her wrist. 'I will not be lied to!'

'You will not threaten me, brother!' She emphasised the word sarcastically, holding his gaze. 'Take your hands off me now.'

'Why should I?' He gave a cold leer. 'There was a time when you liked my hands on you, sister!' He echoed her emphasis. 'Does Gaius know about that?'

'Mama?' Petra's call was anguished.

'I'll go for help.' Sorcha dropped the ladle with which she had been stirring the soup back into the cauldron and turned towards the doorway. She dodged past Flavius and ducked outside before he could catch her. Within seconds she was back with two young men at her side. Dressed in working clothes, their feet swathed in loose-fitting boots, their hair long and unkempt, they stood side by side just inside the doorway looking at each other and then at Sorcha as though uncertain what to do.

He glanced at them and sneered. 'Oh I am so frightened! Is this the best you can do, Lydia, in the way of a bodyguard?' He reached into his belt and pulled out his dagger. 'So,' he said with an exaggerated sigh. 'Who is first?'

'Flavius!' Behind him Gaius had appeared in the doorway, still swathed in his travelling cloak. He took in the scene in one glance. 'Put up your dagger. How dare you!' He stepped forward. 'What in Hades is going on here?'

'He is threatening us, Gaius,' Lydia said coolly. 'As we knew he would. I would like him to leave our house.'

'I don't think so.' Flavius rammed the dagger home in its sheath and turned away from them to sit down next to Petra. He folded his arms. 'I suggest you send these peasants away,' he said. 'This does not concern them.'

'It concerns them if my wife and family are threatened,' Gaius retorted angrily.

'They are not being threatened.' Flavius adopted a tone of exaggerated boredom. 'What nonsense. Lydia is being hysterical. All I did was ask if this man I am seeking has come here to this house.'

'And I told you he hasn't!' Lydia snapped.

Flavius shrugged. 'If you say so, then I must believe you.' He yawned. 'Why not get that girl to serve some supper? If she leaves it much longer it will burn.'

Lydia glared at him. 'I have not asked you to stay and eat with us.'

'No, but you will.' He smiled at her. 'For old time's sake.'

Gaius sighed. He reached up to unpin his cloak, then he stared round. 'Where is Romanus?'

'He went hunting.' Lydia went to his side. She took the cloak from him and folded it over her arm. 'He'll be back before dark.' She looked up at him. 'Gaius –'

'Here we go,' Flavius put in. 'Gaius, darling, your nasty brother is bullying me.' He raised his voice to a falsetto as though imitating her. 'Here. Lydia. A present for you. I bought this from the people I visited today. You see, I didn't bully them or threaten them. I gave them money for something they had to sell. A trinket, but I thought you would like it.' He reached into his pouch and held out his hand.

She stepped closer to Gaius. 'Thank you, Flavius, I do not need trinkets.'

He shrugged. 'Very well, then Petra shall have it. A pretty thing for a pretty girl.' He turned and smiled at her. 'Here you are, sweetheart. This will suit you better than your mother anyway. It will look nicer against a younger face.' He tossed a small packet into her lap. Petra stared down at it, then at Lydia, her eyes full of anguish. Flavius watched, amused. 'So, she doesn't dare open it without your permission. She doesn't have her mother's spirit, does she!' He reached down and picked the packet up. Unwrapping it he exposed a string of coloured glass beads. 'There. Let me put it round your neck, child. See how pretty it is. The beads glitter in the firelight.'

Petra gasped. Her swollen hands went to her throat. 'Mama –'

'That was kind of you, Flavius.' Gaius's voice was acid. 'How thoughtful. My daughter is very grateful.'

Petra opened her eyes wide. 'I can keep them?'

'Of course you can keep them.' Gaius leaned down and kissed

the top of her head. He glanced warningly at his wife. 'Let Sorcha serve the food, then we will all get some sleep. I'm sure Flavius will need to travel onwards tomorrow.'

His brother grinned. 'Tomorrow I am going to borrow your son. He can take me over to Afalon or whatever the place is called. The man I seek is a student there, as I suspected.' He stuck his feet out before him towards the warmth of the fire. 'Once I have seen him and dealt with that matter to my satisfaction, then I shall consider whether to go or whether to stay the winter here. It all depends, doesn't it.'

'Do you have any books about ancient Glastonbury in your library?'

Abi burst into the kitchen where Cal was once more sitting at the table wrestling with her piles of bills. Cal looked up startled. 'Go and look, Abi. You're welcome. There are lots of guidebooks and things in there, on the left of the desk in the window. We shove them all there when we have travelled anywhere so we know where they are. And the older books would be roughly where we found that one the other night. I don't know what Justin took, but I doubt if it was anything you would need.' She frowned. Abi was already heading for the door, her face intense. Shaking her head painfully Cal looked down at the table again, and resumed tapping at her calculator.

Abi let herself into the room. It faced the front of the house, the lawn, the long driveway, the hedges and behind them the road which led from Glastonbury to Wells. The guidebooks were obvious, lying flat on the shelf in a bright well-thumbed heap. She pulled them all out and laid them on the desk. Then came a tatty volume of William Blake's poetry with a curly Celtic book-mark slotted, probably not coincidentally, opposite the page where 'Jerusalem', Blake's own famous celebration of the fact that Jesus himself had walked upon England's hills, was printed. Next to that was another selection of books of local interest. Some of these were modern, some she recognised from her mother's shelves: John Michell, Geoffrey Ashe, Dion Fortune, Sabine Baring-Gould. She smiled. When she had studied history at Oxford the early Medieval period had been her speciality. She remembered some of this stuff from those days, and with them the botch of wishful thinking and confused rubbish which characterised the earliest chronicles and later inventions as England began to try and create for itself a pre-history to match its hopes and dreams as a nation. King Arthur of course was the most important character, his grave found right here in Glastonbury by the monks in the twelfth century. It was customary to put a cynical spin on all the legends these days. The unearthed couple were now thought more likely to have been some Iron Age tribal leader and his lady, if she remembered right. Whoever they were, the discovery of this tall rich man buried with a woman with golden hair, his Guinevere, did wonders for the income of the abbey. Pilgrims came from all over Christendom to pay homage, and it earned the approval and patronage of the king himself, remaining the richest abbey in England until Henry VIII set his greedy eyes on it. The legends about Joseph of Arimathaea and Jesus, as far as she knew, had come much later. She pulled out a small booklet. 'Did our Lord Visit Britain' by the Rev C.C. Dobson, MA. and smiled. The MA gave credibility presumably. She turned to the flyleaf. First published in April 1936. She read for a long time, one book after another. Some of these stories she remembered from when she was a child. She could hear her grandmother's voice now, telling her the old tales.

Joseph of Arimathaea was, it was surmised, a rich merchant, trading in tin, copper, lead and silver. He was, possibly, probably, Jesus' uncle, being the younger brother of Jesus' father. Or mother. (Mind you a lot of the books said great-uncle). Anyway, some sort of kinsman. He was supposed to have brought Jesus with him as a boy on one, or several of his trading voyages west and so the young Jesus had visited Cornwall, and Somerset and possibly other bits of the British Isles as well and he had later come back to Glastonbury to study. It was peaceful and it was sacred, the perfect place to meditate and pray as a preparation for what was to come; the presence here of a druid sanctuary of especial holiness and the fact that druidism was a peaceful religion with a belief in the Trinity had been another draw. She scanned the pages of Dobson, intrigued. The three aspects of the Godhead, represented by three golden rays of light were Beli the Creator of the past, Taran, the god of the present, and Yesu, the coming saviour of the future. A title which Dobson put in capitals. 'The more druidism is studied,' he went on, 'the more apparent is its relationship to the revealed religion of the Mosaic law.' She put down the booklet and stared out of the window. She thought the whole point of druidism, the bit that most people knew, was that as it was an oral culture, so secret in its time that no-one knew anything much about it, beyond the sour complaints of Roman historians like Julius Caesar. But then Julius Caesar was sour about anyone who opposed his plans to conquer the world!

It was wonderful stuff. Intriguing. Mysterious. Irresistible. Abi leafed through some of the books again. All made more or less the same claims, with some asserting that Jesus' mother, Mary, also came when he was a boy and again later, after his death. That was when Joseph returned with the vials or cruets of Jesus' blood and sweat, collected at the cross, and with the Chalice from the Last Supper, which many identified with the Holy Grail and his staff, which implanted in Wearyall Hill became the famous Holy Thorn. Here, in Glastonbury, it was claimed, was the first dedication anywhere in Europe of a church to the Virgin Mary. All the books had scraps of credible history, all had stuff which was to her mind, rubbish. Most made the point that the true Glastonbury of history and the Glastonbury of legend were two different places, two different parallel worlds, co-existing to this very day.

She closed the books and stacked them neatly in front of her on the desk, staring again into the garden. In her previous life she had been, briefly, an investigative journalist and she could feel it again, now. The excitement, the curiosity, the enthusiasm when an idea began to run. How did her story, the story of her vision, fit into this legend? Could she be seeing history as it happened? And Yeshua. Could he possibly be Jesus?

Next morning she parked once more in the abbey car park, this time heading through a narrow passageway towards the entrance to the abbey itself. Her enthusiasm had taken a dive overnight. She woke up early with the firm conviction that she was undoubtedly mad and she thanked God she hadn't mentioned her idiotic theory to Cal or Mat. She glanced up. Behind the high wall she could see the top of the ruined arches of the medieval building, but the entrance to the museum was modern. She paid her money and made her way in to the exhibition where for the time being she appeared to be the only visitor. Coming here was almost certainly going to confirm the impossibility of her ideas.

153

They were playing a CD of plainsong. She smiled. The gentle voices of the monks were soothing, wafting gently between the exhibits; just what she needed. A plaque near the entrance stated: *The Somerset Tradition* and described the whole story, pretty much as she had read it the night before, but of course as a quaint curiosity, not fact. Obviously. Further into the exhibition a glass case was labelled, 'An Ancient Church Built By No Human Skills . . .' So, it was all here. Slowly she made her way round the glass cases staring at the history of the abbey which had been, so famously and horrifically, destroyed by Henry VIII in 1539 after the abbot was hanged on the top of the Tor on trumped up charges of concealing the abbey's treasure from the king's representatives. It was all fascinating, but it was the earliest history she had come to see: the actual origins as far as they were known, of this holy place described by St Patrick as 'this holiest earth'.

The site of Glastonbury Abbey was a huge thirty-six acres, according to the ground plan they had given her at the ticket office, of beautifully tended grounds, with what remained of the once great abbey standing stark and fragmented, the ruined walls neatly strengthened, situated towards the northern edge of the site.

Letting herself out of the museum, she headed towards the Lady Chapel, unusually at the west end of the abbey instead of the east, and built, it was claimed, on the site of the little mud and wattle church, the *Vetusta Ecclesia*, built with Jesus' own hands.

But why, her cynical other self, the self who had gone to theological college, put in, would Jesus have built a church here at all when he hadn't yet invented Christianity? If he invented Christianity, which he didn't. Not really. That was Paul. Wasn't it? The historical Jesus was an observant, probably a strict, Jew. Maybe an Essene, that intriguing ascetic sect who had hidden the Dead Sea Scrolls in the caves at Qumran. He was certainly a rabbi. A scholar. He wasn't, couldn't have been a student here!

With a rueful smile at the contradictions spinning in her brain, she headed towards the walkway which ran at the original floor level of the Lady Chapel, above the now gaping crypt and she stood staring at two signs in front of her describing the building of this chapel after the original abbey had been burned down in the twelfth century. After reading them she turned back to the entrance and made her way to the flight of steps which led down to the floor of the crypt which in the sixteenth century had been turned into a chapel dedicated to St Joseph. The gallery was now behind and above her as slowly she walked forward between the towering, ruined walls towards the apse where a roofed-in area covered a plain altar. A few yards away from it she stopped. She closed her eyes. Could she feel anything special on this most holy of spots? It was hard to say.

Behind her she heard voices. Three people were standing on the walkway. They too had stopped to read the inscriptions there. She could feel their eyes on her back. It was hard to concentrate, to feel any sense of the sacred. It was all so neat, so – the word to describe it wouldn't come. Antiseptic, perhaps. Regulated. Controlled. Where was a sense of the sacred sanctuary of the druids – the place dedicated in even earlier times, so some of the books said, to the mother goddess, hence the later dedication to the Blessed Virgin. Or had it been dedicated to his mother by the young Jesus himself; and where did Gwyn ap Nudd fit in? And who was he? She found herself shaking her head, still too cynical, too hog tied by history, too bound by her own orthodoxy to make any sense of this at all.

She waited. Because of this especial holiness St Bridget, St David and St Patrick had all come here. As a place of pilgrimage it had been called 'the Second Rome'. Domesday Book itself confirmed the gift of twelve hides of land, given by the Celtic king Arviragus to Joseph to build his church. And yet she could feel nothing.

Turning she retraced her way to the steps and almost ran from the chapel, heading out across the grass which marked the position of the old cloisters. In the distance she could see the black silhouette of the Tor behind the trees. Nothing. No feeling of sanctity. She had felt it at Fountains Abbey in Yorkshire. At Dryburgh in Scotland. Why not here? Here of all places she should sense it. She felt a wave of something like panic. She was being excluded from something precious. All around her, as the day warmed up and the sun appeared, lighting up the gold and russet of the leaves on the trees around her, were people immersed in the feelings which she should be feeling.

She sat down on a bench, her hands in her pockets, her shoulders hunched. She had come here to pray. No prayers came. She had come here to feel the ancient sacredness of the land. No feelings came.

A shadow fell across her and she looked up. A figure was standing on the path close to her, a woman's figure.

Abi!

It was a whisper, no more.

Abi!

'Mora?' Abi leaped to her feet.

She had gone. There was no-one on the path at all.

'Mora?' Abi turned slowly around, straining her eyes into the sunshine. 'Where are you?'

Nothing.

Kier drew his car up onto the gravel outside Woodley Manor and sat staring through the windscreen at the oak front door with its elegant, square Georgian porch and frame of scarlet Virginia Creeper. A road atlas lay open on the seat beside him. For several seconds he remained motionless. The house seemed deserted. There was no sign of any cars around; no people that he could see. He sighed. This was a lovely place. No wonder the bishop had chosen it as a retreat for Abi, where she could recover her sense of balance and her faith. Even here in the car he could feel the peace reaching out to him. Groping for the door handle he pushed it open and climbed out. When he rang the doorbell there was no answer. From somewhere deep inside the house he heard dogs barking but no-one came to the door. Maybe he should have phoned. But he had wanted to surprise her and have the chance to convince her that he wanted nothing but her happiness and wellbeing. He wandered round to the side of the house and found a courtyard area with a range of ancient outbuildings, and what looked like a couple of garages. Still no cars. So be it. He would have to come back later. He reached into the car for the map. He had been given the address of Ben Cavendish, her spiritual advisor. Perhaps he should go and see him first.

This time Athena took Abi to a different coffee shop. This one was opposite the Tribunal. As they sat on the comfortable green sofa, teapot and cups on a small tray in front of them, Abi was conscious of the other woman studying her face. She smiled

156

uncomfortably. 'I meant it when I said I needed to buy a book on crystals. I need to know more about them.'

'So you couldn't work it out on your own?'

Abi shook her head. 'I can use it in that it has switched something on. I see these visions. I see –' She hesitated. 'Mora. She's called Mora. My druid priestess. She is trying to speak to me. Just now I went to walk round the abbey and she was there. She came and stood right beside me. She cast a shadow . . .' Again she stopped and shrugged. She reached out for her cup. 'She shouldn't cast a shadow if she's a ghost. Surely that much we know about ghosts.'

'And you spoke to her?'

Abi nodded. 'Well, perhaps I was less than conversational. She gave me a fright! But I called out her name.'

'And did she react?'

Abi shook her head. 'She had already gone. Disappeared.'

Athena picked up her own cup and sipped thoughtfully. 'So you need to know how to speak to her?'

Abi nodded.

'It seems to me, it is nothing to do with the crystal. It is your own doubt and fear which are getting in the way.' Athena set down the cup. 'Is it possible the thought of making contact with another world like this is something you cannot bring yourself to believe in? You have set your own credibility limit.' She leaned back into the sofa, sitting sideways so she could watch Abi's face. 'Or do I mean credulity?' She shook her head. 'You know what I mean.'

Abi smiled. 'I do, and I would say that is undoubtedly one of my problems. The trouble is trying to reconcile what is actually happening here and what I believe is possible.' She still hadn't mentioned the priest bit. It was too big a deal. Bound to be. 'So, how can I reset my parameters?'

Athena laughed. 'My dear, I think that is for you to do. All I can suggest is that you give yourself a good talking to and logically confront what is going on. Look at what is real – have you been to the Tribunal tourist centre across the road, for instance? Upstairs there is a wonderful little museum. They even have an Iron Age canoe over there. That is the reality behind what you are seeing. Study it. Let yourself feel. Does anything come. Does it make a difference, looking at all this as archaeology rather than myth? Then see how you feel about what has happened with your ghosts and decide whether, logically, you can readjust your belief systems.'

Abi shook her head. 'I fear that is easier said than done.'

'I doubt it. If you were too disbelieving you would have dismissed all this as rubbish the first time it happened and shut down. I've seen people do that here. Glastonbury makes things happen for people. There is something in the air!' she sighed. 'They come, all excited and eager and waiting for some wonderful spiritual experience, then when – and if – it happens they go into free fall. It's so sad.'

'I sense there are no half measures here. One is either a Believer or a non-Believer in the Glastonbury experience.' Abi was watching a group of women who had walked in. They went straight to the counter, helping themselves to trays. 'You can tell by the way they dress,' she added absent-mindedly.

Athena snorted with laughter. 'So you have me down as a goddess worshipper, which in your case is not a compliment, right?'

'OK. Sorry. Yes, I suppose I did. It's your skirts. But I love them. I wish I had the courage to wear them myself. They are pretty and floaty and glamorous and they look very comfortable.'

'And they hide the bulges, dear,' Athena added dryly. She stood up. 'I have to get back to the shop; it's Bella's half-day. We'll talk about this some more, but in the meantime, go to the museum, then do some parameter stretching exercises.' She smiled. 'I would think just living round here for a bit would do the job; expanding your open-mindedness.'

Abi watched her make her way towards the door, greeting two people as she left, chatting to them briefly, then moving on. She seemed to know everyone. Abi sighed wistfully. She was an outsider here, an impostor, pretending to be someone she wasn't, but no longer the person she was. She reached for her teacup and sipped from it thoughtfully.

The table jerked slightly and she looked up. The couple Athena had greeted had edged in beside her with enquiring looks to see if the seats were free. They both smiled at her.

'You're a friend of Athena?' the young man said. He was tall and thin and dressed in cargo pants and a cheesecloth shirt. 'Lovely lady.'

Abi nodded. 'I'm just a visitor. She's been very hospitable.'

158

'She said you were interested in crystals,' the young woman said. She put her head on one side surveying Abi critically. Abi was immediately conscious of her own conservative clothes. At least her hair was loose and wild, but the grey slacks and dark blue sweatshirt were unadorned, stereotyped: the female vicar trying to look the part off duty and, she suddenly realised, unremittingly boring. She nodded. 'I was given one which appears to be very powerful and I'm not sure how to interact with it. That was why I went into Athena's shop. For advice.'

'I'm Serena and this is Hal.' The girl held out her hand with unexpected formality. Her accent, Abi realised, was more home counties than Somerset. 'We come down here every year. Hal makes musical instruments.'

'Drums,' Hal said.

'Have you been up to the Tor?' Serena asked. Again she put her head slightly to one side, like a bird listening for a worm.

Abi nodded. 'Not lately but I used to come here a lot as a child. My grandparents lived up near Priddy.'

Serena nodded. 'You're local then. Lucky you.'

Abi was thoughtful for a minute. How strange, just as she had been feeling so much an outsider she was complimented on being a local. She found she was smiling broadly. 'This seems to be a welcoming place. Very special.'

It was obviously the right thing to say. Serena's whole face lit up with excitement. 'Isn't it.' Hal said nothing.

Abi grinned again. Then she levered herself to her feet. 'I'm sorry, but I do need to get on. Perhaps I'll see you around?'

By the time she had reached the door they had taken receipt of two plates overflowing with salad and were leaning over their food with rapt expressions. Abi grinned again.

Athena was right about the museum. As she walked round the two small rooms looking at the glass cases Abi felt a definite pull into the past. These objects had belonged to people who had lived in the Lake Villages around Glastonbury which were constructed in the watery landscape in the years before the Romans came. This was the scene through which Romanus had paddled his canoe. This was the view she had seen with her own eyes. For real. She bit her lip, looking round. *For real?*

159

Those loom weights, spindles, weaving combs, dice. Those cooking utensils. That jewellery and glass. The tools and belongings of a long-gone people. Downstairs, she stood looking at the dugout canoe which had been excavated from its watery grave and she gave a wry smile. Athena had thought it might help, coming here. What it did was to was create a strange ache in her heart, as though she could feel the touch of the men and women who had made these things; hear their laughter. And their anguish. For real. She shook her head thoughtfully. Perhaps Athena was right. Perhaps it was a help.

Pools of mist in a landscape of shadows and milky waters and iridescent light. He smiled. This was a land of dreams and fleeting sunbeams, of numinous tides and dancing wind. A place where leaves fluttered from the trees and floated in patches of gold on silver reflections, where islands vanished into the distances and reappeared as songs on the lips of children . . .

10

Romanus was sharpening his old knife, honing the blade with intense concentration when Flavius sat down beside him on the fallen log overlooking the eel traps. 'Good weapon that,' he said with a friendly grin. 'You are quite the hunter, I hear.'

Romanus blushed. 'I enjoy it. I'm good at it.'

'And you are a fisherman too, I would guess?'

Romanus shrugged.

'Do you have your own boat?'

'We have three dugout canoes. Down there. I can take any of them if I want.'

'And you go across to the island quite often?'

Romanus nodded. 'I like it there.'

'That is where the healer lives, who treats your sister?'

'Mora. She's nice.' The blushed deepened. Flavius noticed. He grinned. 'She sounds a very special person. I look forward to meeting her. Your poor sister seems to suffer very badly. Do they know what it is that ails her?'

Romanus sighed. 'Mora says it is quite common round here. The damp from the meres and fens and the lake gets into the bones. It's old people who usually get it, but when someone young like Petra does it is ten times worse. Poor Petra suffers so badly in the winter she cries sometimes for days.'

Flavius looked concerned. 'Would it not be wiser to move to a land where the sun shines all winter?'

Romanus stared at him. 'I didn't know such places existed.'

'Of course they do. Where do you think your sister was born?'

Romanus bit his lip. 'They don't talk much about where they lived before we came here.' He sighed. 'I'd like to travel like my father used to. It sounds exciting.'

'It is exciting.' Flavius gave the boy an appraising look. Climbing to his feet he looked down at him. 'Right, so would this be a good time for you to take me across to Afalon in your boat? Perhaps if Mora is there you can introduce me. I would like to see a girl who can bring such a sparkle to a young man's eyes.' He slapped Romanus on the back playfully. 'Then tonight perhaps I can tell you some stories about life in the hot countries of the world. It might surprise Petra to know they even exist. She was much too young when your parents left Damascus to remember it. And they don't appear to have told you anything. My guess is that it is because she was born in a different country to a different life, that Petra is so susceptible to the mists and damp of this godforsaken land.'

The smallest of the dugout canoes was a two-seater, narrow and unstable, but fast. Pushing it out onto the shallow waters of the mere Romanus hopped in and took the paddle. Flavius was seated in front of him, staring ahead at the island with its cluster of small hills, the tallest and strangest a cone shape reaching up towards the racing clouds.

Romanus steered deftly between the shallow patches of reed and mud, following the course of a deeper channel all but invisible to the untrained eye. The waters were rich in birdlife and Flavius noted ripples where fish swam in shoals beneath the surface. Two men fishing in the distance raised their hands as they went past; a beaver swam swiftly away from them, its nose cleaving the water leaving a sharp V-shaped ripple on the water.

Romanus aimed for a landing stage where several other boats lay pulled up on the mud and they climbed out aware of the freshening wind tugging at their hair. 'How many people live here?' Flavius asked as he stared round. There was a fair-sized settlement here on the lower slopes of the nearest hill. He could see signs of other habitations above the trees as smoke rose and streamed in torn white wisps towards the east. Everywhere there were apple trees and he could smell the sweet-sour scent of cider presses.

Romanus shrugged. 'There are a lot of people here. There's a village further along the shore called Treglas. Then the druids have many students; this is a sacred island. Up there,' he pointed towards the highest point, 'that's the Tor. There is a sanctuary there where no-one can go but the highest of the initiates. The healers live in a village about a mile from here, along this track.' He waved his arm towards the west. Already he was setting off but Flavius caught his shoulder. 'Wait. How do you know Mora will be there?'

'I don't. I go to her house. If she's not there someone usually knows where she is.'

Flavius was thoughtful for a moment, then he shrugged. 'Lead the way.'

They passed several men and women who greeted them in a friendly manner. No-one seemed surprised to see Romanus or queried his companion. Presumably they knew the boy, and knew he was of Roman descent, not least because of his stupid presumptuous name. Because of that, presumably, any stranger with him was accepted without question. Flavius snorted to himself. The place was populated. He was not going to be able to walk in and despatch his victim openly. First find him, make sure he had the right man, then he could decide what to do once he had located him and spied out the land. After all the young man had no way of knowing that anyone was after him. Romanus had set off up a hillside track. Light-footed and fit, the boy was drawing away. Flavius swore quietly under his breath and hurried to catch up with him.

A blackbird flew out of the bushes, uttering a sharp alarm call. Romanus stopped and looked back. He frowned. 'Am I going too fast?'

Flavius smiled. 'No. I'm a soldier, remember. Fit as a flea, me!'

Mora was outside her house, standing in front of a small table, which was laden with bags of herbs. She looked up as Romanus appeared and smiled at him in welcome. Her gaze moved beyond him to Flavius and her smile died on her lips. 'Who is this, Romanus?'

'My uncle, Flavius. He wanted to visit the island and we thought we could come and collect Mora's medicine to save you the journey.'

Mora frowned. 'But I went to see Petra yesterday, didn't she tell you? I took the medicine with me.'

There was a moment's silence. Romanus looked confused. 'Petra never said.'

'Indeed she didn't,' Flavius added after a moment. He scowled. 'How very odd that no-one mentioned it. I take it you saw Lydia and my brother?'

Mora held his gaze. Her eyes were a deep grey-blue and he

165

felt them probing his very soul. 'I saw Lydia. Your brother wasn't there.'

'Did you go alone?' He folded his arms.

'Why do you ask?'

'No reason. It seems to me a long way to paddle a canoe on your own.' As if realising that he was alienating her with his confrontational questions he relaxed with a broad smile. 'This young man ferried me over just now. I was very impressed with his stamina. I'm not sure many young Roman lads could paddle so swiftly and so strongly at his age.'

She turned back to her table and reached for a bag of herbs. 'How strange. Our young people do it all the time. As do our womenfolk.' She gave him a swift, cold smile.

He nodded graciously. 'Sorry. I didn't mean to offend you.'

Romanus looked from his uncle to Mora and back uncomfortably. He didn't understand this sudden atmosphere of hostility between them. 'I expect Cynan was with you, wasn't he?' he asked helpfully.

'Cynan?' Flavius was watching her hands as she pulled out a wad of dry green leaves.

'My colleague. Yes, he did go with me, as it happened.'

'And who is Cynan? Does he come from a local tribe?'

'Oh yes, his father is one of the druids,' Romanus put in helpfully. 'Cynan taught me how to whistle up the shore birds.'

'So, you know him as well as you know Mora here?'

'You seem very interested in my companion?' Mora said after a moment.

Flavius smiled. 'Forgive me. I am interested in this whole place. It seems very special. I had heard about it long before I arrived here. I gather people come from all over the Empire to study here.'

'The Empire, where to be a druid is an offence punishable by death?' Mora said quietly. 'Have you come to spy on us, sir?'

Just for a moment he looked taken aback but then he was smiling again, all honesty and directness. 'Of course not. The ban, as you must know, is largely directed at the wild men of Gaul who plot and intrigue against the Emperor. They were given their chance to come into line but they refused. Here I gather the studies of your druid schools are directed towards peace and healing. Besides, this place is not part of the Empire yet.'

Mora gazed at him. Something was wrong; she could sense him

166

veiling his mind from her as he studied her face with his wide eyes and his disingenuous expression.

'You expect us to be a part of the Empire one day?'

He shrugged eloquently. 'I think it likely. Why would a small group of isles on the edge of the world want to be independent of the Empire? We bring too many benefits to the peoples we rule. Wealth. Peace. Strength against the barbarian hoards.'

She gave a quiet laugh. 'I fear we are the barbarian hoards.' She turned to her herbs once more. 'Since I have already delivered Petra's medicine, Romanus, your journey was unnecessary, I'm sorry.' She glanced up at the boy with a gentle smile.

He met her gaze anxiously, then glanced at Flavius, eager to help him. 'My uncle wants to meet your student, Mora.'

'Indeed.' Her glance flashed back to Flavius. 'Well, I'm afraid he is out of luck. My student is away on an errand on the mainland. I doubt if he will return for several days.'

Flavius drew his cloak around him as a cold breeze fingered its way through the woodland around her house. 'I am sorry to hear that. It would have interested me to find out how far some of your students have come and why they chose this place. Perhaps I will have the chance to meet him another time.'

Mora inclined her head. She could sense danger here and she wasn't sure why. Gaius was a friend. He and his wife were a part of the community. People liked and trusted them, but this man, Gaius's brother, was a different matter. There was no transparency in his gaze. The wind blew again, a gentle cold warning, touching her cheek. The gods were whispering to her to beware.

Janet Cavendish showed Kier into the sitting room with a tight smile. 'I'll tell Ben you are here. He's working on his sermon.' She pulled the door closed behind her and made her way to Ben's study. 'The evil seducer is here,' she whispered. 'He's rather good-looking.'

Ben stared at her blankly.

'You know!' she went on. 'Abi Rutherford's lovelorn swain. Whichever way you think of him he is here in the sitting room and he wants to see you.'

Ben stood up. 'How did he know about me? Who gave him this address?'

Janet shrugged. 'I didn't hang around to cross question him. That's your job. Shall I bring tea?'

Ben sighed. 'You may as well.'

The fire had not been lit. The room was warm enough but without the companionable crackle of logs in the grate it seemed to lack life and Ben wondered briefly why Janet hadn't brought the man straight into his study as she would most visitors. He held out his hand to his guest and gestured him to a chair, then he went over to the log basket. He reached for a fire lighter, piled up a few birch logs and felt in his pocket for a box of matches. 'So, Mr Scott, how can I help you?'

'I've come to talk about Abi.' Kier sat back in his chair; outwardly at least he seemed relaxed and calm. 'How is she?'

'She is well.' Ben sat down opposite him. In this room Janet had chosen a predominantly pale yellow design for the furnishings. The curtains were flowered with stylised primroses and soft ferns, the chairs a corded light mustard. It was a comfortable room, designed to reassure and uplift. 'May I ask who told you she was in Somerset, Mr Scott? This information was supposed to have been kept confidential.' Flames were licking greedily over the logs now. There were one or two sharp cracks as they grew hot.

Kier looked him straight in the eye. 'Her father told me. Professor Rutherford is as concerned as I am that the Church is not behaving in a responsible and open manner. In fact, I think the bishop's actions in this case have been grossly reprehensible. He has used some remote family connection to give him the excuse for meddling in affairs which don't concern him at all.'

Ben sat back and crossed his legs casually as he surveyed the other man. Kier was dressed in smart brown cords with a rust-coloured sweater over an open-necked checked shirt. There was a silver chain round his neck; Ben could not see what hung from it. Probably a cross, he supposed, but outwardly nothing about the man's appearance betrayed the fact that he was a clergyman.

Aware of Ben's scrutiny, Kier lifted his hand restlessly and brushed his hair back from his forehead. Then he sat forward in the chair, his elbows on his knees. 'I expect you have been given some kind of garbled fabrication of what happened between Abi and myself?'

168

'I have heard Abi's version of the story, certainly,' Ben said carefully. 'But what happened between you and Abi, Mr Scott, only concerns me in that it has affected Abi's spiritual wellbeing. I am her advisor and her counsellor in her role as a priest, I am not a repairer of relationships. And as such, I am sure you understand, I am not at liberty to discuss anything about her with a third party.'

He saw a muscle tighten in Kier's cheek. There was a temper there, tightly under control. He had noted that Kier had not asked him to call him by his Christian name. Odd that, but in a sense welcome in that it kept them at arm's length from one another.

The door opened behind them and Janet appeared with a tray. 'I thought you might like some tea, Mr Scott,' she said with a smile. She laid the tray down on the table near him. 'Shall I leave you to pour out, Ben?'

Ben nodded. 'Please, my dear.' He had not taken his eyes off Kier's face. The man had not even acknowledged Janet's presence. He hadn't risen to his feet as good manners might have indicated. He didn't speak to her or thank her for the tea. His eyes were fixed on Ben's face in some kind of test of strength. He sensed Janet hesitate and he relented. 'In fact, perhaps you could do it for us, Janet. That would be kind.' The man would have to acknowledge her presence if she was handing him a cup of tea. Ben waited curiously to see what would happen.

Kier ignored the proffered cup and after a moment's hesitation Janet set it on the side table next to him. 'I'll leave some sugar here, shall I, Mr Scott?' Her voice was slightly louder than before. Ben could sense her irritation.

And at last he looked up at her and nodded. 'Thank you, Mrs Cavendish. No sugar.' She was dismissed.

Ben looked at his wife. He could see the angry flush on her cheeks as she gave him his own cup and then turned towards the door. If he was any judge of his wife's psychology Abi had just won a useful ally.

'Because of Abi's wild accusations and her more than strange behaviour over the last weeks of her curacy in my parish, she has secured my suspension,' Kier said slowly. 'I don't know if she told you anything about that in your role as her confessor?'

Ben shook his head. 'As I just told you, Mr Scott, I can't

169

discuss anything that I may or may not have talked about with Abi.'

Kier stood up. 'She has ruined my career.' He took a deep breath and walked over to the window. On this side of the house the view was across the lawn. There was already a sprinkling of pale leaves under the walnut tree. 'That in itself is enough to upset me, although I feel sure I will be cleared of any accusations she might have made and any actions I took towards her will be vindicated, but my primary concern, as of course is yours, is with Abi's welfare. I think she's in great danger.'

'Please, sit down, Mr Scott,' Ben said. He waited while Kier returned to his chair. 'Can you tell me what sort of danger?'

'She has a tendency to meddle with psychic phenomena as I am sure you are aware. I rather foolishly accused her of resorting to witchcraft.' He gave a short harsh laugh. 'I didn't mean it literally, but the word frightened her enough for her to go running to the bishop to make another complaint against me. Women are very sensitive to accusations of witchcraft – I am sure you have come across this yourself. They find it deeply offensive. They think it is part of some male plot against them. They equate it with a criticism of feminism. What I witnessed though was something that filled me with horror and I didn't know what else to call it. She summoned ghostly figures into my church and she appeared not only to condone their presence there but also to enjoy their company.'

Ben stared at him incredulously. 'What do you mean, enjoy their company?'

'She said they sang beautifully.'

'That's all? She heard them singing.'

'Isn't it enough?'

Ben looked down at his hands. Kier's description had for a moment conjured up a very much less than holy image reminiscent of some medieval picture of a Satanic bacchanal. He restrained a smile. 'Forgive me asking, but when you say she summoned these figures do you mean she performed some kind of ritual or are we talking about a haunted church and someone with the sensitivity to see the ghosts that frequent it.'

Kier stared at him and for a moment seemed incapable of speech. 'You talk as though hauntings were usual!' he said at last.

'In my experience they are.'

'Don't tell me you're an exorcist!' Kier's face registered deep disgust. His colour had risen and Ben noted the sweat appearing on his forehead. The man was under enormous stress.

Ben shook his head. 'On the contrary, I find a gentle and persuasive attitude to unhappy spirits, and the offer of prayer is usually enough. I take it Abi did not feel these entities were unhappy if they were singing.' He levered himself out of his chair. 'I am sorry Mr Scott but I do feel that it is inappropriate that we should be talking like this. In my opinion Abi and you need some time apart. You have had an unfortunate conflict of personalities and ideologies, as far as I can see, and I truly feel it is no more than that, but a time of reflection would seem to be a good thing for you both.'

Kier leaned back in his chair and reached for his tea cup. 'Very probably, but first I need to talk to her. I shall go over there later and have a word.'

'You know where she is?' Ben was alarmed.

'Of course I know where she is. You think her own father wouldn't know her address? He agrees with me. This has to be sorted out. Bishop David has a lot to answer for! He cannot hide her from the two men who probably care most for her in the entire world.'

Ben sat down again, trying to school his face to impassivity. 'May I ask what exactly it is you need to say to her?'

'That is not your business.'

'Forgive me, but I think it is. I am, as I have already told you her spiritual director. If you are going to say anything which is going to upset her, then I would like to know about it beforehand as I will have to pick up the pieces.' Ben's voice, though still quiet, had gained in emphasis. 'I can't allow you to undo all the good her time down here has achieved and is achieving.'

'I am sure what I have to say will only be of use to her. I am as concerned for the welfare of her soul as you are.' Kier drank his tea and put down the cup with some force, rattling the small silver spoon in the saucer. Then he stood up. 'I will leave you now. I can see you have been drawn in by her charm and her plausibility just as I was. More fool you, if I may say so. I suggest you pray for guidance, because you will need something to sustain you when this all kicks off.'

171

He strode towards the door and pulled it open. 'I am sure we will meet again soon.'

Janet was in the hall, putting fresh water into a vase of flowers on the hall stand. She jumped out of his way as he strode towards the door. In moments he was climbing back into his car.

She went back into the sitting room where Ben was already on the phone. 'Cal, warn Abi that Kieran is on his way over. Get her out of the way. Tell her to hide in the attic. Whatever, just don't let her speak to him. The man is a complete nightmare!'

Slamming down the receiver he turned to Janet with a groan. 'What have we got involved in! You heard all that, I assume?'

She nodded. 'Rude, spiteful and malicious. I am beginning to think that Abi needs to be very careful indeed.'

'Where do you think she is?' Cal was standing at the study window with Mat at her side, staring out across the gravel towards the road. There was no sign of Abi's car.

He shrugged. 'Is it worth me driving around a bit to try and find her? She was going into Glastonbury, you said.'

Cal nodded. 'I think so. There's no point in you going out after her. She could be anywhere. I just assumed she would be back for lunch. She's been ages.'

'She probably forgot the time. She is getting a bit obsessed, you must admit. What do we do when this chap turns up?'

Cal scratched the end of her nose thoughtfully. 'We tell him she's not here. We ask him where he is staying and take his phone number and very politely say that we will ask her to get in touch with him.'

'And what if he refuses to go?'

She sighed. 'I might have to get rough!'

Mat gave an affectionate chortle. He dropped a kiss on his wife's head – she was at least a foot shorter than him. 'I'd better hang around then. Be ready to pick up the pieces.'

'You do that.'

They stood for a moment in silence, then Cal turned away from the window. 'Come on. We don't want him to catch us waiting for him.'

Kier arrived half an hour later. Opening the front door, flanked by barking dogs, Mat noted the silver Audi, then the sturdy, good-looking man striding towards the door. He exuded an air of slightly pugnacious determination.

'Can I help you?' Ordering the dogs to be quiet he put on his best, mild-mannered face. The dogs were not so polite. He could sense them bristling with disapproval.

Kier held out his hand and introduced himself. 'I need to see Abi quite urgently. I am sorry not to have rung ahead.'

Mat grimaced. 'Perhaps it would have been better if you had. I'm afraid she is out for the day.' He was praying she wouldn't choose that moment to drive in.

'I see.' Kier studied his face with care, obviously wondering whether to believe him and, in response to the man's air of cynical superiority, Mat felt his own hackles rising to match the dogs'.

Cal's voice from behind him reminded him of the agreed plan. 'Perhaps Mr Scott would like to give us his address, then we can get Abi to contact him when she comes back.' She manoeu-vred herself in front of him slightly and looked up at Kier with a flinty expression that Mat knew well. People didn't usually argue with it.

'I thought I might come in and wait.' Kier took a step forward. 'If you wouldn't mind. I shan't get in your way.'

A throaty growl from Thiz stopped him in his tracks as he took a step into the hall.

'I am so sorry, but we were just going out.' Cal smiled at him. 'It's really not a good time.' She folded her arms.

For a moment Mat thought he was going to argue, but Kier thought better of it. He shrugged and inclined his head graciously. 'Of course. It was thoughtless of me to come unannounced like this. I'll look in some other time, if I may. I don't know where I shall be staying yet. I'll go and check in somewhere and perhaps try and ring Abi then. And if you could ask her in the meantime to contact me. She knows my mobile number.'

They watched as he slid back into the car.

'Please don't let her turn in at this moment,' Cal murmured as they retreated into the house and closed the door.

They waited, holding their breath, listening to the sound of the car tyres as he reversed and swung round. From the study window they watched him drive to the gate, indicate right, towards Wells, and disappear down the road.

'Call Abi now,' Mat said under his breath.

'I've tried. Her phone is switched off.'

He shook his head. 'Then all we can do is hope she is tucked away somewhere safe where he won't spot her.'

Abi was sitting in the chair which Kier had vacated some two hours before, in front of Ben's sitting room fire. 'Ben, I've got to talk to you. I've got to tell you something –' She broke off as Ben raised his hands as though warding off a stampeding horse. 'What is it? What's happened?'

'Kier was here.'

'Kier?' Her face registered incomprehension. 'What do you mean?'

'I mean, he was here. He was going straight over to Woodley.'

'I should have guessed he would come.' She slumped back in the chair.

'So you knew he'd found out where you were?' Ben cleared his throat.

'My father told him.'

'May I ask how your father knew?'

She shrugged. 'Not from Bishop David. I think someone in the diocesan office probably didn't realise it was supposed to be confidential.' She fixed her gaze on the carpet. 'What did he say?'

'He seemed somewhat disturbed.' Ben heaved a sigh. 'Both in himself and about you. He made some strange remarks, some of which worried me as they have obviously worried David.' He looked up at last. 'Can we get one thing straight, Abi. I take it you did not perform any kind of ritual to summon the spirits of the dead into St Hugh's church?'

'No!' Her indignation was instantaneous. 'Of course I didn't. I told you what happened.' She glanced away from him. 'It was the crystal. It was the first time I realised what it could do.' She paused. The silence was broken by the rustling whispers of the fire.

Ben stood up and moved over to the log basket. He rummaged round in it until he found a section of lichened apple trunk. The

174

room filled with the sweet smell of the apple. 'So, you didn't call up its powers deliberately?'

'No.' She was chewing her lip. 'That was when I first experienced anything so strongly. Clairvoyance I suppose you would call it. The ability to see ghosts. I didn't make the connection with the crystal that time.'

'And you didn't summon this ancient congregation?'

'No. They were just there. Suddenly. Then Kier walked in and they vanished. Like that!' She snapped her fingers. 'As though they had never been. But he smelled the candles and it seems he saw them as well.' She shook her head. 'Which must mean he's clairvoyant too.'

Ben had been standing looking down into the fire. He turned away and resumed his seat with a sigh. 'So it would seem.'

'You do believe in clairvoyance?' She could feel herself growing agitated.

'Of course. By whatever name.' He was watching her as she stood up and wandered over to the window. She stayed there with her back to him, fingering the flowered curtains, looking out at the lawn. He could sense her distress. 'We'll keep you safe from him, Abi. If necessary we'll move you somewhere else.'

'No!' She span round. 'I have to stay at Woodley.'

'Why?' The intensity of her response surprised him.

'Because I want to find out what is happening – what happened,' she amended.

'The ghosts, you mean.'

She nodded.

'Wouldn't it be better to remove yourself from the ghosts? They are unquiet spirits which need to be released, Abi, not called back again and again. You know that as well as I do.'

She made no response. Kier's visit had given him pause. He was uncertain now what she had done. She could sense his ambivalence and it made her furious. She had been going to confide in him the thought that had been tormenting her, that she had seen Jesus. How could she do that now? It would confirm everything Kier had told him. That she was mad!

Turning to face him she gave a wan smile. 'I'll ring Cal and ask if he's there, shall I?'

Ben nodded. 'I would keep out of his sight for now. They can hide your car round the back. There are plenty of old barns and sheds there. He won't stay down here long if he can't find you.'

She shook her head. 'What has he got to rush back for? My guess is that he will stay here as long as it takes. Did he tell you what he wanted to say to me?'

Ben was thoughtful for a minute. 'I'm not actually sure he did. He seemed keen for you to know that he had been suspended.'

'So he wants to have a rant at me?'

He nodded again. 'That's part of it, I'm sure, but there was something else. I think he is afraid you have been corrupted in some way. He wants to save your soul. And he is also a proud man and you have rejected him. Reducing you to a quivering jelly of fear and penitent dependence,' he added shrewdly, 'would make him feel much better about himself.'

She snorted. 'No chance of that!'

'No.' He glanced at her under his eyebrows. 'Repentance is a part of what we do, though, isn't it. If we are worried that we might be doing something not quite right, we try and stop and we ask God to forgive us.'

'We ask God,' she retorted, 'but not Kier!' She folded her arms. 'I'm not doing something not quite right, Ben. My conscience is not telling me to leave this alone.'

That was a lie, she realised. Her conscience was by no means at rest. But then, if she was seeing Jesus . . .

It couldn't be Jesus. That was the point.

In her head she was back in the lecture hall. There were lots of students wandering around in Europe in those days. Europe. She brought herself up short. The Empire was what she meant. It was all part of the Empire. Mainland Europe, excluding the Germanic north and of course at this time Britain, right across to and including the Middle East and all round North Africa. And probably on your gap year visiting even the German and British tribes might sound quite exciting. She smiled to herself. All sorts of students from all sorts of countries. That was what modern studies were showing. Iron Age, even Bronze Age tribal areas weren't isolated, undiscovered territories peopled by primitive barbarians. They were sophisticated communities who traded widely, had done so for a thousand years even before the birth of Christ. Yeshua, whoever he was, would have spoken how many languages? Aramaic, obviously, Hebrew to read the scriptures, Latin in a country ruled by Rome, Greek as an educated man living in an Hellenistic world. Even the druids spoke and wrote Greek. He would have picked up the local Celtic tongue. Maybe, if he had travelled as widely as legend said, he would have learned Tibetan and Sanskrit, the language of the Sutras. Whoever this man was he was an educated, sophisticated traveller of a kind to have put most modern people to shame. He could be anyone. It was her job to find out who. She had to find out what happened. And she didn't need the permission of Ben or Kier or the bishop to pursue her research.

'Abi?' Ben was watching her.

She gave an embarrassed little laugh. 'Sorry. I was thinking.'

'Clearly,' he said dryly. 'May I ask what about?'

She shook her head. 'Just wondering. Can I ring Cal from your phone?'

He gestured towards it. 'Of course.'

She didn't see his worried frown.

Athena Wake-Richards was sitting behind the counter staring out of the shop window, lost in thought. She hadn't been totally honest with Abi and now she was feeling guilty. But then Abi hadn't been fully honest with her either, of that she was certain. Call it intuition, or a shrewd ability to read another woman's face, but she knew Abi was hiding something. She glanced round the shop. The crystals twinkled and dreamed as they always did, creating a strong feeling of energy in the room, but that was all. She had long ago given up believing in them. They were just pretty stones. Giving off energy yes, but beyond that with no particular healing powers, no miraculous ability to divine the future, nor to store the past. She sighed. She had been talking complete balls. Crystal balls. She gave a rueful smile. Oh, she knew the patter well enough. She could reel it off for hours; once she had believed it herself, passionately and completely, as convinced as anyone in the town. She shivered. But she had become cynical in the end as so many did. She had waited and hoped and believed that proof would come; something. Anything. She had dared to hope that a revelation would open her eyes, show her that her rational brain was wrong, that

177

all this magic was genuine. But it hadn't happened. She remembered the last time she and Justin had met. They had had a terrible quarrel. A real break-up-of-any-possibility-of-reconciliation quarrel. Not that they had ever been that close, it was just that he had seemed a kindred spirit; a really nice guy. She screwed up her face in a grimace of disgust. So why had she led Abi to believe that she and he were friends and so claimed a kinship of some kind with Woodley and the Cavendishes? Still, her advice had been sound, hadn't it? Give up on the crystal. She should use her own brain; her talents, whatever it was that was producing these ghostly phenomena. She inspected her fingers and began to chew off a hangnail thoughtfully. Did she believe in ghosts, that was the question. Abi obviously did. She obviously believed everything she had been told and had been presumably convinced as well by the garbage she, Athena, had fed her. She shook her head. At least she hadn't tried to sell Abi a pile of books. She glanced into the back of the shop. There were a great many of them there, some of them very expensive. Good value in their way, with pretty photographs and diagrams of layouts and things, but not for someone with a real problem. Or if they were, she was not the one to explain how they worked.

The bell on the door tinkled as two women came in. She glanced at them and smiled a welcome. Surreptitiously she reached for the writing pad under the counter. She and Bella had a small wager going. These two would buy something, at a guess. Something small like earrings. She put a tick in the column. At the end of the month they would tot up their guesses and whoever won would stand the other a meal at The George and Pilgrims. No cheating, of course. She glanced at her watch. Perhaps she would close early and take a drive down the Old Wells Road and look up Cal and Mat. See Abi on site as it were. See if she could work out what it was that Abi was hiding and at the same time appease her conscience and make sure that nothing she had said could cause any harm. She gave another rueful smile. She knew what people called her in the town. Boadicea. It conjured up the image of a large, florid, aggressive woman with wild Celtic overtones. A strong woman and a wise woman. Well, that was what she had worked at, wasn't it. She should be pleased her image plan had worked so well. Mat and Cal were not going to betray her. They believed the image. Unless Justin had said something. But then Justin didn't talk to them, did he. She looked up and smiled as the customers approached the counter holding out a pair of earrings. Each. She smiled. Two ticks to go on the list.

Abi approached the gates slowly, her eyes peeled for the silver Audi. The quick phone call to Mat before she left Ben's had told her that there had been no sign of Kier returning but she was still nervous. Turning in she drove straight round to the back and tucked her car into an old barn as instructed. The doors were standing open waiting for her and Mat appeared as she climbed out. 'I'll help you shut them. They're a bit warped, but it's worth it. He won't see your car in here. It's much easier to hide you!' He grinned.

'I resent having to hide away from him at all!' Abi said crossly as she reached into the back of the car for the books she had bought across the road from the coffee shop before she left Glastonbury. New books she didn't think they had. One on history, one on legend. 'I'm not afraid of him. Wouldn't it be better if I just told him to piss off!'

'You think he'd go?' He followed her out of the barn and closed the other half of the doors, slotting an iron bar in place to hold them closed.

'I don't know. What else could he do? He can't just sit there forever.'

'He could bully you. He could be unpleasant.'

'But that's all.' They walked across the gravel towards the back door. 'I was afraid of him in Cambridge because he was my boss. He was making unpleasant accusations and pestering me and I was on my own, but once I told the bishop it all stopped.'

'Till he rang you.'

'And I foolishly panicked. But, Mat, I am not going to let him terrorise me. That is nonsense. What can he do? Especially if you and Cal are here to back me up. I'll just ask him to go.'

'OK. It's up to you.' He opened the door for her and ushered her into the kitchen. The dogs, lying in front of the fire looked up, thumping their tails on the ground in greeting. Mat walked over to the sink and washed his hands, drying them on a dish towel before going over to the cooker and lifting the lid on a pan which was simmering gently on the backburner. 'This smells nice. I wonder where Cal is.' He was just replacing the lid when the doorbell rang. The dogs leaped to their feet and raced out of the room towards the front door, barking. Mat and Abi looked at each other.

'May as well get it over with,' she said firmly. To her fury her heart was thudding with apprehension. She waited in the kitchen while Mat went to the door. When he returned moments later there was a woman behind him. 'You seem to have been reprieved,' he said cheerfully. 'I gather you two know each other.' It was Athena.

'There were things I wanted to tell you.' Athena and Abi were seated on either side of the kitchen fire with a glass of red wine each. Mat had disappeared in search of Cal.

'And I you!' Abi had regained her composure. 'But first I'd like to show you the crystal.'

When she reappeared minutes later with the crystal wrapped in its cotton bag Athena was staring into the fire. She looked up. 'I need to make a confession.'

'Look at it first. Please.' Abi glanced at her. 'I think I can guess what you're going to say.'

Athena leaned forward and set her glass down on the hearth. 'I doubt it!' she said sharply. She put her hands out and Abi put the bundle into them. For a moment Athena sat still, her hands on the cloth.

Abi took a sip from her glass, her eyes on Athena's face. For a long time neither woman said anything.

When Athena spoke at last she shook her head. 'I can't feel anything.'

'Unwrap it.'

'There's no point.'

Abi looked dismayed. 'Why not?'

'Because I can't feel anything. That's what I had to confess to you Abi. I've been stringing you along. Well, not entirely. I know my stuff. I've read every book, spoken to every expert, but I can't feel it myself. Crystals do nothing for me. I'm a jeweller. A designer, I can appreciate their beauty but that is all. I'm sorry. I'm a fake; a con artist. I don't believe in it any more.'

'I see.' Abi slumped back in her chair.

'That doesn't mean it's not happening for you.'

'No.'

Hearing the desolation in her voice, Thiz sat up. She came over to Abi and rested her chin on Abi's knee, gazing soulfully up into Abi's face.

'It is happening to me. I can't pretend it isn't,' Abi said slowly. 'And whatever it is, it has something to do with the crystal.'

'You and your mother obviously have the gift.' Athena smiled ruefully. 'I wish I did. I really do. What I've told you is what I've read. And I've brought you a copy of the best book we have on the subject.' She dived into the tapestry bag which she had dropped at her feet when she sat down and produced a book with a selection of brilliant cut crystals on the cover. 'Read it. See if it helps. I still think though that you should go with your own instincts. For you this is real.'

Out in the hall the doorbell rang again. The two dogs raced out of the room barking as Abi looked down at the book in her hands. She didn't open it. 'Thank you.' Her voice was bleak. Then she smiled. 'You didn't mislead me, not really. I feel a little lost, I admit, but after all this is my stone as you say, and my mother's. And I'm not alone. Cal was here when I saw one of the figures in here. Mora. The druid priestess. She came into the kitchen and stood over there by the window –' She broke off at the sound of men's voices in the hall. One of them was Kier's.

Athena looked at her, puzzled as Abi rose to her feet, staring at the door. 'Abi? Are you all right?' By the time Kier and Mat appeared in the doorway she too was standing up.

'So, you are here!' Kier walked in and stared from Abi to Athena and back. 'I need to talk to you. I dropped in earlier, but you were out, so, I thought I might try again.'

'I don't think I want to talk to you, Kier,' Abi said quietly. Her mouth had gone dry. 'Better to draw a line under everything and make a fresh start. For both of us.'

'A fresh start!' he cried sharply. 'How can I make a fresh start? You have destroyed my life.'

'No, Kier. I haven't. You did that yourself.' Abi threw an appealing look towards Mat. He was standing awkwardly in the doorway, the dogs sitting at his feet. 'Please, let Mat show you out. I am sure if you talk things over with the bishop –'

'I have talked things over. I needed you and you turned your

181

back on me. I've told him that instead of helping me, you used the dark arts to bewitch me. You're dangerous, Abi, but I forgive you. And I want to help you. That is why I have come. We can work through this. We can study and pray and ask God to help us.'

Abi was intensely aware of Athena's face. The woman was staring from one to the other of them in astonishment. The crystal, still wrapped in its bag lay on the chair between them beside the book which Abi had dropped there.

'Kier. I think it would be better if you went,' Mat put in at last. 'Give me your address down here and Abi can contact you if she wants to speak to you. Or better still, I think it would be better if you went back to Cambridge.'

'No.'

The single word echoed in the room.

'I have nothing to talk to you about, Kier,' Abi said finally. 'There isn't any point in staying.' Her courage was returning.

There was another long silence. No-one moved.

'Who is this woman?' Kier appeared to have noticed Athena at last. He focused on her with evident distaste.

'This woman,' Athena said with emphasis, her patrician tones ringing round the room, 'is Abi's friend. And if you think Abi is a practitioner of the dark arts, you should see what I can do when I get going. I suggest, Mister, that you leave now!'

Mat rubbed his chin, trying to conceal a smile. He glanced across at Kier to see how well that had gone down. Not well at all, by the look of it. Kier's face had gone an inelegant shade of puce. 'How dare you!'

'I dare.' Athena smiled at him.

Cal chose that moment to appear through the back door. She was wearing her coat and her hair was dishevelled from the wind. She pushed the door closed and stared round in astonishment, putting a hand down to the dogs as they rose to greet her. 'Have I missed something?'

'Kier,' Mat said, 'is just leaving.'

Kier sighed. 'All right. I'll go. There is no point in talking to you, Abi, with all these people around.' He glared at Athena. 'I will come back tomorrow. Perhaps we can have some privacy then to discuss our personal affairs.'

'There are no personal affairs, Kier,' Abi said firmly. 'I am sorry, but you and I have nothing else to say to each other. How much

182

clearer can I make it? I don't want to see you again. I don't want to be harangued by you. I don't want to be saved by you. I have come here to get away from you.'

'That's telling you, buster!' Athena added in an undertone.

Cal was taking off her coat. She went and hung it on a hook by the back door then came back and bustled over to the stove. 'Can you give me a drink, Mat? When Mr Scott has left we can get on with supper.'

Kier gave up. With a shrug he headed for the door. He did not say goodbye.

There was a long silence after Kier left the room. 'Bloody hell!' Athena said at last. 'Where in the world did he come from? You must have some racy past, Abi! Bishops! Witchcraft! I don't understand.'

Abi laughed uncomfortably. 'Long story.'

'Your ex, I gather?' Athena queried.

Abi shook her head. 'Ex boss.'

'And your ex boss is a priest!' She was sounding more and more incredulous.

Abi nodded and took a deep breath. 'So am I.' She forced herself to meet Athena's eye. 'I'm sorry. That's what I should have told you.'

'I thought you said –'

'I did. More accurate to say I was a priest. I resigned. I couldn't hack it any more. It wasn't just Kier. It was the whole thing. I found I couldn't do it.'

'You stopped believing?' Athena didn't sound as shocked by the revelation as Abi expected.

'No, I still believe. At least . . .' She hesitated. *It will destroy your faith, Abi.* Her mother's voice echoed in her head for a moment. *It did mine.* 'Things have happened. To do with the crystal. That's why I'm so confused. I don't know what to believe any more.' She noticed that Mat had vanished. He must have followed Kier out of the room. The dogs had padded after him. She threw herself down on her chair by the fire and closed her eyes. 'I'm sorry. I wasn't honest with you. I'm not feeling very robust at the moment and I'm so used to people who –' She broke off. 'Who aren't believers. They like to have a go.'

Athena nodded. 'With reason usually.' She sat down opposite Abi and leaned forward. 'The church is responsible for so much pain.'

Abi nodded.

'On the other hand, maybe now it is beginning to acknowledge that women exist, there is some hope.'

Abi gave a rueful shrug. 'Maybe.'

Behind them Cal sat down at the table. 'If you go ahead with your resignation, Abi, it will be a great loss to the church for that very reason,' she put in.

Abi scowled. It was Athena who stood up. 'Will you show me your ruins?' She looked down at Abi. 'And the crystal.' Abi hesitated.

It was Cal who nodded with a glance out of the window. 'Go, Abi. Show her. Now before it gets dark.'

They stood in front of the ruined arch for several minutes, watching the evening draw in across the garden. Abi felt strangely relaxed. She pushed her hands into the pockets of her jacket. 'He'll come back,' she said at last.

'The priest?'

Abi nodded. 'Kier. Yes.'

'So.' There was a pause. 'Are you afraid of him?'

'In a way, yes.'

'Why?'

'He has a powerful personality. Corrosive.'

'You don't have to let it corrode you. He can't hurt you unless you let him.'

'True. In theory. I guess he got under my skin a bit. It makes one vulnerable.' She sighed.

'You're not in love with him?'

'No. I fancied him a bit when I first met him, yes.' Abi shrugged. 'But that was all. No, it's this.' She gestured at the flowerbed. 'It's thrown me completely. Instead of healing me, coming here has laid open more wounds. I'm flailing around in territory I don't understand. Bits of my psyche have opened up suddenly and it's not something we covered at theological college. There's a battle going on inside me: orthodoxy versus spiritual mayhem.'

Athena nodded. 'And all this, as you know, will only make you stronger.' She paused. She seemed to have a capacity for silence. 'Can you see them now?' she asked at last. The twilight was dulling into darkness.

Abi shivered. She shook her head.

'Look harder.'

'I can't summon them, it just happens. And I haven't got the crystal with me.'

'You don't need the crystal and you know it. That was what I came to tell you. You are in charge, Abi. You are a strong woman. A priestess. Just look.'

11

He was sitting by the fire, whittling a piece of apple wood, his hands strong and supple as he worked the blade around the grain. Mora came and stood before him with a smile, watching for a moment the sure movements of his hands as he peeled the flakes back with his small knife.

'Do you ever see into the future?' she asked suddenly.

She had looked away from him and was staring into the fire.

'Sometimes.'

'Does it frighten you?'

He flicked some curls of wood from the carving and ran his thumb softly over the surface. 'Yes.' Glancing up, he studied her face. 'You've seen it too?'

She nodded. 'Do you have to go back to your own country?'

He gave a wry smile. 'Oh yes. I have to go back. I've sent word to my uncle that the time has come. Once he has picked up his cargos all along the coast he'll bring the ships in at Axiom and wait there for me. This will be his last trip this year. It's important I go with him. I need to go home.' He glanced up at her face. 'I can see my artistic interlude is over. You have more jobs for me?'

She nodded again. 'There is a whole queue of people come for healing. And after that you can come with me to see a wood-cutter called Sean. A messenger arrived this afternoon to beg me to visit him. He lives in the forest up on Meyn Dyppa. Apparently a tree fell on him when he was cutting it down. His leg is broken in several places. He needs it to be set as well as a knitbone poultice and painkillers. If we cannot help him his family will starve this winter. He has only daughters. There is no son to help him.'

'You know I will come, Mora.' He smiled at her. He set down his knife and the small carving and stood up, brushing the wood shavings off his robe. He glanced up. 'It will soon be dark, do you want to go now?'

She shook her head. 'It is too late. The messenger said one of his daughters is looking after him until we get there. We'll leave at first light.'

He glanced up at her again. 'There are many people, Mora, amongst my people, the Jews, who feel that women have no place in the world of men; no right to stand next to them before God. You and your friends here have shown me that women can be so special, so strong, equal in every way to men.'

For a moment she wasn't sure what to say, she could feel the colour rising in her cheeks. But when at last she managed to master her emotions at his words it was merely to retort, 'I should hope so!'

He nodded with a grin. 'Then after we have seen to the patients here I will go and speak to your father. I am getting behind with my lessons and I need to absorb all I can before I leave. There is so much you learn. Law giving, history, genealogy as well as healing and herbs.' He smiled at her once more. 'The asceticism of your teaching pleases me. And its inclusiveness. Last time he tried to speak to me about the need to control my temper and rein in my impatience,' he laughed, 'and we talked about the wisdom of serpents. I hadn't known that is what some people call the druids. I shall miss you all so much when I leave. So much of your philosophy touches me deeply.'

Mora bit her lip at yet another mention of his coming departure. She had always known that he would go one day, but she couldn't bear to think it would be so soon. She had grown much fonder than she dared admit to herself, of this enigmatic young man with his gentle brown eyes and soft-spoken determination.

'While you do that, I will consult my own gods and I'll go to my herbs and make sure we have all we need for tomorrow.' She reached down and took the knife from him, then the small figure. 'It's a wren!'

He nodded. 'Small and cheeky.'

'And very sacred!' She laughed and handed it back to him. He set it down on the trestle table near the door to his house to join two or three other little carved birds, staring at them critically, his head slightly to one side.

'Yeshua! Your patients are waiting!' she remonstrated with mock severity.

'You're right. Enough of childish things.' He grinned at her, then he turned and clapped his hands once, sharply. The wren shook its feathers, stretched its wings and flew away with a sharp stuttered cry of alarm, followed by the other birds. He turned and winked at her. 'Don't tell my mother! She used to get cross with me for doing that when I was a child. I used to make them out of clay!' Leaving his whittling knife on the empty table he strode away towards the healing complex where their patients waited, leaving Mora staring down at the bare scrubbed boards where the small knife lay abandoned amongst the softly curled wood shavings, its blade glittering in the fitful sunlight.

'Can I come with you, uncle?'

Looking down as he swung himself into the saddle next morning Flavius saw Romanus slipping down from his seat on the wall. The boy had obviously been waiting for him. Above them a flight of crane angled down towards the mere, their bugling cries echoing into the wind.

'I'm riding today,' he said curtly.

'I can run beside you.'

Flavius gave him an appraising glance. 'Very well. I'm going into the hills. Perhaps you can show me the way to the house of Sean the Woodsman?' He gathered his reins, urging his horse towards the gate.

Romanus nodded eagerly as he ran after him. 'He lives up on the edge of the forest, near the great gorge. It's a long way,' he added doubtfully.

'Then let's make a start.'

They turned away from the low ground heading east along the narrow track.

'Why would you want to see Sean?' Romanus asked, looking up at the man in the saddle. He was trotting easily alongside the horse.

'He is expecting the healer.'

'Mora?' The boy's face coloured slightly at the mention of her name.

'Her student. He seems to go everywhere with her.'

'Not everywhere,' Romanus said defensively. 'He didn't come to see us.'

'You like her, don't you?' Flavius slowed the horse to a walk as the track got steeper. Around them the trees were ablaze with autumn colour. Leaves, red and crimson and scarlet fluttered around the horse's hooves as it trod the path, tossing its head with a jingle of harness.

Romanus shrugged.

Flavius glanced at him. 'It must be hard to have a rival, with her all the time. I hear this man is handsome.' It was a deliberate goad.

Romanus shrugged again. 'She likes Cynan. Mama says they will marry one day.'

'I thought she was a priestess.'

'She is. And he is a priest. But druids are allowed to marry.'

'Really.' Flavius grimaced. 'I'd heard they serve their goddess with orgies in the forest like the followers of Dionysus. Hardly a background to marriage, I would have thought.'

Romanus shook his head, puzzled. He had never heard of Dionysus. 'I don't think they do that.'

Flavius gave a cynical smile. 'Perhaps they haven't told you, boy.' He nudged his horse into a canter and Romanus had no more breath for talking. When they next slowed down, the trees had thinned. Around them lofty green pines clung to rocky outcrops and here and there bushes of gorse were still alight with golden flowers. Romanus caught up and looked up at his uncle eagerly. 'Do you really work for the Emperor?'

Flavius leaned forward and slapped his horse's neck. 'I do. Why, has my brother said otherwise?'

Romanus shook his head. 'No, no. He has said nothing. I just wondered. It sounds so exciting to travel the world on secret missions.'

Flavius nodded. 'I suppose it is.'

Romanus looked round. He hadn't noticed that the autumnal sun had disappeared and the creeping tendrils of mist were winding through the trees around them.

Flavius reined in his horse. 'Is it much further?' His voice was tense.

Romanus shook his head. 'We are nearly there. We cross the heath here, and then we follow a track down towards the gorge.' Where only moments before they had been making their way across the rock-strewn hillside, now they were surrounded by a wall of white. The boy shivered. He turned round, staring over his shoulder.

'You aren't lost?' Flavius's voice sharpened.

'No, of course not.' Romanus glanced up at his uncle. 'You won't hurt Mora, will you?'

Flavius held his gaze coldly. 'There must be no witnesses to what I do here.'

'But –'

'No, Romanus.' Flavius interrupted him. 'I will not hurt Mora if you help me. When we get there you must see to it that they are separated. If you and Mora leave us alone, then neither of you will be witness to what happens and you will be safe. This is up to you, boy. Her life is in your hands. You will tell no-one of this conversation, do you understand? No-one. Not your sister, not your mother. Certainly not your father. If you do, I shall know and Mora will pay the price.' He fixed Romanus's face with a frightening stare. 'You have it in you, boy, to be a servant of the Emperor. If you do this well, maybe I can get a position for you when you are a little older. It is up to you. Show me what you can do.'

'He doesn't kill him. I know he doesn't kill him!' Abi found she was clenching her fists, her knuckles white. She looked round. It had grown dark, the last light in the western sky a pale salmon behind the black silhouette of the Tor.

'Who doesn't kill who?' Athena's voice was almost a whisper. Abi swung round. The other woman had retreated to the bench and was sitting watching her, her hands wedged into the pockets of her jacket. Somewhere nearby an owl hooted.

Abi shook her head. She couldn't, shouldn't talk about this. At least, not the Jesus part. She managed a smile, walking over to Athena and sitting down next to her. 'My Roman family is riven with hatred and jealousy. Two brothers who seem to hate each other.'

'Common enough, alas,' Athena said wryly. 'Especially here. Mat and Justin.'

'But they wouldn't kill each other?' Abi was shocked.

'No, I don't think it's that bad.'

'My Roman brothers seem to have fallen out over a woman.'

'How corny!' Athena gave a deep throaty laugh. 'Not so, Mat and Just. I don't know why they fell out, but it certainly wasn't

190

over dear old Cal.' She stood up with a shiver. 'At least I don't think so.' She paused thoughtfully, then she made a move towards the path. 'Come on, it's getting cold. Have you done enough eaves-dropping for the night?'

Abi nodded. 'You're right. That's what it is. Eavesdropping.' She paused for a moment as they turned towards the house. 'What did I do while that was going on? Did I say anything?'

Athena shook her head. 'The only thing you said was, "I know he doesn't kill him" or something like that when you came to. You were talking to yourself. Before that, all was silence. You seemed lost in thought. You just stood there, staring out across the garden.'

'For how long?'

'I don't know. Long enough for me to get damn cold. Twenty minutes? Half an hour perhaps?'

'It's weird. I saw Mora this time, but she didn't see me. She was across there, on the Isle of –' She hesitated. 'I was going to say, Avalon.'

'Why didn't you?'

'Because it wasn't. Not then, was it? That's Arthurian. What I am seeing is way before Arthur. But they seem to call it that. Ynys yr Afalon.'

'The Isle of Apples. It has had so many names. Glaston, from the Welsh word Glas, which was the colour of the waters of the lake. Thence the Isle of Glass, Ynys Witrin.' Athena moved on across the grass. 'That was in Anglo-Saxon times I think. Most people go for Avalloch, but whether that was to do with apples too, or named after some ancient chieftain, who knows. I like Afalon. The hard f in Welsh sounds like a v. That would make sense. Next time you see your Mora to talk to, ask her. It would solve a lot of puzzles over which historians and myth-makers argue for hours!' Athena was heading back towards the house. Abruptly she stopped and turned to face Abi again. 'How long were you a vicar?'

Abi grimaced uncomfortably. 'A couple of years. I'm still a curate technically. I've never had my own parish.'

'But you can do all the priest stuff, right? Communion? Bury people?'

'Yes.' Abi looked at her uncomfortably. 'I became a proper priest after my first year as a curate.'

191

'Then you resigned.'

Abi nodded. 'But I'm still a priest.' She found she was whispering. 'It's not something you can just undo.'

'Blimey!' Athena grinned. 'Who'd have thought it. Me being friends with a lady vicar.' She reached out and squeezed Abi's hand. 'Don't look so forlorn. I expect you're still human deep down.' She gave a teasing smile.

Opening the kitchen door they went inside to find Cal and Mat laying the table. 'Supper in twenty minutes,' Cal said sternly. 'And Ben wants you to ring him at once, Abi.'

She put the call through in the study, standing at the window staring out at the darkness while Athena, having accepted Cal's invitation to stay for supper joined her and Mat in a glass of wine.

'What did Kier say?' Ben sounded agitated.

'Quite a lot, but he went when asked.'

'Was it very unpleasant?'

Abi hesitated. 'Not as bad as I had feared, to be honest, but there were other people here. It might not have been so good if I had been on my own.'

'David is going to contact him and call him back to Cambridge.'

'You've spoken to David?'

'Yes, of course. This can't be allowed to go on. The man is obsessed. You have to be protected from his bullying.'

Abi grimaced at the darkened window. 'Thank you, Ben.'

'You are happy staying there? I don't want you to feel that you are vulnerable now he knows where you are.'

'I'm OK, Ben. Really. I feel completely safe here, thanks to your brother and Cal. They are fantastic. And Athena.' She grinned as she thought of Kier's reaction to meeting her.

'Good. Well, you know where I am if you need me. Call any time. I mean that, Abi. Even in the middle of the night. And in a day or two we'll fix up another meeting, OK?'

She stood staring out into the darkness after he had hung up, feeling the silence of the night beyond the glass. It was several minutes before she reached up and slowly drew the curtains.

Outside, Kier gave a final distasteful look at the dented blue car which was parked outside the front door. It had been easy to see that it belonged to the large, silver-haired woman who had been sitting by the fire in the kitchen. A worshipper of the goddess.

In the back window was a small poster for an exhibition of sculpture in the town. It depicted a pottery figure of one of those hugely obscene naked females which these women seemed to find so necessary to their so-called worship. He shuddered. That the woman should be sitting there in the same room as Abi was grotesque. It was a disaster. It reinforced everything that he had most feared about the route Abi was taking out of the church. Didn't she realise that she was still a priest? Once a priest always a priest. She could resign from her curacy, from a parish, but she could never resign from her priesthood. Facing the car he made the sign of the cross, then he turned and walked slowly down the drive towards the road.

Abi woke suddenly, every sense alert. She could hear footsteps downstairs in the room immediately below her bedroom. It was still dark outside. She groped for her bedside clock and stared at it. Three a.m. Sitting up, she slid her legs over the side of the bed and groped for her slippers. It was probably Cal or Mat. It had to be, otherwise the dogs would have barked but there was no harm in checking. Her heart was, she realised, thudding unevenly in her chest as she slipped on her dressing gown and quietly opened her bedroom door. Halfway down the stairs she stopped, listening. There was no sound now. And no light on anywhere that she could see. She crept down a few more steps. Surely if someone had come downstairs they would have switched on the lights? She paused in the hall. The sounds had been coming from the library. The door was closed. There was no sign of any light under the door. She crept closer, listening. Yes, there it was again, the quiet pad of footsteps, the sound of a chair or something, being moved. She put her hand on the door handle and turned it softly. As she pushed the door open and reached for the light switch a torch beam swung violently towards her, raking up and down her body. Dazzled, she let out an exclamation. Justin was standing by the desk, the two dogs beside him, tails wagging furiously. 'Turn off that light!' His furious whisper cut across the room.

'Why?' She spoke in her normal voice, suddenly furious. 'What on earth are you doing here, skulking round like a burglar?'

'I don't want to wake my brother, that's why!' He strode across

193

towards her, manhandled her away from the switch, clicked off the light and quietly pulled the door closed. 'I'm sorry to wake you. I was trying to be quiet.'

'Well, you didn't succeed.' She rubbed her arm where he had grabbed it none too gently. 'Why on earth do you have to behave like this? Surely you and Mat are grown adults? You don't have to creep around like some kind of unwelcome intruder.'

'I am an unwelcome intruder.' He glared at her, taking in her bare feet, her tousled hair, her short, unexpectedly revealing nightshirt, and suddenly he grinned. 'Sorry. I can't expect you to understand. It's just easier if we don't meet. I wanted to grab another couple of books before I leave. I'm going home tomorrow.' He glanced at his wristwatch. 'Today. There won't be any time to hang around until Mat goes away somewhere so I can come here in daylight, so I thought I would pop in on my way by.'

Abi shook her head. A smile, however charming, was not going to win her over. 'Well, I suppose it's none of my business. And the dogs seem to think it's all right.' They were sitting one on either side of Justin gazing up at him with every sign of adoration.

'Indeed. They will vouch for my good intentions. You can search me if you like. No stolen silver. No hidden cash. No stolen credit cards. And I will leave a note for Cal as I always do, telling her what books I've taken. I will leave it somewhere Mat won't see it.' His smile disappeared at the mention of his brother's name.

Abi raised her hands in surrender. 'OK. I'm off back to bed. I'll pretend this was all a dream.'

'Do that.' He stood waiting. With a shrug she turned back to the door, then she paused. 'I don't suppose you would tell me why you and your brother hate each other so much?'

'No, I couldn't.' He folded his arms. 'Goodnight, Abi.' He smiled again. 'Sweet dreams.'

To her annoyance she found herself smiling back.

She woke late. When she reached the kitchen it was empty. A note on the table informed her that Cal and Mat had gone to Taunton and wouldn't be back until late evening. 'Sorry about this. Unexpected appointment. Don't worry. We've got the dogs.' She raised an eyebrow as she set about putting on the kettle and making coffee. So she was alone in the house. Unless . . .

The library was empty. She stood in the doorway looking round. The room felt deserted; there was no resonance there from her altercation with Justin in the middle of the night. Nothing. She wandered towards the shelf where Justin had been standing, running her hand across the backs of the books until she came to a space. What was it that was so interesting here that he had to keep coming back? She squinted at the titles on either side of the gap and pulled out Mrs Leyel's *The Magic of Herbs*. Thoughtfully she ran her finger down the edge of the rough, handcut pages. Beyond it there were several other books on herbalism and ancient remedies. To the right of the gap was a set of Victorian guide-books to the counties of England. She frowned. Were they all still there, or was one of them missing? She ran her eye along the shelf. So, he had either taken a guidebook or he had taken a book on herbalism. She wandered over to the desk. He said he would write a message to Cal. She wondered where he had hidden his note. The sound of car tyres on gravel disturbed her train of thought and she glanced out of the window. Kier's Audi was pulling up outside the front door. He drew to a halt and climbed out. She froze. She was standing right by the window. He only had to glance her way and he would see her. He stood for a moment looking up at the front of the house, looking, she realised with a shiver of distaste, directly up at her bedroom window. Had he seen her up there last night, silhouetted against the light before she had drawn the curtains? She took a step backwards. Then another, not daring to turn her back on the window. If she could just reach the door she would be out of sight. Please God, let the outside doors be locked. His attention snapped back to the front door and he strode towards it. Seconds later the bell pealed through the house. She held her breath. He would be expecting to hear the dogs bark. As far as he was concerned her car was missing, it was still hidden round the back, and so was Cal and Mat's. The house would look empty. Surely he would give up and go away. She tiptoed into the hall and as soon as she was out of sight of the windows raced along the passage to the back. Reaching the back door she turned the key and shot the bolt across before retracing her steps back to the passage. At least there was no window there; no way he could see her if he walked round the house peering in. Were there any other downstairs doors to the outside? She wasn't sure. None that she had seen. Except the glass doors in the living room which led into the conservatory. She held her breath. They would be locked, surely. She crept back to the main hall, listening intently. There was no sound now from the front door. She pushed open the living room door and peered in. The doors to the conservatory were closed, but that didn't mean they were locked. She threw a quick look at all the windows. There was no sign of Kier. Running across the polished oak boards with their scatter of old oriental rugs she reached the glass doors just as Kier appeared at the conservatory door.

He smiled and strode towards her. 'So, there you are.' She could hear him through the glass. She threw herself at the doors, groping for the key, but he was already there, effortlessly dragging them out of her hands. 'I know the others are out. I saw them on the road. So there is nothing to stop us having a nice quiet talk.' He turned and closed the doors behind him, turning the key and putting it in his pocket. He stopped suddenly, staring at her. 'There is no need to be frightened, Abi. I'm not going to hurt you.'

'Of course you're not.' Somehow she managed to keep her voice steady. 'I just had no wish to speak to you. Not now. Not today. Not ever. And I don't like the way you keep locking me in with you. You did that in church and it freaked me out. Anyway, I'm just going out.'

'Then I won't keep you long. Can we go and have a cup of the coffee you're making? I can smell it from here. You always did make good coffee, Abi.' He walked ahead of her to the door and opened it for her. She had no alternative but to precede him to the kitchen.

'I don't think there is anything else for you to say, Kier.' She pulled down two mugs from the dresser.

'Abi, whatever you think of me, you must agree that I have your best interests at heart,' he said slowly. He sat down at the kitchen table. He was wearing a navy blue three-quarter-length coat with an open-necked shirt under it. No dog collar. Heavy silver cross plainly in view this time. 'Please listen.'

She said nothing. She poured him some black coffee and pushed a mug towards him. 'You've got five minutes.'

'Did you know who that woman was who was in here last night?'

'Of course. And before you say anything I should remind you that she is a friend.'

'She is a witch.'

'No she isn't. She is a talented artist. A jewellery designer.'

'And a goddess worshipper.'

Abi smiled thinly. 'She may well be. That is her business. It doesn't make her a witch. Not in the way you mean it.'

'Associating with her is putting your immortal soul in danger.'

'Rubbish.'

He linked his hands around the mug, his knuckles white. 'It is not rubbish, Abi,' he said gently. 'And you know it. You must let me help you.'

'I thought you were the one who needed help, Kier. I don't. Not from you. I have told you that. Your five minutes are nearly up.' She walked over to the fireplace and stood with her back to the cold ashes. 'Two minutes more, then you go.'

'No!' Kier slammed his mug down on the table and stood up. 'No, I will not be hounded out of here. I will not let you be endangered in this way, Abi. Can't you see what danger you are in? For God's sake listen! At least let me pray with you. Let me protect you. I can make you happy, Abi. I can look after you. Come away with me, now. Far away from this godforsaken place. We can pray together, we can beg God to forgive you. We can start again.'

'No, Kier!' Abi felt her stomach tighten as his voice grew more frantic.

'I can't go, Abi. Not without you.'

Abi eyed the telephone which was on the table behind him. No chance of grabbing it and ringing Ben or the police. He would take it from her before she even touched it. 'Please, Kier. Just leave.'

Behind Kier the door into the hall suddenly opened. She spun round in astonished relief to see Justin standing there. 'You heard the lady.' He had obviously overheard at least the last part of the conversation. Abi had never been so pleased to see anyone in her entire life.

Kier's mouth dropped open for a second. 'Who are you?' He backed away from the table.

'I live here.' Justin narrowed his eyes. 'And I don't remember asking you in. Neither, I suspect, did my brother. Please leave.'

'Not without Abi.'

'Abi stays.' Justin stepped into the kitchen. 'Quite apart from threatening her, I heard you making some very disparaging remarks about a friend of mine. That kind of thing makes me angry. I don't think you would like to see me angry.'

Abi held her breath. She watched Kier's face intently. His mouth was set with fury. He was, she was sure, trying to decide as he eyed Justin, whether or not he could take him on. Justin was taller than him, but slimmer, more lightly built. But he was younger and, Abi suspected, far lighter on his feet. Whatever the reality, Kier obviously decided that he would not chance his luck. He raised his hands in surrender. 'OK, OK, I'm sorry. I'll go.' He turned to Abi. 'But I will come back. I can't leave you to this. My conscience won't let me. You are too good a person at base, Abi, to lose you to the devil. Who knows, you might even come back to the church. Don't throw that chance away, I beg you. Let me help you. Please.' He was backing away from Justin, towards the door. 'I'll ring you. I promise. I won't leave the area without you.' He was walking down the passage now, with Justin right behind him.

'Kier!' Abi called suddenly. 'The key!'

Kier stopped and turned. For a moment she thought he was going to refuse, but he put his hand in his pocket and fished it out. It was Justin who put out his hand and after a second's pause Kier gave it to him. Then they were both out of sight. Two minutes later Justin reappeared. He walked over to the table without speaking and sat down.

Abi left the hearth and came to sit opposite him. 'Thank you.' Her voice was husky.

'You are a priest?' Justin held her gaze. His whole demeanour had changed. He looked cold and angry.

She gave a tight, miserable smile. He was no longer the enigmatic, good-looking mystery man who she had, she had to admit, secretly found rather attractive. He looked suddenly frightening. 'I was.'

'In which church?'

'The Church of England.'

He held her gaze for several seconds more without speaking, then unexpectedly he smiled. 'Does Athena know?'

Abi nodded.

'And that prick was a priest as well?'

She nodded again.

His smile broadened. 'I take it my sainted brother and his wife know?'

'Yes, of course they know.'

'And you are some project of Ben's?'

'You could say so.' She was beginning to feel angry in her turn. The shock of Kier's arrival was wearing off, and she resented this supercilious line of cross-questioning. So Justin was another hater of the church. The knowledge didn't surprise her but she was shocked to realise how much it upset her. 'I'm glad you were still here,' she said stiffly to change the subject. 'I take it you knew Mat and Cal were going to be out for the day and changed your plans.'

Justin gave a barely perceptible nod. 'Cal told me. Don't worry, I have her permission to be here. I spoke to her before they left.'

'It is none of my business why you are here,' she retorted crisply. 'I'm just glad you were. I don't know how to get the message across to that man. I don't like him. I don't need him. I want him to leave me alone. What will it take to get through to him? Perhaps I need to scream at him a few times!'

He grinned. 'I'd like to be there when you do.'

'At this rate you will be!' she replied grimly. She was not going to be placated by a smile now she knew how he really felt about her. She stood up abruptly. 'Well, I think I will leave you to it. I don't feel particularly safe here. I think I shall go into Glastonbury for the day.'

He stood up too. 'May I ask why you don't feel safe? Not because of me, I trust.'

She gave a small snort of laughter. 'No, Justin, not because of you. It is because I suspect he is waiting round the corner to re-appear when you go.'

'Well, I won't be going for quite a while, so feel free to be here safely.' He surveyed her silently for a moment. 'I can't quite see you in a dog collar.'

She felt the colour rise in her cheeks. 'I wouldn't bother to waste your imaginative powers on me.' She moved towards the door.

He folded his arms, watching her. 'Actually I think it would be rather appealing.' He paused. 'You don't like me, do you.'

'Is there any reason why I should?'

'Christian charity?'

She gave a wry smile. 'That is in short supply today, I'm afraid.'

'OK.' He shrugged. 'I'll be gone when you get back. Take care.' He turned away from her back to the table and reached for the telephone. For a moment she didn't move, then she headed for the door. It didn't seem worth saying goodbye. He was already engrossed in his call.

Athena was serving a customer when she opened the door and let herself into the shop. Abi hovered for several minutes, studying a small table laden with incense burners and candlesticks, waiting until they had gone. 'Kier turned up again this morning,' she said as soon as the door was closed behind them.

Athena sighed. She pushed the drawer of the till closed and heaved herself onto the stool behind the counter. Leaning forward, her chin on her cupped hands, she surveyed Abi. 'He's persistent, isn't he?' This morning she was wearing a saffron-yellow low-necked blouse with multiple stranded filigree necklaces with brown agate and copper drops strung along the wires. 'You could come and stay with me. He'd never dare follow you there.'

Abi smiled. 'That's true. He thinks you're a witch and a goddess worshipper.'

'He's not necessarily wrong.'

'No.' Abi paused. 'It's kind of you Athena, but he is not going to chase me away and I do have a reason to stay where I am.'

'The ghosts.'

Abi nodded. 'It's not that I haven't seen them elsewhere, it's just that that is the epicentre. I sort of feel it's meant to be, that I am there.'

Athena straightened and looked at her watch. 'Listen, I'm off duty at twelve. As soon as Bella comes in why don't you and I have a spot of lunch, then this afternoon we'll climb the Tor. How does that sound? We'll see if your Mora follows you there. That is the true epicentre of power, the focal point. In every era, pagan and Christian it has been recognised as special. Let's see what you make of it. Have you brought your stone?'

Abi shook her head. It was at Woodley, tucked back in the bottom drawer of the chest of drawers in her bedroom.

'Doesn't matter. You don't need it. As I told you, you can do it without, whatever it is it does or doesn't do. Go and buy yourself a pretty skirt, Abi Rutherford, and some low-necked sexy blouses and dump those churchy blue shirts. I'll meet you at twelve thirty.'

'Go and see what the situation is,' Flavius whispered. He had dismounted several hundred paces from the woodman's hut and tied his horse to a tree. Around them the grey limestone cliffs reared up out of the trees towards an intensely blue sky. 'I'll wait here.' He frowned as in the distance something moved on the distant rocks. He recognised the outline of a wild goat and nodded, satisfied.

Romanus crept forward, russet leaves rustling under his feet. The hut seemed deserted. Listening intently he moved on a few more paces. The place was utterly quiet. No smoke seeped through the roof and the door was closed. He glanced over his shoulder. He couldn't see the horse or its rider any more; the forest seemed empty. He glanced up as a shadow flicked across the sunlit track at his feet. A bird had flown overhead to perch on a tree near him. A crow. He shivered. It was watching him intently and after a minute it called, the three raucous caws echoing across the trees. The door of the cottage was pushed open and a dog raced out, barking wildly. It came straight at him and he had no alternative but to stand up in the sunlight. He held out his hands soothingly. Dogs liked him as a rule and this one was no different. It stopped its headlong rush and began to lick his hand, its tail wagging.

'Hello?' A weak voice called from the cottage. 'Who is there?'

Romanus glanced back over his shoulder in an agony of indecision. He was supposed to be spying out the land, but there was no hiding now. The dog had seen to that. Straightening his shoulders he walked up to the cottage and stooped in the doorway. 'Hello, Sean.'

The man was lying on a pallet on the floor. In the light from the doorway Romanus saw a pale face, sweaty with pain, the big man propped uncomfortably against some rough pillows. There was a rug across his legs. He was alone, but someone had left him a cup of water and a plate of bannock with a chunk of sheep's cheese. He didn't appear to have touched the food. Romanus decided the truth was probably the best option. 'I heard Mora the healer was on her way to see you,' he said. 'I thought I would bring you the message. Reassure you that you hadn't been forgotten.'

Sean managed a smile. 'That was kind. My daughter said she would try and send word to the island. She left yesterday to find someone to take a message.'

'And she hasn't come back?' Romanus frowned.

The man shook his head.

There was a pause. The boy didn't know what to say next. Why would she not return to her father when he was in such pain and all alone? He glanced round the shadowy hovel. The dog had followed him in and was lying at the foot of the pallet. The man's tools were neatly stacked by the doorway. Axes, mattocks, hooks. His needs seemed to be simple. A small pot for cooking. The plate and cup by his side, his breeches and a leather jacket lying by the bed. Someone had taken his clothes off. He could see the bloodstains on the torn fabric. 'Shall I fetch you some more water?' he asked at last, noticing that the cup was empty. The man nodded gratefully. Romanus picked it up and looked round for a jug.

'There is a spring. Behind the house.' Sean was speaking through teeth gritted against the pain. Romanus nodded and ducked outside into the sunlight.

Behind the hut a narrow track showed where a clear spring trickled out of a rocky outcrop. High above a raven soared upwards from the cliffs. Romanus held the cup under the water and swilled it round before refilling it.

'What the hell did you go in for?' The whisper at his elbow nearly made him drop it.

He swung round. 'I had no choice. The dog saw me.'

Flavius glared at him. 'No harm done, I suppose. So, he's alone?'

Romanus nodded.

'And he's expecting the healers?'

He nodded again.

'Good. We'll hide over there near the door. If we keep still long enough the dog will grow used to our presence. It seems to accept you. Come.'

'I'll just take him the water.'

'No. We need to hide! Leave it.' Impatiently Flavius struck the cup out of Romanus's hand. It hit the rock and shattered. The boy stared at it in horror. 'That was his only cup. He's thirsty.'

'I'm sure the ever competent Mora will bring something with her. He can wait,' Flavius said curtly. 'Come.'

Romanus looked from his uncle to the ground where the shards of broken pottery lay scattered. 'You shouldn't have done that,' he said stubbornly. Then he thought of something else. 'What happens if his daughter comes back? You're not going to hurt her, are you?'

Flavius glared at him 'She won't come back. She's had a message telling her that the healers have taken her father back to their island. By the time she finds out that's not true this will all be over.'

'But –' Romanus began.

'But nothing!' Flavius glared at him. 'You are beginning to annoy me. Has no-one ever taught you obedience? If you want one day to serve the Emperor, that is something you are going to have to learn, and learn fast. Sentiment has no place to play in my world, Romanus. You obey or you fail.'

Romanus stared at him, terrified. 'I do want to serve the Emperor.'

'Then obey me.'

Romanus followed him without a further word. They skirted the hut at a safe distance and found a hiding place from which they could watch the entrance. As they settled down out of sight amongst the bracken Romanus saw his uncle loosen his sword in its sheath. He bit his lip. 'You won't hurt Mora, will you? You promised.'

'Be silent!' Flavius narrowed his eyes. He had seen a movement on the path in the distance.

Mora glanced up at the tall pine on the edge of the forest. The crow launched itself into flight as she watched and again the three caws echoed over the treetops. She frowned, stopping in her tracks. Yeshua stopped beside her. 'What is it?'

'Something is wrong.'

He looked up at the bird. 'We have disturbed it.'

'It's more than that.' She looked round, narrowing her eyes against the sunlight. They had travelled more quickly than they had expected, hitching a ride on an ox cart through the lower slopes of the hills, setting off on foot across the heathland on the edge of the forest as the sun began to settle into the west. Even from here as they followed the track they could see the sharp silhouette of the Tor against the pearly western sky far away through the trees. Below it the marshy levels and the water of the mere were shrouded in mist.'

'We must go back,' she said suddenly. 'There is danger here.'

He shook his head. 'There is an injured man here, Mora. We need to help him.'

'But the bird has spoken.'

'Even so, we need to give help where it is requested. If we have been warned of something, then we can be on our guard.' He threw a glance over his shoulder. 'You are right. I sense all is not well, but there is a sick man out here somewhere, that is true and he needs our aid.' He smiled at her. 'Come.' He held out his hand.

She gave in. 'It isn't far.' She looked up at the tree. There was no sign of the crow now. 'Thank you, brother bird,' she said, 'wherever you are. We will be careful.'

It was not long afterwards that Yeshua stopped her with a hand on her shoulder. He pointed up ahead to the spot where the hovel lay in the shadow. 'Is that the place?' he whispered.

She nodded. 'Where is the woodman's daughter? Why isn't there a fire?'

He eased his pack off his shoulders and gestured her to do the same. Then he pushed her gently out of sight into the bushes. 'Wait here. I will go and see.'

'No!' She caught at him. 'No, it is you who is in danger.'

He shook his head. 'Why me?'

'I don't know. I just sense it. Something is wrong.' She looked round wildly. 'I don't know what to do.'

'Leave it to me.' Yeshua took a firm grip on his staff and stepped back onto the track. 'Wait here.'

Cautiously he approached the door to the hut. Seconds later the woodman's dog began to bark.

Mora watched as he pushed open the door and stooped to go in. She saw the dog jumping around him, its tail wagging, then she saw the movement in the bushes beside the hut. A tall figure emerged into the clearing, followed by a boy. She froze. The man was carrying a drawn sword.

'Abi, are you OK?' Athena's voice in her ear woke Abi with a start. 'You called out. You sounded terrified.' They were sitting side by side on the grassy slope below the old tower of St Michael's on the summit of the Tor. Around them the view stretched away on every side into the hazy distance. Abi shook her head, trying to rid herself of the image of the woodman's hut and the clearing in the forest. Yeshua had gone inside to heal the man and outside Flavius was waiting to kill him. She groaned with frustration.

'I'm sorry.' Athena stared at her. 'I shouldn't have interrupted.'

'No!' Abi rubbed her eyes fiercely. 'I was watching someone. He was in danger. I wanted to stop it. To be there. To be able to do something.' Scrambling to her feet she walked across to the tower – all that remained of St Michael's church which once stood on top of the Tor. The tower stood four square, the entrances on each of the four sides open to wind and rain and sun.

As she ducked inside and stood looking up at the sky Athena followed her. 'But you couldn't?'

'No.'

Behind them two strangers walked into the space beneath the tower, looking round. 'I can feel the power of this place,' Abi said suddenly. 'Rising up through me. It's amazing.' She held out her arms, pivoting round in a circle. She smiled, and stood still shading her eyes with her hand as she looked towards the east. 'Somewhere up there in the Mendips, there is a woodcutter's hut, near some limestone cliffs. It might even have been in Cheddar Gorge. Mora went there to heal him after a tree fell on him.'

'And did she?' Athena held her gaze steadily.

'I don't know.'

'She went there alone?'

Abi hesitated. Why did she not want to mention Mora's

205

apprentice? Because who he was, or might be, was still such a huge deal. Because, she realised, she wanted so much for it to be true. Because she still couldn't believe it herself. Because she couldn't bring herself to put her vision into words. 'Romanus was there,' she said at last, 'with the wicked uncle, Flavius, lying in wait.'

'I see. And I interrupted at the wrong moment?'

Abi nodded ruefully.

'Do you want to try again?'

But it didn't work. However hard Abi tried to summon her vision of the past nothing happened.

After a while she shrugged. 'It's gone.' She stood staring out across the levels towards the distant Bristol Channel with beyond it a faint haze which shrouded the hills of Wales.

Retrieving the crystal from the drawer where it was stowed, Abi made her way slowly to the bench by the ruined arch. There was still no sign of the Cavendishes when she got home. The house was very quiet. The afternoon was drawing in fast and already she could see the mist beginning to form over the flat fields. She went to sit down, pulling her jacket close around her. 'OK, Mora. What happened next?' she whispered.

She turned the stone over and over in her hands. She could feel nothing. No warmth, no vibration, no tingling in her fingers. A shot of panic went through her. Supposing she couldn't do it again? Supposing she never found out what happened?

'Mora?'

She stared round at the ruined arch, the old crumbling remnants of the walls, the fragment of pillar poking up through the flowerbed. In the light of the low sun all she could see was the shroud of ivy which protected it. The air was full of the smell of damp moss. Shivering she tried to still her thoughts, concentrating on letting her mind stay blank. Allow it to come. Don't try and force it. She cradled the stone on her lap, touching it gently with her fingertips. 'Mora, where are you? What happened next?'

The shadow of the arch stretched across the grass at her feet, its shape elongated, irregular as it crawled across the flowerbed and onto the grass.

'Mora? What happened? I know Flavius didn't hurt him.' She held her breath, listening. 'He didn't attack you, or Romanus?' The words were no more than a whisper. 'Mora?'

Supposing he had killed her? Supposing in his rage and frustration at somehow missing his target, he had struck out at the druid priestess. Perhaps that was why she felt the need to haunt the place where her story had unfolded. Clutching the stone, Abi rose to her feet. 'Mora? Where are you? What happened?' She stepped forward onto the flowerbed and rested her hand against the arch as though somehow it would connect her to the past. In the orchard a blackbird shrieked its warning and flew past her. She stared round, desperately trying to see into the shadows, trying to sense the past which must be there, just out of sight, but nothing came. She looked down at the stone in her hands. 'Was it Kier? Has he frightened you away?' She gave a bitter smile. Or was it the priestess of the goddess with her pretty skirts and lovely necklaces? She turned slowly looking towards the house. If Cal and Mat were home the lights would have come on in the kitchen by now and the dogs would be rushing across the lawn towards her. All was silence. The place was still deserted. With a sigh she rammed the stone into the pocket of her jacket and began to walk down through the orchard at the end of the garden.

Opening the door she made her way inside the little church and closed the door behind her. Silence enfolded her. That was why it kept drawing her back. Her own church. Her own sacred space. It was a novelty, this special feeling, this certainty that she had to come back here constantly to be safe, and that here everything would in the end begin to make sense. It was just possible to make out the aisle in the gloom and she made her way towards the chancel as for the first time she registered that there didn't appear to be any electricity in the church. That explained the proliferation of candles. Besides those on the altar there were more on the window sills, a candelabra hanging from the ceiling on a heavy black chain, another standing at the back near the font. All the candles looked well used, half burned down, decorated with patterns of waxy drips. She sat down in one of the chairs at the front. The east window was in total darkness with no light from the eastern sky outside to illuminate the figure of Christ. It was as though he wasn't there. Behind her a faint rosy light flooded low onto the floor as the setting sun found a momentary gap in the racing clouds. The church was cold. As was the stone in her pocket. She reached in to touch it briefly, her fingers stroking the rough surface, then she withdrew them. Perhaps she shouldn't have brought it with her.

Slipping to her knees she folded her hands together in prayer. 'What happened?' she whispered. 'Is it true? Were you here? Did what happened here become a part of your teaching?'

Somewhere in the body of the church a timber creaked as the temperature outside dropped. She shivered again. 'Our Father . . .' She paused. She could sense someone behind her. Not Kier. Surely he hadn't followed her here. Swallowing hard she levered herself into a sitting position, straining every nerve to hear any movements in the nave behind her. There was nothing. Whoever it was, if there was anyone at all, must be holding their breath just as she was. After a minute she began to turn round, staring into the shadowy spaces of the church. Nothing moved. If there was someone there he must be deliberately hiding, down amongst the rows of chairs. Another small sound echoed into the silence. Something had dropped and rolled a little way before coming to a stop. She could feel her heart banging against her ribs. 'Who is it? Who's there?' She could hear the fear in her own voice. 'Come on. Show yourself.' She paused for a second. There was no reply. 'Kier, is that you?'

Nothing.

Standing up, she stepped into the aisle, straining her eyes as the light grew fainter. The pink light on the floor was beginning to fade now into the grey of evening. Taking a couple of steps towards the back of the church she paused, then she took two more. There was a box of matches lying in a saucer on a shelf near the door. With a shaking hand she lit a candle and as its faint light spread feebly into the darkness she stared round. There was no sign of anyone there. Picking up the candlestick she looked round again, not giving herself time to think. She was not going to be driven from this place of refuge. There was no-one there. It was a small church. There was nowhere to hide. No vestry, no pillars, no curtains. The noises had been natural ones, the creak of ancient timbers, the small sounds of mice or bats, the branch of a tree tapping a window. With a final look round she went back to the altar step to pray.

'No sign of Abi?' Mat walked into the kitchen and looked round. He had brought in an armful of logs and he let them fall into the hearth.

'Her car was there.' Cal followed him in. 'I hope she didn't mind us going off so early. We should really have spoken to her before we left.'

'I should think Abi welcomed some time to herself,' he said cheerfully. 'It was worth it though, wasn't it!' He smiled at her suddenly. The trip to Taunton had been to discuss a new job for Mat; or to be strictly accurate, an old one. A follow up for one of his previous clients. Nothing large or permanent, but a huge help financially in the short term. 'Abi will be fine. You don't have to watch over her the whole time. Unless – you don't think the ghastly Kieran was here again?'

Cal shook her head. 'His car isn't here. I expect she is out viewing the ghosts in the ruins.' She went over to the window and looked out at the rapidly darkening garden.

'What do you think is actually going on there?' Mat stooped to pile the logs over some kindling and struck a match.

'Not sure. They may be our ghosts technically, if one can have ownership of ghosts, but she is obviously connected in some way.'

'And rapidly becoming obsessive. Ben is worried.'

'I'm sure he is.'

'As is the ghastly Kier. The man is genuinely concerned. I know Abi is furious and resentful, and even frightened of him but he does have a point.'

Cal made a face. 'Don't let Abi hear you say that.'

The phone began to ring.

'Heaven forbid.' He walked over to answer it, listening for a few seconds before replying. 'She's not here, Athena. We were just wondering where she was ourselves. We've only just got in. OK. I'll get her to call you.'

He put down the phone and turned to Cal. 'They went up the Tor this afternoon.' He walked over to the door and opened it. 'Go on, dogs, have a scout round. Where is Abi? Find her!'

They watched as the dogs streaked off into the darkness, barking. 'Do you think they know who you mean?' Cal grinned.

'Of course they do!'

'OK. Let's see how long it takes them to come back.'

'Are you sure Romanus went with his uncle?' Lydia had found Sorcha in the byre. She had taken an empty jug outside to the girl who milked the goats, dipping it into one of the cool clay storage bowls and had stayed to gossip.

Sorcha nodded. 'I'm afraid so. They went off together early. Romanus was running behind his horse.'

'And do you know where they were going?'

'Flavius had heard that Mora had been called to visit someone who had had an accident up in the gorge. He was sure the Galilean would have gone with her.'

'And you didn't think to tell me?' Lydia's voice was frozen with horror.

'I've only just found out where they were going,' Sorcha said defensively. She glanced at the milkmaid. 'Rhiannon has just told me.'

Lydia turned to the girl who had gone as white as the milk in her pail. 'Who told you this?'

'The lad who brought the fish, ma'am. He heard it from the woodman's daughter who had told his brother to fetch the lady Mora from the island. The lord Flavius had offered good coins to anyone who could give him information about where she was going and why. I'm sorry. Was it wrong?'

'No.' Lydia shook her head impatiently. 'You weren't to know. None of you was.' She stared out across the palisade, down the fields, towards the island. Darkness had come early, a white mist hanging over the water of the mere. 'They should be back by now, surely.' It wasn't just that she was worried about Romanus. Petra's pain had worsened sharply and she had retired to her bed, feverish, trying to suppress the agonised sobs which she knew so upset her mother. Lydia needed Mora to come back with the stronger medicine she had mentioned.

'Romanus will be all right,' Sorcha said reassuringly. 'Flavius will look after him.'

210

'You think so?' Lydia turned on her. 'The man is a professional killer.'

There was a shocked silence behind her. She turned and surveyed the two young women. 'I'm sorry, but it's true. He is not to be trusted. I told Romanus!'

'He's a boy, lady Lydia,' Rhiannon said quietly. 'To him the man is exciting. Exotic.'

'And I am someone whose orders can be ignored,' Lydia murmured to herself as she turned away again and began to move back towards the house.

Sorcha picked up her jug and made to follow her. 'Let me know if you hear anything,' she whispered under her breath.

Rhiannon nodded. 'I'll ask the men when they come in. Someone will know something. The lord Flavius is not someone you see and instantly forget.'

'Though he would have it so,' Sorcha said wisely. 'He seeks to creep around and listen and watch, spying on everyone and plotting against the family. The lady Lydia is right. He is not one to be trusted. I would not like my son to choose him as a hero to worship.'

Both young women swung round as a group of men appeared at the gate. Laughter rang out in the misty air as they jostled into the yard and began to stack hoes and rakes and mattocks in a corner of the byre. Rhiannon called out and they came over. They all knew Flavius had offered rewards to people who could give him information about Mora; none of them knew that someone had accepted his bribe and sent him on a quest into the hills.

The men looked at one another uncomfortably. 'Was it wrong to listen to him?' one of them ventured. He looked guilty.

Rhiannon shook her head. 'We are only worried because young Romanus went with him and no-one knows where they are. They should have been back by now.' She looked across at Lydia and shrugged. 'All you can do is wait, my lady. He'll be all right. Romanus is a resourceful young chap.' She smiled reassuringly.

Back inside after a quick glance at her daughter who was sleeping fitfully, huddled under the covers, Lydia sat down by the fire, wrapped in her cloak against the evening chill. If only Gaius were there, but yet again he had made the long ride north towards the coast to meet up with the last batch of traders of the season. It had been a wet summer; the rivers had flooded, the summer-lands had never properly dried and now once again the meres and lakes were filling and spilling over one into another to make wider and wider lakes across the levels to the west. Mora said the wise men in the druid school were predicting a stormy autumn and a cold winter. Gaius had been reluctant to leave her, but there would be no more overseas trade after this until the spring. She shivered. It was imperative that Flavius leave too on the last boats. The gods forefend that he be trapped with them for the winter. She glanced up as Sorcha followed her inside. 'Petra is asleep.'

'Perhaps Mora will come back with them. She often senses when Petra needs her help.'

Lydia nodded miserably. She was full of misgivings about Flavius's intentions towards the young woman. What if he hurts her? What if he hurts Romanus?

12

Abi jerked awake with a shiver. Had she dozed off, there on her knees in the church? The place was in total darkness; she looked round nervously. She had been dreaming about Petra, here in church, just a brief glimpse of the girl with her poor swollen hands huddling into her bed to keep warm as the wind rose, stirring the fire, blowing wisps of smoke around the interior of the house. Lydia too was worried. There was no news. No word from Mora.

'Mora?' Rising to her feet, Abi called the name out loud. 'Mora? What happened?' She made her way back down the aisle and fumbled for the door latch, pulling the door open. It was full dark now and she had no torch. She walked outside, closing the door behind her and stood for a moment staring round. There was still a faint glow of light in the west, but above her now the stars were appearing, bright in the clear night sky. In the distance she heard a bark, then again, closer. The dogs were back, which meant so were Cal and Mat. With a smile she turned towards the lych-gate. Before she was halfway there the two dogs had found her and leaped up in greeting.

It wasn't until after they had eaten supper and were sitting round the fire nursing their coffee that Abi mentioned Kier's visit that morning.

'He let himself in through the conservatory. If Justin hadn't still been here I don't know what I would have done –' She broke off mid-sentence, wishing she could bite off her tongue as she saw Cal's look of anguish.

'He only came to borrow some books, Mat,' Cal said quickly.

Abi saw the fury on Mat's face in astonishment. 'You didn't think to mention the fact that he had been here?' He was addressing his wife.

She shook her head. 'Why? When I know how much it upsets you.'

'You know I have forbidden him to come anywhere near the house!'

'It's as much his house as yours, Mat,' Cal said quietly. 'Your grandfather left it to the three of you equally.'

'And he chose not to take up his share. This is my home and I will not have him set foot under my roof!' Mat stood up. 'Has he been here before?'

'You know he has.'

'I mean recently. Tell me, Cal!' They seemed to have forgotten that Abi was there. Thiz came and sat beside her uneasily, leaning against her legs and she lowered her hand to fondle the dog's ears. She glanced down. Her hands were warming up. Instinctively she was seeking out the animal's aching shoulders where arthritis was beginning to make its mark. She let her hand rest where it was for a moment with a small silent prayer. No-one noticed save the dog, who looked up at her with a small moan of pleasure.

'He's been here once or twice. He's never stayed for more than a few minutes. He takes one or two books, and he's always brought them back.'

'Why didn't you tell me?' Mat turned away, his voice suddenly quiet.

'You know why, Mat. Because I don't want scenes like this. He's every right to come here. You know that as well as I do. He does no harm. He touches nothing except the books. And they are as good as his. You know your grandfather meant them for him.'

'And what does he do with them?'

Cal shook her head. She went over to her husband and kissed his cheek tenderly. 'He reads them, you ninny.'

There was a moment of silence, then Mat shook her off and headed for the door. Banging it behind him they heard his steps running up the stairs.

'Sorry,' Cal said after a few seconds. 'You didn't need to see all that.'

'It was my fault,' Abi said sorrowfully. 'It's me that should be sorry. I knew you didn't want me to mention him. It just came out.'

'Mat's not rational when it comes to Justin. I don't suppose he ever will be now. It goes back a long way. Forget it happened. We'll all be back to normal tomorrow morning.'

214

'What does Justin do, Cal?' Abi asked. Withdrawing her hand from the dog's back, she picked up her coffee mug again.

Cal hesitated. 'He writes books. He's a historian.'

Abi smiled tentatively. 'That doesn't sound so bad.'

'No.' Cal sounded bleak.

'Does he live near here?'

Cal shrugged. 'I don't know where he lives, Abi. He's never told us.'

Abi knelt for a long time in prayer that night when at last she went upstairs. A hazy moon was hanging low in the sky as she stood up at last and went over to look out of the window. The garden was misty; she could make out little detail beyond the dim silhouettes of the trees. Somewhere an owl called, a sharp urgent shattering of the silence, answered from a long way away by a wavering hoot. She pushed open the casement and leaned out on her elbows. It was cold outside and smelled of dead leaves and wet earth. The smoke from the house chimneys wreathed around the rooftops, wafting the incense of burning oak and apple into the air. 'Was it you, up there in the hills?' she whispered again. 'Were you here? Did you know Mora?'

There was no answer. Turning away from the window at last she pulled it shut and went over to the drawer where she kept the stone. She had tucked it away before supper but now she brought it out again and unwrapped it on the bed. It lay there, an inert lump of rock with its crystal faces dim. She laid her hand on it gently. Nothing.

'Mummy?' She whispered the word into the quiet room, lit only by the dull moonlight at the window and the bedside lamp with its aged ivory shade. 'Mummy, are you there? I need to talk to you.'

Again there was no response. She picked up the stone and held it in her hands. 'Why aren't you working?' She carried it over to the window and held it up to the moonlight, angling it back and forth to catch the pale gleam on its surface. With a sigh she left it on the window sill and finally climbing into bed she switched off the lamp and lay there staring up at the ceiling.

*   *   *

'Athena isn't in today.' Bella glanced up from her magazine as Abi went into the shop. 'Sorry.'

'Do you know where I could find her?' Abi was amazed at the lurch of disappointment she felt at the news. She had counted on speaking to the woman again. Her combination of certainty and doubt, of knowledge and ignorance and reassuring experience of life suited Abi's mood perfectly.

Bella shrugged. 'I don't know if I should tell you.' She looked anxious suddenly.

'Her phone number then?'

Athena sounded as though she had just woken up. With a groan she gave Abi the address. The flat was only minutes away, reached by an iron spiral staircase which led up out of one of the attractive little courtyards lined with small shops, which lie behind the high street. On the inner corner of every other step there was a plant pot. Athena opened the door dressed in an exotic black housecoat decorated with scarlet dragons and led the way into her kitchen. It was small and chaotic. Abi liked it immediately. Heavy greeny-blue pottery, plants, jars of herbs, a crystal ceiling chime, a lump of wood for a breadboard, still with her breakfast loaf, seedy, crumbly and smeared with Somerset honey. It was exactly the sort of kitchen she would have expected this woman to have.

Hitching herself onto a stool at the breakfast bar she watched as Athena brewed fresh coffee. 'I'm sorry to come so early.' It was nearly eleven. 'But I had to talk to you. The crystal still isn't working, so maybe you're right and it is all imagination. And I know you said I should rely on myself now, and not the crystal anyway, but I'm obviously not working either. Nothing is happening, and I have to know. Did he kill Mora? I haven't slept all night.'

Athena grimaced. She reached onto the counter for a pack of cigarettes and shook one out. 'Sorry, I know it doesn't go with the image, but I can't think straight until I've had one.' She struck a match and lit up, inhaling deeply. Then she shook her head, eyes closed. 'Abi, dear, don't you think it would be more sensible to worry about real people and real things?'

Abi's mouth fell open. 'I'm sorry.' She felt ridiculously chastened. 'But I thought you understood.'

'I do understand. All this crap is too beguiling, isn't it?

216

Romantic. Wonderful. It seduces you away from the real world. Then you turn back and find the real world has moved on and passed you by. That's Glastonbury for you all over. Bloody Avalon!'

Abi was silent. 'What's wrong, Athena?' she said at last.

'Someone died.' Athena was staring out of the window. A basket of pink pelargoniums hung there, from a brass hook.

Abi sighed. 'I'm so sorry.' She watched as Athena poured the coffee and hauled herself onto a stool next to her. 'Do you want to talk about it?' she asked at last.

'That's your job, isn't it. Talking to the bereaved.'

'It was part of it, yes.'

'Do you still believe in it all? Heaven, I mean. Now you've seen the poor buggers hanging around in the ether acting out their lives again and again and again!' Athena took another drag on the cigarette.

Abi put her hands around her mug, warming them. 'It's something I have been thinking about a lot. My faith has had to change over the last few months. I haven't lost it.' She hesitated. 'At least, I don't think so. But I am having to adapt.'

'How bloody convenient!'

Abi bit her lip. 'I don't think it's just convenient,' she said after a moment. 'It's taken a lot of heart searching. I'm not there yet.' She took a sip from her mug.

'Tim. That's who died. My husband. My ex,' Athena said after another long pause. 'Cancer.'

'You still loved him?' Abi said cautiously.

'I suppose I must have.'

'That's hard.'

Athena nodded. She sniffed. 'I can feel him here. In the flat. Through there in the living room. Every time I go in there I can see him sitting at the clavichord; I never knew why he didn't take it with him, he was the one who played it. I've never even tried. Not after he went. I always thought he would come back for it, but he never did.' She wiped the back of her hand across her eyes, slid from her stool and went over to the kettle. 'This coffee's cold.' She flicked the switch. 'He loved that thing.'

'Would you like me to say a prayer?' Abi asked cautiously. She gave a half-smile and shook her head. 'It's what I do. Sorry. Perhaps not.'

217

'Say one in there if you want.' Athena indicated a door across the narrow passageway opposite the kitchen. 'I'll stay here if you don't mind. Abi, the goddess thing. I don't think I ever really believed it. I tried to. I enjoyed all their rituals and stuff to start with, or most of them,' she said, grinning. 'But then I started to have problems with it all. For instance, I could never bring myself to sit on the egg-stone! Did you see it, the Tor Bur behind the abbots' kitchen in the abbey grounds? Someone has left it there at the foot of the wall and so many legends have built up round it. There is a depression in it which could look as though it was made to hold your crystal! Don't even ask what they use it for. It would really upset your vicarly susceptibilities. I had swallowed the whole "this is the authentic religion of the British Isles, it is as ancient as time itself" thing for a while, but it wasn't. I began to feel a shallowness. It was all made up. Part of the feminist movement. It had no substance. They wanted it to be real so badly, and who knows, perhaps I'm wrong and it is, but it just didn't do it for me.'

Abi didn't know what to say. She slipped off her stool. The main room of the flat was large with full-length windows leading onto a narrow wooden balcony which overlooked the courtyard below. On it a cluster of ceramic pots held a riot of flowers. The curtains and drapes were all shades of the same green-blue as the mugs and plates in the kitchen. She looked round. There was an old sofa, spread with a sequined shawl, piled high with cushions, a couple of soft armchairs, a low table, loaded with magazines and books and a huge chunky candle, an ancient TV and a modern sound system, and against the wall the small keyboard instrument, its lid open, music on the music rest. Abi went and stood looking down at it. Mozart. She reached out a finger and stroked one of the keys. The sound was so quiet she barely heard it.

'He's gone, hasn't he.' The voice behind her made her jump.

She glanced round and nodded. 'I think so. Perhaps he just came to say goodbye.'

'I wonder?' Athena's voice was bitter. 'More likely, "Now I can really fuck you up, Athena! I'll come and haunt you for the rest of your days. That will be fun!"' She threw herself down on the sofa.

Abi perched on a chair opposite her. 'It sounds as though you two had a lot of unfinished business.'

'You could say so.'

'You're a wise woman, Athena. You know what to do. Let it go. Let him go.'

'Do you think I don't want to?'

'I think you didn't want to.'

'And now I do?'

'Now you can.'

Athena leaned back, studying her face. 'I suspect you were a bloody good vicar.'

Abi gave a rueful smile, shaking her head. 'Obviously not good enough. But this I think I do understand. Whatever unfinished business there was between you is over now. It's up to you to forgive him and send him on his way with your blessing. It will free you both. Then you can move on.'

'The usual, sadly rather trite piece of advice. Next comes, "Get on with the rest of your life". Counsellors' psychobabble.'

'It's a bit of psychobabble that works.' Abi shrugged. 'If you nurture your hurt it will stay with you. Spoil your life. That would be your fault, not his. You're worth more than that, Athena. You are a strong woman. You can do it.'

'Why did you come here this morning, Abi? To ask me what to do about your vanishing ghosts? It seems to me you know all the answers yourself.' Athena gave a quiet chuckle. 'OK. Give me a few minutes to get dressed and we'll go out. Leave Tim to tinkle away here if he wants to.' She went over and threw open the windows. 'There. Now his spirit can leave unimpeded. *Bon voyage*, my dear.' She waved at the window.

Abi waited for her in the kitchen. Then they went to the Chalice Well.

'It seems the right place for both of us, today.' Athena walked ahead of her up the cobbled path and through the gardens. The place was deserted.

Abi looked round in delight. 'I had forgotten it was all so beautiful and serene.'

'There is so much love here.' Athena paused as they reached the well head itself. The ornate wooden lid decorated with the iron *Vesica Piscis*, the interlinked circles whose ancient symbolism brings together pagan and Christian, East and West, lay open, ferns growing out from under the iron grid which covered the dark, still water. One or two flowers floated on its surface and someone had left a ring of tealights on the well's rim. The flames flickered slightly in the breeze. 'People come here with their prayer and blessings,' Athena said quietly. 'It is the right place for both of us, today. Your Mora would have come here all the time. And Tim loved it here. It was here he told me he was leaving me. He thought it would soften the blow, saying it here.'

Abi bit her lip. 'Athena –'

'No. This is the place to lay the demons. You are right about that. I won't have him destroying my relationship with one of the most sacred places in England. I never came back after that day.' She sat down on the wall which bounded the flowerbeds. Behind her a small pink cyclamen, caught for a moment in a ray of sunlight echoed the delicate shade of the drooping flowers hanging from a fuchsia bush. 'He spoiled it for me. What an irony. I don't think he meant to. I think he really did feel it would make it easier.' She paused as behind the neighbouring yew trees a young man, sitting down on a hidden bench, began to pluck a quiet, doleful tune from his guitar. 'He knew how much I loved it here,' she went on in a whisper. 'That was part of the trouble. He felt I loved this town, the whole Avalon experience, more than him. He wanted to get back to reality.'

'Reality is such a subjective thing,' Abi said after a long pause. 'What you and I think of as beauty and truth someone else considers a complete cop out.'

'I think that someone else is probably right.' Athena sighed.

Abi was staring down at the water in the well. It was dark and still. As she looked a leaf drifted down and settled beside the white daisies someone had left there, floating on the surface. It made a small ripple. She could see the blood-red traces of the iron chaly-beate staining the wall of the well below the moss. This was the red spring, so sacred to the ancients, in the depths of which, so legend had it, after the Crucifixion, Joseph of Arimathaea on his return to Glastonbury hid the Chalice of the Last Supper. Above it the two yew trees lazily scattered crimson berries around their feet.

'It's the blood of the earth.' The voice beside her was soft. She looked up. Mora was standing there, staring down into the water of the well. Except it wasn't a well any more it was a spring, surrounded by trees, yew trees, perhaps the ancestors of the same yew trees under which they had been sitting moments before. Mora looked up and smiled at her. 'This is the most sacred place.'

'I know,' Abi whispered. 'I can feel it.'

'He came here with me,' Mora went on. 'Yeshua. He understood.'

Abi felt her eyes filling with tears. 'What happened up there in the hills? Did Flavius find you that day?'

Mora nodded. 'Oh yes, he found us.' She looked down into the water again. 'Look deep into the crystal. It will tell you Yeshua's story. He was such a special person. A man who would change everything –' Already she was fading, a shadow in the sunlight, no more.

'Don't go!' Abi jumped to her feet. But where Mora had been standing there was nothing but the shadows of the trees. The well was once more enclosed by a stone rim with an iron-clad lid to close it out of sight.

Athena smiled at her. 'Mora was here?'

Abi nodded. 'Did you see her? She told me to look in the crystal. She knew about the crystal. She knew who –' She paused. 'Who Yeshua was.'

Athena shook her head. 'Did you bring it with you?'

'No.'

'Go and find it then. Go home now, Abi. I think I'll stay here for a bit.' It was a dismissal. She had not asked where Yeshua fitted into the story.

Kier switched off his phone and stared thoughtfully out of the car window. He was parked outside Morrisons and had been about to drive away when Professor Rutherford had phoned him. 'Have you seen her? How is she?' The professor sounded thoroughly irritable.

Kier sighed. Poor Abi. No wonder she had wanted to escape if that was her father's usual demeanour. 'I've seen her a couple of times,' he said cautiously. 'She is still adamant sadly that she doesn't want to speak to me.'

'What are these people like who she is staying with?' Harry Rutherford asked after a moment's thought. 'I believe my wife knew them, but as far as I know she hadn't seen them for a long time.'

'They seem decent enough,' Kier replied cautiously, 'but obviously they are shielding her. They believe that I have somehow offended her, I am not very welcome in their house.'

There was another short silence. 'Have you found the wretched stone yet?'

'What stone?' Kier flicked an imaginary speck of dust off his trouser leg. He was watching a woman manoeuvre a heavy trolley closer and closer to his car. In a moment he would have to get out to show her that he was there and would not appreciate his car being rammed by her wretched shopping. No, she had spotted him and yanked it back on course. He sighed with relief.

'Didn't I tell you about the stone?' Rutherford sounded incredulous.

Kier shook his head. Good grief. She had got one, two, three six-packs of beer in that trolley. And now came the wine. No wonder it was so heavy. 'Sorry, Harry, what were you saying about a stone?'

Ten minutes later Kier was still listening. The woman had long since driven away.

'Yes, I can see why you would hesitate to tell anyone about it,' he murmured. 'It sounds like complete fantasy.'

He sat still for a long time after the call. Clearly Harry Rutherford was right. This explained everything. The change in her attitude, her obsession, sudden supernatural powers which were, he now realised, beyond her control. Nothing to do with her. He had to find this ridiculous stone and dispose of it. He was as certain as the professor that the legend Abi's mother had attached to it was complete rubbish, but that made it no less potent. After all Laura Rutherford had believed it and now, so did Abi herself. It was the stone which had destroyed their relationship. It explained everything if it was after she had been given the thing that she started to turn against him.

He chewed his lip thoughtfully. She was not going to give it to him calmly, that was for sure. So, how in the world was he going to get hold of it?

He was staying at a small hotel in Wells. He loved Wells, the cathedral, the ancient city, the bishop's palace. The whole place soothed his soul and, he glanced at his watch, if he set off now, he could be there in time for evensong. Resolutely he drove past the gate of Woodley Manor without even looking. Tomorrow, after a night of prayer and careful planning he would return and think of a way of retrieving this superstitious lump of rock. Then he would take it and throw it in the Bishop of Bath and Wells's moat. It would be a fitting resting place for it. He shook his head with a wry smile. 'I don't believe I've agreed to do this. This is ridiculous. Mad! Insane!'

At the Rectory next morning Ben was scraping the last fragment of boiled egg from its shell, *The Times* folded open at the leader page on the table in front of him, when Janet came back into the kitchen after answering the phone in the hall. He glanced up.

'Abi,' she said. 'I couldn't put her off. She sounded distraught.'

He put down his egg spoon with a sigh. 'Is she coming straight over?'

Janet nodded. 'I've checked the fire in your study and I'll make sure you're not disturbed.'

He glanced at her. This was a change of tune from last time. Kier had annoyed her so much she was prepared to accept Abi now without comment. Standing up he refolded *The Times* and handed it to her.

'Shall I make the coffee now?' Janet asked.

'Please. Meanwhile, I'll go and say a prayer before she comes.'

Ben stood at the window in his study staring out across the grass. The wind in the night had brought down a lot more leaves. Under the maple tree at the edge of the lawn a fresh carpet of gold lay in an exact circle on the grass beneath its branches which were almost bare now. With a sigh he closed his eyes and tried to marshal his thoughts.

Abi waited until Janet had set the tray of coffee down on the side table and left the room before she turned to Ben. 'I've lost her.'

'Lost who?' Ben was expecting to talk about Kier.

'Mora. I can't contact her. I've lost the thread of the story. She

223

appeared to me at the Chalice Well yesterday, just briefly, and she said I should look in the crystal, but the crystal is useless. It isn't working. I can't do it any more.' She paced up and down the room a couple of times. 'And now Mora has gone. I tried all night.'

Surreptitiously Ben studied her face. She looked drawn and utterly exhausted. 'And you got no sleep at all,' he said quietly.

Abi nodded. 'There is something I haven't told you.' She sat down on the edge of the chair.

Ben walked over to the tray and began to pour the coffee. He said nothing for a few moments, waiting for her to go on. When he turned back to her with the cup in his hand she was staring down at the floor.

He put the cup down on the table beside her. 'What is it you haven't told me, Abi?' he said at last.

'I've seen Jesus.' She looked up at him and he saw defiance in her expression. And fear. Was she expecting him to laugh? To ridicule her? To have her sectioned, or to send to the bishop's office to have her made a saint?

He turned away and took the chair opposite her. 'Supposing you tell me exactly what happened.'

'He was here, at the druid school. Studying. The story, the legend is true. He came here, to England. He spent time here. With Mora.' She was twisting her hands together nervously as she told him the whole story. 'Obviously he wasn't called Jesus. They all call him Yeshua, but that is all right, isn't it? Some people say that was his real name. Obviously we know Flavius couldn't have killed him because he went back to the Holy Land to begin his teaching there but what happened when he tried to get near him? Did Flavius kill Mora? Did Romanus help him? What happened in that hut? I have to know.' There was a hint of something like desperation in her voice.

Ben stared thoughtfully into the fire. 'It seems strange that suddenly your visions should have been stopped. Did that coincide with Kier's arrival?'

It was not the response she had expected. Why hadn't he pounced on her revelation?

She frowned. 'No. Yes. I don't know! Why?'

'I wondered if his presence down here, his belief that this is a demonic visitation, had acted as an inhibitor to your,' he hesitated, trying to find the right word, 'your experiences. Your imaginative faculty might have shut down and your rational good sense reawakened.'

She leaped to her feet. 'My imaginative – you think I've imagined all this?'

'Some of it, possibly. Abi, you know you might have. The ghosts, well Cal has substantiated your reports of those, but this other story – the detail – we have to keep an open mind. Having said that, whatever is happening here was, at least at first, a viable experience for you. It was tied up with experiences of otherworldly beings that others have seen. At the same time it is possible that you have been drawn in to the whole Glastonbury thing, my dear. I don't want to belittle what you have seen, or think you have seen, but you know as well as I do that the idea that an historical Jesus came to England is complete rubbish. It is not possible. Why on earth would he have wanted to come here, to the ends of the Earth, to study with a bunch of pagan savages who were immersed in human sacrifice?'

She shook her head in despair. 'No, you've got it wrong. You've got them wrong. There was no human sacrifice. They were learned men and women, the druids. They were wise, cultured, respected across the world. Jesus went to Egypt to study first, everyone knows that, then he went east, to India and Tibet.' She ignored Ben's slowly shaking head. 'Then he came west. He needed to absorb and understand the learning of the Gentiles as well as that of the Jews. He had come to save the whole world. He needed to understand the scale of what he was undertaking. Everyone thinks he was just focused on the local scene. The small area round Galilee, but he wasn't. He had visited other countries. He knew about other places, races, beliefs.'

Ben clasped his hands together and studied his knuckles for a few moments. Then he looked up. 'I'm sorry, Abi. I have no right to denigrate what you are saying. It only shows how rigid are my own beliefs. Maybe you are right.' He paused again. 'But I don't know where to go from here. I know you are praying for guidance as to what the right thing is that you should do, and I will do the same. It's just that it is an area I know so little about.'

He reached for his cup. Abi was watching him in something

like despair. 'You haven't asked me what he looked like,' she said at last.

Ben shook his head. 'You said you thought he was in his mid-twenties.'

'Did I?' She shrugged. 'He was amazing. Strong, yet gentle. But he was confused. He had a temper. He was a healer, but he was impatient as well. So human. Attractive.'

Ben smiled. 'Just as I – and perhaps you – would have imagined him to be.'

She nodded. 'So, I can't win. You are not going to believe me.'

'I want to, Abi,' he said. 'You have no idea how much I want to.' He took a thoughtful sip from his cup. 'There is someone who could help us, perhaps. Someone who could look at this more objectively; who might understand the technicalities of what is happening to you. My brother, Justin.'

'Justin!' Abi stared at him in astonishment.

He looked up. 'You've heard about him?'

'I've met him. Twice.'

It was Ben's turn to look astonished. 'Where?'

'At Woodley. He seems to make a habit of breaking and entering in the middle of the night or when he thinks the place is empty. How on earth could he possibly help with this?'

Ben was silent for a moment. 'Did you speak to him?'

'Not much. He did help to chase Kier away, for which I am grateful, but he still seems to me to be an arrogant, conceited man, bent on outwitting poor old Mat. I don't like him, to be honest.'

Ben hid a smile. 'That sounds like brother Justin all right. Neither of us exactly gets on with him. But he does have certain fields of expertise. The trouble is I don't know where he lives at the moment. I don't suppose he told you?'

'No, he did not.' Abi shook her head. 'And Cal and Mat don't know either. Cal mentioned the fact.'

'Pity. Well, if you see him again, perhaps you could swallow your pride and ask him to get in touch with me. Or if the moment seems right, talk to him about all this yourself. What he has to say may surprise you.'

*   *   *

226

It wasn't until later that day that Abi had the chance to speak to Cal alone. 'I didn't want to mention him in front of Mat. Not again. But how on earth could Justin help me with all this? Ben wouldn't explain when I asked, he just looked quizzical!'

Cal was standing by the back door, a woven willow trug on her arm, a pair of secateurs in her hand. For a moment she reminded Abi almost unbearably of her mother who had so often carried a similar basket round the garden at home. Swallowing the wave of grief which threatened to overwhelm her she pulled on her coat and both women headed into the garden. The stone crystal, retrieved from the drawer upstairs, weighed down Abi's pocket. 'Justin knows a lot about local history; much more than any of us. He says he's writing some sort of book on the area,' Cal said cautiously. 'I suppose Ben thinks he could throw light on what you've been experiencing. He's also always been interested in what you might call occult practices.'

'Occult –?' Abi stared at her. 'Black magic, you mean?'

Cal shrugged. 'Something I think he called the Western Spiritual Tradition.' They had walked towards the rosebeds and Cal began to select some long-stemmed buds. 'I don't even know if he still does it; maybe he grew out of it, but it was one of the things Mat hated. Strangely I think Ben respected him for having any kind of interest in spiritual matters at all. They used to discuss it. I don't know why Ben and Justin fell out in the end. With Mat it was something that was there even when they were kids – and he was so much older he should have known better. I've always thought Justin had a raw deal with the other two.' She concentrated on reaching some deep red blooms in the centre of the bed.

'And Justin is a very attractive man,' Abi said.

Cal glanced at her sharply. 'You think so, do you?'

Abi blushed. 'I'm human! But it's you he fancies. Just a bit?' she added quietly.

Cal shook her head. 'No. At least, maybe a long time ago. Yes, I suppose that didn't help.' She smiled sadly. 'I've always liked Justin, but not in the same way I liked Mat. The old stick doesn't seem to realise I still adore him. I always did. Justin never stood a chance. Not like that.'

227

Abi smiled. The affection in Cal's voice was very genuine.

'Justin seems a difficult man,' she said after a pause. 'Yes, I do find him attractive, but I didn't take to him. I'm amazed Ben would recommend I get in touch with someone like that. Surely it goes against everything he should be doing to keep me in the church.'

Cal laughed. 'Justin's not that bad! No, I expect he was a bit acerbic when you met him! After all, you caught him in the act. He would much rather have slipped in and slipped out again. It is going to be much harder for him to use the library from now on. What Mat didn't see, he didn't worry about.'

'Why should Mat begrudge him the library? Surely Justin could come when Mat is not here.'

'Dog in the manger.' Cal laid two more roses on the pile in the basket. 'I've got two bed and breakfast visitors coming this weekend.' She changed the subject abruptly. 'So I thought I would make the house look nice. They won't get in your way, so don't worry. They will only be here at breakfast time.'

'I was supposed to be helping you with things like that,' Abi put in. 'You must let me do things to pay my way.'

'The bishop is paying your way, Abi,' Cal said firmly. 'So no more of that nonsense. You are a double joy. A nice guest, a good friend and you bring a bit of lovely money!' She laughed. 'Sorry. Does that sound too crude?'

Abi smiled. 'Not at all. But I'm glad the friend bit crept in there. I was afraid I was causing you too much hassle what with my ghosts and Kier and everything.'

'They are our ghosts too,' Cal reminded her gently. 'And as for Kier, well, he makes life more interesting, to be honest!' She headed for the next flowerbed and began to cut some Michaelmas daisies. 'Quite exciting, in fact. Wretched man!'

For a moment Abi thought about returning to the fascinating topic of Justin, but she swiftly thought better of it. Cal had changed the subject. Better to let it rest.

When she went back indoors Abi walked on down towards the ruins. The sun was low in the sky again, highlighting the colour of the autumn leaves. Sitting down on the bench, her fingers lying lightly on the crystal stone in her coat pocket, she saw the robin hop at once nearer, watching her with a beady black eye.

Suddenly it flew away. Something moved on the edge of her vision near the archway. She leaned forward. 'Mora?'

She was there, an insubstantial shadow, no more. Barely visible against the spray of scarlet Virginia creeper. Abi clutched at the stone in her pocket. 'Mora? Can you see me?' She was overwhelmed with relief and anxiety.

The young woman was less hazy now, her outline distinct. She was wearing a light-coloured rough woollen robe with a greeny-grey cloak around her shoulders, the hood draped over her hair. She took a step towards Abi and Abi was aware that Mora's eyes were fixed on her face. Slowly she stood up and took first one then another step towards her, as cautious as she would have been approaching the robin which had retreated to a tree nearby and was making anxious little alarm calls.

'Mora?' Abi whispered the name. 'Can you see me?' Slowly she reached out her hand.

The colours in the garden leached away suddenly. Abi glanced up at the sun. A huge cloud had drifted across its face. She looked back at the flowerbed. Mora had gone.

'Blast!' She sighed. Then she reached into her pocket again and drew out the stone. 'Mora? Was this yours?' The robin bobbed up and down and flew closer. 'Please, come back. I want to talk to you.'

There was no response.

She waited a long time before she turned and walked back to the house.

The kitchen was empty. Abi glanced at the two flower arrangements standing on the table. The late roses had been distributed between them. They were beautiful but there was no sign of Cal in any of the downstairs rooms. Slowly she made her way up the staircase and paused on the landing. Cal was coming out of her bedroom. 'Abi! I'm sorry. I should have locked the front door. I don't think he touched anything. He left the second he heard me come upstairs.'

'What? Who?' Abi felt a clutch of fear in the pit of her stomach. 'Not Kier?'

Cal nodded. She stepped away from Abi's door. 'The cheek of the man!'

Abi went into her room and stood staring round. 'What was he doing?'

'He was standing by the chest of drawers when I came up. None of the drawers was open or anything. As soon as he heard me he came out of the room, gave me a half-apologetic, half-embarrassed smile and raced down the stairs and out of the front door. I must have left it open. I often do. He didn't say anything!'

Abi shivered. She opened the top drawer and looked inside. It was there she kept her underwear. It was impossible to tell if anything had been touched. Surely he wasn't that sort of man. What on earth can have possessed him to take a risk like this?

Cal shook her head. 'What did he want? He could see you weren't in here. Did he just want to be near you?'

Abi sat down on the edge of the bed and felt the bump of the Serpent Stone in her jacket pocket against her thigh. She extricated it and stared down at it. 'I wonder,' she said after a moment, 'if he was looking for this.' She turned it over in her hands. 'It might explain why when he saw I wasn't here he might have decided to look round. If my father has told him about this and shown any of the fury and antagonism about it he showed me, then there was more than enough reason for Kier to try and find it.'

'If you're right, what would he have done with it if he had found it, I wonder?' Cal said thoughtfully.

Abi gave a rueful smile. 'Goodness knows, but I think you can be certain I wouldn't have seen it again.'

'You will have to hide it somewhere better than that,' Cal said. 'You can't risk it.'

Abi stared at her. 'You think he'll come back?' She nodded in answer to her own question. 'Of course he will. You're right. If this is what he's after he will probably get obsessed by it the way he does about everything.'

'You could go to the police, Abi,' Cal said after a few moments' thought. 'The man is stalking you.'

Abi shook her head. 'I can't. Think of the scandal. He was rummaging through my knicker drawer. Two priests in the Church of England. Ex-priests. Lust. Passion. The Occult as you called it. We'd have the nation's press camped on the doorstep within hours.'

Cal nodded. 'It might put off my B & B guests, certainly.' They both laughed uncomfortably. 'I'll remember to lock the front door

230

in future. If we had been indoors we would have heard him. He must have known Mat and the dogs were out.'

'Which means he's been watching the house.' Abi glanced towards the window. 'Oh God, I hate this!'

'Do you want to go and stay with Ben?' Cal eyed her sympathetically. 'Just for a few days. Kier won't hang around forever.'

Abi shook her head again. 'No, he'd guess where I'd gone at once. Besides, I am not going to let him chase me away.' She hesitated. 'Unless you would rather –'

'I've told you before.' Cal headed for the door. 'You can stay here for as long as you like.'

'It will be good if you've got guests this weekend, though, Cal.' Abi followed her to the staircase. 'More cars outside. More people in the house at night.'

'And I'll make sure Mat leaves the dogs here when he goes out. They may not be the world's greatest guard dogs, but they do bark at the right moment.' Cal reached over and touched her arm. 'Don't worry. You have the Cavendish clan behind you. If he comes back we'll be ready for him. He's not going to be allowed to pester you and he's not going to find your stone. I can show you somewhere to hide it which Kier will never find in a million years.'

It was in the garden. Cal left Abi to tuck the stone away and walked back to the house. Abi watched her go with a fond smile, then, almost without realising she had done it she turned aside to the bench and sat down, with it still in her hands. 'What happened?' she whispered. 'Mora? Romanus? What happened next?'

'Tell me about Judea. I've never been anywhere very far from here. My sister was born near there, wasn't she?' Romanus and Flavius were walking side by side now, the horse's rein over Romanus's shoulder, the horse plodding behind them. The fog had grown thicker.

Flavius nodded. 'Indeed she was. My first posting when I was a young man was to the service of Herod the Great in Jerusalem. I was in the legion which went to Galilee to put down the uprising at a town called Sepphoris. We taught them a lesson they wouldn't forget in a hurry. I was noticed by my commanding officer and selected to join an elite force of undercover agents and we were ordered to look for a family of insurrectionists who claimed to be descendants of King David. They were expecting the birth of a child who people claimed would inherit the throne according to some sort of prophecy. The Jews are always talking about prophecies.' He shook his head disparagingly. 'Herod knew they would use it as an excuse to revolt again, so our mission was to find the kid and kill it.'

Romanus frowned. 'A baby?'

'Yes. A baby who would grow up to be a traitor.'

'And did you?'

'As it turned out, no. We killed a good few babies while we looked, but it turned out none of them was the right one. The parents knew we were after them and they fled to Egypt. It took us a while to find out. All the time we were a few steps behind them. They returned to their home town eventually, but they were protected all the time by people who knew about this wretched prophecy of theirs and hid them, and the boy grew up and left home.'

'And this is the man you are searching for now?' Romanus was frowning.

'That's it. He's dangerous.'

'But how can a healer be dangerous?'

Flavius looked down at him again. 'Because he's bright and lippy and thinks a lot of himself, or he did as a child, and the Jews think he is a king, that's why. And so he is a danger to the Empire.'

'And so you are still working for Herod?'

'For his son. The old king died. His lands were divided. A new Herod, Herod Antipas was given the governorship of Galilee by the Emperor, and I work for him.'

'I see.' Romanus was still frowning. He was wondering how his uncle had found it so difficult to catch up with this man and kill him. He obviously wasn't a very good assassin. He didn't say so, of course. 'And you've travelled the world in the search for him?'

'It wasn't as easy as you may think.' Flavius had picked up on the unspoken criticism. It infuriated him. 'Everywhere he goes he blends in. He is hidden. People like him. They fall for his charm. Somehow I am thwarted every time I come close. It is

232

as if he is protected in some way.' He scowled. 'But here, at last, I have caught up with him. I know where he is. I just had to get him away from the druid school. I have no intention of going there and finding they have hidden him, or that once more he has slipped away in the night as I arrive or that I am spotted and forced to back away. He is waiting for a ship to take him back to the port of Caesarea. I have to do the deed before it arrives. And it has to be secret. Rome does not want me to be seen. Rome must not be involved. When this man dies, he dies from an accident, or he disappears. No-one must ever suspect that I have had a hand in it. That part of the Empire is always on a knife edge of rebellion and for the Jews to find out that a Roman agent has killed one of their number could cause another rebellion. He must disappear silently and without suspicion. I thought maybe he would drown in the lake, but up here in the mountains with these great limestone crags, he could as easily slip and break his neck or be savaged by a bear. And when his uncle arrives he will find that his nephew has disappeared without trace and all their prophecies and plans will have evaporated into this confounded fog.'

One glance through the shop window next morning told Abi that Bella was again on duty. Athena opened the door of her flat so quickly Abi realised she must have seen her walking across the courtyard from the balcony. 'It occurred to me that you were the only person who might know where Justin lives,' Abi said as they at down in the living room. She saw at once that the clavichord had gone. 'Please, Athena. It looks as though he might be the only person who could help me.'

Athena gave a humourless chuckle. They were drinking herb tea this time, from the same pretty green mugs. 'OK,' she said. 'I grant you Justin might have more knowledge than Ben about some of this stuff, but summoning him back to the OK Corral might not be the way to tap into it. He's likely to tell you where to get off in no uncertain terms.'

Abi scanned her face. 'You said you and he fell out?'

Athena nodded. 'Oh yes.'

'Can I ask why?'

'No.' Athena sat back against the cushions, and shook her head.

She was wearing a peacock-blue sweater with lapis and silver beads.

'All right. Sorry. Well, at least tell me, he made it clear he's no Christian. Is he a fully paid up pagan?'

Athena smiled. 'Oh yes, I think you could say that.'

Abi bit her lip. She was silent for a moment, then she shrugged. 'Can I have his phone number?'

'I can give you his mobile number. But it may not be up to date.'

'I'll try it and see.' Abi waited. When nothing else was forthcoming she went on, 'And can I have his address? Then if the phone doesn't work I can at least drop him a line. Unless he has an e-mail address?'

Athena snorted derisively. 'As if.'

'Why not? He's a writer, he's doing research. It would make sense, surely.'

'It might make sense to you, dear,' Athena said, caustically, 'but I doubt if he would go in for that sort of thing.' She shrugged. 'OK, I'll give you his address. He lived in Wales. But for all I know, he left there a long time ago. He might even be back here by now, after all he seems to drop in at Woodley quite regularly.' She got up and went over to her desk which stood between the two French doors onto the balcony. After a lot of rummaging around amongst piles of papers and notebooks she produced an old address book and began to flip through the pages. Eventually she found what she was looking for and reaching for a notepad copied it down, tearing off the piece of paper for Abi.

'Powys?' Abi looked down at it curiously. Her heart sank at the thought of how far away that sounded.

'It's a little cottage, high up on a mountain. Very remote. Which is just as well as I'm sure he would annoy the hell out of any neighbours he might have!' Athena said tartly.

Abi smiled. 'You and he really don't get on any more, do you?'

'I told you.'

'I'd love to know what he did to you.'

'Well, you're not going to. Are you going to come and have some lunch with me over the road or are you going to rush off and ring him now?'

'Lunch,' Abi said decisively. 'I've got lots to tell you. My priestly stalker is back. He searched my room and he's giving me the creeps.' It helped to talk about it and Athena was a good listener. The irritable and mysterious Justin could wait.

The wind had risen. It screamed across the countryside, tearing leaves from the trees, whipping the water into waves. The sky was the colour of lead, the clouds towering columns of darkness promising thunder and lightning across the length and breadth of the land. He smiled, feeling the tingle of excitement through his blood. He could feel no threat, no promise of retribution here. This was the land and the sky speaking their own words.
Why still the rage of the storm when it was glorious?

13

Kier had driven faster than he had ever driven in his life after Cal caught him in Abi's bedroom. His face hot with humiliation, he threw himself into the driving seat and accelerated out of the gate, his seatbelt flapping, turning onto the road almost under the wheels of another car which hooted violently. Heading towards Glastonbury he slowed down slightly as he reached the first round-about then he headed on into the town, keeping going resolutely until at last he pulled into the coach park outside the abbey. There he sat for a long time, his head resting on his hands on the steering wheel. He knew her room was at the front, he had seen her there at the window, but once inside he had only found it by accident. It was the second he had looked into and he had recognised the jacket thrown on the bed. At least he hadn't touched anything. Never again would he put himself in such a stupid, insane position. How could he have even thought to do it? Why had he listened to Professor Rutherford? The man was obviously deranged. A magic stone indeed. A bewitched, stupid, magic stone. 'You have to find it. You have to get hold of it and dispose of it.' The man's voice echoed in his head. Stupid.

When at last he looked up he stayed where he was, staring blankly out of the windscreen. It was some ten minutes later that he saw a man striding across the car park away from him. It was Justin Cavendish. Kier frowned, watching. He was heading towards the entrance to the abbey.

Opening the car door Kier climbed out, intrigued. Where he was going? He glanced round, spotting the pay and display meter only feet from his car and cursed under his breath. Knowing his luck he would be clamped if he didn't buy a ticket. He scrabbled in his pocket for change as Justin disappeared out of sight, following a high stone wall at the back of the car park. Seconds later Kier had slapped a ticket inside his windscreen and ran to follow, keeping far enough back to stay out of sight. Justin was going into the abbey; into a sacred Christian place. Why? Kier followed cautiously, close enough to hear him exchange cheerful banter with the woman inside the ticket kiosk; he obviously knew her. His curiosity piqued, he crept after him. Justin turned right into the museum. Kier paid for his own ticket and followed him at a safe distance, listening to the sound of monks chanting in the distance as he made for a display cabinet and ducked behind it. He was consumed with curiosity about what Justin was doing here, but he didn't want him to turn round and spot him. After all, he had shamed and humiliated him in front of Abi. Another surge of anger shot through him and he clenched his fists, forcing himself to breathe steadily. He had to know what the man was doing in here. He peered round the glass case. Justin was standing staring at something in another display. Moments later he turned and headed for the doors that led out into the abbey grounds. Kier watched him from the window. He was walking slowly along the path which led towards the west end of the abbey ruins and in seconds he had disappeared behind a stone pier. Kier let himself out of the museum and hurried after him.

The grounds seemed very empty. He felt exposed as he walked past the huge wooden cross which stood by the path and headed towards the archway where Justin had disappeared, hoping the man wouldn't reappear suddenly in front of him. He stood and looked at the notice which informed him that this was the Lady Chapel, then he ducked inside the archway and cautiously he made his way down the steps into the open area of the chapel itself. It was deserted. He stared round. At the east end there was an altar, under a roof area but here the place was completely open, the high ruined walls soaring up towards the open sky. He was suddenly regretting the impulse which had brought him charging in in Justin's wake.

'I take it that you are looking for me.' The voice came from immediately behind him.

He spun round. Justin was standing in the shadow of the wall, his arms folded. He regarded Kier with what appeared to be an expression of calm interest. He was dressed in shabby moleskin trousers and a dark green much-worn Barbour with frayed pockets and cuffs and yet he made Kier feel like an ingénue schoolboy caught in the act of perpetrating some pathetic little felony. Kier

240

felt his face colour with embarrassment. 'I saw you in the distance, yes.'

'And you felt we had unfinished business.' Out here Justin seemed far more in his element than in the kitchen at Woodley.

'I suppose I did, yes.' Kier shrugged. Perhaps Justin was right and that was his real motive. 'You interfered in matters which were not your concern.'

Justin smiled. He was a good-looking man, with a shock of fair hair and a weatherbeaten face which seemed to indicate an outdoor life. He exuded a quiet confidence as he stood without moving, his arms still folded. 'Abi made them so.'

'What is she to you?' Kier felt a surge of jealousy as the man used her name.

'Nothing at all,' Justin said quietly. 'I barely know her.'

'Then why were you there?'

'As I believe I told you, Woodley is my house. At least, I share its ownership with my brothers. Abi therefore is in a sense my guest. She is there by invitation, you, it seemed were not. If she wanted you out of there, it was for me to see that her wishes were adhered to.'

Kier glanced up as a jackdaw settled high in the tracery of a ruined window behind Justin. It looked down at them, head on one side, then it called loudly, the sound echoing round the chapel walls.

Justin smiled. 'My friend has come to remind me that it grows late. If we have no further business to settle you will have to excuse me. If on the other hand you are spoiling for a fight, then I would ask you to follow me outside. We stand here on holy ground, and I am sure you would be as reluctant as me to brawl on it.'

Kier felt himself colouring again. 'I have no intention of brawling anywhere.'

'Good.' Justin grinned at him. 'Then I will bid you farewell.' He bowed slightly and moved towards the steps which led up out of the chapel.

Kier stayed where he was. 'Wait!' His voice brought Justin up short. 'What did you come in here for?'

Justin turned and surveyed him. 'I saw you sitting in your car. I thought I would see if you followed me.'

Kier's mouth dropped open. 'You knew I was there all along?'

241

Justin inclined his head slightly. 'I saw you turn in as I came round the corner from the high street.'

Above them the jackdaw called again. The urgency of its cry echoed round the walls. Justin acknowledged the sound with a raised hand and turned away. This time Kier remained silent.

He had begun to shake violently. Sweating with fear he glanced up at the bird. It had gone.

'I was going to ring Justin myself, but I thought, maybe, it was better coming from you.' Abi had phoned Ben straight after breakfast the next day. Inadvertently she had overlapped with the B & B guests and found herself seated at table with two sets of strangers. They were going to spend the day in Glastonbury and listening to their enthusiastic plans reminded her exactly how romantic this place was. Their interest was all in King Arthur. They were going to go straight to the abbey to lay flowers on his grave, then later they were going to head over to Cadbury Castle which may or may not have been Camelot. Abi had excused herself from the table with a smile and headed for her room. Ben was right. It was very easy to get sucked into all this. Something to do with the atmosphere, the light, slanting across the low-lying fields, the mists which wreathed the magical island which was Avalon.

'Any more signs of Kier?' Ben asked over the phone.

'Not after he ran out of here yesterday, no. I doubt even he would come back soon after that debacle.' She laughed bitterly. 'And he must guess that I would have hidden the stone somewhere else by now. If that is what he was after.'

'And I take it you have?'

'Yes.' She laughed again. 'Cal found me the perfect spot.'

'Good. Well, don't tell me in case he comes and tries to torture it out of me.' Ben sounded amused. 'I'll try this number and see if I can reach Justin. Then I'll call you back, OK?'

'OK. Ben, about Justin –'

But Ben had rung off.

Abi reached for her jacket. Slipping the phone into her pocket she let herself out of the room and hesitated for a moment. Cal had made sure she had a key but it went completely against the grain to lock her door. Eventually she left it. She ran down the stairs and headed out into the garden. The morning was grey and cold.

The mist still hung across the lawn as she walked towards the archway. She paused for only a second then she headed down towards the orchard and the church. She was halfway there when the phone rang. She groped for it. 'Ben?'

'I left a message for him,' Ben said. 'I'll call you when – if – he gets back to me, OK?'

She felt a moment of disappointment. She may not have liked the man, but at the moment he seemed to be the answer to her problems. She shrugged. 'Thanks for trying, Ben.'

'That's all right. Come over if you feel you want to. I'm going to spend the day working on my sermon for tomorrow. And, Abi. Remember. Surround yourself with prayer, my dear. Whatever is going on here, protect yourself. We don't know exactly who your Mora is, do we.'

Abi stared down at the phone in her hand after she had switched it off. What did he mean? Did he think Mora was some kind of evil entity? Mora, who was Jesus' friend and mentor.

If she was.

She was standing in the orchard and she looked round with a shiver. A cold wind was cutting through the trees, tearing off the golden leaves, shaking off one or two last small wrinkled apples.

Justin was unloading his car when his mobile rang. He juggled a couple of boxes, put them down and fished in his pocket. Glancing at the number he grimaced and switched it off. Then he went back to his parcels, lugging the first towards the door. Ty Mawr was a small, white-washed stone cottage, built close to a ridge of the Black Mountains. If he turned his back on the door and surveyed the view he could see a vast swathe of the Wye Valley laid out like a panoramic map far below. Behind him the hills unfolded ridge upon ridge up towards distant flat-topped summits, shrouded in cloud. He took a deep breath of the cold clean air and smiled to himself. He was always happy to come home.

He stacked his purchases on the table in the centre of the room. Food, writing materials, the necessities of life. Then came the books from Woodley. Some half-dozen this time. Methodically he put everything away, lit the fire in the large old fireplace, and went out to the lean-to shed at the side of the building where the postman left anything that came for him when he was away. There were two packets from Amazon. He smiled with satisfaction and taking them indoors set them on his desk to open later. A glance out of the window showed rain coming in from the north-east. In ten minutes or so it would be pouring down, slanting across the garden, isolating him in a grey pall. Before it arrived there was just time to glance at the garden. He let himself out of the back door and went to stand at its centre, silently greeting the plants, apologising for days of neglect. Then and only then did he fish in his pocket and glance again at his phone. He wasn't sure why he even had his brothers' numbers stored in its memory. Some atavistic acknowledgement of connection, he supposed. More interesting was why Ben had rung him. His thumb hovered over the delete option, then at last he gave way to curiosity and held it to his ear.

'Justin, I believe you've met Abi Rutherford. She's staying with Mat and Cal at the moment. She has what I suspect is a very major problem. Paranormal. Possession. I'm not sure what is going on here. I should be able to deal with it, but I don't think I can. Not alone. It seems to have pre-Christian elements.' There was a slight hesitation as though he wasn't sure how to word his message. 'I gather you're in the area. I'd really like it if you could drop in. Thanks, mate.'

Mate! Justin snorted.

The first drops of rain were falling as he pocketed the phone and went back indoors. Walking over to his desk he picked up the first of the parcels from Amazon and began to unpack yet more books.

Abi sat for a long time in the church. She wasn't praying. Meditating perhaps, her eyes fixed on the east window with its enigmatic portrayal of the crucified Christ. It was dull this morning, the colours drab and cold. His face was impassive. Not agonised. Not pleading. Not angry. Blank. She sighed, ramming her hands down into her jacket pockets. The church was cold and very silent and smelled of beeswax from the candle she had lit last time she was in here. She should go over to Ben's. Talk things through with him. Not just about Mora, but about her future. And Kier. Abi closed her eyes. When she opened them again Mora was standing on the chancel steps in front of her. Abi blinked a couple of times, holding her breath. Mora was still there. She was shadowy, insubstantial, and yet Abi could not see through her. The folds of her dress seemed to stir slightly, as though in a draught. Abi could see the plaited girdle at her waist, the enamelled clasps which held her cloak at the throat, her hand, slim sensitive fingers, holding a fold of the material just below the clasps as though she was afraid the garment might slip off her shoulders. Her knuckles were white.

Abi's mouth had gone dry. She didn't dare move. It occurred to her that Mora was as frightened as she was. She didn't take her eyes off her. Each time she had seen her before Mora had vanished when she looked away. This time she was determined to keep the woman in focus, to hold her there by sheer willpower. She opened her mouth to speak and found the words dying on her lips. She tried again. 'Mora?' It came out as a whisper. The woman was still there. She saw a reaction in her face. A slight frown. Eye contact. An effort to speak. Maybe to understand. Slowly Mora was holding out her hand towards her. 'Mora, talk to me.'

For a moment the two women were immovable, facing each other, straining across some divide too deep, too impenetrable to cross. Mora reached out her hands and the expression on her face was one of despair. *Help me*. Had she really said those words, or had Abi imagined them? 'Mora! Wait!' Abi called out, but slowly Mora was beginning to fade before her eyes. 'No!' Abi stood up. 'Wait. Don't go. We can do this!' Throwing herself out of the chair she reached out, her hands clawing at the space where Mora had been standing. There was nothing there but a slight frisson of cold in the air.

Abi stood still. She was trembling, she realised suddenly. She turned round slowly, studying the church, searching every corner as though expecting Mora to appear behind her, in the aisle, or near the old stone font. There was no-one there. The silence was absolute. It was some time before she slowly realised that she was becoming aware of sounds around her again. The moan of the wind outside; a branch tapping on a window, a rustle from a flower arrangement on a window sill. She swung round, in time to see a small mouse poking through the leaves, looking for berries and ears of corn in the autumnal arrangement. She smiled. Mora had gone. Reality had reasserted itself. Time was moving smoothly forward again.

*   *   *

She had to scrabble through the leaf mould to find the small hidden hollow at the base of the ancient oak tree. The Serpent Stone was there where she had left it, tucked at the back in the darkness. She pulled it out, wrapped in its cotton bag. The material was damp and stained from the hiding place and the crystal was cold. She knelt there on the damp grass staring down at it, fully conscious for the first time of the generations of women who must have held it as she did and who, maybe, had seen the same things she had seen and felt the same emotions and she found she was near to tears.

Then the story came back.

Mora had stirred the fire in the centre of the woodcutter's hut into life. She piled on twigs and small logs from the pile near the door and set the iron pot of water from the spring on the trivet over the flame. Then she glanced across at Yeshua. He had folded back the man's blankets and was running his hands gently over the twisted leg. 'How is he?'

'Feverish. Delirious. He is drifting in and out of consciousness and he doesn't know we're here, which is as well. I will set the leg quickly while he is asleep.' He glanced up. 'Where is the man's daughter? She should be here!'

Mora shrugged. 'She went to fetch help. When we didn't come perhaps she went out again.'

She had heard the irritation in his voice, seen once again the flash of anger. She smiled quietly to herself. The first thing he had done when they entered the hut was to go out again to fetch the thirsty man some water. His anger when he had found the broken cup had been formidable. She had watched him control it firmly as gently he raised Sean's head and allowed him to sip from one of the bowls they carried in their pack.

She searched through the pouches of herbs in her bundle, concentrating on the infusion she would make when the water had heated. Behind her she heard the man groan, the grating of bones as Yeshua manipulated the leg, the gentle, reassuring words he spoke as he cleaned the wound and bound the leg straight. She glanced round. Yeshua was sitting beside the man now, his eyes closed, his hands resting on the man's forehead in blessing. She smiled. He wouldn't need her infusion now.

He probably wouldn't even need a bandage. Yeshua's blessing was enough.

It was as they sat together in a silence broken only by the cracking of twigs as the fire licked higher, that she became aware that all was not well outside. She tensed, withdrawing her concentration from the fire, letting her attention expand, listening beyond the licking flames. Someone was out there. Someone hiding. She heard the urgent warning alarm of a wren, then the sharp pinking note of a chaffinch. She glanced across at Yeshua. His eyes were closed. He was praying. Silently she rose to her feet and went over to the doorway and peered out. The area in front of the little house was a clearing in the middle of which was a ring of blackened stones, with ash lying heaped in the centre. Obviously the woodman preferred to do his cooking outside. Mora glanced round. She and Yeshua had left their walking staffs leaning against the side of the house as they ducked inside. From here she couldn't reach them without going out. The birds were silent now, waiting. Someone was out there. Not the woodsman's daughter. She would have come in at once and made herself known. No, this was danger. She could feel the skin on the back of her neck prickling. There was a movement behind her and she looked round hastily, putting her finger to her lips. Yeshua came over and stood behind her. 'There is someone out there,' she whispered. 'Someone who means us harm.'

He frowned. Behind them the sick man stirred and groaned, his head moving from side to side in his dream. Mora glanced at Yeshua. 'What do we do?'

He moved a couple of paces back into the hut and groped around in the wood pile. Seconds later he was back beside her, a sturdy makeshift club in his hand. 'You wait with him. I'll go and see,' he whispered.

'No!' She caught at his sleeve. 'It is you he wants.'

He looked at her, his brown eyes on hers. 'You know this?'

She nodded. 'A flash. A knowing. Don't go out there.'

'I have to go out there at some point, Mora,' he said quietly. 'Now is as good a time as any.'

Ducking out of the doorway he stood up, hefting the piece of wood in his hand. There was another moment's silence, then a rustling from the bushes nearby. The branches parted and Flavius straightened up as he emerged into view. He was holding a drawn sword. 'So, we meet at last.' He took two paces towards Yeshua and stopped. 'Our Jewish king, dressed like a peasant and covered in ash!' He laughed grimly. Behind them Mora hid in the doorway out of sight, looking round desperately for a weapon. She glanced at the wood pile, then at the woodcutter behind the fire. He was sitting up, watching her. In the light of the flames she saw his face. He was clear-eyed and he gestured towards his pack which was lying in the darkness beyond the reach of the flames. She crept back towards him and taking hold of it pulled it towards the light. He leaned across and opened it. Inside there was a sharp bronze knife. He pulled it out and handed it to her. With a quick gesture he ran his finger across his own throat and then pointed to the doorway. Gripping the handle tightly she ran back and looked out again. Yeshua hadn't moved. Flavius was standing about six paces from him, the short Roman sword held out in front of him. He was enjoying the moment. She could see it in his eyes. A cat with a mouse.

'The time hasn't come, my friend,' Yeshua said quietly. His attention was fixed on Flavius. 'My end has been foreseen by the prophets, and it is not now. Not here.' His anger had gone to be replaced by calm confidence.

Flavius smiled. 'Prophets can be wrong.' He transferred the sword lightly from his right hand to his left and then back again. 'Have you done your work with the sick man?'

Yeshua nodded. 'He is healed.'

'Pity. Then I will have to kill him as well. We want no witnesses here. It suits my purposes that you quietly disappear in the wilds of Britannia. History and your prophets will have to acknowledge that this time they got it wrong. There will be no word that you ever came to this country.' His glance shifted past Yeshua for a moment, towards the hut. 'Is Mora there too? It is sad but she also will have to die –'

'No!' There was an explosion of movement behind Flavius as Romanus hurled himself out of the bushes. 'You can't kill Mora. I won't let you.'

Mora stepped outside, the knife in her hand. 'And nor will I, Romanus!' That one moment of distraction was all it needed.

Yeshua stepped forward, his club upraised and struck the sword from Flavius's hand. 'Enough!' he shouted. 'You are not going to interfere with my destiny or with the destiny of these innocent people.'

His face was white with anger again, his careful calm gone. 'You are an evil man with no conscience and no shame! I will not let you hurt anyone here.' His eyes narrowed with the fury that had gripped him.

Flavius staggered back, cradling his broken hand against his stomach. It was Romanus who picked up his sword. The boy's face was white. 'You were going to kill Mora.' It seemed to be the only thing that had registered.

Flavius looked down at him with an expression of complete contempt. He snatched his sword from the boy's hand, then he turned and began to walk away. Several paces on he paused and looked back. 'I will do my duty to my Emperor,' he called. 'This may not after all be the time or place, but do not think you will escape me.'

Seconds later they heard the thud of hoofbeats on the ground, rapidly receding into the distance. They looked at each other.

'Why?' Mora gasped. 'Why did he try to kill you? I don't understand!' She was trembling violently. The knife had fallen from her hand.

'I didn't realise what he was going to do,' Romanus said miserably. 'At least, he told me, but I didn't believe it.' The boy's eyes filled with tears. 'He said you were a traitor. Then he said you were a king.' He brushed the tears away with the back of his hand. He was looking at Yeshua with curiosity and something like awe.

'A king? I thought you told me your father was a carpenter and a mason and an architect!' Mora put in. Her face was white. She turned to Romanus, Yeshua's antecedents forgotten in the wave of indignation that swept over her. 'You told him we would be here and you brought him here. You betrayed us. Why?'

Romanus looked devastated. 'He made me come. He makes it hard to refuse. My head was in a muddle.'

Yeshua stepped forward and put his hand on the frightened boy's shoulder. 'I have a feeling it would be hard for anyone to refuse Flavius. Don't blame him, Mora. You did the right thing in the end, Romanus, when you shouted. You saved our lives.'

Mora shook her head. 'I still don't understand. Why would he want to kill you? He's a stranger. I thought he was Gaius Primus's brother.'

'He is his brother,' Romanus said. 'He's my uncle. He came here all the way from a place called Sepphoris in Galilee, specially to find Yeshua.'

'And kill him!' Mora was distraught. 'Why?'

Yeshua walked over and put his arm round her shoulders. 'It's complicated,' he said. 'I will explain when we get back. For now, we came here for a purpose. Come, let's see how our patient does. We need to find his daughter to take care of him, then Romanus can come back with us. We have a long walk ahead of us.'

'He was completely better,' Romanus said as they walked down the track later. 'His leg wasn't broken any more.' He was staring at Yeshua with something like hero worship.

'No, it wasn't. It was as if it had never been broken.' Mora too kept glancing at him. 'That was more than just a healer's job. That was magic. The goddess Bride could not have done better.'

'You are right, she couldn't.' Yeshua smiled. He rumpled Romanus's hair. 'It was God's work. All I did was line up the bones, that was all.'

'No, it was more than that.' Mora was still looking at him, eyes narrowed. 'I could not have done what you did today.' They had left the man sitting up by the fire, drinking his daughter's hot broth. She had returned at last just after Flavius left, explaining that a message purporting to come from Mora had sent her all the way back to the island, delaying her and keeping her away from her father. She was however carrying a bow and two skinned hares for the pot. She too had stared at her father's leg in something like awe.

'But it was broken in at least three places. The bone was protruding.' She looked from Mora to Yeshua and back.

Yeshua shook his head. 'Maybe it was not as bad as it looked.' He hesitated. 'As I said, it was God's work. I prayed and He healed him. But your father will need nursing. The shock will return tomorrow so he should rest and drink more of your broth.'

It was growing late when they at last regained the lower ground, heading south towards home. At one point Mora stumbled on the track and dropped her bag. Yeshua lifted her to her feet. 'Take care. You are tired.'

250

She shook her head. 'I'm all right. We will be at Lydia's soon.'

'Will Flavius be there?' Romanus looked up anxiously. Not for the first time he seemed uncertain.

Yeshua and Mora glanced at each other. 'It's possible,' Mora said eventually.

'Then you mustn't come home with me.' The boy straightened his shoulders, looking at Yeshua. 'You must stay away from him.' He looked at Mora pleadingly. 'Mustn't he?'

She nodded. 'We have to avoid your house until we are sure that he has gone. I still can't believe that happened today. The man is mad to think he can get away with such a wicked deed. He wouldn't escape with his life if the people round here heard he had so flouted the laws of hospitality. Surely, he must realise,' she added hopefully, 'that he can never go back to his brother's house. Mustn't he?' She glanced across at Yeshua.

'I don't think we can be sure about anything,' Yeshua replied. 'Supposing he has gone back. Would the boy be safe? He won't exact revenge on him?'

Mora's hands tightened on Romanus's shoulders. 'Perhaps you should come back to the island with us.'

Romanus shook his head. 'My mother will be so worried if I don't go home. I went without telling her this morning. Besides,' he added bravely, 'Uncle Flavius won't hurt me.'

They both looked at him doubtfully. Mora shook her head. 'That was wrong of you, to go without telling anyone. If something had happened to you, how would anyone have known where to look?' she said gently.

He shrugged. 'I was with Uncle Flavius.'

'Exactly.' She gave his shoulder a squeeze. She sighed. 'Will you be all right if we leave you here? It is only a short step home for you and from here we can take the hidden trackway over the mere.' She looked at him closely. 'You haven't told Flavius about the hidden ways through the marsh, have you?'

The boy shook his head vehemently.

'When you brought him to see me before, you didn't bring him that way?'

Romanus shook his head again. 'I took him in the boat.'

She nodded in relief. 'That was well done. We can take no chances.' She glanced around in the dark. 'I don't feel him near –'

'He isn't,' Yeshua said. 'We are safe for now. May God's blessing be on you, Romanus,' he added quietly. He reached over and touched the boy's head. 'And may He keep you in His hand.'

'Abi? Abi, are you all right?'

Abi was kneeling in the wet leaves, the crystal still between her hands. She looked up. Cal was standing a few feet away from her, holding a torch. It was dark.

But Mora was still there, standing in the shadows, looking at Abi, her hands outstretched. There was no sign now of Yeshua or Romanus.

Help us. You must help us. You have to tell the story . . .

'Abi?' Cal touched her arm. 'Are you OK?'

Mora was still there, but she was fading. Abi reached out, grasping at the air. Already the figure had gone, fading back into the dark. In seconds the night was empty.

She looked up at Cal, her eyes blank. 'I'm fine.' She staggered stiffly to her feet. She was clutching the crystal, her fingers rigid with cold. 'Let me put it back. The tree kept it safe, just as you said it would.' She was shivering. How long had she been kneeling there as the evening drew into night? She had no idea. Behind them the house was ablaze with lights. They spilled out across the grass, drilling pools in the gathering mist. Tucking the crystal out of sight again and covering it with dry leaves, she followed Cal back inside and went upstairs to have a hot bath to soak the ache of cold out of her knees.

It was about nine o'clock when Ben rang her. 'Justin just got back to me,' he said. 'He's agreed to come tomorrow to talk to you. Can you be here about ten?'

She bit her lip. Was this what she really wanted? 'Abi?' Ben's anxious voice rang in her ear. 'Can you make it?'

'Yes,' she said at last. 'Yes, of course.'

Athena was sitting on the sofa in her living room, once more attired in her red dragon dressing gown, her bare feet tucked up under her. She was reading one of the books on crystals from her shop. She leaned forward and took another sip from the whisky glass on the table, hearing the ice cubes chink companionably as she set it down again. Outside she could hear voices and laughter

252

from the courtyard below. Someone let out a shout and she heard a glass breaking on the paving stones. She sighed and picked up the book again. Did she believe in ghosts? Did she believe in the goddess? Did she believe in Atlantis? If she did, she read, it was possible that the priestesses of Atlantis used crystals as repositories of their wisdom. Sort of primitive tape-recorders. No, not primitive. Up to the mark. The latest thing. Crystal technology. Was that it? Was that what Abi's crystal was? A record of past events, events so momentous that someone had felt they should be dictated into the rock and kept forever. She thumbed through the pages. There were dozens of photographs of all the different crystals and their structures. Complicated, intricate, multi-formed. Then came the instructions on how to decode them. Ah, that was the rub, of course. How to decode the secrets. Something Abi seemed to have stumbled on by accident, and now seemed to have lost. Perhaps she had just switched off the machine. Reaching for the glass she took another sip. Tim had always hated her drinking whisky. It was man's drink, he used to say. She gave a rueful smile and raised the glass in a toast to the dear departed. 'My drink still, my dear, and I'm all the better for it,' she said out loud. 'Unlike you, it seems.' She let the book drop on her lap. 'Bloody crystals.'

Abi woke to find the eastern sky flooded with crimson. She lay in bed staring towards the window, still lost in her dream, but already it was going. 'Red sky in the morning, shepherd's warning,' the words ran through her head like a mantra as she recalled the vision of the sacred spring on the hillside beneath the ancient yews. And this had been a dream, she was sure of it. And yet.

Mora and Yeshua had been standing at the foot of a processional way. Abi could see it stretching through an avenue of yew trees winding through the ancient orchards up towards the Tor. There was a mist hanging over the fenland, shrouding the reedy waters. Mora glanced at Yeshua and smiled as she recognised the distant look in his eyes. So much about him was familiar to her now, the mysticism, the tendency to dream, the profound inner life, the constant need to pray and then the sudden mood swings when anger and frustration bubbled up in the face of the injustices and pain they saw around them.

253

'It's time to go,' she said gently. She walked up to him and, facing him, took his hands in hers. 'Yeshua?'

He was far away. He didn't seem to realise she was there. With a fond smile she raised the hands to her lips and dropped a gentle kiss on them. Then she gasped. His hands were sticky with blood. There were gaping wounds in his wrists, blood was pouring down his palms. 'Yeshua!' She couldn't hold back her cry of distress.

He blinked and looked down at her, focusing on her face, seeing her dismay. Slowly pulling his hands out of her grip he reached up and touched her face. 'Mora?' The blood had vanished. 'What is it?'

She shook her head, too upset to speak, turning her head away. Out there on the waters of the mere a stray beam of sunlight pierced the mist, highlighting the ripples to a glittering carpet. 'You saw something?'

'Nothing. I saw nothing.' She blinked away the tears.

He moved round slightly so he was facing her again and she felt his gaze on her face. She refused to meet his eyes and after a moment he sighed. She felt his finger touch her cheek, stroking away a tear. 'The time has come for me to go home, Mora,' he said after another moment's silence. 'Joseph will soon be arriving in Axiom. I have to go and speak to your father and tell him.'

Somehow she forced a smile. 'He is going to miss you. He looks forward to your talks together, your exchange of stories.

He nodded. 'The way of your people, to instruct with stories and poems. Never to write the important things down. It intrigues me. There are clear messages there in the stories for everyone and yet only the initiates understand the hidden meanings. We write down our laws and our histories, the rules of our religion. You remember yours.' He sighed. 'Sometimes by writing things down they are cast in stone. That is not always good either.'

She nodded. She lifted her hand and put it over his, where it lay on her shoulder. She felt the muscles and bones, the strong sinews under her fingers, warm and vibrant, without scars, and she quickly brushed away another tear.

Abi slipped out of bed and went to kneel by the window, watching the crimson light flood across the sky. Through Mora's eyes she had seen a vision of Jesus' wounds. Out there, on the hillside above the Chalice Well, a druid priestess had touched the hands of Jesus and traced the wounds of the Crucifixion with her finger; felt his blood warm on her hands. Awed, she closed her eyes and began to pray.

It was half an hour later that she was interrupted by a quiet tap on the door. It was Cal. 'I don't know if you want to have breakfast before the B & B guests appear? Up to you.'

Abi was out of the house by nine, glancing up at the stormy sky. The old saw was right. It was going to rain. Already the wind was tearing at the leaves, whirling them into the air, and heavy clouds were racing in, piling up into threatening masses over the Mendips. The first heavy raindrops began to fall as she headed for the car.

Justin was already at the Rectory, closeted with Ben in his study. Janet let Abi in and took her coat from her. She had managed to get soaked in the short run from the car. She shook back her hair and ran her fingers through it in an attempt to restore it to some kind of order. She saw her hostess glance at it.

'Wild weather!' Janet said brightly. 'Come in. They are waiting for you.' Her sudden look of disapproval as she opened the door led Abi to suspect she was not one of Justin Cavendish's fans either.

Justin was sprawled in one of the fireside chairs, Ben standing with his back to the hearth. Spits of rain were hissing on the logs behind him.

Justin climbed to his feet. 'Come and get warm.'

'I've been telling Justin a little about the background to your case, Abi,' Ben said. He glanced at the window as a squall threw leaves against it from the lawn.

'My case?' Abi took Justin's chair. She shivered.

'Your situation would be a better way of describing it,' Justin said thoughtfully. He was standing looking down at her.

'And am I allowed to know what your exact qualifications are for being wheeled in as consultant to my "situation"?' Abi asked. She was feeling uncomfortable under his intense gaze. Her hair was dripping down her neck. What she wanted was a towel and a hot drink, not an instant launch into theological dispute.

'My *exact* qualifications?' Justin grinned. 'I don't know. What has my big brother told you about me? Both my big brothers, come to that. Mat, I can guarantee, would have had nothing good to contribute to my CV. I'd be interested to know how Ben described me.'

Ben grimaced. 'I'm not sure that I did. Beyond saying that you were the expert on matters of an occult nature. What I do is sometimes called deliverance; maybe for you it is something similar?'

Justin moved back and sat down in the free armchair. 'The word occult always has pejorative overtones I find. And deliverance implies that someone or something feels they need to be delivered. So, can we get our definitions straight before we start? To my mind, most Christians who think they are seeing Jesus Christ in a vision of some kind would be rejoicing and clamouring for more, not sending for the nearest druid to stop it happening.'

Abi stared at him. 'Druid?' she echoed blankly.

'Ah. So you didn't even tell her that, big brother?' Justin looked at Ben.

Ben shrugged. 'I hadn't got round to it, no.'

'So, you are a full-paid-up pagan,' Abi said slowly.

Justin grinned. 'Ah, now that would also be leaping to conclusions. In Christian circles pagan is a bit of an iffy term.'

'In Cambridge where I was a curate there are a lot of pagans,' she went on thoughtfully. 'Some were viciously hostile to Christians, others were interested in talking, seeking for areas of mutual understanding.'

Justin inclined his head. 'Then put me down as one of the latter.' He sat forward on the edge of his chair. 'I think in this case, though, it is my areas of expertise which are needed, not narrow definitions of what I may or may not believe. I am trained in various techniques, shall we call them, which are for whatever reason not often available to Christian ministers. Soul retrieval. Shamanic travelling. There are Christians who do these things. My brother is not one of them, bless his heart,' he glanced at Ben, 'and neither, obviously is the Reverend Scott. He and I met and had a little chat after our first encounter at Woodley, and since then I have been hearing about some more of his exploits. I gather it is his interference in your life which has caused you so much grief with his accusations that what you are experiencing is in some way evil.'

Abi smiled doubtfully. 'I think you've put the case very succinctly.' She frowned. 'Where did you meet him?'

'In Glastonbury. There is no need to worry. It was accidental and no blood was spilled.' He smiled mischievously.

'If he was rude, I'm sorry.'

'He is not your responsibility, Abi. That much is clear.' He paused. 'Now, having heard my qualifications for helping you, you haven't as yet run screaming for the door, crossing yourself in horror.'

'No. Not yet. I'm finding my experience very positive.'

'Good. Then we have a basis for proceeding.' Justin turned to Ben. 'If you could lever Janet's ear from the far side of the door and get her to make Abi and me some coffee, then you and she can go out for the day. That will give us a chance to talk.'

Ben scowled. 'There is no need to be offensive, Justin.'

'No?' Justin rose to his feet and in three strides he was across the room. He pulled open the door. Janet was outside in the hall, a duster in her hand. She looked flustered. 'Is everything all right in there?'

'Everything, my dear sister-in-law.' Justin looked down at her coldly. 'Coffee, if you please.'

'Justin, you are being gratuitously unpleasant!' Ben stood up too. 'All you had to do was to ask me to leave you alone. If that is all right with Abi?' He turned to her.

Abi looked from one brother to the other in dismay. The tension was crackling between them suddenly. 'I think I would rather that Ben stayed,' she said after a moment. 'If you don't mind.'

'Ye gods!' Justin looked skywards. 'I can't work like that. Do you want to learn or not?'

'I don't know what I want to learn,' Abi retorted. 'I don't know what you are offering.' She had been on the point of telling them about her dream; about the vision of the stigmata. Glad now that she hadn't, she looked at the two men again. 'All I want to know is how to control these visions I'm having. How to switch them on and off, and what significance my mother's crystal rock has. Nothing else. I don't want to learn shamanic drumming or druid rituals or whatever else it was you mentioned.' She too stood up. She looked from one man to the other with a sudden surge of resentment. 'In fact, I don't want to learn anything. I am sick to death of men telling me what to believe and how to do it! First my father, then Kier and now you two. I think we'll leave it now. I'm going.' She made for the door.

Justin swung round. He caught her arm. 'Wait, Abi –'

'No!' She wrenched her arm free. 'No, I won't wait. I want nothing more to do with this. It was a bad idea. I have no intention of getting involved in the Cavendish family row, whatever it may be. In fact I can see clearly what it is about. You seem to enjoy making a mockery of as many people as possible, Justin. Well, count me out. I'm going back to Woodley.'

She didn't wait to see what they did. Grabbing her coat from the hall stand she opened the front door and stormed out into the rain.

The abbey car park was almost empty. Turning in, Abi parked and sat still. She was still shaking from head to foot with fury. She wasn't sure why she had come straight here. Perhaps because she hadn't wanted to go to Woodley and have to explain her sudden return to Cal; she hadn't wanted to go to Athena's either. There was nowhere else she could go. She sat back miserably and closed her eyes.

When at last she had calmed down she climbed out and headed in towards the ruins. The Lady Chapel was empty. Rain splattered down on the stone and dripped from the ancient walls all around her. She stood there shivering, staring up at the broken arches of the windows with their drooping adornment of late valerian. Jesus was here. He had to be. He was everywhere. So why couldn't she feel him? Suddenly there were tears in her eyes.

'You look a bit wet.' The cheerful voice behind her shocked her out of her thoughts. She turned to see an elderly man standing a few feet from her. He was wearing a long stockman's coat and a broad-brimmed hat. He had a neat white beard. She managed a smile. 'It suddenly didn't seem such a good idea to come in here.'

'It's always a good idea to come here.' He looked at her shrewdly. 'Give it a few minutes and its peace will begin to work. Put the day behind you. Don't try and sort it all out in your head, just let it happen by itself.' He grinned and rather rakishly touched the brim of his hat. Then he turned and left, walking steadily through the rain up the steps which led out onto the grass and out of sight. Abi found herself smiling. That at least was good advice. The best yet today. She felt a shiver of excitement.

258

The interruption, the comment of a stranger had indeed cleared her head. The lines of one of her favourite hymns were running through her head:

> Be still for the presence of the Lord
> The Holy one is here . . .
> We stand on holy ground

'We stand on holy ground,' she whispered the words out loud. Suddenly, standing there in the rain, between one moment and the next, she could feel it all around her, the holiness and the magic of this place.

Athena was in the shop. She had a set of small tools spread out on the counter in front of her and seemed to be working on an amber brooch, twisting silver wire into an intricate knot. 'Hello.' She looked up.

Abi stopped in her tracks. 'You're busy.'

'No, I've nearly finished.' Athena laid down the pair of narrow pliers. 'You look like a drowned rat. I take it you were hoping for a hot drink and somewhere warm?'

Abi shrugged. 'That would be nice. Maybe I am. But above all I want to know about Justin Cavendish.'

'Why?'

Abi told her what had happened.

Ten minutes later Athena tucked her tools into their soft suede roll, locked away the piece she was working on and closed the shop – 'No-one is coming in this afternoon anyway in this weather –' and they were once again on the green sofa in the cafe two doors up.

'Are you sure you want to know?' Athena ventured.

Abi nodded. It was warm and comfortable in the café, pleasantly noisy, the overlay of quiet chatter backed by a soundtrack of some sort of Celtic harp music. She warmed her hands on the mug of hot tea in front of her. 'I need to know. It's not just curiosity. Not now. It may be that he can help me.'

'You don't need help, Abi. Not his nor anyone else's,' Athena repeated firmly. 'How many times do I have to tell you?'

'I do need help. I haven't the courage to do it alone.'

259

'Do what?' Athena pushed herself forward to the edge of the seat. 'What is it you need to do so badly, Abi?'

'Find out what it is that Mora is trying to tell me. She is trying to say something to me. And before you ask, yes, I have tried to talk to her. I have tried to have some kind of to and fro with her. She sees me and she wants me to listen. I'm not afraid of her or of what I am seeing. I'm prepared to try anything. I don't think it's evil. I don't think I'm dealing with demons. We are just in two different places and there is some sort of barrier in between us.' She put down her mug. 'This is not just a ghost story, Athena.'

Athena was sitting back on the sofa now, her cup cradled between her hands. She was studying the reflection of the lights on the surface of her green tea. She sighed. 'Don't trust Justin, Abi.'

Abi studied her face. 'Why?' she said at last.

'Just don't.'

'I know you don't like him now, but he must have been a friend of yours once.'

Athena shook her head. 'Once perhaps.'

'So, what happened?'

'Let's say he can be dangerous.' Athena sat back and folded her arms.

'I think you need to tell me,' Abi said quietly. 'After all, Ben seems to trust him.'

There was another pause, then Athena sat forward. 'OK.' She held Abi's gaze. 'Justin caused the death of someone very close to me. Not deliberately. He was trying to help her, but he was in way over his head and he killed her.'

Abi stared at her. She felt a shiver pass right through her body. For a moment she was incapable of speech. It was several seconds before she could ask, 'How?'

Athena looked up. 'I don't want to talk about it. I'm sorry. Just keep away from him, Abi.'

14

Bishop David looked up from his notes and waited while Kier took the chair in front of him. The younger man looked tired and he had lost a lot of weight. 'I know I shouldn't have gone after her,' Kier said.

The bishop laid down his pen. He stifled a sigh.

Kier glanced up under his eyebrows and flinched as he saw the flash of anger cross the bishop's face. David Paxman's summons back to Cambridge had been peremptory, his fury barely controlled. Kier had obeyed the command at once. 'I'm sorry I went against your orders and I'm sorry if I've made things worse, but I had to go.' He rushed on before the other man had a chance to interrupt. 'I had been to see Abi Rutherford's father. I though it would help me get over her,' he shrugged with what appeared to be genuine embarrassment, 'if her father told me to sod off! It would have made it easier somehow, but he didn't. He begged me to go and find her. He begged me to help her. He seemed genuinely distraught.'

'So you made that an excuse to disobey my orders.' David Paxman was finding it hard to curb the surge of anger and impatience which was rising inside him.

Kier nodded. He kept looking at his hands, folded on his knee. He no longer seemed able to meet the bishop's eye.

'And what happened when you got there?'

'I saw her. She is staying –' He paused and gave his head a small shake, as if trying to keep himself awake. 'But of course you know where she is staying. Professor Rutherford gave me her address and I went to try and persuade her to give up a piece of rock that her mother had left her when she died. The rock is some kind of pagan talisman. The professor felt it was having an evil influence on her and I agreed with him.'

'You agreed with him.' The bishop repeated the words without emphasis as if to make sure.

The flat delivery made Kier even more nervous. 'Yes. I wanted to find it and dispose of it. Throw it away somewhere where it could never be found. I had planned to throw it in the moat at Wells Cathedral.' He gave a rueful grimace.

'But you failed to find it.'

Kier nodded. 'Abi was very angry. I thought she would have complained by now. She was angry and rebellious. She seems to have forgotten all her vows as a priest of the church.'

'She has offered her resignation as a priest of the church, Kier.' The bishop leaned back in his chair and recapped his pen slowly.

Kier's eyes were riveted to the action. 'She mustn't be allowed to resign. She is far too good a priest.'

'I seem to remember that you told me she was quite the opposite. That she was practising witchcraft in your church.'

'She was being influenced in a way she could not control, but that was because of her inexperience. I want you to take her back. Help her.'

'She has all the help she needs down at Woodley, Kieran. She has a spiritual supervisor there, and she was supposed to have peace and quiet to allow her to spend some time in contemplation.'

'But she isn't.' Kier was becoming agitated. 'Don't you see? She is using this stone as some kind of key to access a supernatural world. There are ghosts everywhere down there.'

'Ghosts which you too have seen?' David looked up and fixed Kier's face with an intense glare.

Kier shifted uncomfortably. Then he nodded. 'I know she's telling the truth. I watched her. She didn't know I was there. I saw figures. I saw people around her. Sort of swirling, misty lights and shapes and shadows.' He sighed. 'I don't know what to do.'

'What did you do at the time?'

Kier shook his head. 'Nothing. I was so afraid. I couldn't move or speak or even call out to her. I watched it all happen and then I fled.'

Flavius was back at the house, and had shouldered the entire blame for taking Romanus with him without informing his mother, and for their late return. He had explained away his injured hand by saying he had fallen from his horse and landed on it. Sorcha had

262

cleaned the wound and bound it up for him with a warm poultice. Romanus, shaken and silent, watched his uncle grit his teeth against the pain, and felt an overwhelming wave of relief that his mother's wrath at his all-day disappearance without a word had been directed at someone else. When their supper of mutton stew and bread and beans was over, Lydia and Sorcha reached for their sewing, whilst Rhiannon brought her small harp to the fire and gently began to strum a slow melodious tune. Lydia glanced at Flavius. He was sitting in silence, the shadow of the flames playing across his face as he nursed his bandaged hand. She caught the thoughtful look her son threw at him from time to time and wondered what had really happened up there in the hills. With a sigh she laid aside her sewing. She found it harder to see these days in the dim light of the flames. 'Petra was worse today, Rom,' she said quietly. 'I think I am going to have to ask Mora to come back with the stronger medicine she promised.'

Romanus froze. He looked up at his mother with an expression of utter horror.

'It's all right. She stayed in bed today, and she has eaten some supper.' She had interpreted his look as concern for his sister. 'We've wrapped some hot stones for her and put them in her bed to keep her warm.'

'Perhaps you should volunteer to go and ask Mora to come to see your sister tomorrow, Romanus,' Flavius said suddenly, raising his voice over the sound of the harp. 'And to bring her colleague with her. He can perform miracles, so we heard today. He seems to be more successful than she is at curing people.' He eased himself back on the bench with a groan, flexing the fingers of his injured hand. 'He can take a look at this while he is at it.' He gave a strange harsh laugh which made Romanus flinch with terror.

A short while later he rose to go outside and beckoned Romanus with him. The boy hesitated, then reluctantly he followed his uncle to the door. The night was bright with stars. They walked across the yard and stood leaning on the gate, looking out across the fields down towards the marshes. Romanus could see the great cone shape of the Tor in the distance outlined against the luminous sky.

'You will go over there tomorrow, and you will tell them that I have left.' Flavius turned to him. 'You will beg them both to come and see your sister. Then you will return and if you do not want your mother and sister to see what happens you will make sure they leave the place and do not return until after dark. Is that clear?'

Romanus shook his head. 'I don't think I can –'

'You can, boy and you will. Do you want me to kill Mora?'

Romanus went white. His eyes were round and huge in the starlight. Flavius smiled. 'I saw how you looked at her. That was the reason you cried out her name and ruined everything for me today. You like her. Do you want her to die horribly? It is up to you, boy. Do you want to serve the Emperor, to be regarded as a warrior? Do you want to write your name in history with any woman you want, or are you going to remain no better than a petty tribesman in an unknown corner of this godforsaken island? You want her to notice you, don't you?' He paused. 'Well, I will let you save her. How is that? She won't know what has happened to her precious Yeshua, I shall make sure of that. You can take her away. Be a man. But of course, you are not yet a man, are you. How old are you boy? Have you had a woman yet?' He laughed. 'Well now is your chance. Do you want her to go to that filthy druid priest we saw on the island? What was his name, Cynan? What kind of name is that?' He spat over the gate. 'Or what about Yeshua? Do you think she lets him sleep with her after they have discussed their medicines and their bandages? I saw them looking at each other. She likes him. You want her to look at you like that, don't you?' Finally he stopped. He glared at Romanus. 'Right?'

Romanus nodded. His mouth had gone dry. He felt like a fish, pinned wriggling into the mud by a toothed bone harpoon. He watched as his uncle turned away and went to piss into the ditch by the kitchen house. He saw him hitch his clothes back into place and then walk back towards the main house. In seconds he had ducked into the entrance and out of sight and Romanus was alone.

Abi sighed. She was sitting outside on the bench, the crystal on her lap in the darkness. She glanced up at the stars. The rain had blown away and the night was clear now. She could see the Big Dipper low on the horizon, just as Romanus and Flavius had seen it all those years ago. She shivered as the wind cut through the orchard, lifting the hair on the back of her neck. The scene had ended. She had looked away and when she looked back the view had changed. It was almost imperceptible, this shift of perspective, a change of focus between one breath and the next. She didn't need Athena or Justin to show her how to use the crystal after all. She had found the way again on her own. She had come out with it in her pocket and seated herself in the darkness and waited. She looked over her shoulder towards the house. The windows were in darkness now. Everyone must have gone to bed. She glanced at her watch. It was after two a.m. Stiffly she rose to her feet. She still didn't feel sleepy. She carefully re-wrapped the stone and groped in her pocket for her torch. The hiding place was a small leaf-lined hole, almost cosy in the light of the beam. She tucked the stone inside and pushed some leaves over it, then she turned back to the garden. Switching off the torch she wandered on down towards the orchard in the starlight. When she came home after speaking to Athena she had found the B & B guests were back. Cal had invited them to supper to cheer them up because of the rain. Abi had slunk past the kitchen and up to her own room. There was too much to think about to volunteer herself for social duties.

Justin the killer. Justin the druid. She felt absurdly cheated. Even betrayed. The whole family obviously knew about his history and yet Cal had mentioned nothing and Ben had thought it safe to bring Justin back to advise her.

She had sat for a long time on the end of her bed, staring into space before putting on her jacket and coming outside to look for the stone in its hiding place at the base of the old oak tree. And now she had a new worry to distract her: Flavius, who was forcing Romanus to betray his family and Mora. Surely the boy hadn't believed that bit about sparing Mora's life. But he was a child. This man was his uncle and he was dazzled by the brush with Imperial purple.

So, was Mora dead? Abi gave a rueful smile. Of course she was dead. But somehow she wanted her to have lived to a happy old age, not to have been murdered by the vengeful and vicious Flavius. She couldn't bear that to have happened. She had become involved. And it mattered. Jesus. Her Jesus, her lord and saviour would not, could not, have allowed these innocent people to have died to

265

save him. But then, over the millennia how many people had died for his cause? That was what he did. He inspired loyalty and love – to the death. She clenched her fists in her pockets.

Somewhere nearby a fox barked suddenly. She felt the hairs on the back of her neck prickle. She turned round, staring into the darkness. Here under the apple trees the starlight wasn't so bright. The orchard was full of shadows. She was looking for signs of movement. He could be here now. Justin. She knew he poked around Woodley in the dark. She had caught him at it before. What was more natural than that he would come here after their farcical meeting this morning? He had a key to the house. He had a right to be here. She moved quietly towards an old apple tree, reaching out her hand to the rough bark, feeling the reassuring touch of the cold lichen under her fingers. The night smelled cold and fresh, of moss and grass and flowers and suddenly the acrid tang of fox.

She ground her teeth together in frustration. She was not going to be terrorised by this man any more than she was going to let herself be terrorised by Kier. 'Where are you? I know you're there?' Her voice rang through the silence and there was a panic-stricken squawk and flap of wings as roosting pheasants soared up into the darkness. She waited, listening to the fall of broken twigs as the birds disappeared out over the fields. Nothing. Silence slowly fell back across the orchard. She felt for her torch and defiantly she switched it on, following the narrow beam as she swung it round. Nothing but grass and trees and a small flash of white from the rapidly disappearing scut of a rabbit fleeing into the brambles.

Taking a deep breath, she turned back towards the gate, fighting the urge to run, forcing herself to move steadily across the long grass until she emerged back into the garden.

Cal had left the back door unlocked. She pushed it open quietly and heard a small enquiring bark. The two dogs were lying, head on paws, by the fire which had been banked up for the night behind a guard. Thiz climbed to her feet and came over, tail wagging.

'Hello, girl,' Abi whispered. Pym had lowered his head again and closed his eyes, bored. Abi reached for the light switch. The kettle had nearly boiled when the door opened and Mat appeared, swathed in a dressing gown, his grey hair on end.

'Ah, I thought it might be you. Everything all right?'

'Sorry, did I wake you?'

He shook his head. 'Would you like to make me one of those?' She had reached down the tea caddy from the lintel over the fire. 'Ben rang. He said to give you a message. He said he had looked it up and,' he scrabbled for a piece of paper by the phone, 'Yeshua – is that how it's pronounced? – is thought to have been a Hebrew short form of Yehoshua, or Joshua, and yes, you could be right.' He glanced up. 'Does that make sense?'

Abi smiled. 'Oh yes. It makes sense.'

'And he said to tell you he was worried about you.'

'He told you what happened?'

'He's an idiot. He should have known better than to get in touch with that blasted brother of ours. I hope he didn't frighten you.'

'No, he didn't frighten me. He made me cross. I'm afraid I left rather precipitously.' She handed him a mug. He took it and lowered himself with a groan onto one of the chairs by the fire. Thiz went and sat next to him, leaning fondly against his knees. Abi took the chair on the far side of the fire. 'Did he really kill someone once?'

'Who?' Mat took a sip of tea.

'Justin. Athena told me he had killed someone.'

Mat shook his head. 'No. I believe almost everything I hear about Just, but not that. Why on earth would she tell you that? He has a temper. He is still the same spoiled brat he was at seven years old in some ways, but he's no killer. What a ludicrous suggestion.'

'So, that's not why you hate him.'

Mat gave a hollow laugh. 'No. I hate him because he told me once that he could have Cal off me any time he wanted. I know he couldn't. She wouldn't. But –' He paused and shook his head, 'There is always that lurking fear at the back of one's mind that he could do it. Against her will. And the fact that he even threatened it . . .' His voice trailed away. 'He's ten years younger than me. So is she.'

'Oh Mat. She loves you so much. Even I, a stranger, could see that the first time I met you.'

He smiled. 'I know. It's not logical. But there is nothing I can do about it. The fear is always there.' He reached down and fondled the dog's ears. For a second she thought he was going to cry.

She looked away, giving him time to compose himself. 'Is he really a druid?' she asked after a moment.

Mat laughed. 'Oh yes, I think that is what he would call himself, or something like it. He's very knowledgeable about alternative beliefs and paganism and comparative theologies. I'm not sure what his own gods look like, but he's very sincere about whatever it is. I gather there are people who think of him as some sort of priest. He's conducted marriage ceremonies and funerals. He has written a couple of books and I understand he's writing another. That's why he comes here. Grandfather had a huge collection of books on folklore and stuff. He used to talk to Just about it when he was a little boy. Neither Ben nor I were interested, but baby brother lapped it all up.'

'So he doesn't believe all this just to spite Ben?'

'No. No, I don't think so. He's very sincere. Ben actually has a lot of respect for him. Why else would he have called him in to try and help you. I think Ben is a bit wary of the church's teaching on some things. He's not very happy about exorcism and hell and damnation. He's a gentle soul, is Ben. He would prefer to ask nicely for ghosts to leave.' He smiled. 'He's genuinely worried about the Kieran Scotts of this world and their approach. He sees that as very damaging, not just to you, but to the souls involved.'

Abi's eyes widened. 'I didn't realise he felt like that.' She was silent for a moment. 'But that leaves the question, has someone suggested that I be exorcised? Someone apart from Kier, I mean? I don't want to be exorcised and I am sure you don't want your resident ghosts to be moved on. We are all very happy as we are. Has the bishop suggested it?'

Mat shrugged. 'I've no idea. We were only asked to give you bed and board.' He gave her a weary grin. 'Ben is in charge of the spiritual department.'

'Is he furious with me for running out on him?'

'No. He's furious with Justin.'

'And Justin has gone?'

'I can't help but say I hope so.'

Abi nodded. 'I can see why he's such a disruptive force around here.'

Mat stood up. 'Well, it's very late. I'm for my bed. Will you turn off the lights when you go up?'

She nodded. 'Of course. I'll sit here for a few minutes longer and finish my tea.' Behind the wire mesh of the fireguard a lone flame flickered, throwing shadows up into the chimney.

Why had she said the ghosts were happy? Mora wasn't happy. Mora was worried. Afraid. Frantically trying to contact her. And she, Abi, had seen off the one man who might be able to help. She sighed, picturing Justin for a moment. His eyes with their steady half-humorous gaze, his face with the same strong bones as his brothers, the long straight nose, the smile which like theirs could be so attractive and had, she had thought for a while, that extra something that makes a man irresistible to women. She bit her lip. He could have helped her feel her way through the enigma which was that small family, out there in the garden, trapped in some eternal cycle of fear and retribution. Were they trying to explain? To exonerate themselves for their actions? To tell the world what had happened? Or were they, whatever she had felt to the contrary, merely replaying an endless video, trapped somehow in the ether, shadows without souls who were doomed to re-enact forever some small part in what was arguably the most momentous piece of history ever.

She leaned forward to stroke Thiz as the dog came over to sit beside her, leaning against her legs. This animal at least recognised her as some sort of a healer. She smiled. She could feel it too, the warmth and reassurance flowing through her hands. So why could she not do it any more for people? For a while she sat in silence, enjoying the dog's trust, then slowly her thoughts turned back to Justin. Why had Athena said he was a killer? She wouldn't have made it up. But surely his own brother would have known about it if he was. Especially if he had reason to hate Justin so much.

But he had got away with it, hadn't he. Otherwise he would be in prison.

The dog sensed Abi's withdrawal of attention and with a huge sigh she climbed to her feet and went back to the fire. She lay down with a thump next to Pym and closed her eyes. It was a clear hint that all this thinking in the early hours was a bad thing. Abi gave a rueful smile and stood up. Tomorrow she would go and see Athena again. Force her to explain what it was exactly that Justin had done.

'She's gone away for a couple of days.' Bella looked up as she went into the shop. 'Her ex is being buried today and she's gone to the funeral.'

Abi murmured a quick silent prayer for the deceased, who she had felt wandering so disconsolately around Athena's flat. 'Where has she gone, do you know?' It was wrong to be indignant, to resent the poor man for being buried when she needed so badly to talk to his ex-wife. No, it wasn't just wrong, it showed how completely skewed her values had become.

'London somewhere.'

So, she was not going to find out from Athena what she meant, not today at any rate. That left Ben, to whom she owed a huge apology.

There were no cars parked outside the Rectory, and no reply when she rang the bell. She stood for a few moments looking out across the leaf-strewn lawn, bereft. The world moved on. Everyone was busy, going about their lives. At the manor the B & B guests had packed and paid and driven away; Cal and Mat had gone off on one of their trips to Taunton. That left the Serpent Stone and Mora.

'You were weeping just now?' Mora came and stood near Yeshua as he sat near the sacred spring. She had waited for him to notice her, studying his face. He was lost in a reverie, his attention far away in the spaces of time where she could never dream of following him. She sat down a few paces away from him, under one of the sacred yews.

He looked at her and nodded, his eyes still full of unhappiness. 'So much cruelty, so much hatred in the world. Sometimes in my meditations, I see such terrible things. The suffering of my people. I want to help them, but they won't listen. They will never listen.'

'Your people?' she said gently. 'That Roman said you were a king.'

Yeshua raised his hands in a gesture of despair and confusion. 'Sometimes I feel like a king. Other times,' he shrugged, 'I am no-one.' He paused. 'When I was born,' he went on quietly after a while, 'there were signs in the sky. Two planets came together to form a brilliant great star, a star that foretold the birth of a king in the town where I was born, over the house where I was born. My mother was visited –' He paused and shook his head. 'No matter. You wouldn't believe me if I told you. Suffice to say that my father wasn't my father, although he too came from the royal house generations before. Wise men, astrologers from far away, came to speak to my parents and they brought me gifts. They too had heard the prophecy; they had followed my star. They explained the gifts were symbols of my destiny. It made my mother terribly afraid for me and for them. Gold for kingship and myrrh for death.' He reached across and took her hand. 'King Herod heard about me and decided I was a rival for his throne. He resolved to have me killed, toddler as I was, and when no-one would tell him where I was – I was protected, Mora, by everyone – he ordered that all the little boys of around my age in the area should be killed.'

Mora caught her breath.

'Herod was a vicious and ruthless man, even with his own family.' He withdrew his hand from hers and sat, his arms around his knees, gazing down into the water of the spring. 'Even then, after he had done such terrible things, people cared for me. They hid me and helped us when my family decided to flee the country to get away from him.' He looked at her, and for a moment she saw, still lurking below the surface, the restless unhappy boy he must have been as he fled with his family far away from his home. 'Those children died, Mora, to save me. That man, Flavius, represents the Roman will to stamp out any threat to their power. Herod Antipas is one of King Herod's sons. He now governs in my country. He is different from his father in many ways, but it appears he still maintains this secret band of men dedicated to finding me – or, perhaps not just me, but anyone who might be a threat to the stability of the countries around the eastern end of the great sea. I don't know if Flavius was one of those who slaughtered those little boys all those years ago. He is old enough to have been there, but he is one of them in his heart. And now he works for Antipas or for Tiberius himself, and he has followed me across the world, always just behind me. Never before have I seen his face except in my nightmares.' He paused thoughtfully. 'Never before has he come this close to killing me.'

A cold breath of wind strayed across the spring, throwing a line of ripples across the clear face of the water. He stared down into it silently. They both saw the shadows there, red, like blood. 'When my kinsman Joseph returns with his ships I will go with him. I will meet Flavius and his like face to face, but in my own country. It is there I must confront my destiny.' He glanced up at her. 'Your cold, windy western winter will come soon and close the seas. I am in God's hands. I'm so sorry, Mora, but I must be gone before then.'

She had realised long ago that there was no point in arguing. 'How will we outwit Flavius and get you away safely?'

He shrugged. 'I am sure we will think of something. I am sure God's hand is over us. I will pray.'

She frowned. His single, all-powerful god was lord of all things and all men and women. It was a strange concept, and yet it wasn't. To her, god was in the wind and the sea; he was in the trees and the waters and the clouds. God and goddess were everywhere; but maybe his idea was the right one. There was one great all-encompassing godhead and all the other gods were aspects of his power; angels and spirits that served him.

She bit her lip. 'I shall miss you.' Her voice cracked with misery.

He smiled and reached across to touch her face with a gentle hand. 'And I you, Mora of the druids. And I you.'

Abi smiled to herself as she sat on the bench. The sun was shining and it was warm here in the shelter of the trees. Her fingers were stroking the crystal as it rested on her knee. There was so much affection between Yeshua and Mora, affection and genuine understanding each of the other. Affection, perhaps even love.

She closed her eyes against the sunlight, aware that she was back in the present day yet reluctant to open her eyes and return to the world. It was several seconds before she became aware that she was not alone. Her eyes flew open.

Justin was sitting on a rock close to the edge of the pool near her, watching her in silence. She felt herself grow tense. 'How long have you been there?'

'Not long.'

'Are Cal and Mat back?' She was, she realised suddenly, uncomfortable at being alone with him.

He shook his head. 'I would hardly be here if they were. I came over on the off chance of catching you alone. We didn't make a very good start yesterday, did we. As you know, I think it would be better if we talk by ourselves.' He rose from his seat and came over to stand in front of her. 'May I see it?' He held his hand out for the crystal.

She hesitated.

'I won't harm it.'

She held it out reluctantly. Their hands brushed as he took it from her. He turned to face the sun, and scrutinised it carefully, turning it this way and that, watching the light reflect from the faces of the crystal. 'This is a lovely thing.' He cupped his hands around it and held it against his chest. 'It has a nice feel. I can sense your mother. It has brought you close.'

'What about the past?' She felt very uncomfortable, seeing it in his hands like that, almost as though she was feeling him touching her. Getting up she went to stand near the ancient stone arch, leaving several feet between them.

He closed his eyes in silence. 'When you want it to talk to you,' he said at last, his voice very soft, 'all you have to do is listen. It has much to tell.'

'That much I already know.' She couldn't keep the tartness out of her voice. He opened his eyes and glanced at her. To her surprise she saw amusement there. 'Then you have cracked the code on your own.' He held it out to her and dropped it into her cupped hands. 'You were right. You don't need me.'

He turned and began to walk back towards the house. She stared after him. 'I know how to listen,' she said. 'But I want to talk to her!' The words erupted out of her without thought. 'And I don't know how.'

He stopped.

'Please, show me how to get through to her.'

Mora walked slowly up the hill following the long serpentine route which generations of priests and priestesses, the servants of many gods, had trodden, her eyes on the grass below her sandals. She was thinking. About Yeshua and Cynan. Cynan, the

273

young man to whom she had been betrothed almost since she was born, her companion and fellow student, and colleague. One day they would be arch druid and druidess of this school, and in years to come their children would succeed them. She pictured his kind, gentle face, his green, thoughtful eyes, the smile which hovered from time to time around his mouth, the calm serious expression he habitually wore. Then she thought about Yeshua. Taller than Cynan, with a darker, more olive skin, brown hair, deep brown eyes. His hands. Why was it she always thought about his hands; she was always watching them. His long strong fingers, gentle and artistic, always moving except when he was at prayer when at last they were still. He spent so much time at prayer; sometimes she watched him, seeing him go so far away from her where she could never follow and she had surprised herself at the occasional sudden resentment she felt at whatever, whoever, it was that took him so far from her. And now he was going. She had known the moment would come, but had hoped against hope that he would change his mind and stay. Just a while longer. Over winter, perhaps, and then perhaps another spring. But she knew he wouldn't. Part of his charm was his certainty. And an equal part was his doubt. And now, when he looked deep into her eyes and told her he was going, she realised that more than anything or anyone she loved him and that if he asked her she would give up everything to follow him. She stopped in her tracks and looked up at the summit of the Tor above her in the sunlight. The great menhir which had stood there for thousands of years caught the light, white and almost luminous. It marked the place of greatest power, the concentration of the forces of earth and sky, of storm and wind, of star and sun. It was the place where one could speak directly to the gods. And the place, she sensed, where she could speak most easily to the woman who was following her around the island, trying so hard to contact her from another plane of existence beyond the mists. She looked round. She was there now. She could sense her reaching out. A priestess as she was, an initiate in all probability, somehow lost in the otherworld. On an impulse Mora stepped off the path and found herself a sheltered spot to sit down out of the wind. At once, in the silence, below the shoulder of the hill she heard her calling.

Mora! Mora? Are you there?

Mora closed her eyes and waited, opening herself to whatever came.

She was not expecting it to be a man.

He was walking uncertainly up the serpent path, dressed in strange clothes, his hair, short like a Roman's, blowing around his head. His eyes were fixed on the top of the Tor and he had walked right past her without seeing her when somehow he sensed her presence and stopped. She saw the look of puzzlement on his face, then fear, as he scanned the hillside. Then she saw him shiver. Crouching down she kept still, willing him not to see her, drawing down the cloak of mist which her father had taught her to use if ever she felt herself in danger, wrapping it around herself. All he would see now would be a patch of nothing on the hillside, a place where the morning mist had lingered in a hollow between the gorse bushes.

'Hello?' He was very near her, and she saw him shake his head as if clearing a buzzing in his ears. He was looking straight at her now. He had bright, searching brown eyes; not warm brown, like Yeshua, but hard, the colour of hazelnuts, his hair was reddish and his complexion florid. He could sense her there. She cowered down, not moving, like a small animal freezing before a weasel.

'Bloody place!' She heard his words clearly. They meant nothing to her. He turned away from her at last and looked back up towards the summit before him. It was a steep climb to the top from here and he was already out of breath. She could hear him panting, almost feel the beat of the blood in his ears. Then at last he was back on the path and once more following it towards the top. He had cut across the serpent path. He was following some track she hadn't noticed before. There were steps in it, a well trodden way. She frowned, still not daring to move. Once he was out of sight she would retrace her steps towards the bottom of the hill. She had no desire to be up there with a stranger in that sacred place. Now her fear was receding and her senses were once more working, she could feel his anger and his fury as tangible streaks across the air around her. Why would he go up there if he was so afraid? She glanced up towards the menhir and frowned. For a fraction of a second she could see what he could see, the man from the other world. A tall square tower on the place where the ancient stone had stood. Then it was gone, a grey shimmer in the sunlight, no more.

*   *   *

Kier had driven back overnight. He shouldn't have come. The bishop had expressly forbidden it but he couldn't keep away. Ever since his interview he had tried to put Abi and her affairs out of his mind but his conscience wouldn't rest. She was in danger. Of that he was sure. It wasn't her fault, but her natural psychic ability had driven her into the arms of the worst possible situation. David Paxman still didn't understand how stupid it was to send her down here, to Glastonbury! Of all the places on earth he could have sent her, this was the last he should have chosen.

He completed the final scramble to the top of the Tor and stood looking round, trying to regain his breath. After the interview with the bishop and then the long tiring drive through heavy traffic his head was spinning and he felt tense and unhappy. After he had parked the car he sat for a long time wondering what to do next. He wasn't sure what had made him head for the Tor. It seemed the perfect place to clear his head. High. Windy. Full of sunlight. There were several people up there when he arrived on top. The usual eclectic mix. Dog walkers. Hippies. He turned down his mouth, glancing at three young women in white robes. They were giggling and he suspected it was out of extreme embarrassment as they realised how silly they looked. A couple of ramblers. He eyed their state of the art rambling poles and heavy laced boots with extreme disfavour. Did they think this was the Matterhorn? There were a couple of earnest men. He classified them as probably academic, but who could tell. They might be astrologers on a day out from Mars. He snorted to himself. The day was clear. He could see for miles. He went and stood, his back to the wall of the tower, hands in pockets, feeling his hair being swept back by the sharp cold wind, then he frowned. How strange that on a day like today, there were still patches of mist on the lower slopes of the hill. He moved round to look down at the path he had followed upwards, seeing small groups of people slowly wending their way up and down. No mist. Not anywhere. It must have dispersed in the wind.

He found himself a place where he could sit in the comparative shelter of the lee side of the tower, and began to think out his strategy. He had to get the wretched crystal ball away from Abi. He shuddered at the thought. And he had to get Abi away from Glastonbury. The bishop was not going to help; and nor obviously was Ben Cavendish. A fine spiritual adviser he was turning out to be. The rest of the Cavendish family were going to be no use either, and that third brother was especially dangerous. He had recognised the type. Absolute certainty was always dangerous; absolute certainty in a religious fanatic of whatever persuasion was lethal. He snorted again. Druid indeed. What in God's name did the man think he was playing at? He was presumably educated. Of sound mind. Yet he was no better than those girls, who were now decorating themselves with little wreaths of ivy, giggling even more as the wind tugged playfully at their hair and wound green tendrils into their eyes.

What he had to do was persuade Abi to come with him back to Cambridge. But how? He began to gnaw the knuckle of his thumb. She wasn't going to listen to him. He couldn't threaten her. She was a strong woman. She knew her own mind. Could he lure her in some way? He shook his head slowly. What could he offer? She wasn't interested in him romantically, that was for sure. Supposing he told her that David wanted her to go back? But that would be a lie. He closed his eyes. 'Please, God, tell me what to do. Help me make the right decision here.'

The right decision was of course to do nothing. To leave well alone and go away.

They were sitting side by side on the bench in the sunshine. Abi threw a quick glance at Justin out of the corner of her eye. She had been careful once more to keep a safe distance between them. He was sitting absolutely still, eyes closed and she had the feeling that he was listening. She said nothing. The stone was resting in her lap. Was it her imagination or did she sense a change in it? Almost as if it too was listening. She took a deep breath and tried to calm herself. What was it Ben had said to her?

'"My daughter, in time of illness do not be remiss, but pray to the Lord and he will heal you. Keep clear of wrong-doing, amend your ways, And cleanse your heart from all sin."'

But surely sitting here, with this man, was not a sin. She couldn't picture him as a killer. Or even as some kind of sorcerer. She didn't sense anything evil about him at all. Arrogance, maybe. But Ben would not have summoned him if he was truly dangerous. She thought back to her first meeting with Ben as her religious advisor. He had given her the tools to keep her safe. It was up to her to use them. 'You feel uncomfortable. You are uncertain. I can only suggest you pray. Surround yourself with the love of God. If you feel you shouldn't be doing this, Abi. Stop. Recite the Breastplate. "Christ in quiet, Christ in danger, Christ in mouth of friend and stranger", remember?'

Abi opened her eyes to find Justin looking at her. There was a speculative glint in his eye. 'If you are uncomfortable with this, Abi, stop now.'

It was an uncanny echo of her thoughts. She shrugged. 'I don't know much about druids.'

'It's a term, that's all. A title that appeals to people.'

'A title that you gave yourself, or did you train to be one?'

He grinned. 'I have trained. But it takes a thousand lifetimes, so I'm not there yet. In ancient times the training of a druid was said to take twenty years and yes, by that measure I am, as it were, qualified.' He smiled. 'Your next question is going to be, do I practise human sacrifice. The answer is no.'

She gave a shocked little laugh. 'Actually, that hadn't occurred to me, but I'm pleased to hear it.'

'Is there anything else bothering you?'

She shook her head meekly. 'Ben has vouched for you. That is enough.'

It was his turn to laugh out loud. 'I fear his recommendation would be ringed with caveats, but we will find that out as we proceed. I don't think there is much I can teach you, to be honest, as I take it you are not seeking training as a druid yourself. You obviously have a natural propensity to see beyond the normal range. You listen and you don't panic. What is preventing you from being able to step fully into your experiences is your own in-built monitor. That comes from conditioning. No doubt at school you learned to keep quiet about any so-called psychic experiences you might have had as you would have been mocked. Sadly that is inevitable. I am sure it is the same at a training college. The less sensitive brethren in any community always trumpet their scorn of anything they don't understand. Sadly they are also inevitably the majority, so they win by default unless you are exceptionally tough or learn to use your talents to entertain them in some way, which devalues the experience but usually gets them off your back. The threat of being more powerful than they are usually frightens bullies enough to stop them.'

278

'That sounds as if you are speaking from experience,' Abi said softly.

He grimaced. 'Public school is not a place for the sensitive, to my mind.' He leaned back with a sigh. 'In your case, whatever your experiences as a child and as a student, they will have been more than reinforced by your training at theological college. I cannot understand why the church as a spiritual body, which has within its own creed the words "I believe in one God, maker of all things, visible and invisible," then goes on to deny the existence of a huge portion of the so-called invisible world. Well, no, I lie. I can understand it only too well. It is a matter of control. They want to keep the masses battened down and in ignorance. But it is something you have to learn to put behind you if you want to explore the invisible world. You already know it is all too visible to people who can see a slightly wider than average spectrum. Your church acknowledges the existence of angels, as do Jews and Muslims. Hindus have Devas. Use that belief to give you permission to see and to believe. Otherwise you will never get beyond your own inhibitions. Do not fear any of this contradicts or conflicts with your beliefs. It doesn't.'

'Wow.' Abi shook her head. 'That is telling me.' It was what Athena had said, after all.

'You needed telling.'

'So, where do I go from here?'

'That's up to you. You are on your own from here.'

'You mean, that's it. That's the extent of your help?'

'That's it. You can do the rest yourself.'

'And the stone?' She held it out in her cupped hands.

'The vibration of the crystal has been programmed, either by accident or deliberately – probably the latter – to hold a story. If you believe in computers, you can believe in crystals. Accessing information is marginally easier than with a computer in my experience. Suspend disbelief. Keep calm and quiet. Empty your mind and wait. It is unlikely to crash or slow down or pause while Windows updates.'

She laughed. 'That does please me. I think I could feel more comfortable with prehistoric technology.'

'And by prehistoric you mean?'

'Its technical meaning. Pre-written history.'

He nodded. 'OK. You pass the test. I think you can be left in charge of your stone. Which is something very beautiful and special. I would say magical if I didn't think the word would freak you out.'

'Magickal spelled with a k in the middle?' She cocked her head to one side with a small grin.

'Never!' He stood up. 'I spell my magic the right way. I don't need whimsy. When your friend, Mora, tries to speak to you, allow it to happen and reply naturally. You will find there is a knack to it. It might not come at once, but keep trying. Be calm. Don't be afraid. Maintain a degree of serenity. The rest will follow.'

He turned and walked away across the lawn. She sat still gazing down at the crystal and realised she was almost disappointed that he had left so abruptly. She was beginning to enjoy their verbal sparring. Looking up again she watched him surreptitiously as he walked around the side of the house and out of sight. Not once did he look back.

Romanus was sitting by the fire whittling a stick with his knife. He was listening to the sounds coming from behind the screens which separated off his sister's sleeping room. Sorcha was sponging Petra with warm water, changing her bedgown and laying her back as gently as she could onto the sheets of the bed. Romanus put his hands over his ears as he heard Petra crying out with pain. She tried so hard to be brave. He could picture her biting back the sounds, clutching at Sorcha's arm, desperate to keep her agony from her mother. He glanced at the doorway. Lydia was outside with Flavius. He could hear their raised voices. Again and again she was begging him to leave, to go back home, to abandon his stupid quest for this man, Yeshua. His attention was abruptly brought back into the room as Sorcha appeared, a bowl of warm water in her hand, a towel over her arm. She looked pale and upset. 'Go and talk to your sister, Romanus. See if you can take her mind off her pain,' she whispered. She went to the doorway and threw out the water. 'I can't bear to see her like this. I don't know what to do. Your poor mother spent the whole night sitting up with her.'

Romanus climbed to his feet. He looked down at the piece of wood he had been carving and with a grimace tossed it into the fire. Ramming his knife back into the sheath at his belt he went through to Petra's small room. 'Hey. How are you?' He sat down on the stool by her bed. 'Do you want your gifted brother to sing for you?' He grinned. It was a standing joke between them. She could sing. He couldn't. Not a note. She shook her head, blinking back tears. He leaned forward and took her hands between his. Tending for his adored sister had given him surprising gentleness for a boy. 'Poor you. I wish I could do something.'

'Can you fetch Mora?' Her voice was husky. 'Mora and her healer friend. She said he would be able to help me.' She tried to smile. 'Please, Rom.'

He scowled. 'I'm not sure I can.' He had been thinking about Flavius' command all night.

'Why?' Glancing up he saw the panic in her eyes.

He looked away. 'I don't know if she's there.'

'She is. I heard Uncle Flavius tell Mama. He told her to send for them, but Mama felt we should wait. She doesn't want to ask too many favours at the druid school, I don't know why.' Her eyes filled with tears.

'Because we can't pay them back. Because I wanted to go there to study and I've told her I don't want to any more.' He looked away from her shamefacedly. He wanted more than anything to go with Flavius back to Rome and then on to Judea. He couldn't tell them that though. Not any of them, not even Petra. And he was ashamed of wanting to go. Of wanting to go with a man who was planning to murder the one person who could help his sister. His hands tightened over her swollen fingers and he heard her gasp of pain. 'I'm sorry.' He released them guiltily. 'Oh Petra, I don't know what to do.'

He looked up and found her gazing at him. Her lovely eyes and long lashes were still full of tears, but he saw the love and trust there. He scrambled to his feet and turning away from her ducked out from behind the screens and ran across the main room. Outside he fled across the yard towards the gate in the palisade. In seconds he was running down the field as fast as he could go.

Lydia watched him in astonishment. 'Petra?' Suddenly frightened she ducked back into the house, leaving Flavius on his own. It was only seconds before he turned to follow Romanus out of the gate.

He caught up with him at the edge of the lake. 'So? What happened? Why haven't you gone to the island as I told you?'

Romanus shrugged. He kicked hard at an old willow stump, protruding from the reeds and was pleased when it hurt.

'Your sister is in pain. She needs her medicine.'

'She wants me to fetch the healer.'

'So why don't you?' Flavius's voice was suddenly persuasive.

'Because if I do you will kill him.'

'If you don't, as I told you, I will kill Mora.'

There was a moment of silence. The boy's knuckles whitened as he clenched his fists.

Flavius gave him a cold smile. 'I tell you what. I will intercept him on his way back after his visit. That will give him time to look after your sister. Remember what I told you. It is up to you. If you can distract Mora and keep her back she will never find out what happened to him and I will spare her life. It is up to you, Romanus. Everything is in your hands.'

'And if I do what you ask? You will take me with you?'

'If you have proved yourself worthy, I will take you with me.' His gaze was watchful, reading the conflicting emotions on the boy's face. 'You will have to convince them that it is safe to come here. That will be up to you. If you don't do it I shall have to resort to other means. If that happens, I can't guarantee that Mora won't be hurt.' He looked down thoughtfully at the dugout canoes pulled up on the mud. 'Go now. The sooner the better. Think of poor Petra's agony. She needn't go through another night like last night. I could hear her crying even in my guesthouse. Think how pleased and relieved your mother would be.'

Romanus was standing looking down at the boats, a picture of indecision. His hand strayed to the mooring rope, looped round the willow stump. 'You swear you won't hurt Mora?' He didn't appear to be worrying about Yeshua, Flavius noted. In fact the boy was probably jealous of the man's closeness to Mora. Perhaps secretly he would welcome the disappearance of a rival. It had obviously never occurred to him that his uncle might break his word and kill her too.

'I swear.' Flavius brought his right fist up to his heart with a thump. 'The word of a soldier of Rome.' He stooped and loosened the painter. 'Go on. Hop in. I will give you a push off.'

Romanus hesitated for just one more second, then he nodded. He stooped and scrabbled under the seat for the paddle. 'Will you tell Mama where I have gone?'

Flavius nodded. 'I'll tell her. And Petra. Be as quick as you can, for her sake.'

'Silly boy!' Abi came to with a start. 'Can't you see he doesn't mean it! For God's sake –' She stopped in mid-sentence, aware suddenly that Mat and the dogs were approaching across the lawn.

'Hello there! You looked lost in thought. I'm sorry. I always seem to be interrupting.' Mat grinned at her comfortably.

She stroked the two dogs. 'No. I was thinking about coming in. It gets cold as the sun goes down.' How long had she been sitting there, for heaven's sake? Last time she had been aware of the sunlight it had been hot, shining across the lawn, sending the shadows slanting towards the house. Now the garden was dull and overcast and wisps of mist were trailing in across the hedges. From somewhere she could smell bonfires, rich with spicy apple smoke.

She hesitated. Mora. She had to see Mora. Had to try to speak to her. She had expected her to appear, but the story she had been watching was about that little fool, Romanus.

'I'll follow you in.' She shrugged. 'Just trying to think a few things through. I'll wander about for a few minutes more if you don't mind.'

Mat nodded. 'Take as long as you like. See you later.' He whistled the dogs and strode on past her down towards the orchard.

Abi turned round slowly and picked up the crystal which at some point had slipped from her hands onto the bench. It was ice-cold. Tucking it into the pocket of her jacket she glanced over her shoulder. She wanted to walk towards the orchard, but if Mat had strolled on that way her chance of solitude was gone. Instead she retraced her steps through the flowerbeds and back in a circuitous route which would take her round the far side of the house. From there she could cut across the paddock and down the steep hillside towards the churchyard wall, the churchyard which was, she now realised, Cynan's island. The ancient church had been built on his hermitage, his private sanctuary, his druid shrine.

The grass was wet with dew and she shivered as the hems of her trousers grew rapidly cold and damp. 'Mora? Can you see me?' Her fingers closed over the crystal in her pocket. 'Can you hear me? What happened when Romanus reached you? Can you tell me? Can I help?'

There was no answer.

'Justin was here this afternoon.'

Cal was peeling potatoes when she walked back into the kitchen. Mat was still out with the dogs. Cal looked up sharply. 'I thought Ben said it didn't work out. He made a mistake asking him.'

Abi smiled. 'He came over to give it another go. We talked. It was easier without Ben there.'

'I can imagine.' Cal selected another spud. 'So, was he any help?'

'I think so. He made me see things in a different light.'

'Don't tell Mat he came.'

Abi shook her head. 'Of course not.'

'Has he gone back to Wales?'

Abi shrugged. 'He didn't say. He just walked away.' She picked up a knife and selected a potato. Digging out an eye she rinsed it and threw it into the bowl. 'He's a bit enigmatic, isn't he?'

Cal smiled. 'I suppose he is.'

'Did you never really fancy him? Honestly?'

'No.' Cal stared at her. 'No, of course not. That's an outrageous thing to say.'

'Tell Mat. Then the quarrel can be over.'

Cal shook her head. 'Is that what Justin thinks? That I fancy him! The conceited bastard!'

'No, Cal, it's what Mat thinks. He told me.'

For a moment Cal froze. She stood without moving, a potato in her hand, her eyes on the bowl of peelings in front of her. 'He doesn't. He can't. Not still! That's crazy.'

'Of course it's crazy. But who says love is logical.'

Cal looked up suddenly. 'Is this with your little miss vicar counselling hat on?'

'The very same.' Abi nodded. 'I'm sorry, I should mind my own business, but I can't bear to see you all hurting so much.'

Cal threw down the potato. 'Where is he?'

'Mat? He was out with the dogs. In the orchard. He must be coming in soon.'

Alone in the kitchen after Cal had taken down her jacket from

284

the peg and run outside, Abi finished the potatoes, left them on the side and threw some logs on the fire. Then she settled down to wait. It was half an hour before Cal reappeared. Her hair was rumpled by the wind, her face worried. 'I can't find him. I've called and called. Are you sure he was going to the orchard?'

Abi frowned. 'That's what he said.'

'He must have decided to walk a bit more. The dogs have been cooped up all day in the car. They will have been egging him on.' She smiled uncomfortably.

'Don't worry about him, Cal. I'm sure he's OK. He seemed quite cheerful just now when I talked to him.'

Cal looked pensive. 'I was lying just now,' she said suddenly. 'Mat's right. I do find Justin attractive. But he never fancied me.' Automatically she reached for the potatoes and put the pan on the cooker.

Abi said nothing.

'Mat had already asked me to marry him. I had never met his brother. Justin is always away somewhere. Then suddenly he walked in one day and smiled.' Her eyes filled with tears. 'I was lost. Mat knew it. It has always been like that. Justin arrives and everyone in the room looks at him. It's as though the rest of the cast have walked into the shadows leaving just the one spotlight on the stage.'

'But you chose Mat.'

She nodded. 'I couldn't bring myself to hurt him, not like that. Not when it was what he expected. And anyway, Justin wasn't for me. One day he will find a priestess who will perform a sacred marriage with him up in the mountains or down in the forest, attended by fairies and spirits of old.' She wiped her eyes with the back of her arm and cleared her throat. 'You are right. Mat knows. He has always known. And he always will know.'

'But he is the one you chose,' Abi repeated. 'It wasn't too late. You could have changed your mind. You could have run away with Justin. You could have dumped Mat. But you didn't. You might have fancied Justin, but it's Mat you love.'

Cal nodded again.

Behind them there was a sudden hiss of overflowing water on the hotplate as the potatoes came to the boil. Cal stood up and went to turn down the heat. Then she sat down again. 'He comes here so seldom. Sometimes he is away for literally years without

285

a word. That is what has brought this all to a head again. He started coming to borrow books, trying to do it without being seen. I caught him, just as you did.' She gave a rueful smile. 'After that I was somehow complicit. And now he is coming more openly. It's bringing stuff out into the open again.'

'So now is the time to lay the ghost,' Abi said gently. 'Talk to Mat. If you hide things he senses it. Blame me. Or even Ben. Reassure him that Justin has only come back because of me.'

Cal sighed. 'I will. I'm a coward, that's the trouble. I prefer to pretend things aren't happening, hoping it will all go away. But it doesn't of course.' She paused. 'What about a glass of wine while we wait for him to come in? I've a casserole in the oven, so supper is nearly ready.'

'I'd love one.' Abi stood up. 'But first let me go and have a quick look outside. I know where I saw him last.' She reached for her coat and for the torch which was kept beside the back door. 'By the time you've poured one out for me, I'll be back.'

She had a feeling she knew where he would be. She walked steadily, the torch beam on the ground ahead of her, through the garden, past the ruins, heading for the church.

It never seemed to be locked. Perhaps it was too far off the beaten track to be in danger from vandals or thieves but she knew when she turned the handle and heard the latch lift in the silence that he was there. He was sitting in the front row of chairs, the two dogs lying beside him in the aisle. They thumped their tails as she entered but made no move to greet her.

'Mat?'

He didn't move. She felt her throat tighten with fear. 'Mat, are you all right?'

She walked towards him, the torch throwing a faint pool of light on the paving slabs. He was sitting staring at the altar. 'Mat?' She laid her hand gently on his shoulder.

'I'm OK,' he said at last. He sounded as if he was waking from a dream.

'We were worried. Cal has been looking for you everywhere.'

'I'm sorry.' His voice was husky. For a moment longer he sat without moving then he gave his head a slight shake. 'I saw her. I was watching her. Your priestess. She was here looking for you.'

Abi sat down next to him. She switched off the torch and they sat side by side in the darkness.

'I've never seen a ghost before, Abi. I've heard so much about them. Imagined what it would be like. Ridiculed Cal and Justin, even Ben, and then suddenly there she was standing looking at me. I could smell her. A sort of static electric smell. I've never smelled anything like it before.'

Abi frowned. 'I've never smelled anything like that.'

He shook his head. 'It was wonderful. There was no mistake. I wasn't imagining it.'

'Why do you think she was looking for me?' Abi's eyes were growing used to the dark now. She could make out the faint outline of the window against the stars, the black silhouette of the altar. She stared round, wondering if Mora was still there.

'She was searching for something. Someone.'

'Perhaps it was Cynan. He was the man –' she paused, 'one of the men, she loved. This was his special place.'

'This was certainly a sacred place long before the Christians came,' he nodded. 'It is in the guidebooks. You know Glastonbury,' he grinned suddenly, 'a place where the veils are thin. Technically we may be on the "mainland" now,' he drew the inverted commas in the air with his fingers, 'but we are on our own little island, and so is this church. We share those ancient Celts' "mysticality", their sense of mysticism.'

Abi smiled. 'You are right, of course. I sensed it too, but I am distracted by the fact that it is a church. I was wrapping myself in prayer, not allowing her in.'

He glanced at her. In the darkness they were no more than two shadowy silhouettes. 'Does it get in the way a lot?'

'Being a priest?'

He nodded.

'It shouldn't. It is who I am.' She paused. 'But yes, I think that is one of my problems. I don't seem to know how to integrate my belief in Jesus Christ with my knowledge that other things, things which are not officially compatible with Christianity, are out there. Things I find important. Things I can't deny just because I am not supposed to see them.'

'It sounds as if you need a concentrated seminar with both my brothers, one after the other.'

She gave a muted chuckle. 'You are right.' She sighed. 'We must go back. Cal is opening the wine and supper is ready.'

'And Mora has gone.'

She nodded. 'I don't sense her here. I'll come again in the morning, and work at stripping away the fabric of Christianity so that I can talk to her. Although –' She stopped. She had been about to say that Mora of all people would understand about Jesus Christ.

He was there ahead of her. 'I don't think it matters, Abi. She needs to talk to you and she has consistently followed you around. Just stop and listen.'

How many people was it now, who had told her the same thing? As she stood up and turned to follow the dogs to the door Abi glanced over her shoulder into the darkness. It wasn't that she hadn't tried. She had tried again and again. Perhaps tomorrow Mora would come to her and this time they would find a way to talk.

'Please come, Mora.' Romanus was standing in the doorway of her house, his hair blowing in the wind which had risen over the marshes. 'Petra is so ill. And she needs Yeshua. He could cure her, couldn't he? His God is so powerful.'

Mora looked at him thoughtfully. 'And your uncle? Is he still there?'

The boy nodded miserably, unable to tell a direct lie. He looked away from her. 'He won't be there when we get there. He said he was going out. He will be out all day. I can go ahead to make sure. Please, Mora. She was crying all night. It was awful, Mama and Sorcha took turns to sit with her, but we could all hear her.'

Mora looked past him out of the door. The sun was shining but the wind was bringing with it a wrack of stormy cloud. She was torn between the suspicion that Flavius would be there somewhere waiting, and her desire to help Petra. That the girl was in intolerable pain she knew was true. With the wind in this direction it was always worse and she doubted if Petra would be able to bear the long winter of cold and damp. Yeshua was her only hope. And yet to visit Petra's house would put him in immediate danger. She brought her attention back to the boy's face. He was watching her in an agony of doubt, twisting his fingers together in the folds of his woollen tunic. She noted the serviceable knife in his belt. A man's knife. But he was still in so many ways a boy.

She made up her mind suddenly. 'I will talk to Yeshua,' she said. 'I will see if he thinks it would be safe to come.'

Watching him closely she saw the sudden shift of his eyes, the tightening of his knuckles. 'Romanus,' she said quietly, 'I know you love Petra. I know you would do anything to help her. But to trap Yeshua would be so wrong. Petra would not want that.'

'My uncle said he was going to be away today,' he repeated stubbornly. 'I am sure it will be safe. You – he – wouldn't have to stay long.'

'Very well. Go and wait by your canoe. I will speak to Yeshua and I will collect my medicines and bring the extra strong doses for her.'

She had told her father and Cynan about the Roman and his ambush up in the hills and both men had frowned in consternation. 'You must not go onto the mainland alone with Yeshua again,' her father had said sternly. 'Take Cynan with you and some of the young druids. I want no violence, but their presence would probably be enough to protect you. Invoke the gods to wrap you with concealing mists so the man becomes lost. If he should wander into the mere, so much the better.' He looked at her thoughtfully. 'Don't be led astray by Yeshua, Mora. Strange forces surround him. His god is very strong but so are his enemies.'

Yeshua was standing by the spring. Mora made her way along the track, feeling the wind drag at her hair, pulling the cloak back from her shoulders as she walked. The sacred yew trees were whispering to one another, the rattle and hiss of their agitated branches drowning the gentle bubbling of the waters. She stood there in silence, waiting for him to look up at her, aware of his thin shoulders in the woollen robe of a druid, his bent head, his neck so vulnerable beneath his blowing hair.

When he spoke it was without taking his eyes from the waters in front of him. 'We are to go and see Petra?'

She felt herself tense. 'You have seen it in the spring?'

He nodded.

'And do you see if we are being tricked?'

He nodded again. 'Don't blame the boy. He is torn. His loyalties are pulled every way by the scheming of this man. But I want to go and see this child. It is not right that she should be left to suffer because we are afraid.'

'We should take Cynan and some of the others with us,' she

289

said reluctantly. 'My father is not happy for us to go across alone any more.'

Yeshua shook his head. 'I don't want druids to be involved in this. Rome fears and resents them. In Gaul they are proscribed. I don't wish to bring trouble to people who have been my hosts and my teachers and whose way is peace. Don't worry. My father will protect us.'

'Your father?' She raised an eyebrow. Then she understood. She could never get used to the familiar way he sometimes spoke of his god. 'Even if we go alone, it won't do any harm for us to protect ourselves as well,' she put in sharply. 'At least we know what to expect.'

He turned to face her, smiling. 'You make a formidable body-guard, my Mora. With you beside me, how can we fail?'

She met his eye and for a moment they stood looking at each other. She reached out and put her hand on his chest. 'I can't bear it that you will be going soon.'

Gently he put his arms round her. 'I shall remember you always, you know that.'

'Couldn't I come with you?' She reached up to kiss him and for a second they stayed, lost in each other's arms.

Then he pushed her away. 'You know that's not possible. What I have to do, I have to do alone. You have a duty here, Mora. It is your home and your destiny just as my destiny lies far away in Galilee. We have to do as God directs. Besides you have a good man here in Cynan. He loves you. He would die for you.' For a moment he stood looking down at her, then he turned to the track. 'Come, let us go and find young Romanus. You have your bag of herbs?'

Blinded by sudden tears she couldn't move for a moment. He glanced back and held out his hand. 'Be brave, my Mora. You are a strong woman. Think now about Petra and how we can help her.'

15

The hotel in Sadler Street still had a vacancy and Kier found himself in the same twin bedroom, looking out towards the towers of Wells Cathedral. The room was very quiet. He looked round with satisfaction, dumping his bag down on the bed nearest the window. Perfect timing. He would go to Evensong, then have a meal in a local pub.

The next morning he drove back to Woodley and parked several hundred yards away from the house in a lay-by on the road where it ran straight and flat across the drained fields with their deep rhynes, symmetrical ditches punctuated by pollarded willows, the route of the causeway between the Isle of Avalon and the mainland. He was heading for the hill upon which the little church was built. He had seen Abi from across the field, threading her way down through the orchard then climbing the steep track on the far side. He watched her pause in the churchyard, then let herself in, leaving the door open behind her. The bright sunlight and fresh cold wind had swirled in with her, tugging at her jacket and tangling her hair. He frowned. She seemed to wear her hair loose all the time now. It seemed too young and frivolous, to him. And wild. Not at all suitable for a woman of the cloth. She was wearing a bright skirt, too. He could see it blowing round her legs. He walked slowly towards the church, following a footpath along the field edge. When it got to the hedge around the churchyard he found a stile and climbed over. Sheltered by yews and ancient oaks the churchyard was an island in the wide flat landscape. From here he could see the other conical hills, once islands in the wetlands, rising up in the distance. Behind him the Mendips rose as a phalanx to the north-east. It was a starkly dramatic landscape.

He walked quietly towards the church door, still uncertain what he was going to say to her and paused in the porch to listen.

No sound came from inside the church. Cautiously he stepped towards the inner door and peered round it. She was sitting, staring at the altar. She looked as though she was praying. He watched her for a few moments, his eyes lingering over the beam of sunlight which illuminated her wild halo of hair and brought out the soft greens and browns of her jacket, the swirling patterns of her skirt. He could see her profile, the long straight nose, the high cheek-bones and the strong, determined mouth. He smiled and stepped back, tiptoeing outside once more, unwilling to interrupt her, hearing the murmur of her voice. He paused and almost turned back, but that was wrong. If she chose to speak out loud to the Almighty then who was he to interrupt. This was why she was here. To pray and meditate. To clear her conscience with God. He stood for a few minutes in the windy churchyard, watching the four ancient yew trees sway and dance in a stately quadrille, then he turned and made his way back towards the stile. He was halfway there when he stopped and looked back.

Then he began to retrace his steps.

Abi could see her now. She was still hazy and somehow hesi-tant but the expression in her eyes was clear. It was pleading, desperate. 'Mora, speak to me. I can see you. What can I do to help?' She spoke clearly but she didn't dare move. Behind her the heavy door swung open in the wind, scraping on the ancient paving stones. She had the feeling that if she stood up or moved closer she would scare Mora away again. 'Please, tell me what you want. I am listening to your story.' She fell silent, trying to open herself to whatever came. The figure hadn't moved. Shadows from the trees outside fell through the stained glass of the window and played across the altar. She frowned, afraid she would lose sight of the figure in the shifting beams of light. 'Mora, speak to me.'

'Who in the name of Our Lord Jesus Christ is Mora!' Kier's voice just behind her made her spin round, rigid with shock. 'Just who are you praying to?'

She turned back to the altar but Mora had gone. With a mixture of rage and disappointment, she fell back onto the chair. 'Get out, Kier.' She spoke through clenched teeth.

'Not until you've told me. Who is Mora? Are you praying to

some sort of goddess?' He sputtered over the word as he stood over her.

She shook her head wearily. 'No, Kier, I am not praying to a goddess.'

'What then?'

'It is none of your business. Please go away. I thought you had gone. I thought you had realised you had made a huge mistake coming down here.'

He shook his head wildly. 'Please, don't look so cross, Abi. I only want to talk to you for a few minutes, then I will go. I promise. I need to explain –' He paused and looked away, anguished. 'I didn't mean to come and hound you.' He tried again. 'I don't want you to feel you've got to run away all the time. It's only because I care so much that I have come here. It's not your fault I've lost my job. I know that now. I went back to see the bishop. I handled everything appallingly but it will all come right. I know it will.'

Abi put her hands in her jacket pockets and waited in silence. He glanced at her, then looked down at the floor. 'You are a sensitive woman, Abi,' he said at last. 'Exceptionally so and as an ordained priest you are a prime target. You know that as well as I do.' He paused as though expecting her to say something.

She waited, looking at him, amazed that she could feel so much hostility towards a man who had once attracted her. 'I don't know how to get through to you,' she said at last. 'I don't want to see you any more. I don't want you interfering in my life.'

'When I first came it was because your father asked me to,' Kier went on. 'He begged me to help you. He knows how dangerous that rock crystal is. He says it destroyed your mother. It has demonic powers.'

'Rubbish!' Abi felt a surge of anger. 'Look, Kier. I am trying to be reasonable. I don't care what my father asked you to do. My father hates anything that smacks of superstition to him, and that includes the Church of England, I may say. I left home because he and I do not agree on a great many important subjects. Our relationship is none of your business. Please go now.' She saw him hesitate. 'Now, Kier!'

'I'm not going anywhere. I can't leave you here like this. Your immortal soul is in danger –'

'No, not again!' Suddenly she was so angry she couldn't contain

293

her rage. She stood up and turned on him. 'My immortal soul is my affair, Kier. If I want to pray to the devil himself I will! Now I want you to go away and leave me alone and never, never come near me again. If you don't I shall go to the police and charge you with harassment, do you understand me?'

He took a step back. 'Abi! There's no need for that. I want to help you.'

'You are not helping me.'

'Then explain. Who is Mora?'

'All right. I'll tell you.' Her eyes were blazing with rage. 'Mora is a ghost. She was a druid priestess and she has been trying to speak to me.' His face had gone white, his eyes narrowed with shock. She didn't notice. 'She is a healer. Yes, a healer, Kier. And what is more she was a friend of Jesus. She loved him. He was a student here, on the Isle of Avalon. The legends are true. He came with Joseph of Arimathaea, a trader who came to pick up cargoes of tin and lead round the coast here, and he studied with the druids and he healed the sick and I have seen him. Watched him at work. And this church is one of the most sacred places in the whole of England and you have walked in here with your petty jealousy and anger and your puritan ignorance and you have spoiled everything!'

He was silent for a moment, staring at her. When at last he spoke it was just two words. 'Oh, Abi.'

'Yes, oh Abi!' Ducking away from him she threw herself into the aisle near the pulpit, and turned to face him. 'Go away, Kier.'

'You poor child. You are completely deluded.' He took a step back away from her. 'It is far worse than I thought. Far worse.' He paused again. 'Have you told Ben about this delusion?'

'It is not a delusion.' She was so furious she could barely speak. 'Yes, I've told Ben about Mora. She has been seen around here for hundreds of years by generations of his family. She has a story she needs to tell, about Jesus, Kier, and she has been trying to find someone who can understand her. Someone who will listen.'

'And that person is you.' His voice was flat.

'Yes, that person is me.'

'I see.' He sighed. 'OK. I can see why you were angry with me for interrupting you. I'm sorry.' He glanced round the church with a shiver. 'I take it she isn't here any more.'

'No, she's gone.'

'I saw the ghosts at St Hugh's, you know.' He shook his head. 'I've always seen ghosts. They terrify me. They are evil. They take you over. I wanted you to help me stop them, but you made them worse.' His voice was shaking. 'Can we pray together, Abi? Then I'll go.'

She hesitated, her anger short-circuited by his sudden capitulation. What harm could it do to pray? With a nod of her head she relaxed visibly. 'All right.'

He walked past her to the altar step and turning beckoned her to come and stand beside him. He gave her a brief smile, then he turned to face the window, staring up at the crucified Christ. The sun was shining directly in, highlighting the colours. The face of the man on the cross was inscrutable. 'Dear Lord,' he murmured. 'Bless us and hold us in your hand. Especially look with mercy on your servant, Abi, and cast from her the devil, Mora, and all her illusions –'

'No!' Abi turned on him once more. 'How dare you!'

Kier was ready for her. He grabbed her arm and twisted it behind her. 'I'm sorry, Abi, I truly am. But I have to do this. Kneel down.'

'No!'

'Yes!' He was forcing her to her knees on the step. With her arm held so painfully behind her back, Abi gave in and subsided. He could hold her easily now with one hand. She couldn't move. She watched in real fear as he groped in his pocket and produced a small bottle. 'This is holy water, Abi. It will remove her. Don't be afraid, my dear. In a moment it will all be over.' He looked up at the window again, addressing the man on the cross. 'Lord, be with us here in this place and help me reclaim it for you. Begone from this place, every evil haunting and phantasm; depart for ever, every unclean spirit –'

'No! Kier, stop! You don't know what you are doing. Don't be so stupid!' Abi's protest was cut short as he gave a small vicious jerk on her wrist, forcing it up between her shoulder blades. Her shoulder was agony.

Flipping the stopper out of the bottle with his thumb he held it over her head. 'Almighty God, your nature is always to have mercy and to forgive: loose this your servant from every bond of evil and free her from all her sins. I ask this though Jesus Christ our Lord, Amen.' He was sprinkling the water over her hair, she could feel it, warm from his pocket. Splashes of it fell on the step where she was kneeling. The sun had gone in and the window in front of them had lost its colour. He waited for a full minute, as though expecting something to happen, then he released her arm. She fell forward, trying not to sob out loud as she cradled her shoulder in her other hand. Kier was watching her closely.

'There,' he said at last. 'Now you will be safe. Pray, Abi. Ask for God's forgiveness and protection.' He turned away and walked back down the aisle. Near the door he stopped and pulled out his mobile phone. As Abi staggered to her feet and turned to look after him she heard him speaking urgently. 'Ben? It's Kier Scott. Can you come at once? I'm in St Mary's Church. Abi is here. I've prayed with her and cast out this demon who has been possessing her, but it would be good to have you here for back up.' He flipped the phone shut and put it back in his pocket. Then he went to sit down at the back of the church.

Abi sank onto the altar step. She had begun to tremble all over.

Lugging her suitcase up the steps after her, Athena inserted her key in the door and pushed it open. She was exhausted. The last couple of days had been hell. Funerals were never good, but this one had been particularly bad. The service, if that was the word, had been held at the West London Crematorium. It had been arranged by Tim's sisters. She had never got on with them or they with her. They had shaken hands with her, tight-lipped, when she arrived and then turned away to go into the chapel which was fairly full. Apart from them, every person there was a stranger. How could she have so completely lost touch with him? Their parting had not been acrimonious. Sad, yes. Regretful, even cross. But the anger had been fleeting and directed at circumstances and belief systems, not at one another. She turned into a row at the back and sat down. The order of service was bleak. Two hymns. A prayer. An address. The man who gave the address did not seem to have known him at all. He certainly hadn't known the Tim she remembered from the past. The funny, energetic, artistic, musical man who had wooed her and lured her away. She expected to hear some wonderful music blasting round the chapel. Some of Tim's own recordings; harpsichord music, a symphony, piano. Anything. All they got was a recorded placebo on an organ.

She wanted to leap up and tell them what kind of man he had been but she didn't. She sat quietly and looked at the pine coffin with its wreath of chrysanthemums and wished she had thought to bring some flowers herself. Her own farewell would have to be private, somewhere only Tim could hear her.

She had spent a second day in London, then a sleepless night with a long-suffering friend who had agreed to put her up in exchange for a visit to Somerset the following spring and she had set off for home at six a.m. She needed tea and breakfast, a shower and bed. Dropping the case in the hall she walked into the kitchen and stopped dead. Justin was sitting at the table reading a newspaper. At his elbow she saw he had found her percolator and the pack of coffee she kept for visitors. 'What the hell are you doing here?'

'Waiting for you.' He folded the newspaper and set it down. 'Where have you been?'

'None of your business. You get out now.' She paused. 'How did you get in, anyway?'

He raised an eyebrow. 'And how nice to see you too.'

'Justin, I am very tired. I have just had a long drive. I am in no mood to mess about.'

'OK.' He gave her an appraising look. 'I'm sorry. I asked Bella for the spare key. Don't blame her – I charmed it out of her.' He gave her his best heart-warming smile. 'I knew you'd be back soon or you would have asked her to come and water your plants.' He glanced out of the window where a hanging basket was gently swinging to and fro in the breeze. 'And I need to ask you something. Just answer me this one question, then I shall go. Why did you tell Abi Rutherford that I had killed someone?'

'Because it's the truth.' She held his gaze.

'You know it's not.'

'You claimed you could help my sister. You reassured her. You drew her into your stupid belief system. You told her not to bother with doctors. You convinced her she could get well without the help of orthodox medicine so she cancelled that last operation. She refused chemo. And she died. And that was your fault!' There was a sob in her throat.

He nodded slowly. 'She made her own choices, Athena. All I did was show her that she had choices. You know as well as I do that surgery would not have helped her in the long run. Her family, and that includes you, were desperate to do something, anything, to keep her with you and that was understandable, but you were thinking of yourselves, not of her. This way, she had a few months at home, happy and positive months, and she was in a position to say her farewells with dignity. It was what she wanted.'

Athena slumped down into the chair opposite him. 'She would have still been here. She would have been alive now.'

'No, Athena, she wouldn't.'

He reached up to the shelf for a mug and poured her a cup of coffee from the percolator beside him. 'Drink this. Calm down. Think about it. I was very fond of Sunny. I wouldn't have done anything to hurt her, not in a million years.'

She reached for the mug and took a sip. She winced at its bitterness. 'I've just been to Tim's funeral.' She changed the subject abruptly.

'I heard he had gone. I'm sorry.'

'I don't even know where he died. His sisters had arranged the most god-awful cremation.' Her eyes filled with tears.

'You can do something for him here. That's what he would like. He always loved you, Athena.'

'Did he?' She looked up at him. 'How do you know?'

'Because I do.' He gave a slow smile. 'Believe me.'

'You're always so damn certain about these things.'

'Some things, yes.'

'I'll tell Abi I was wrong to say that about you.'

'I wish you would. She is in deep trouble and I want to help her. It's not very reassuring to be told that the man who can set you on the right path is the next best thing to Dr Crippin.'

She gave a watery grin. 'Sorry.' She stood up and went to throw her coffee down the sink and rinsed the mug under the tap. Switching on the kettle she reached for a tin of herbal teabags instead. 'You think she is in real trouble?'

'She is very sensitive. In every sense of the word.' He took a sip of his own coffee. She watched for him to grimace, but he appeared to enjoy every mouthful. She couldn't believe that someone who claimed to be spiritually advanced, a druid and a shaman, could allow anything so bitter and strong and filthy to pass his lips. 'It's really strange,' he went on thoughtfully. 'As a priest she should have been given the tools to deal with the

298

situation which has arisen, but either she wasn't, or she doesn't have the experience, or the right training.' He paused. 'And she's too inhibited. On the one side by the church and on the other, so Cal tells me, by a formidable bully of a father. She needs instruction.'

'And you can help her.'

He nodded.

'By destroying her Christian faith.'

'No.' He looked up sharply. 'Absolutely not.'

'Then how? What on earth can you do to help a Christian?'

He smiled at her. 'I'll think of something.' He stood up. 'In fact I might go back there now.' He leaned forward and gently touched her cheek with the back of his hand. 'Go safely, Athena. If you need me, you know where I am.'

Neither Abi nor Kier spoke, each sat sunk in their own thoughts as the minutes ticked by. The church felt very empty. Abi could feel the desolation. It was as if the heart of the place had been ripped out. She could still see the spots of water on the stone floor. How could he have used holy water against her? Against Mora. Against Jesus himself. It was crazy. And wrong. So wrong. When the door latch clicked up and the door swung open she didn't move.

Kier stood up. 'Ben, at last!'

Ben came in, shaking raindrops from his jacket and looked round, seeing Abi still sitting on the altar step. She didn't move or greet him. 'What's happened?' He swung to face Kier. He was speaking in a whisper.

'I performed a minor exorcism.' Kier straightened his shoulders. 'Nothing heavy. Prayer and holy water. To get rid of this presence that's been haunting her. It worked well I think.'

'You think,' Ben echoed. 'Wait here.' He pointed back at the seat and Kier sat down.

Ben walked towards Abi, studying her demeanour. She still hadn't looked up. 'Abi? Are you all right?' He paused beside her. 'What happened?'

'Didn't he tell you? He assaulted me! He twisted my arm. And he splashed me with holy water and bade Mora begone. He tried to exorcise the church. The church, Ben!' At last she looked up.

He saw fury and despair in her eyes in equal measure. 'This special, beautiful, sacred place. He tried to exorcise it.'

Ben sighed. He shouldn't have touched her. 'Prayers and holy water will harm no-one unless they are evil, Abi, you know that.'

'But she's gone! She knew he meant her harm. He banished her. Just as we were going to talk.' She was suddenly aware that Kier had tiptoed up the aisle behind them.

'Did she tell you that this fiend, Mora, was a druid priestess, Ben? And did she tell you that Mora claimed to have made love to Our Lord Jesus Christ!' Kier's voice was heavy with disgust.

Ben looked at Abi sharply. 'You told him about your theory that Jesus himself was here?'

'It was a mistake. I shouldn't have.' She was still sitting on the step, her arms round her knees. Then she looked up again. 'And I never said Mora made love to him. She was in love with him, that is a very different matter.'

Ben was struck dumb for a moment. He looked at each of them in turn, then he shook his head. 'You shouldn't have told anyone.'

'I know.' She buried her face in her arms. 'And Kier has made it seem dirty and evil and heretical.'

'It is heretical, Abi,' Kier put in. 'She needs care, Ben,' he went on. 'I think she's having some sort of nervous breakdown. This is the result of the strain she's been under. You should have taken this whole episode more seriously. You've breached your role as her spiritual mentor. This has escalated out of all control now and we have to act at once. To save her.'

Abi looked up. 'I've had enough of this.'

Ben hesitated. He looked from one to the other and shook his head. 'I think we should go back to the house,' he said at last. 'Come on Abi, let me give you a hand.' He held his hand out to help her up from the step.

She ignored it. 'I want Kier to leave.'

Ben looked up at Kier. 'She's right. I think you should go. Leave this to me.'

'I left it to you last time,' Kier retorted. 'And look what's happened. You did nothing!'

'Abi and I have been working on all this slowly,' Ben said patiently. 'There is no cause to be dramatic. Abi's experiences need to be explored and prayed about and that's what we have been doing. Please go. Your presence can only exacerbate matters.'

Kier's face reddened in anger. 'It seems to me I am the only person who cares about her!'

'Go away, Kier!' Abi scrambled to her feet. 'For God's sake! How many times? You don't understand me. You don't understand what is happening to me. Your reactions to this whole thing are archaic. I came down here to get away from you!'

'Go, Kier!' Ben said forcibly before the other man had a chance to react. 'Go now.'

Kier shook his head. 'My conscience won't let me. I have to deal with this. You're obviously not going to. "Your enemy the devil walketh about, as a roaring lion, seeking whom he may devour." Don't you see it, man! In God's name, open your eyes.'

Behind them the door opened. For a second none of them turned round, then Kier looked up. His eyes widened and Abi saw the skin over his cheekbones blanch.

'What have we here? A gathering of vicars. Does that make a synod?' Justin's voice rang out with authority as he walked slowly towards them up the aisle, sweeping his rain-soaked hair back from his eyes with his hand. He gazed round, hastily taking in the situation. 'You don't look happy, Abi.'

'I'm not. I want Kier to leave.'

'Why doesn't that surprise me?' Justin gave a grim smile. 'And Ben?'

'Ben is fine,' his brother retorted. 'But he would also like Kier to leave.' He turned to Kier. 'If you would be so kind.'

Kier stared from one to other of the men, his eyes wild. 'No!'

'It is strange how we seem to have been in this situation before,' Justin said calmly. 'You seem to make a habit of being where you are not wanted, my friend. I think it would be as well if you left. I would be sorry to have to use force in a house of God.'

'You don't believe in God!' Kier spluttered.

'My beliefs or lack of them are not the issue here.' Justin did not raise his voice. 'This is a Christian church and you are a Christian priest and you have been asked to leave. I think it behoves you to do so. And if you don't go in the next ten seconds I shall throw you out.'

Kier looked at Ben. 'Are you going to let him talk to me like that? A foul heathen!'

'One. Two.'

'He's my brother.' Ben shrugged. 'We don't talk theology much, but he seems to have reiterated what Abi and I have been saying. I would have found it much harder than Just to resort to violence in a church, but I might have done so had he not appeared.'

'Five. Six. Seven –' Justin said slowly.

'Right. I'm going. And I'm going to phone the bishop as soon as I'm out of here,' Kier said, already moving towards the door. 'This is not the end of the matter. Abi has to be saved. If neither of you cares, then I am going to have to do it myself!'

They watched as he gained the door and went out, banging it behind him.

Abi subsided onto the step again. 'He tried to exorcise the church,' she said to Justin. 'He tried to banish Mora.' Her voice was shaking.

Justin glanced round slowly. 'I can feel the rage in here. The place is vibrating with anger and fear. If I take Abi back to the house, Ben, will you pray to settle the church?' He held out his hand to Abi.

Unsteadily she climbed to her feet. She stared round. The place seemed to be full of an angry mist.

'Who is Cynan?' Justin asked suddenly.

Abi stared at him, then she turned slowly, glancing round the church. 'Is he here?'

Justin nodded. 'He is angry and confused and afraid for Mora.'

Abi stared at him. 'Where? Where is he? I can't see him.'

'He comes here to be alone. Here on the hill top. In his time there is no building here. This is a sacred place. He prays here, just as you do. And he senses that it has been desecrated.' He paused for a moment. 'Kier's obsession has allowed something very powerful to worm its way into his soul. Not love, though I'm sure he feels he loves you, Abi. I'm afraid it is something much more sinister. Come with me. He held out his hand. 'Leave Ben to sort this out here. We will speak to Cynan outside.'

He took her hand and led her up the aisle towards the door. She stopped abruptly. 'Suppose Kier hasn't gone?'

'He has.' Justin didn't seem to have any doubts on the matter. With a glance at his face Abi meekly followed him out into the rain.

The churchyard was deserted. She glanced round in relief. 'I had no idea he had followed me in there.'

Justin shrugged. 'Forget him for now. We have to speak to Cynan.'

302

'How? I've left the stone –'

'We don't need the stone.' He stood for a moment in silence, staring round, then he set off at a brisk walk towards the gate. 'Follow me.'

Abi glanced behind her towards the church door. There was no sound from inside. She wondered what Ben was doing. More holy water, or just prayers to try and settle the jangling echoes? After a second's hesitation she followed Justin out of the gate and down the steep path towards the orchard.

So, there wouldn't be another winter here, to stand and watch the frost-sparkled lacework on the graceful branches of the willow, the bright icicles on the bare angles of the old apple trees, the splintered ice out on the shallow immovable waters, their spears of reed and sedge rigid with cold. He shrugged the robe more comfortably onto his thin shoulders and turned full circle, looking out across the distances. God's world, at every season, had its beauty and its infinite mystery.

16

Cynan was standing looking out across the water of the lake. The brisk wind had made it choppy. He could see the reeds thrashing to and fro, the yellowed leaves on the willows rustling back and forth and there in the distance he saw the dugout canoe with Romanus paddling in the stern. Yeshua had taken the other paddle and between them Mora sat low in the boat, cradling her bag of herbs. He narrowed his eyes. She had gone without a backwards glance. He shook his head. He could feel danger crackling in the air around them, like summer lightning on a humid, luminous night. He closed his eyes and tried to pray, but he wasn't calm enough; he couldn't reach deep into himself to touch the silent core of his being from where he could speak to his gods. He opened his eyes again. They were further away now, almost too far to recognise, heading for the landing point below Gaius's fields. Glancing round he saw another boat pulled up among the reeds. He paused for only a second before he ran to it and began to push it into the water. At least he could be there. At least if they needed him, he could help.

Janet Cavendish parked her car beside Cal's in front of Woodley Manor and climbed out. The front door opened and the two dogs came hurtling out, followed by Cal. 'Thanks for coming over.' She leaned forward to kiss her sister-in-law's cheek.

Janet looked at her in concern. The urgent message had been totally unexpected. As a rule the two of them rubbed along in a state of happy incomprehension. They came, as Janet often thought, from two different worlds; two different planets. All they had in common was the surname and the two brothers. When they met it was always to sort out something one or the other of them felt could not be done alone. A Cavendish problem. Both of them realised that at some level that joined them at the hip. If a phone call came, it meant drop everything and listen.

Cal led the way into the kitchen, settled Janet into a chair and put on the kettle. The two dogs threw themselves down in front of the fire recognising the fact that this was obviously going to be a conference. No prospect of an imminent walk, then.

'We have to be prepared to do something about Kieran Scott,' Janet said without preamble. 'And soon.'

Cal was spooning coffee into the percolator. 'Horrid man.'

'More than horrid, Cal. Dangerous.'

Cal turned and glanced at her. A word like dangerous from Janet was serious.

'He rang earlier and called Ben, did you know?'

Cal shook her head.

'He was in St Mary's with Abi. Ben took off like a scalded cat. I've never seen him look so worried.'

Cal pursed her lips. 'Wretched man. Why can't he leave Abi alone?'

'He's obsessed, that's why. Dangerously obsessed.' Janet took the cup of coffee, sipped it and winced as it burned her mouth. 'I've seen men like this before, Cal. Fundamentalist; absolutely convinced he is right and that everything he is doing is for God. I know Ben has tried to calm him down, and will be trying to calm him down as we speak, but he won't recognise any possibility that he could be wrong or that Abi's views and feelings are the remotest bit relevant. I gather she is troubled too, and she seems to be quite a feisty lady. The combination could be disastrous. The problem is that Ben is such a gentle, good man. He believes that prayer and reason can sort out anything.' She shrugged and shook her head, knowing instinctively that Cal would recognise that this was probably not a realistic outcome.

Janet looked round suddenly. 'Where is Mat?'

'He had to go back to Taunton to collect some papers.'

Janet looked relieved. On the balance of things this was probably just as well. Mat was a bit of a wild card. And if anyone mentioned Justin in front of him . . . She glanced back at Cal. 'Did you know that Ben called Justin in?'

Cal nodded. 'Abi told me.'

'That implies that Ben feels out of his depth.' She sighed.

'What are you afraid of, Jan?' Cal sat down, warming her hands around her mug. 'Do you think Kier could be violent?'

Janet nodded. 'Oh yes. I've seen that expression in men's eyes before. He doesn't rate Ben at all. He thinks he knows more, is holier, is "chosen", is Abi's only hope. All that and more. And my dear sweet husband will have walked over to the church like an innocent to the slaughter.'

Cal stood up. 'Then let's go over there now.'

Janet gathered up her handbag. 'I've been thinking what to do. We have to be careful. If we rush in, we could exacerbate things. I don't think Kier is armed or anything like that. He's not going to shoot anyone. He is more likely to be hurling thunderbolts. Bible quotes. Holy water. Plus the whole John Knox bit. Blasting the monstrous regiment of women. That may or may not hurt Abi. I suspect she has inured herself against the Rev Scott to a certain extent, but it will shock Ben. It will be awful for him. I don't know if he can cope.'

Cal was astonished to see tears in Janet's eyes suddenly. She leaned forward. 'Ben is tougher than you think, Jan. He'll cope.'

'Will he?'

'He's a senior churchman. He can deal with the likes of Kieran Scott. It's Abi I'm afraid for. You're right, she knows what to expect from Kier, but she's vulnerable at the moment. She is fighting her own demons. She doesn't need him putting the knife in and twisting the blade.'

The two women looked at each other. 'OK. You're right. Let's go. But we'll approach quietly and see what's happening, OK?'

They put down their mugs and reached for their coats. The dogs stood up eagerly. Cal looked at them, thought for a moment, then nodded and opened the door. The dogs had adored Abi from the first moment they met her. If there was any trouble, she knew who the dogs would ally with.

The air was full of the rushing of wind, splatters of raindrops from the speeding clouds, shadows racing across the ground from the west. The yew trees were hissing gently, guarding the path as the two women crept nearer to the church. Janet gripped the door handle with both hands and began to turn it as quietly as she could. The door creaked as it opened a crack. They held their breath and listened. There was no sound from inside the building. She pushed the door open and they stood looking in.

Ben was standing in front of the altar, staring up at the window. He turned as he heard them and they both saw the anxiety in his face. When he recognised them he broke into a smile. 'Janet! Cal! What are you doing here?' He had lit the candles on the altar and they flickered and streamed in the draft from the open door.

'We came to see if you were all right?' Cal called the dogs back sharply as they ran up the aisle and they came back to heel and sat down beside her, looking sheepish. 'Where are Abi and Kier? What happened?'

Ben gave a rueful smile. 'Ah, I see. You've come to pick up the pieces. Well I'm pleased to say no blood was spilled.' He shook his head. 'It was pretty bad though. Just turned up and saved the day.'

'Justin?' Cal echoed. She looked round. 'Where is he?'

'Kier left rather abruptly and I fear probably temporarily. I was afraid that that was him when you came in just now. Just has taken Abi out into the orchard to try and sort out her ghosts.' He shook his head. 'I stayed in here to pray. The atmosphere was appalling.'

'It's all right now,' Cal said. 'Isn't it?'

He shrugged. 'Better than it was. I should have left the door open. A technical point, but an important one. I had closed it against Kier, but it allowed some of the anger to remain trapped. But now you're here, with the dogs,' he smiled down at the animals fondly, 'it is better.'

'We came through the orchard,' Janet said suddenly. 'We didn't see anyone there.'

They looked at one another. 'It doesn't mean anything bad has happened,' Ben said reassuringly. 'Just will look after her. I'm sure he could defeat Kieran if it came to blows. He is younger and I suspect a lot fitter.'

'He too is a priest, Ben,' Cal said quietly. 'He isn't a man of violence.'

Ben smiled wryly. 'That description applies to Kier as well, my dear. Or at least it should.' He sighed. 'But we must try and find them. Are those dogs of yours any good at tracking?'

Cynan pushed the dugout into the reeds and jumped out. He glanced round. There was no sign of anyone. The reed beds swayed in the wind; a sheet of ripples spread swiftly across the water behind him and was gone. He frowned. He could hear birds calling from the osiers on the bank; from somewhere nearby he heard the bark of a deer. He reached back into the boat for his staff, then he turned and began to walk steadily up the track towards the house.

'I can see him,' Justin whispered. 'He is a brave man.'

'He's in love with Mora,' Abi breathed. They were standing on the edge of the field, by one of the deep straight drainage ditches which had so long ago taken the water from the lake over which Cynan had paddled. He strode past them, his eyes on the track ahead, his sandaled feet padding softly over the muddy grass, then he paused and looked round. They saw his knuckles whiten on the wood of his staff.

'He can feel us,' Justin said quietly. 'We are very close.'

Abi held her breath.

Cynan stood still for several seconds, then he set off once more, but they could see he was wary, his eyes flicking left and right towards the undergrowth. After a few more paces he stopped again and turned back, this time looking straight at them. He fumbled at his waist and with a sharp irrational jolt of fear Abi saw him draw a knife. So he was armed after all.

'Can he see us?' she murmured.

Justin nodded. 'I think so. Wait here. Don't move. I will speak to him.'

She watched as he took one careful step forward. He paused, then he took another. Cynan frowned. He was peering round now as though trying to see through a mist. 'Greetings, my friend.' Justin spoke out loud at last.

Abi saw the other man's fist tighten over the handle of his knife.

'You know there is danger up there at the homestead,' Justin went on slowly. 'We are here to help if we can.'

'He can't understand what you are saying,' Abi whispered.

'He can. Just as you could understand them,' Justin retorted. 'The Roman has tricked his nephew,' he went on, turning back to Cynan. 'The man lies in wait to kill Yeshua and Mora.'

Cynan backed away a few steps, looking increasingly confused. While holding the knife out in front of him with one hand, he rubbed his eyes with the back of the other.

'Listen to me, my friend. Beware. Listen to your heart. You already suspect treachery. You must hurry to help them. Mora needs you.'

'Mora!' Kier's voice ripped through the sound of the hissing reeds. 'Again, Mora! The witch's goddess! Begone, you foul fiend!' He was standing so close to them Abi couldn't believe they hadn't seen him coming. He had raised his hand and he made the sign of the cross in front of them, then he stretched forward and grabbed Abi's wrist. 'Come with me. I can't let you listen to this pagan mumbo jumbo. You have to be saved!' He sounded desperate as he dragged her towards him and for a moment she felt herself fall off balance, unable to pull away.

'Let her go, you fool.' Justin recovered himself fast. Behind them Cynan had disappeared into the mist. The sun reflected on the water of the ditch and the wind shook the leaves on the pollarded willow nearby.

'Let me go!' Abi tried to wrench herself free. 'You are insane, Kier! Help Cynan,' she shouted at Justin. 'Don't be distracted. Please, help him.' She was struggling hard now, trying to wrench her wrist away from his grasp but Kier was too strong for her. Slowly and inexorably he was dragging her away from the ditch and towards the hedge behind which was the road.

The two dogs were on them before they realised what was happening, barking wildly as they raced across the field. Abruptly Kier released her. He swore under his breath as the two women appeared by the gate. 'Don't think this is the last of it!' he muttered to Abi. Turning, he walked swiftly down the field away from them.

'Leave him,' Justin called. She wasn't sure if he was speaking to her or to the dogs. Rubbing her wrist, Abi saw Cal and Janet hurrying towards them.

'What was he doing!' Cal called as soon as she was close enough. 'For goodness sake, Abi, are you all right?'

'I'm fine.' Abi shook her head angrily. 'Ignore him.' She spun round to Justin. 'What happened?'

Justin shook his head. 'He's gone. I've lost him.'

'Who's gone?' Cal asked, puzzled.

Justin gave a dry laugh. 'A visitor from the past, Cal. Don't worry about it.'

'There was a ghost. Here?'

'There are ghosts everywhere, you know that as well as I do,'

Justin retorted. He went over to Abi and took her arm. 'Let me see that wrist. He hasn't broken it, has he?'

She winced. 'It's just painful.'

'Do you want us to call the police? The man is a menace,' Janet put in as Justin gently probed the back of Abi's hand.

'No. I just want to keep away from him!' Abi pulled her hand away. 'Sorry, that hurts. It's not broken! I'll be fine.' She stared round. 'Where has Kier gone?'

'Back to the road,' Janet said. 'His car is parked up there in a lay-by. We saw it.'

'You have to tell the police, Abi,' Cal went on. 'This has gone on long enough.'

Abi shook her head. 'We just need to get on with what we were doing. If he's gone, then that's fine. Please, I'm sorry, but this is important.'

'No Abi,' Justin said. 'It's over. We were there at a particular moment in time. It's gone. Time moves on. The past waits for no-one. Whatever happened, happened.'

'No!' She looked at him in despair. 'No, we can help, I know we can.'

He looked back at her resolutely. 'Not now. It's over.'

'But –'

'No, Abi. I'm sorry.'

'But there will be another chance?'

'There might.' He watched her gravely. 'What you have to do is learn to observe and listen and then you will know when you can communicate with them. But for now you will have to go back to being a passive observer. I'm sorry, but that is the way it is. It's to do with the tides.' He gave her a rueful smile. 'Not just the tides in the sea, but the tides out there,' he gestured up towards the sky. 'Moon, sun, stars, atmosphere, a thousand different possibilities have to coincide to make it happen.'

'And they coincided just now?' She was staring at him.

'For a brief moment, yes.'

'What a load of bull, Justin!' Cal said. 'Leave the poor girl alone. She's been through enough. Isn't it sufficient that she can see these poor bloody ghosts without you trying to turn the whole thing into some sort of mystical time warp fest!'

Justin shook his head in despair. 'You of all people should understand, Cal.'

313

'No. That's enough. She's a vicar, for goodness sake.'

'And what has that to do with anything?' Justin said. 'Can't vicars understand quantum physics?'

Abi gave a watery smile. 'No, to be honest they can't. At least this one can't. I just wanted to help Mora.'

'And maybe you have.' Justin put his arm round her shoulder. 'Already you have changed what was and what was to be. You have shaken the waves of time. Who knows, Cynan may have heard us. He may have hurried up the hill a little faster. He may have looked out a little more carefully and he may have warned her what was going to happen.'

She looked up at him. 'You really believe we can alter the past?' His arm around her was firm and comforting. Without realising it she had relaxed against him.

He shrugged. 'I believe in all possibilities.' He released her abruptly and turned to Cal. 'I need to go back to talk to Ben. Will you take care of her, Cal? If you need me, ring me on my mobile.' He turned back to Abi. 'You, look after yourself and keep away from that maniac.'

Before any of them could speak Justin was striding away across the field and heading back towards the gate.

Abi stared after him, overwhelmed by a sudden sense of loss.

At the edge of the copse Romanus paused and hesitated. 'Wait,' he said anxiously.

'What is it?' Mora followed him into the shelter of the black-thorn scrub which bordered the track. Her nerves were at breaking point. 'Did you hear something?' All around them trees and bushes seemed to cluster together to make hiding places; the birds were wary, she could sense it. Something was wrong.

Romanus shook his head. 'Let me go ahead and make sure he's gone.'

She scanned his face. 'You said you were sure.'

'And I am. It's just –' He was pale, his eyes darting round them anxiously.

She looked at Yeshua. 'We should go back.'

He shook his head. 'Not when we have come so far. I sense no danger here. Not yet.'

'Not yet?' Her voice rose to a squeak.

314

He smiled. 'We are here for Petra, Mora. She needs to see us.'

She looked at him doubtfully, then back at Romanus. 'Go, then. Quickly. Make sure your uncle isn't there.'

Romanus was back within a short space of time. He was smiling. 'Sorcha saw him go,' he said. 'She watched him go a long way down the track. It's quite safe. This way.'

By the time they got there Petra was lying by the fire, propped against several cushions. Her hair had been brushed and the rugs covering her shaken and straightened. Sorcha and Lydia were standing beside her, their faces anxious as they waited for the visitors. Romanus remained in the doorway as Mora led the way in.

Yeshua went straight to Petra and knelt beside her. 'You mustn't be afraid. I'm here to help you.' He laid his hand on her forehead. She was burning with fever, her eyes bright, the fingers of the hand he took in his were swollen and red. He smiled gently. 'Do you believe that I can help you, Petra?'

She nodded shyly.

'Then come. Stand up.'

Behind him Lydia drew in a quick breath. 'She can't. She's in too much pain.'

Yeshua looked up at her. 'You must have faith, too. God can heal everything and everyone.' He turned back to Petra. 'Stand up, my child. Your pain has gone.'

She held his gaze for a long minute, her eyes full of hope, then slowly she reached down and pushed back the rugs. Carefully she swung her legs off the low couch and rose to her feet. She stood there for several seconds, breathing carefully, not moving. Yeshua stood up too and held out his hands. 'Come. Walk to me. It won't hurt.'

There wasn't a sound in the room. The eyes of the three women were fixed on Petra as she took first one step then another. She reached out her hands towards him uncertainly and then slowly she began to smile. 'It doesn't hurt any more!'

He smiled. 'Good. Come, try a few more steps.' He backed away from her, slowly encouraging her to move forward.

'It doesn't. It doesn't hurt!' Her voice rose in delight.

Mora stared at her, then at Yeshua. She could see the child's hands. The swollen joints had subsided. The pain had left the girl's face. She looked at Yeshua and he met her eye with a grave smile. 'You've cured her,' she whispered.

315

'God cured her,' he said.

Lydia was staring at him in awe. Stepping forward she took his hand in both of hers. 'How can I thank you?'

'By thanking God, and then by being happy with your daughter. She has suffered too long. She needs to learn how to have fun; to dance, to run like other children.' He looked across at Sorcha. 'You mustn't be afraid.'

Sorcha blushed scarlet. 'I've never seen anything like that before. Mora has been trying for so long.'

'Mora is a brilliant healer,' Yeshua said quietly. 'She is the best and you must use her medicines and her help whenever you need it.'

'And you'll show her how to do whatever it was you did just now?'

Yeshua glanced at Mora. 'I'll show her.'

Silently Mora walked over to Petra and took her hands in her own. The heat had gone. The hands, the wrists were cool to her touch. She looked up at Petra's face and smiled. 'You won't need me again. I'm so pleased.' She looked at Yeshua. 'Another miracle?' She too was suddenly in awe of him. 'This is your god?'

He nodded. 'My father.'

There was a long silence. They were all looking at him. Suddenly he shook his head. 'Come! Petra needs something to eat. We all do, then Mora and I must return to the island. We have things to talk about before I leave.'

'You're leaving?' Lydia looked distraught.

He nodded. 'I fear so. I have to return to my own country, but I shall pray for you all. I shall ask God to keep you safe.' He turned to the doorway. 'Romanus? You have kept watch well. Come in and eat with us.'

Romanus had seen what had happened from the doorway. He looked at Yeshua with something like hero worship in his eyes, but he was frightened. He shook his head. 'I must stay here and watch.'

'Because you know your uncle is coming back?' Yeshua said gently.

Romanus blushed scarlet. 'I'm afraid he might.'

'So he hasn't gone on a long journey today?'

Romanus shook his head.

'And you were prepared to allow us to walk into a trap?'

316

'Romanus?' Lydia's voice was sharp. 'Tell me that's not true!'

Romanus shrugged miserably. 'Uncle Flavius wanted Petra to get better so he went out. He knew Yeshua wouldn't come if it wasn't safe.'

'He knew Yeshua was coming here?'

Romanus glanced from one to the other of them nervously. He was beginning to look like a trapped animal. 'He guessed.'

'He didn't guess. He had sent you to fetch him!'

Romanus nodded uncomfortably. Lydia looked at Yeshua, her face white. 'My son has betrayed you!'

Yeshua shook his head. 'It's not his fault. Don't blame him. Your brother-in-law is a clever and forceful man. He will have used arguments a boy of Romanus's age could not have countered. Blackmail. Bribery. Threats.' He glanced at Romanus and smiled. 'The important thing is that you have told us now. Mora and I can leave quickly and get home –'

'No!' Romanus shook his head. 'You don't understand. He's lying in wait for you. He promised me he wouldn't hurt Mora but he means to kill you. He needed to get you off the island. He didn't want any witnesses to what he was going to do –' He broke off in horror, looking at Mora.

'So, finally you see the truth,' Sorcha put in. 'You stupid boy! You think he would let Mora live?'

Romanus was speechless. Suddenly there were tears in his eyes.

'We'll give you an escort back to the lake,' Lydia said suddenly. 'The men on the farm can go with you. And we can go too. If there are enough of us he can't do anything. Once you are there you are safe.'

'Until he tries to leave,' Sorcha put in.

Yeshua shook his head. 'My father will protect us.' He went over to Romanus and put his hand on the boy's shoulder. 'You did right to tell us. We'll go now. There is still time to get to the lake before your uncle returns. God bless you. Look after your sister and your mother.' He ducked out into the sunshine. Mora followed him. The others stayed where they were in silence.

'Are you sure he won't come back 'til later?' Mora whispered as they headed towards the gate.

Yeshua grinned at her. 'Not entirely. But I don't want to put them all in danger. The man is a vengeful bully by nature. He won't hesitate to hurt people who get in his way. That little family have suffered enough. We have been forewarned. That gives us an advantage, and God is with us.' He caught her hand. 'This way. We won't use the track. We'll cut down through the wood. Listen to your friends the birds. They will warn us if there is someone about.'

The path down through the wood was steep. The carpet of dead leaves rustled beneath their feet as they made their way cautiously back towards the place where they had left the boat. 'Romanus isn't coming,' Mora whispered. 'We'll have to paddle the boat ourselves.'

He grinned at her. 'So, you think that's a problem?'

She shook her head. 'What you did for Petra,' she said after a few more paces, 'that was a miracle. I have tried so hard for so long to make her better.'

'That was God's power working through me,' he said slowly. He paused and they stopped, looking at each other. He looked troubled. 'This was another sign that my work in this country is done, Mora. I have prayed so often about this. I am needed in my own country. It is there my teaching is to be done. Others will come after me, to spread the word across the whole world.' He shook his head. 'I feel the weight of it all on my shoulders. Sometimes I think I see what is to come, then the future is once more shrouded in mist and I know I am not supposed to know yet. I'm not strong enough yet. I haven't studied enough yet.'

She moved closer to him and put her hands on his shoulders, resting her head against his chest. 'I have seen your future in the sacred spring.'

He frowned. 'Tell me?'

She clung to him. 'I can't.'

'Mora?'

It was a moment before she looked up to meet his gaze. She shook her head.

He nodded slowly. 'I think I know.'

'You will one day be the most famous man of all time,' she whispered.

He smiled. 'At least I escape the clutches of Flavius.'

She swallowed. 'For now.'

'And you. Did you see the future for yourself?'

She pushed him away. 'Come on, we have to get down to the boat. There is no point in waiting for the light to go. It will be even easier for him to jump on us!'

318

'Mora?' He caught her hand. 'What happens to you?'

'We don't see our own destiny,' she said, with a brave attempt at a smile. 'That is kept from us by the gods!'

He frowned. 'Mora –'

'I know. Your god does not recognise our gods. Well, maybe in some things our gods know best. The gods of the rain and mist, the gods of the restless ocean, the gods of the sacred well . . .' Suddenly she was crying.

He took her hands and drew her to him, then he put his arms around her. 'Mora, my little love.'

She buried her face in his chest again and stayed there for a long time. Then at last she raised her head. 'Come on. To the boat.'

Abi was staring into the fire. The kitchen was deserted, she realised. The others had gone. Not even the dogs were there. Wearily she stood up. Had she been asleep? Was that a dream? She couldn't tell the difference sometimes between her dreams and the visions which happened when she was awake. She noticed the cup of coffee on the table. It was cold. Beside it there was a note.

Abi! Didn't want to wake you. Mat rang. His car had broken down. I've taken the dogs and gone to fetch him. Back soon. If you go over to St Mary's, Lock yourself in. Be vigilant!! C xx

Abi glanced at her watch. It was three p m. She looked up at the window as a squall of rain swept across the garden and smacked against the glass and she shivered. Part of her wanted to stay indoors, but another part wanted to go back to the church. In spite of Kier she loved it there and it was there that Mora had tried to speak to her. Besides, she wanted to see if she could sense what Ben and Justin had done.

She sighed. What if Kier's exorcism had driven Mora away? What then? She had to find out. And where was Cynan, who had been on his way to help them? She took her jacket down from the hook near the door and pulled it on. Then cautiously she opened the door. A blast of wind hit her. Leaves were racing round the garden in spirals, mini whirlwinds of scarlet and yellow. The sky was grey and heavy with bulging clouds. Trees bent and whipped before the wind, their leaves streaming out, some falling, whipped away, others hanging on in streamers of carmine and scarlet and ochre. Closing the door behind her she rammed her hands into her pockets and leaning into the wind, she walked resolutely across the garden. The place seemed deserted. She kept her eyes skinned for Kier, searching the corners and shadows behind tree trunks and bushes, turning round every so often to look behind her, refusing to give in to her insane urge to turn and run for it back to the house where she could lock herself in and build up the fire and wait there until the others came back.

The walk down through the orchard seemed steeper than usual in the face of the wind and she felt herself breathless as she reached the lych-gate. Above her, the squat grey church was huddling down behind its yews, used to the wild weather. Abi ducked into the porch, looking round. Anyone could be hiding behind those huge old trees with their impenetrable arms flung wide. The wind whistled through the foliage, tearing the flowers someone had laid on an ancient grave near the gate out of their container and whipping them away to lie at the foot of the hedge. It was as she pushed the door and heard it creak as it opened that she realised that this was where he would be hiding. Her heart seemed to stop beating for several seconds as she peered in. All was silent. 'Kier?' Her own voice seemed like an intrusion, a sacrilege as she called out, and heard the silence echo back. She went in and pulled the door to behind her, glad to be out of the wind. In here the quiet was almost shocking. She felt in her pocket for her matches – she had borrowed a box several days ago to make sure she would always be able to light the candles when she got there – and she went to the candelabra which stood near the font, lighting the six candles, throwing flickering light up into the roof beams. Only when she was completely satisfied that there was no sign of Kier did she go back to the door and draw the rusty wrought iron bolt across.

It took a long time for the atmosphere to grow still. She sat with her eyes fixed on the window as the light in the eastern sky faded, feeling her way into the silence. Ben had obviously done a good job. She could sense his prayers weaving around her, restoring the tranquillity of the place. As it grew dark she got up from her chair and walked up to the altar. She lit those candles too, then she knelt down. It was hard to voice the words of the prayer. Dear Jesus. Is it you? Are you Yeshua? Did you come here, to this peaceful place? Did you meet treachery and mayhem here as well as good and learned men? Did you meet a woman here whom you felt you could love . . . The words faded. She couldn't speak them out loud. She sensed a ripple of movement in the air above her head and looked up. Nothing. She knelt in silence, trying to still her own thoughts, listening, waiting.

It was full dark when at last she stood up. There had been no answer to her prayers, no words, no ghosts. She felt in her pocket for her torch and extinguished all the candles one by one before making her way back to the door by the wavering beam of the torch. Her hand on the bolt, she paused. Supposing he was outside, waiting for her? She switched off the torch and waited in the dark, listening. She could hear the wind roaring across the levels behind the church, moaning in the yew trees, hissing through the oaks by the lych-gate. She couldn't think how she had been unaware of it before. Cautiously she wriggled the bolt back and twisted the ring handle to lift the latch. She could feel her anger simmering again. How dare this one man intimidate her to this extent? What rights did he think he had over her? How could he be allowed to get away with stalking her to the point of making her life a misery? Well, it wasn't going to go on. Tomorrow she would go to the police and make a formal complaint. She stepped outside and pulled the door closed behind her, then, pulling the collar of her jacket up around her ears, she headed down the path towards the lych-gate.

'She's gone out!' Cal was on the phone to Ben. 'I cannot believe she would be so stupid! Well, I can actually. To the point where I left her a note telling her to lock herself in if she went over to St Mary's. And now it's dark, and I'm worried!'

'She's a stubborn woman,' Ben said ruefully. 'Huge amounts of charm and so much to give to the church, but very wilful. And now –' He stopped mid-sentence.

'And now?'

'Jesus. Here.'

'You think she has flipped?'

There was a wry laugh from the other end of the phone. 'I don't know what to think, to be honest. I have been questioning myself. Why do I find it completely OK to believe in Romans and druids and other assorted ghosts, but not My Lord? How do we know he didn't come here? He had to be somewhere in the missing years. He had the whole world to choose from and plenty of time to visit every corner of it if he so wished.'

'What's the official version?' Cal put the phone to the other ear and walked over to flip the switch on the kettle. She glanced at the clock and frowned. It had been dark for over an hour now. Mat was walking over to the church with the dogs and a large torch and the wind was getting stronger every second.

'That he studied to be a rabbi, I suppose.'

'And suddenly popped up out of nowhere to be the Messiah?' She shrugged. 'Surely someone would have noticed him getting more and more learned and charismatic over the years.'

'Perhaps they did. It's just that none of the official versions of the gospels which have come down to us tell us about it.' Ben sighed. 'She hasn't gone out in her car, I suppose?'

'No, it's still there!'

'I just hope Kier didn't come back, I genuinely fear for that man's sanity.'

She heard a muttered aside, then Ben came back on the line. 'Sorry, Cal. I've got to go. Call me, please, the second you hear anything.'

Cal sighed. She made herself a cup of instant coffee and went to sit down beside the fire, staring into the flames. If she was a druid she would be able to read the messages there, she thought idly. She would know where Abi was. She would know what had happened, and whether Mora and Jesus had made it to safety in the end.

Abruptly she put down her coffee mug and stood up again. She might not be a druid, but she knew someone who was and maybe by now he was back on the end of the phone.

'Justin, where are you?'

'I'm back home.' He sounded exhausted. 'For goodness sake, Cal, you haven't lost her again!'

'She's gone, Just. I know it's stupid but we couldn't keep her locked up. I just wondered whether she had come with you?'

There was a moment of silence the other end of the phone. 'You know she didn't. I left alone.'

'I know.' Her voice fell. 'But for all I know you might have met

322

up later. No. Silly idea. It's just that I'm so worried. Kier is still wandering around. He really scares me.'

'And my indomitable brother is . . . ?'

'Out looking for her with the dogs. He's gone over to St Mary's, just to make sure.'

'Then he will probably find her there.'

'You couldn't look into the fire and do some scrying could you?'

There was a moment's astonished silence. Then Justin laughed. 'Did I just hear you right?'

'Please, Justin. I know you can do it.'

'You think so.'

'Yes.'

There was an other chuckle. 'Ring me when you find her, Cal!'

She looked at the receiver and banged it down in exasperation. He had hung up on her.

Back in Wells, in the lounge of the pub after his meal, a coffee and a small dish containing two chocolate truffles in front of him on the low table, a local guide-book open on his knee, Kier began to gather his thoughts into some sort of a plan. The trouble was that Abi was surrounded by people who seemed to have made it their mission in life to thwart him in his desire to save her from herself. It wasn't their fault. They thought they were doing the right thing. They had believed her when she told them he was pestering her. He glanced up as someone sat down at the far end of the same low sofa, nudging the table and inadvertently slopping some of his coffee into the saucer. The man apologised profusely, offering to buy him another coffee and there were several minutes of general palaver before he sat down and allowed Kier to settle down to his own thoughts again. The room was very pleasant. A low hum of conversation from the people around him, the sweet smell of logs from the large open fire, were seductive. Reassuring. He blinked several times to keep himself awake.

He had to get Abi away from the Cavendish family and somewhere where he could speak to her, and have even half a chance of persuading her of the danger she was putting herself in. He shivered as he thought about Justin Cavendish. Before he came out, he had dug his notebook out of the bottom of his bag in the hotel bedroom and Googled Justin on the off chance. Somewhat to his surprise, there had been several entries. He scrolled though them with interest. Justin was the author of two books, one a history of local folklore, little more really than a themed guidebook. The other was a book on the ancient druids. This sounded far more academic. He looked it up on Amazon. Four and a half stars. Loads of reviews, nearly all respectful and even laudatory. The man seemed to have been attached to Oxford University at some point and he was also part-author of a book on druid philosophy with another Oxford graduate, Meryn Jones. Kier didn't bother to look that one up. He went back to Google. There he found newspaper references to the death of a young woman, Sunny Wake-Richards. She had, in the last stages of terminal cancer, left hospital to embrace various complimentary therapies, including spiritual healing. He frowned. Justin Cavendish had been called as a witness at the subsequent inquest after the family had accused various alternative practitioners of hastening her death. The police had investigated and said there was no case to answer, that Sunny had left hospital of her own free will, without coercion, but Sunny's mother had stood up in court and accused Justin of murder.

Kier raised an eyebrow. So, he had given up a lectureship at Oxford University to become a spiritual healer. There were lots of advertisements for second hand copies of his books listed, but no website, no other articles, no comments. He was about to shut the laptop when he decided he might as well look up Justin's co-author, Meryn Jones and here he struck gold. Another list of books – these druids didn't seem to be able to keep out of print these days! But far better, he found an article which had been written about Meryn in a Scottish Sunday newspaper two years before. It described him as shaman, druid priest, author, mystic and psychic investigator and it mentioned that he had moved to Scotland via the USA from Mid Wales where he had lived near Hay-on-Wye and where his co-author and colleague, Justin Cavendish, still lived. Kier snorted with derision. 'So, Justin, my friend, this is the kind of company you keep,' he murmured softly. Justin, who had targeted Abi Rutherford, who because of her ordination as a priest in the church would be a trophy he could never have dreamed of.

He leaned forward to sip his coffee and picked up one of the chocolates in the dish in front of him. It was rich and delicious.

A plan had begun to form in his head. It would need some careful thought, and organisation, but he thought he could pull it off, and once he had Abi would be safe where no-one would find her. In the meantime he would keep out of sight. It wouldn't take long for them to let down their guard. They would imagine he had given up and gone away. A couple more days would do no harm if it meant he could help her in the end, and in the interim he would surround her with prayer, find out where Justin was based, and take steps to ensure that he never interfered with any God-fearing Christian ever again.

Cal was furious when Abi finally came in that evening. Tight-lipped, she did her best to hide it, but Abi was contrite. 'I feel awful. I assumed you would know I had gone to the church. I'm really so sorry. I just needed to pray. To go back and make sure it was all right after the vile things Kier had said and done. I assumed you would know. You'd left the note telling me to lock myself in.'

'I did. I'm sorry.' Cal sighed and shook her head. 'I'm more wound up about all this than I realised. It's just, it got dark and I was imagining all sorts of things. That evil man has completely spooked me. There is something so sinister about him.' She pushed Abi into one of the chairs by the fire and poured her a glass of wine. 'And Mat said he was going to the church but he isn't back yet.'

Abi stared at her in horror. 'He hasn't gone out to look for me?'

Cal nodded. 'He's got the dogs. He'll be fine.'

'How could I have missed him?'

'I don't know.' Cal shrugged. 'I thought he would be twenty minutes.'

They looked at each other for a few seconds, then Abi stood up again. 'I'll go and see –'

'I knew you'd been in the church!' The door opened and Mat appeared, his hair dishevelled and damp from the cold evening air. 'The candles were still warm when I got there.' He grinned as he came in. 'My passion for Sherlock Holmes has not been in vain! I put two and two together and realised you must have only just left and lo and behold, here you are.'

Abi was grateful for his good humour. It somehow defused

Cal's anxiety which was still hanging in the kitchen in a palpable curtain.

'I promise I won't scare you like that again,' she said later when they were preparing to go up to bed. It was only when Cal had rung Ben and Justin back that she had realised just how much of a panic she had been in. Mat was banking up the fire, putting the guard in place: 'I was thoughtless and you are both being so kind to me.'

Cal gave her a quick hug. 'This is a new experience for us. I just don't want you to come to harm.'

Mat stood up with a grin. 'In fact it's been quite exciting. Not the sort of thing one gets involved in as a routine. Please don't feel guilty, Abi. None of this is your fault. If this obsessive piece of work hadn't come after you everything would be fine. I thought,' he hesitated, 'I thought, if you don't object, I'd have a word with Ben and suggest that he gets in touch with the bishop. David needs to know what sort of a man Kier is. He may not realise just how far down this obsessive route he's gone. I don't know if he has any authority to rein him in, but if he has he should do it.'

'Do you think he's still round here somewhere?' Cal folded a tea towel and began to turn out the lights. Involuntarily she glanced towards the window.

'Yes,' Abi said after a moment's thought. 'I don't think he's going to give up. I'll go and see Ben tomorrow if he's got a moment and I'll mention David if you like. I agree, he might be able to say something to Kier.' She hesitated. 'It's just, when I looked into Kier's face, there was something there which filled me with compassion as much as horror.'

'Stay with the horror,' Cal said tartly. 'The man is threatening you.' She had turned out all the lights save the one by the door.

Abi went over and kissed Cal on the cheek. 'Thank you for everything.'

It was when she reached her bedroom and turned on the lights she remembered the crystal. It was outside in the hollow base of the tree. She bit her lip. She didn't need it tonight. She would have a hot bath and read in bed for a bit and tomorrow in broad daylight she would retrieve it, follow Justin's instructions, and summon Mora to see what had happened when she and Yeshua had found the dugout canoe and headed back to Avalon.

Unless something had happened to Mora.

326

She had bathed and washed her hair. Her bed looked inviting and warm in the pool of lamplight, a pile of books on the table beside it. She was safe. But she needed the crystal. She couldn't wait until tomorrow. She had to know what happened. She sat on the bed, trying to put it out of her mind. Everyone had told her she didn't need it. She knew she didn't need it. She was becoming as obsessive as Kier.

She swung her feet into bed but it wasn't going to work. She was not going to sleep unless she collected it and brought it into the safety of her room. If she did that, she could be sure. She could warn Mora, make her understand that Flavius would as soon kill her as smile at her. Supposing Justin was right, that she could interact with them in the past, that she could alter the outcome, the very timeline of history?

With a sigh she climbed out of bed and reached for her dressing gown. Tiptoeing to the door she pulled it open and looked out. The house was in darkness. Mat and Cal were probably asleep. The place was locked up, the dogs asleep in the kitchen. She couldn't disturb them. She closed the door again, biting her lip. How likely was it that Kier would be out in the garden at midnight on a rainy windy night, however close he might be staying. She paced up and down a couple of times, chewing her thumbnail. How long would it take her to retrieve the crystal? Ten minutes? Five? Cal would never forgive her if she went out now in the dark and inadvertently woke them up. The dogs would bark if she went down. There was bound to be some noise.

She paced round the room again.

You don't need the crystal. Athena's voice echoed in her ears.

Mora had programmed it. It contained the last message she had ever put there. Supposing it was happening now. Flavius was creeping ever closer to them through the sedge and reeds, his sword in his hand, and she, Abi, could somehow have saved the situation.

Torn, she turned back into the room.

You don't need the crystal.

Reluctantly she climbed into bed again and sat with her back against the pillows, helping herself to the pile of books which she had stacked on the bedside table: two novels which Cal had passed on to her, one of the histories of Glastonbury and then at the bottom her own Bible. She laid her hand on it affectionately. It was strange how her reaction to it had changed. Every time she looked at the New Testament now, she was reading it from a new angle. Jesus was a living breathing person to her now. Still the son of God. Still the teacher and the storyteller and her Redeemer, but also a living breathing man, full of doubt and uncertainty, fearful and brave, kind and gentle, but angry and frustrated. All that was shown in the gospels, but now for her it meant so much more. She let the Bible fall onto her knee unopened. She had to fetch the crystal. She had to.

It took less than ten minutes. The dogs didn't bark. They thought it was exciting. They came with her; if anyone had been there they would have barked. They waited while she knelt in her dressing gown on the wet ground and fished into the dark wet hollow of the oak tree by the light of her torch, then they bounded ahead of her back to the house. She let herself indoors and bolted the back door. Then, with a conspiratorial whisper she swore them to secrecy as they returned to their beds by the fire. She turned off the light and padded upstairs, her hair wet with rain, her dressing gown smeared with mud, the crystal clutched against her chest and quietly let herself back into her room.

Cynan had walked cautiously up the track towards the house, then veered off into the alder scrub to the north of the farm. Something told him that if Flavius was lurking close to the house this would be where he would hide. He gripped his staff, and slipped into the shadows of a stand of ancient willows, flattening himself against the trunks of the trees as he peered round towards the fenced pasture near the house. He could see the smoke coming from the roof. There was no sound. He eased himself towards another tree, flitting like a shadow ever closer, aware that the wind in the autumn leaves masked the sound of his movements. Then he saw him. The Roman was standing still as a statue, hidden as he was, in the trees, only fifty paces from him. The man's face was half-turned away but Cynan could see his hand, gripping the hilt of his short sword. So Mora and Yeshua were still inside the house. Cynan glanced out across the fields down to the lake. The Tor stood out against the grey clouds, illuminated by a ray of sunlight. He gave a grim smile. Blessed Gwyn, son of Nudd, be with me. Be ready to take this feeble and inexpert warrior into your kingdom of the dead. He ducked out of the shadow of the tree and moved closer to Flavius, counting on the wind to mask the sound of his footsteps and the fact that the man seemed to be concentrating so hard on the door of the house. Suddenly Flavius stepped back. Cynan paused, holding his breath. He too could see them now, a group of figures emerging from the low doorway.

First Mora, then Lydia, then Yeshua and Sorcha, bringing up the rear. They all embraced. They looked happy. Then Yeshua and Mora began to make their way towards the gate. Alone. How could they be so trusting? So stupid! Cynan felt his fist tighten round his staff.

He glanced back towards Flavius and his heart stood still. The man had vanished. He looked round frantically. Where had he gone? The woodland was alive with dancing shadows, rustling leaves, the crackle of twigs on the ground. He could be anywhere. He took a step forward. If he called out Flavius would hear him. He was torn between remaining hidden and running towards them. He was still too far away to help. He turned away, intent on making his way down through the trees to intercept the track closer to the lake. If he could get to them in time to warn them they could duck out of sight and avoid Flavius. That way they would be safe.

He set out following a game trail through the undergrowth, his eyes on the ground. He wasn't sure what made him look up. As he did a black shape, which he barely had time to recognise as the silhouette of a man, appeared in front of him, there was a bang and a blinding flash as something hard met his head, and he crumpled to the ground.

Abi ran her finger over the milky face of the crystal. There was nothing there now. She cupped her hands around it, willing the picture back. What had happened to Cynan? Dear, kind, faithful Cynan. She almost shook the crystal. What was happening? Was Cynan dead? She knew that Mora had been more than fond of him. Had they been lovers before Yeshua had arrived? Certainly he loved her; they had been promised in marriage. She looked up at the window as a stronger than usual gust of wind outside rattled the panes and the curtains shivered and she reached out to touch the Bible again, lying near her on the bedcovers. The story of Jesus. The sum of all that was known about him.

Mora stopped and looked round. They were nearly at the edge of the lake now. She could see the two dugouts pulled up amongst the reeds. She put her hand on Yeshua's arm and looked at him, putting her finger to her lips. Somewhere nearby she heard the strident triple caw of a crow and she shivered. It was an ill omen. She pulled him with her off the track and behind some trees, staring back the way they had come. 'There's someone there,' she whispered. 'Following us.' He nodded and she saw his hand tighten on his staff.

She could sense it now. Something was wrong. She could smell blood and violence in the air. Lydia? Petra? Surely he wouldn't have gone back to the house and killed his own family. She looked at Yeshua and saw him frowning. He pushed her behind him. 'Stay here and don't make a sound.'

'No!' She caught at his sleeve again. 'You mustn't. It's you he wants to kill!'

But already he had stepped out onto the track. When Flavius appeared, his drawn sword in his hand, Yeshua was standing in front of him. 'Greetings, my friend. It seems you cannot be dissuaded from trying to kill me.'

Flavius paused. His jaw set, he took a few steps forward, then stopped again. 'I have no choice. I obey orders.'

'And you have been told to act in secret, where there are no witnesses.'

Flavius glanced round. 'I see no witnesses. No doubt the healer is with you. If she is it will not take long to despatch her too.'

'And the boy Romanus? He will know what happened.'

'He is expendable. As are his family.'

'Your family,' Yeshua corrected him.

Flavius sneered. 'Not any longer!' He took a firmer grip on his sword. 'Prepare to die, healer!' He smiled greedily, then abruptly the smile left his face and he was frowning. His sword hand fell to his side as two men stepped out of the shadows, one on either side of Yeshua. Flavius gazed at them in disbelief, then he shook his head and rammed the sword into its scabbard. 'So, you're not alone after all. So be it! I can wait.' With a scowl he turned and ran into the undergrowth. In seconds he had disappeared. Had he turned back he would have seen Yeshua standing alone on the track.

Mora ran to Yeshua. 'Why did he run away like that? What did you say to him?'

Yeshua smiled. 'On this occasion my father sent help. Did you not see them?'

She stared at him and shook her head. 'I saw a flash of light on the road. I don't understand.'

'We're safe, that's what matters.' He put his arm round her.

'And the house, are they safe there?' She could still sense the violence in the air but he nodded reassuringly. 'For now they are all safe. But the only way to keep them safe is for me to go. Tonight.' He looked down at her. 'Come. Back to the boat. I have farewells to make.'

Abi saw her face, the misery, the hunger, the desperate yearning love as Mora looked back up the track, then turned to follow him down towards the lake. Of Cynan there was no sign.

17

Kier had bought an Ordnance Survey map of the area and taken it to what was rapidly becoming his favourite coffee shop. Opening it on the table, he carefully folded it open at the right place and began to study the terrain. The only hard part of his scheme would be to lure her away from her companions, and already he had had an idea how to do that. Finishing the coffee, he asked the waitress where he could find the nearest electrical shop.

Only an hour later he was driving back towards Glastonbury, heading once more for the abbey car park.

'I phoned Bishop David last night, Abi.' Ben bent to throw another log onto his study fire. Janet had already brought them coffee. There were two slices of cake as well this time, Abi noticed. Did that mean she had been in some way promoted on the scale of acceptance? 'We had a long chat about Kier. Did you realise he went back to see the bishop last week?'

Abi nodded with a shrug. 'He told me he'd spoken to him again. I didn't really take it in.'

'I don't think I'm betraying any confidences in saying to you that David is very concerned for you. He was horrified to hear that Kier was here again. He had specifically forbidden him to go near you.'

'And the first thing he did was come back and look for me.' Abi felt her stomach clench with apprehension merely at the sound of the man's name.

Ben nodded. 'We wondered if it was safe for you to stay where you are. You are a sitting target there, Abi. He knows the house now. He knows how to get in, he knows where you go.'

'What does David think he is going to do to me?' She picked up her cup and realised that her hands were shaking.

'He doesn't think Kier would hurt you.' Ben walked restlessly up and down in front of the fire a couple of times, then he subsided into the chair opposite hers. 'Kier is contrite, and too horrified by the fact that he laid hands on you before. We both feel that he means you well. He is genuinely frightened at the thought of the contact you are making with a spirit world. It is that which he finds terrifying and evil.'

'You don't agree with him about that?' She looked up anxiously.

He shook his head. 'No, of course not.' She heard the qualification in his voice. 'Although I think you should be wary of what is happening. We discussed that as well.' He leaned forward, his eyes on her face. She saw nothing but kindness there, but there was also a hint of anxiety. 'We do both however feel you need to be far more cautious than I think you are. You are dealing with a people from a pagan age. People whose beliefs and practices were unpredictable. You are dealing with a pre-Christian era. I know,' he held up his hand as she opened her mouth to protest, 'I know that you feel you are watching Our Lord when he visited this country. I know it is a distinct possibility. But it is also possible, Abi, that you are watching a demon in disguise. A phantasm. Something directed specifically against you as a Christian priest.'

Abi stared at him. 'No, Ben.'

'In all the years the ghosts of Woodley have been recorded, I don't think there has ever been a mention of the man you call Yeshua.'

'But he came with Mora to see them. She was a healer from Glastonbury. From the druid college there.'

'We don't even know if there was a druid college there, Abi. Not for certain.'

She stared at him in dismay. 'But I thought . . . There was a ceremonial way. The Chalice Well was a pre-Christian sacred spring. The Tor was the centre of a sacred landscape. I've read about it. It was sacred to the cult of Gwyn ap Nudd.'

'A pagan Celtic god.' He sighed. 'The ghosts of Woodley have all been Roman, Abi.'

'Until I brought my crystal down here.'

He shrugged. For a moment he said nothing. He reached for his cup and sipped the coffee appreciatively. Janet had made it rich and strong and spicy.

'I thought you were on my side,' Abi said at last. It sounded childish even as she said it.

'We are not taking sides, Abi. And we are not understating the problem of Kier, I promise you. That is why I am saying that you should be very wary. That you must test your contact with the other world which surrounds you. That you must allow people to have doubts and have doubts yourself. Question the stories. For instance you mention Jesus meditating at the red spring, which you feel is the Chalice Well, but that was not the only one. There was a white spring too near it; it's still there. And what about St Joseph's well in the abbey, which is under the Lady Chapel, and the holy well of St Edmund, for many centuries that was the most sacred spring of all?'

'But none of that proves anything,' she said weakly. 'Just that he, or they, preferred the one place.'

'I think it proves you are being influenced by modern legend.'

'No!' She shook her head violently. 'No. What I am seeing is real.'

'You can't be sure, Abi.'

'And where does faith fit into all this?' She could hear the harshness in her own voice.

'Faith is everything.' He smiled. 'But we must beware of false gods.'

'When you stayed behind in the church yesterday to pray and cleanse it,' she looked at him through narrow eyes suddenly, 'did you see anything?'

He shook his head.

'But you felt something?'

'I felt anger and rage and fear. But they were all very human emotions, left by Kier's intrusion into a quiet and sacred place.'

'You didn't see Mora or Cynan?'

'I told you, I have never seen a ghost.'

'But you believe that other people have? Cal, Justin?'

He nodded. 'I believe they exist.' He took a deep breath. 'Abi, it was wrong of me to bring in Justin. I should have realised he carries too much baggage to be of any use in this situation, however knowledgeable he is in some respects. So, what we were wondering is, would you talk to someone else about this, someone who has studied ghosts, and believes in them, a friend of David's, a member of his deliverance team in Cambridge? David feels it would help you to have someone to talk to, someone on your side as you put it. An impartial expert on the paranormal who happens also to be a parson.' He paused, waiting for her response.

She shrugged. 'I'm not going to stop consulting my crystal.' Once again she heard the sulky child talking.

'I'm not asking you to. All I am suggesting is that you talk to this man. His name is Greg Solway. David thinks you would like him and that it would be helpful to you. We are both thinking of you. He's prepared to come down today. He can stay with us here and you can talk to him wherever you like. At Woodley. Here. In the garden by the Roman site, in St Mary's. In Glastonbury. On your own, or with me. Wherever. However.' He smiled. 'Abi, please, will you eat some cake! I don't feel I can unless you do. I'm not supposed to eat Janet's cakes, they are too scrumptious and rich and bad for me. You don't know how honoured you are to have been offered a piece.'

Abi gave a wan smile. She reached for her plate. 'For Janet.'

'Thank you.' He reached for his own slice with alacrity and took a huge bite. It was several seconds before he could speak. His action had given her time to think. 'So, can I go ahead and ring to say Greg can come?'

She nodded tolerantly. 'Why not? He sounds an interesting man.'

'And meanwhile, pray, Abi.'

She nodded.

'If you go to St Mary's, check the atmosphere. Surround yourself with the love and peace of God. If Our Lord truly came there then you have nothing to fear and neither does your Mora.' He smiled.

Gaius was standing on the quay at the port of Axiom looking across the decks of several ships moored alongside. They had almost finished loading their cargoes of lead and silver and were riding low in the water. Nearby a group of great hunting dogs was howling into the wind as though aware that soon they would be embarking for the long voyage away from the land of their birth. Beyond them a compound held some two dozen slaves destined for the same ship. All had the blonde hair so beloved of Roman buyers. All looked cold and miserable and frightened.

Gaius nodded slowly, folding his alderwood notebook shut and tucking it away into the leather bag on his shoulder with his stylus and pens and wax tablets. It had been a good year for trade. He was well satisfied. He smiled as he saw the ship owner approaching in a small tender. The sailors tied it to the ladder and he climbed up stiffly to stand on the quay beside Gaius.

'It has gone well, my friend.' He held out his hand. Gaius clasped it. Joseph was one of his regular customers, arriving almost every year on one or other of his ships. Of sturdy build, with grizzled hair and bright intelligent eyes Joseph from Arimathaea was one of the owners he most looked forward to meeting each year. In his early sixties, wealthy and extremely well read, the man was a fascinating conversationalist and a mine of information. Gaius always hoped there would be time for a drink or a meal together and a chance to gain news of the wider Empire beyond this distant outpost.

'You sail on the tide?' Gaius led the way to the *mansio*, one of the cluster of *tabernae* and *cauponae* which had mushroomed around the little port. This was the most respectable of the buildings and served, besides ale and the local cider, passable imported wine.

Joseph shook his head. 'Not quite yet. I am waiting for my nephew. He left word here that he is ready to go home. I sent messengers yesterday to tell him my captains say we have to sail within the next few days. The weather is about to change. Hopefully he will take the hint and leave at once.' He glanced up at the lowering skies with a shiver, noting the wheeling gulls with a professional eye.

Gaius smiled. 'Your nephew has been causing a certain amount of excitement in our community.'

'Really?' Joseph smiled fondly. 'Why does that not surprise me!'

The two men commandeered a table near the fire and Gaius beckoned a serving girl over. He ordered wine and, with a regretful sniff at the luscious aroma of roasting boar which permeated the building, asked for fish stew in deference to his guest's religion.

'There has been a problem, to my enormous regret. My brother Flavius arrived from Galilee.'

Joseph's eyebrow shot up. 'I didn't know you had a brother, never mind out there.'

'No.' Gaius pulled a wry face. 'Not something to brag about. We don't get on. He works for Herod Antipas and it appears that your nephew has been targeted by the Roman authorities. You need to get Yeshua away from here as fast as possible. It is a blessing from the gods that you are here now, and in a position to take him home.'

Joseph frowned. 'I thought he would be safe so far away from Galilee,' he said with a sigh. 'But I suppose am not surprised to hear he has been followed. He was destined to catch the attention of the authorities since he was born. His mother, my niece, fears for him every moment of the day. We hoped that if he went away to study he would be safe and allowed time to prepare for his destiny in peace.'

'His destiny?' Gaius reached for the jar of wine and poured two beakers. The two men clinked them together.

Joseph pulled a face. 'If the prophecies are to be believed, it appears God has a very special mission for him.'

Gaius studied him over the rim of his beaker for a moment. He saw a mixture of emotions flit across his companion's face. Sorrow. Pride. Regret. Determination.

'So, that is why you brought him here. To get away from the Empire.'

Joseph smiled. 'I didn't exactly bring him by force. He has travelled all over the world in the last few years. But he recalled these islands from when I brought him as a boy, do you remember? He loved this land and he wanted to study with the druids. Their reputation as philosophers and theologians stands very high amongst men of learning.'

'But not with the Emperor, I gather.'

Joseph shook his head. 'The Emperor won't tolerate any stratum of people who are organised enough to oppose him. It is very hard in Gaul.' He sighed. They fell silent as the girl brought their plates. The stew, thick with leeks and flavoured with chives and mustard seeds was excellent. It was served with chunks of bread and savoury bean and mushroom fritters. For several moments the two men ate in silence.

'I take it that it was no coincidence that your brother came here,' Joseph said thoughtfully at last. 'He had information about Yeshua's whereabouts?'

Gaius nodded. 'He wasn't paying a visit out of fraternal affection.'

Joseph noted the grim line of his friend's mouth and nodded slowly. 'As you say, Yeshua is in danger. We must leave as soon

337

as he arrives.' He shrugged. 'I have to go soon anyway. Another day or so and it will be too late to sail this year.'

'Is your crew trustworthy?'

Joseph nodded. 'They have been with me for years. I can vouch for every man and boy on the ships.'

'You had better take no more passengers then, my friend,' Gaius said grimly. 'Collect your nephew and go on the first tide.' He stood up. 'I will head back home tomorrow. If he is still at the college when I get there I will speak to Fergus Mor and precipitate matters and in the meantime try and delay my brother, much as it pains me to think of him for even another minute under my roof.' He paused with a grimace. 'Yeshua will be much missed. From what I gather he has made many friends here.'

Joseph nodded. 'He is a very special young man.'

'Then we will do our best to look after him.' Gaius reached out to clasp the other man's hand. 'I shall see you next spring if the gods are willing.'

Joseph nodded slowly. 'If God wills,' he echoed, but so quietly his friend did not hear him.

Greg Solway was tall, completely bald and wore rimless glasses. He arrived at Ben's door at midday in a bright red open-topped MG and, climbing out, leaned in to extricate a shabby overnight bag, a laptop and a rucksack.

He turned as the door opened behind him and raised his hand in greeting. 'Sorry. I expect you heard the old girl. Bit noisy these days. I shall have to get rid of her. My carbon footprint must equate an entire small country but I try and make up for it in other ways.' He strode forward and held out his hand. 'Greg. I take it you are Ben?'

Ben nodded, wincing under the force of the man's handshake. He led the way in and took Greg straight to his study where Janet had set a tray with a decanter of sherry, another of whisky and an array of glasses. Greg rubbed his hands together appreciatively as he headed for the fire. 'A bit colder than I expected with the lid down, in spite of the sun. Whisky please, Ben. No water. OK, tell me everything you know. I take it Abi is not here?'

The two men talked for an hour, then continued their discussion over the cold lunch which Janet had laid out in the dining room.

She had tactfully left them alone. It was when they went into the kitchen to brew themselves some coffee afterwards that Ben reached for the phone and put in a call to Abi. There was no reply from Woodley or her mobile.

'Doesn't matter,' Greg said easily. 'Why don't I go over to your brother's house on my own, if he doesn't mind, and take a look at the places all these things have been happening. The ruins; the little church. The orchard.'

He found it easily and left his car in front of the house. There was no-one else there as far as he could see. The back garden was warm, ablaze with autumnal colour in the sunshine. He strode towards the far end of the lawn, looking about him with interest. So far he had felt nothing untoward.

Heading up the deliverance team which served part of David's diocese, he had a wealth of experience in dealing with the paranormal. Before his ordination twelve years before he had been a practising psychologist for ten years, then he had quit to study parapsychology at Edinburgh. He had been psychic his whole life. Most of the stuff he had to deal with was low key; unhappy souls, restless spirits, egos trapped by the power of their refusal to let go. He had visited houses and public buildings, pubs, the scenes of fatal car crashes where the deceased hung around in confusion and misery, not sure what to do, even on one occasion a supermarket plagued by a poltergeist, but never yet a Roman ruin, nor yet an active church.

He found the ruined arch easily and sat down quietly on the wooden bench to pray.

Abi had climbed the Tor once more, inexorably drawn to it and its strange powerful energies. This time she had sat alone, staring out across the levels, her back to the other people up there, trying to imagine herself into the distant past. It hadn't worked. The day was still and bright. The sound of voices carried round her, dragging her back to the present. On the flanks of the Tor the grazing cows were restless. She could hear them mooing disconsolately. On a road in the distance she saw the glitter of car windscreens. In the end she climbed to her feet and began to descend.

339

The first thing she saw when she reached the drive was the bright red car. She stared at it dubiously as she let herself into the house. There was no sign of Mat or Cal or the dogs. She was just going out into the garden when the phone rang.

'Abi?' It was Ben. 'Have you met Greg yet?'

The church was empty. She went back outside and looked round the churchyard once more, walking slowly between the ancient graves, listening to the gentle sad song of the robin perched on a lichen-covered elder bush. The air was unnaturally still. And then she heard it. Far in the distance the sound of monks singing. She stopped in her tracks, listening hard. The sound was very faint. She looked back at the church, but the sound was not coming from there. It seemed to be shifting, now coming from the orchard below, now from the flat green fields of the levels with their straight watery rhynes. Slowly she made her way back towards the lychgate, following the sound. She could feel the skin prickling slightly on her arms.

'Greg?' she called softly as she came back towards the orchard. The apple trees rustled in the breeze, the sound drowning out the voices of the monks, then it returned. She could hear the words: *Kyrie eleison*. 'Greg?'

The sound was louder now. She turned away from the house, towards the far side of the orchard, and finding a rotten gate dragged it open and made her way out onto the track. It led towards an old stone barn which stood starkly on the skyline some half a mile away. Surely the sound couldn't be coming from there? Walking slowly, drawn irresistibly towards it, she followed the old cart ruts which led out onto the levels. She glanced up. A kestrel was hovering nearby, balancing its wings against some imperceptible thermal as it scanned the ground beneath. She could almost feel the fear of whatever tiny rodent was hiding there in the grass.

The sound was coming from the barn. Curious rather than afraid now, she pushed tentatively at the huge double doors. They didn't move. Slowly she walked round the building and found another door. This one was unlocked. Pushing it open she peered inside. The sound was clear now, the gentle cadences rising into the high rafters. She looked up. Sunbeams filtered through spaces between the tiles, illuminating dust motes which danced between them.

'Hello?' she called. 'Is anyone there?'

She took a step inside. Behind her the door swung slowly closed, cutting off the sunlight.

For a moment she stood where she was in the semi-darkness, looking round, then she heard the sound of a key turning in the lock. With a shock of fear she flung herself at the door. It wouldn't budge.

'Abi!' The voice outside brought her up short. It was Kier. 'I don't want you to be afraid. You are not going to come to any harm. I have left food and water and blankets there for you. I knew sooner or later you would hear the music and follow it.' He gave a short laugh. 'It was sooner than I expected, I must admit. I want you to stay there for a few days. You will be quite safe.'

'Kier!' She rattled the door. 'Don't be ridiculous. Let me out!'

'Not now, Abi. There are things I must do. This is for your own good. Don't be frightened. I have left a Bible for you. Pray. Pray as though your life depended on it, do you hear me?'

'Kier!' She was shouting now. 'Kier, open this door now! What are you thinking of? Kier!'

There was no answer.

Phone. She groped in her pocket for her mobile. No signal. With an exclamation of disgust she held it up in the air and waved it round slowly. Nothing. Oh God! she let out a groan of frustration. Now what was she going to do? How dare he do this to her!

She turned round furiously and surveyed her prison. There must be a way of getting out. The huge old double doors at the end of the barn appeared to have been nailed shut years before. She fingered the wooden bars across them, looking at the rusty nails in despair, then she walked on round the stone walls. To one side were a couple of doors. They led into what looked like small stalls or sties built against the wall. In one was a bucket and a roll of loo paper. She let out a groan. He had thought of everything.

She discovered her bed in the far corner of the main barn. A pillow, three blankets and a sleeping bag. On the sleeping bag, as he had promised, lay a copy of the Bible. There were two plastic water carriers, a box of food and there, playing softly, was the portable radio CD player. The CD had been bought at the abbey shop in Glastonbury. There was no torch, no lantern and no candles. Clearly he did not mean her to sit up reading once it got dark. Trying to curb her anger, she toured the barn again, searching every corner for a way out. There appeared to be none. The only external doors were the large ones and the smaller one she had entered by. How could she have been so stupid as to fall into his trap! She cursed softly and stared round yet again. Why had he done this? What was he going to do with her? She tried the phone again. Still no signal. Furiously she shouted again. She only stopped when she grew hoarse.

They would come and look for her the moment they discovered she was missing. The dogs would find her. All she had to do was wait. With another groan she flung herself down onto the sleeping bag and reached for a blanket. She was only wearing a light jacket over her T-shirt. As soon as the sun went down it was going to get very cold.

Pushing open the church door, Greg looked inside. The sun was going down now. He stepped in and looked round. The place was quiet. There was no sense of disturbance. He frowned. Earlier he thought he had heard the faint strains of plainsong drifting through the orchard. He had stood listening. For a moment it had spooked him, he had to admit that, but you could tell very easily when something was genuinely not from this world. This had been a recording. A good one. Beautiful. Perhaps Abi had taken a CD player out with her. He walked slowly towards the altar feeling carefully into the shadows. No, Ben had done a good job in cleansing the place of any unpleasantness. There was nothing to fear in here. He turned back to the door and stepped outside, closing it carefully behind him. The churchyard was growing shadowy now. The sun was slipping into the west. Somewhere he could hear a bird singing. He listened until it stopped and then slowly he turned back towards the gate. He must have missed her. He would go back to the house, choosing a different route and meet her there.

He was halfway across the orchard when he felt it. Suddenly the air was hot with pain. The shadows were screaming. Someone had died here. He groped in his pocket for the little cross he carried with him all the time, reeling back from the suddenness of it. He had been open, searching, listening. He had not protected himself and now he was suffocating under the overwhelming pall of fear and anger. He was seeing red. He could feel the blood, sticky and hot and thick, running over his hands and across his face. He couldn't breathe. He reeled aside, and cannoned into the trunk of a tree. Clutching at the rough bark with desperate fingers he felt the rasp of lichen, he could smell the sharpness of sap mixed with the blood. He gasped, trying to find the right words. 'In the name of Jesus!' It was all round him. He could hear nothing but the thunder of blood in his ears. 'In the name of Jesus Christ!'

And as suddenly as it had started it was over. The orchard was silent. He stood clutching the tree, his forehead against the trunk, his face pouring with sweat. He had lost his specs. For a long moment he didn't move, then slowly he released the tree. His fingernails were broken and split; he had torn the knee of his jeans and he was shaking uncontrollably. He stared round, not daring to move his feet in case he stepped on his glasses, one hand now holding a branch as though his life depended on it. 'Christ be with me, Christ within me, Christ behind me.' He looked down at the grass and spotted the spectacles lying a few feet away from him. He reached for them frantically. They weren't broken and he stuck them back on with relief. The orchard was growing dark. Somewhere an owl hooted. He took a deep breath, still clutching the cross. 'Christ before me, Christ beside me, Christ beneath me, Christ above me.' Somehow he had to get back to the house but before he left the orchard he had to pray for the soul in torment here. Someone had died in this place, violently. Someone had been murdered and their spirit was not at rest. Closing his eyes he clasped his hands together around the little cross. 'Our Father, which art in heaven . . .'

'Abi's car is back so she must be here somewhere.' Cal and Mat had searched the gardens with the dogs as soon as Greg had returned. It had still been light enough to see then, but even so Mat had taken a large torch with him. At the gate to the orchard they had hesitated, glancing at Greg, then all three had walked in under the trees, calling her. There was no sign.

Ben arrived as they filed back into the house. He glanced at Greg with a grimace. 'I'm sorry. I had no idea things were this bad.'

'I suspect I stirred it up.' Greg threw himself down on one of the chairs by the fire, shaking his head. 'Idiot! Rushing in without proper preparation. I should know better after all these years. The church was so peaceful. I let down my guard.' He broke off as the phone rang.

Cal picked it up, listened for a second and passed it over to Ben. 'It's Janet.'

Ben took the phone and listened, his face growing grave as his wife spoke. 'I'm on my way,' he said at last and slammed the phone down on the table. 'Kieran Scott is there. He is claiming he has kidnapped Abi. Dear God!' Ben looked at Greg. 'Can I ask you to come with me? He's a bit intimidating, this guy. Mat, can you two wait by the phone?'

'So what has he done with her?' Cal whispered.

Ben shrugged. 'We'll see if we can make him tell us. He wants me to speak to the bishop for him, apparently.'

'Sounds as though he's lost it,' Greg said succinctly. He hesitated. 'Can I suggest that you both stay away from the orchard for the time being?' he said hesitantly to Mat and Cal. 'I'm aware that this is very much your patch, but I think I may have awoken some problematic influences. My fault and I should deal with them.'

Mat nodded. 'I for one am certainly not going to go looking for trouble.' He sighed. 'Phone us as soon as you know anything, Ben.'

When he had closed the front door behind them he came back to the kitchen to find Cal standing in front of the fire. 'Has it occurred to you it might not have been Greg who stirred things up? It might have been Kier. Or even Abi,' she said.

Mat nodded. 'What are we going to do?'

'We are going to take the dogs out again to look for her.'

He gave a wan smile. 'They are getting used to hunting for missing people!'

'We don't have to go near the orchard,' she added doubtfully. 'What could he have done with her?' She shivered.

'She could be anywhere, Cal, if he persuaded her to get into his car with him.'

She shook her head. 'She wouldn't have.'

'Perhaps he drugged her or something.'

'Surely not.' She looked down at the floor. 'Is he deranged, Mat?'

344

Mat shrugged. 'Ring Justin, Cal.'

She raised an eyebrow. 'Are you sure?'

He nodded. 'We need his help. That chap Greg didn't inspire me with confidence, to be honest. If he is the expert on the paranormal that Ben said, why is he making elementary mistakes? And Just might be able to locate Abi somehow.'

She glanced at him quizzically. 'With his super magic powers?'

'Something like that, yes.' Mat didn't smile.

Cal went to the phone. She did not have to look up the number, Mat noted. When she put the phone down she looked at him uncertainly as though she had read his mind. 'He's on his way,' she said.

Mat nodded. 'I'll take the dogs out again.'

'No. Wait. I'll go with you.'

'I'm not going near the orchard.' Mat smiled at her. 'That's my brother's job! No, I'll just wander round a bit with the torch and see if these two little blighters can get a sense of where she went. 'Abi, dogs! We really need you to find her.'

Pym and Thiz sat up. Neither seemed very enthusiastic. Cal frowned. 'That's not like them.'

Mat shrugged. He walked over to the door and reached for his jacket. At that the dogs leaped up, tails wagging. 'Don't leave this room, Cal. There has to be someone near the phone at all times.'

She nodded. 'Have you got your mobile?'

He checked his pockets, held it up then headed for the door. Then he stopped. 'Isn't that Abi's bag?' He had spotted it on the counter half-hidden behind a pile of books.

Cal went over to it and after a second's hesitation, picked it up. 'She wouldn't have gone anywhere without her bag,' she said quietly. 'Not voluntarily.'

'Where is Mora?' Cynan stopped to enter the house and looked round. Lydia was brushing Petra's hair. She looked up at him and smiled. 'Look. Petra is healed! Can you believe it, Cynan? Yeshua healed her.'

Petra smiled at the young man and rose to her feet. She stumbled slightly, still unsure of herself, but her smile told him all he needed to know as she slowly pirouetted in front of them. 'The pain has gone, Cynan. It has gone!'

He forced himself to grin, genuinely pleased for her. 'That is good news. Such good news. But where are they? Have they gone already?' He tried to hide his anxiety.

Lydia nodded. 'They went a while back. I'm afraid you've missed them.' Her expression changed as she saw the young man stagger forward. 'Cynan? What is it? Are you hurt?' In the dim light she had not noticed the blood seeping through his hair.

He collapsed onto a stool near the fire and put his head in his hands. 'I'm sorry. Someone hit me. I was in the trees looking for them . . .'

Lydia went white. 'Who hit you?'

He shook his head painfully. 'I didn't see.'

'Flavius?' Lydia spoke through pursed lips. 'Of course it was Flavius! He must have come back. We thought he had gone away for the day. I knew we shouldn't trust him. He must have been waiting.' She blinked back furious tears. 'What if he has hurt them!'

'I'll go back down to the boats.' Cynan staggered to his feet again. 'If they have already gone they will be safe. He wouldn't dare follow them across to Ynys yr Afalon. You take care of Petra.' He forced another smile. 'If any of the men are around I will take them with me. Flavius won't harm you or Petra. You will be safe. It's Yeshua he's after.'

'Romanus!' Lydia whispered. 'Yeshua told him to stay here, but he followed them.'

Cynan shook his head. 'He won't hurt the boy either, lady. Don't worry. It is Yeshua who is in danger.' And Mora. He didn't say her name out loud.

He ducked out of the door and stood for a moment as his head reeled in the bright sunlight. The compound was empty. There was no time to go and look for back up. Grabbing a staff which was leaning against the wall outside the house to replace his own which he must have dropped when he was hit he headed for the gate and the track back down across the fields and woods towards the water's edge.

Both canoes had gone. He studied the ground carefully, trying to read the footprints, but so many people had walked there it was hard to make head or tail of the tracks in the mud. In one place he saw the marks of a smaller boot. Perhaps that was Romanus. Then he saw a sandal print. Small and neat. That would be Mora, but it was difficult to see which way she was going. They might have made these marks when they arrived. 'Lord Gwyn, watch over them and keep them safe,' he breathed. He turned north alongside the mere and began to run. There were hidden ways across to the island, threading through the reeds. He could get back without a boat.

A hundred paces further on he stopped again, listening. Somewhere behind him he had heard a shrill sound. He spun round, scanning the track. The day was warm and still. His skin began to prickle a warning. Carefully he backed into the shelter of some osiers and gripped the staff tighter. Then it came again. A scream from the direction of the house. There was no mistaking the desperation in the sound. He crept off the path and began to thread his way back the way he had come, watching for any sign of movement, keeping to the shelter of the trees and bushes, hurrying as fast as he could go. He could hear it now. The shout had turned to a painful sobbing. It was the boy. He was almost certain of it. He crept on, keeping his eyes skinned and then suddenly he saw him. Romanus was leaning huddled against the trunk of a tree, clutching his stomach. Cynan stared round cautiously. Romanus seemed to be alone. Running on his toes to stay silent Cynan approached him. 'Rom? Are you all right, lad?'

He gasped as Romanus looked up. His hands were running with blood as he tried to staunch the wound in his belly. Only a rope tied around the tree was preventing him from falling. 'Flavius told me to call Yeshua back,' Romanus sobbed. 'He said if I didn't call him he would kill me.' His words came in tight, thready sobs. 'He stabbed me with his sword to make me scream.' His voice was fading. 'No-one came.'

'I came.' Cynan groped at his belt for his knife. It wasn't there. The bastard must have taken it from him when he hit him. Swearing, he reached for the rope, groping through the blood, trying to find the knot. 'Hang on, Rom. You'll be all right. Let me get you free.' They couldn't be more than five hundred paces from the house. He wondered if he dared call out, or was Flavius still within earshot?

'Yeshua and Mora have gone back to the island or they would have come for you,' he murmured. He found the knot and tried to pull it open. The boy was failing. He could see the gleam of sweat, the pallor on his skin. 'Your bastard uncle must have gone after them. Both boats have gone.' He tugged violently at the rope with both hands. Romanus's struggles must have tightened it too far to loose it. He had to find something to cut it with. He gave up pulling and looked round desperately. Then he stooped and picked up an armful of dead leaves from the track. It was all he had. He wadded them together and pushed them between the boy's fingers. 'Here. Hold this against your stomach. Hard. Push!' He stooped and picked up some more. 'These are willow. They will help staunch the blood. I'm going to have to run to the house to find something to cut you free. I'll bring help. Hang on, Rom, do you hear me? Hang on.'

The boy's hands grasped feebly at the leaves, then they fell away. Cynan swore softly. 'Yeshua, where are you? We need you now, man.' He stepped away from the tree, his own hands scarlet to the elbow and found himself facing Flavius. He drew in his breath sharply, swept with impotent rage at the sight of the man's apparent calm.

'You are right. Where is Yeshua when he is so badly needed?' Flavius gave a cold smile.

'This is your own nephew!' Cynan shook his head. He was beyond fear.

Flavius shrugged. 'Indeed, my own nephew. The spawn of my brother.' He reached to his waist for his sword. 'And you are an interfering priest. You can accompany the boy to Hades, my friend. That will comfort him and ensure there are two less people to stand in my way.'

The sun glinted for a moment on the blade of the sword, then the world turned red.

18

Janet was lurking inside the front door as Ben and Greg hurried into the Rectory. 'He went straight into your study,' she whispered. 'I've taken him some tea, but he's pacing up and down like a caged animal.'

Ben glanced at Greg. 'Stay within earshot,' he whispered at his wife. 'Just in case.'

She nodded and tiptoed towards the kitchen.

Ben led the way towards the back of the house. Outside the door of the study he paused. He glanced at his companion. 'Ready?'

Greg raised his eyebrows. 'We have God on our side,' he murmured.

Ben pushed open the door and they went in.

Kier was standing in front of the fire staring down at the smouldering logs. He swung round to face them. His face was drawn, his eyes red-rimmed. 'I suppose you think I'm mad,' he said harshly. 'And perhaps I am, but if so it is her fault. She drove me to it. All I want is for you to put it all right.' He was addressing Ben. He didn't appear to have registered Greg's presence.

Ben went slowly towards the windows and pulled the curtains closed against the night, then he turned and made his way across to his accustomed chair. He sat down with a sigh. 'Tell me what has happened, Kier. I am not sure I have understood.' He kept his voice carefully level.

Greg quietly moved towards the sofa where he eased himself into the corner, crossing his legs. Both men were focused on Kier's face.

Kier took a deep breath. They saw him flex his hands, visibly trying to calm himself. The tea lay untouched on the low table in front of him 'My career is over unless you can convince the bishop that she has lied.'

'I can only convince him if you can convince me,' Ben said

firmly. 'Sit down, Kier and tell me what has happened.' He found it hard to keep an edge of irritation from his voice.

Kier perched on the edge of the chair opposite him, but only for a second, then he stood up again and went back to the fireplace. 'I should have known. I should have seen it when I first met her, but I liked her so much.' His voice rose in anguish. 'I was blinded. I thought we could work together. I thought she would be so good for me. For the parish. She seemed just what was needed.' He paused. 'It took me a long time to see through her, but she wasn't clever enough to keep it up forever. Her disguise wasn't quite good enough.' He paced over to the desk and back. 'And I was too weak! It was too late. I had been snared. She bewitched me. She was working with the dark arts. She was conjuring devils. I love the woman, Ben!' He perched back on the chair and put his face in his hands, running his fingers through his hair.

'So where is she now?' Ben asked softly.

Kier looked up. 'I haven't hurt her. She is safe where she is; as long as she is there she can harm no-one else.'

Ben nodded quietly. 'The bishop will need to deal with her himself,' he said after a moment. 'This is too serious for any of us to cope with, you do realise that?'

Kier narrowed his eyes, but he nodded. 'Once the bishop has realised it is not my fault.'

'He knows that already, Kier,' Greg said firmly. 'I am the bishop's envoy. I have come down especially to deal with this matter and report back to him. He is very concerned that he allowed Abi to come here. I do need,' he paused, 'to see her as a matter of urgency.'

Kier looked up, seeming to realise there was someone else in the room for the first time. 'I have told you, she is safe. And she can't hurt anyone else.' He clenched his fists.

'If she has indeed been taken over by demonic forces,' Greg said slowly, 'where she is, is not relevant. She can manifest her curses non locally.'

There was a moment's silence. Kier appeared to be trying to work out what he meant.

'He is trying to tell you that she can cast her spells over you from wherever she is. She doesn't need to be near you,' Ben put in. 'So keeping her a prisoner somewhere will do nothing but make her more angry, and therefore more powerful.' He paused. 'If she is as evil as you think.'

'Oh she is!' Kier rounded on him. 'Believe me. She can conjure spirits. I have seen her do it.'

Greg nodded. 'Then you need to leave her to me, my friend. For the sake of your own safety.' He reached into his pocket for his cross and held it out. 'I have special powers she would never have dreamed of. I have been trained for just this sort of eventuality, which is why the bishop sent me, so you must allow me to cope with her from now on. Ben will see to it that the bishop is informed what is happening, and make sure he understands that you have been the innocent victim here.'

Kier looked from one man to the other, his eyes like slits. 'I don't believe you,' he said after a long pause. 'You are just trying to find her. You're on her side.'

Greg shook his head vehemently. He had not looked at Ben. 'I can assure you I am not. I have never met the woman. If you doubt my qualifications you can look at our diocesan website under Deliverance. You will find me there.'

Kier was shaking his head. 'You can't save her, only God can do that,' he muttered.

'God has entrusted me with my calling, Kier,' Greg said reprovingly, his voice carefully even. 'I work in his name.'

Kier stood up again. 'That is as maybe, but I think you will find that my way of dealing with this is better.' He faced Ben. 'Are you going to ring the bishop?'

Ben caught sight of Greg's quick nod.

'Of course I am. If you tell Greg where she is, I will ring him now. The sooner the better. But there is no point in speaking to him while Abi is still out there able to channel her malign thoughts in your direction.'

Kier grinned wildly. 'You must really think I'm mad. I'm not telling you where she is. Not until I have the bishop's word that my future is secure.'

Ben inclined his head. 'OK. If you insist. I will ring him now.' He stood up with a sigh and walked towards his desk.

'Thou shalt not suffer a witch to live,' Kier said softly, almost to himself.

Ben stopped in his tracks. 'What did you say?'

'I think you heard me.' Kier sat down again. 'I am as qualified as you two gentlemen, to deal with someone like Abi. Perhaps more so. I don't want her to suffer. It is up to God how he punishes her. But it would be better if she were dead than that she go on with her apostasy. You must see that. I thought she would listen to me. I thought she would see the error of her ways, but if she doesn't and if she stays where she is, then she will die. I have put something in the food I have left for her. She won't feel any pain. I'm not a monster or a sadist. She will just go to sleep.'

Ben looked at Greg. 'I will ring the bishop now,' he said.

Kier smiled. 'I thought you would.'

'How do you know she hasn't eaten it already?' Greg said sharply.

Kier shrugged. 'I don't.'

'You haven't given her any poison.' Ben's eyes narrowed shrewdly. 'You haven't got what it takes to be a killer. Don't make matters worse for yourself, Kier. You still have the possibility of coming out of all this with your job and your credibility. But only if you cooperate.' He turned his back on the desk. 'Abi isn't a witch. She isn't a conjuror of spirits. Grow up, man. The woman doesn't want you and your pride has been hurt. Get over it!' He folded his arms.

Kier stared at him. 'Aconite,' he said softly. 'They used to call it wolf's bane. One of the deadliest of poisons. Tasteless, so I'm told. I wasn't sure of the dose, but I put it in some samosas. I thought the flavour would cover any bitterness there might be.' He smiled sadly. 'I so hoped we could work together on this, but it appears not.' He sighed and stood up. He made his way towards the door. 'I promise she won't suffer. At least not until she gets to God's great tribunal.'

'Kier, wait!' Greg was on his feet and at the door at the same moment Kier reached for the door handle. 'You can't go. We have to know where she is.'

Kier shook his head. 'I'm truly sorry.'

'Wait, man!' Greg reached him, and grabbed at his arm.

'Not a chance!' Kier gave him a violent push which knocked him off balance. Before Greg had recovered he had run down the passage and out of the front door.

He was in his car, gunning the engine before Ben and Greg were halfway across the drive. Narrowly missing both men he drove out of the gate, swung onto the road, overtook a van with a scream of tyres and disappeared.

'Did you get his car number?' Ben gasped. 'I'll call the police.'

Abi had explored every corner of her prison. Acutely aware that it was getting dark she walked around the walls, examining them in detail. There were no other doors, no windows, no weaknesses that she could see in the stone, nothing to use as a lever or a battering ram. The floor was interesting. Two thirds of it was beaten earth. The other third, up a step, and raised about a foot above ground level, was boarded and when she stamped on it, it sounded resonant. It appeared to be hollow. There were rotten holes in the boards. Kneeling, she peered in. She could see nothing. Down there it smelled of damp earth. She glanced round. There were still stray sunbeams threading their way inside round the cracks in the big doors as the sun sank lower. As one ray of light caught the floor as she knelt there she glimpsed something white lying in the darkness beneath. It looked like a bone. She drew back in shock, then she leaned forward again and stared in. Whatever it was it had long ago dried clean. After a moment's hesitation, she reached into the dark and grasped blindly at the bone. It was large and cumbersome and might just give her some sort of tool with which she could dig her way out. With a wiggle she pulled it free and found herself staring at a horse's skull.

Laying it down on the floor she wiped her hands on the seat of her jeans with a shiver. There was something deeply disquieting about finding it; she had expected the bones of a sheep or a cow perhaps, but a horse? Horses were special. Horses in pagan times had been sacred. Its burial under the floor was probably part of some ancient superstition, designed to bring luck or fertility or protection to the barn. She backed away from it, aware that the light was now going. In minutes the place would be dark.

'Bugger you, Kier,' she whispered.

How dare he lock her up like this! The self-righteous, sadistic, power-crazed, bloody man! A dangerous man. She paused. Yes, he was dangerous and she was at his mercy. She made her way back to the sleeping bag and sat down on it, pulling a blanket round her shoulders. At least he had left her food and water. And entertainment. Reaching forward she switched on the radio.

Thiz and Pym stopped in their tracks, their ears pricked. 'What have you heard, dogs?' Mat was shivering, his hands in his pockets. 'Can you hear Abi?' He had taken them towards the churchyard, sensing that she would have gone there and guessing that perhaps that was where Kier might have jumped her. He flashed the torch around into the dark trees, starting as a bird launched itself out of a bush in panic and blundered past him in the darkness. 'Find Abi!'

Thiz was pointing, paw raised, head arrowed down towards the levels, concentrating so hard she was almost vibrating. 'What is it, girl?' He glanced at Pym. Then both dogs were running. Taken aback he was left behind as they tore through the gate and down the track away from the church, down towards the fields with their regular criss cross of watery ditches. Stumbling, he ran after them trying to keep sight of them with his torch beam as they drew further and further ahead.

Athena looked across the table at Justin as he slipped his phone back into his pocket and shook her head. 'Just as well you were here!' Justin smiled. 'Thank you for giving me supper. I'm glad we've sorted our differences.' He leaned forward and put his hand over hers for a second. Then he pushed back his chair. 'I'd better go. It sounds as though all hell has been let loose over there. Cal was frantic.' He hesitated.

'So why are you waiting?' She glanced up at him and gave him a stern shake of the head. 'To keep your brother on tenterhooks?'

Justin shook his head ruefully. 'Partly, maybe.'

'And?'

'Vicars.' He gave a snort of laughter.

'As in Abi Rutherford?' She was watching his face closely.

'Stop looking at me in that shrewd all-seeing mode!' he said tolerantly. 'Yes, as in the beautifully sexy Abi and also the fearsome Kieran and something dangerous in the orchard.'

She sat back in her chair. 'Something dangerous that is worrying you?'

He nodded. 'There is something very unpleasant lurking in that place at the moment.'

'Apart from this man, Kier, you mean? Something you should be dealing with?'

'Indeed.'

She pushed back her chair and whisked his plate away. 'Go. Now.'

He didn't argue. Standing up he leant forward and planted a kiss on her cheek, then he reached for his jacket. 'They didn't ask where I was. I suspect they think I am driving down from Ty Mawr. I'll surprise them.'

'Have you got everything you need?'

'In the car. Always. I'll call you.'

She sat still long after he had gone, staring down at the half-eaten food on their plates, then at last she stood up. Turning her back on the kitchen, she walked through into the main room. In the corner on a low table stood a small figurine. It wasn't the goddess, not the great hollow-bellied goddess of the statues sold in the town, but a young beautiful woman in a long dress and with shrouded hair, a kind, loving woman with a baby in her arms. Not the Virgin Mary with the baby Jesus. Isis and Horus, maybe, or Semiramis with Tammuz. The *mater* of the tribes. The universal mother and child. Whoever she was, it was comforting sometimes to pray before her and ask for her intervention. She hadn't turned on the lights. Reaching for the matches she lit the one small candle which sat on the table. 'Take care of him,' she whispered. 'He's not for me, I know that, but maybe for Abi. She's right for him.' She kissed her fingertips and rested them for a second on the head of the woman, then, feeling marginally happier she went over to the sofa and threw herself down to listen in the candlelight to the music drifting up through the open window from the courtyard below. Her neighbour was playing his saxophone quietly to himself. When he was drunk or drugged the music had an unearthly beauty which was almost unbearable. Tonight he must be stoned out of his mind.

Justin drove fast, reaching Woodley within twenty minutes. Cal gaped at him as she opened the door. 'Jet-propelled broomstick?'

He shook his head. 'Car. I was only up the road.'

He followed her into the kitchen and glanced round. No Mat and no dogs. 'Tell me what's going on. Exactly.'

He stood with his back to the fire, listening without comment as she filled him in on the events of the evening. 'Even Mat agreed we needed you,' she said when she had finished.

He raised an eyebrow. 'Wonders will never cease.' He let out a deep thoughtful sigh. 'We have three separate problems here. Kier and whatever it is he thinks he believes, which is a matter for his bishop, Ben's right. And whatever it is that has been awakened out there in your garden.'

'And Abi.'

He nodded. She saw the crease between his brows deepen. 'And Abi. She has been sucked into the story out there, and Kier, rather than supporting her, has I fear added a very unwholesome energy to the mix.'

'Can you do something?' It was almost a whisper.

He shrugged. 'I wish Meryn was here.'

'Meryn?'

'The man who taught me all I know.'

'The sorcerer to your apprentice?'

He laughed dryly. 'Exactly. I'll do my best. I wish Mat and the dogs were back here safely. I don't like the thought of my brother crashing around in the undergrowth all open and unprotected in the psychic sense.'

She shook her head. 'Nor do I.'

He gave her a quick smile. 'I'll do my best for them all, Cal. You know I will. But as I'm here and the others are presumably on Kier's tail, I'll start in the orchard. You wait here, OK? Please do not come outside no matter what happens. I need to know you at least are safe.'

She nodded dumbly and he gave her a quick pat on the shoulder. First he went out to the car and retrieved a canvas bag from the boot. Slinging the strap onto his shoulder he raised a hand to her and walked off round the back of the house into the darkness.

He could feel it all around him. An electric tenseness in the air which he had never felt here before. The place was very quiet. Not a breath of wind. No sound of small animals or night birds. Nothing scuttling busily in the undergrowth. It was all totally silent.

356

He walked out across the lawn and paused near the log seat, sending out feelers into the night, trying to sense where his brother was with those two irrepressible dogs. If they were anywhere nearby there would not be this silence, this sense of nothing.

He tensed. He was wrong. There was something. Just for a moment he had sensed someone else out there listening and waiting for him. He frowned, trying to keep his mind empty of expectation. 'Don't give the enemy anything to work with.' Meryn's voice echoed in his head for a moment. 'If he or she senses that you are expecting to see a figure in a bedsheet that is what you will see. If you are sure it is the Loch Ness Monster or Black Shuck, be ready, for they will appear.' It had seemed funny at the time, but it was shrewd advice and very hard to follow. He deliberately blanked his mind of visions of Roman soldiers and bloody swords.

He held his breath, surrounding himself with a shield of protection. The old condom from head to toe trick. His mouth twitched into a smile again. Meryn's words were supporting him. Making him strong. He stayed immobile, waiting. Someone was nearby, watching him. But who? Not Mora. Not Lydia or Petra. No-one from the homestead. Much too powerful and sophisticated for that. A druid? His senses sharpened. He wanted to step forward, to get closer, but he resisted the urge to move.

The cauldron of silence grew deeper. A small patch of moonlight drifted across the grass from the waning crescent, half-shrouded in clouds. He took the chance to take two slow unhurried steps towards the bench and sit down. Carefully, without any hurried movements he reached into his bag and drew out the small drum. For a long time he sat without moving, waiting to see what would happen. It was like watching a nervous animal, trying to win its trust. No. That wasn't right. There was nothing nervous about this energy. His fingers strayed to the taught drumskin made with his own hands from the hide of a deer he had hunted and slain himself, giving thanks to the soul of the animal for its sacrifice. Its meat had kept several families in food for a while, up there in Scotland, when he had been training with Meryn. The antlers had been used to make handles for crooks and staves and knives. What remained, and there was precious little, had been buried with honour on the hillside where the young stag had lived. It had been destined for the cull. It was better that he kill it with honour and respect, than a man

357

with a gun who had paid money for the fun of slaughter. The wood of the drum was ash from a storm-felled tree on the same wild mountainside. The animal and the tree between them could conjure life out of rock; they could summon the future and they could enchant; above all they could carry him far away into the distant past. Slowly he began to tap, feeling the drum wake, feeling it respond like a lover to his touch.

He drummed on, gently, hypnotically. 'Don't lull yourself, boy.' Meryn's voice came to him and he remembered their long sessions as the druid taught him his art. 'Keep alert. Be watchful. The drum has a mind of her own. She may not call those you expect. She may take you to places you would rather not go.'

It was his turn to smile. How true. So, who or what was this shadow? Why did they not reveal themselves?

Almost as he thought the words he sensed a drawing away. What had changed? Was there someone or something else out there?

The sound of the drum went on, a soft heartbeat, conjuring matter out of darkness. He could feel someone else there now. He didn't turn his head. Whoever it was would reveal himself soon. It was a child. A boy. He could feel the aggression, the hesitancy, the uncertainty. The fear. He resisted the urge to speak. The cast was assembling. All he had to do was wait.

The call of the night birds echoed in the moonlight and he heard the splash of a fish jumping in the darkness of the water. In this land of ever-changing light and dark, of liminal beauty, neither land nor sea, the silvery wind breath was full of the scents of mud and flowers, of soft grasses and damp woodland moss, of sweet air from the distant hills and sharp salt from the faraway sea.

He had come here to pray for the last time before he left.

19

'Are you ready?' Mora peered in at the door of Yeshua's little house on the edge of the sanctuary. A patch of new wattle showed where he had been mending the wall. 'It is time to go. I sent a message to Cynan and asked if he would meet us at moonrise with a boat. By dawn we will be halfway down the river.'

Yeshua was sitting staring down into the small circular hearth in the centre of the floor. He was deep in thought. She ducked in and came to sit beside him, settling gracefully on the matting and watching him in the flickering light. His eyes were closed in prayer. She studied the planes of his face, the long strong nose, the firm mouth, the high cheekbones, the straight eyebrows and felt herself aching to put her arms round him, to protect him, to draw him close. She looked away guiltily, biting her lip. 'Yeshua?' she whispered again. 'It is time.'

He opened his eyes and looked at her. 'My presence here has caused you nothing but unhappiness, Mora,' he said softly. He reached out and took her hand.

She shook her head. 'You have cured Petra. You have brought so much good and love and healing with you.'

'I have brought death and destruction to those you love.' His voice was suddenly anguished. 'It is something I am going to do to my followers again and again!'

'No.' The denial was automatic but even as she said it she knew she was wrong and he was right.

They sat for a moment clasping hands, looking into each other's eyes. He looked away first, back towards the fire. 'Will you keep faith with me Mora?'

'Of course.' She gave a sad smile.

'Even if I asked you to give up your gods for mine?'

She hesitated.

'I need you to believe me, Mora. I need you to have faith in me.' He looked anguished suddenly. 'If you don't, who will?'

She frowned. 'You told me an angel foretold your birth. Your mother believes in you.'

'My brothers don't.' He shook his head with a wry grin. 'A prophet, as I am sure you know, is not without honour save in his own land and in his own house! And I have to convince the whole world as well as them.'

They were looking into one another's faces. I have to remember him like this, she thought. After today he will be gone. I will never see him again. He smiled again, that melting, beautiful smile which went straight to her heart.

'I believe in you,' she whispered. 'And I believe in your god.'

'Bless you.' He tightened his grip on her fingers.

'We have to go.'

He nodded. Standing up suddenly he picked up the shovel by the fire and pushed the ashes over the flames. It was a symbolic gesture; without the light, the house grew dark.

Picking up his pack he led the way outside.

'I'll come with you, down to the boat,' she whispered.

There was no-one there to say goodbye. His farewells had been made earlier to Fergus Mor and Addedomaros and his friends and fellow students. Only Mora followed him down the grassy path towards the water's edge.

The mere was deserted. There was no sign yet of the boat. They stood side by side staring out across the dark water listening to its gentle lap amongst the reeds and sedge at their feet.

'There is no moon yet,' Mora said quietly. She stared out into the dark. A small kernel of worry had lodged somewhere deep in her chest. Cynan should be here. He was always early and he needed no moonlight to navigate across the peaceful waters of the mere. He could do it with his eyes shut. She could see the golden loom in the sky now behind the hills where the moon was climbing higher. Soon they would see it hanging over the black silhouette of the trees. 'Where is he?' she whispered.

Yeshua took a step forward to the water's edge. Somewhere out there a duck quacked uneasily. They heard the splash as a fish jumped.

'Something's wrong,' Mora murmured. She clutched his arm.

He grasped her hand and held it. They could see the tip of the moon now, the sharp crescent hauling itself higher into the sky, spilling pale gold light across the land. Waiting in silence, they watched the sickle turn from gold to silver as it climbed higher, and the light it spread across the summer country changed from warm to the cold of ice.

Mora shivered, clutching her cloak around her. 'He's not coming. Something has happened.'

Yeshua nodded. 'The boy's uncle?'

She dropped his hand and moved a few paces away, staring out, trying to listen. Somewhere in the distance a dog barked. 'We have to go. We'll take a boat from the landing stage. We can paddle it ourselves.' She was hurrying him now, leading the way along the edge of the island back towards the small bay which in summer was a grassy meadow. This year with the early rains it was an inlet teaming with fish. They took the first boat they came to, untying it from the post near the water's edge, throwing in his bundle. Mora jumped in and freed the paddles from the place they were wedged beneath the polished oak thwart while Yeshua pushed the boat out into the water and hauled himself in. For a moment the narrow craft wobbled violently then, as he reached for the second paddle it steadied. In seconds they were both paddling, driving the boat away from the island, towards the river which wound inland from the sea. 'He's coming after you,' Mora murmured, already out of breath. 'I can sense it. We have to get out of sight, into the river before he realises where you have gone.'

'And Cynan?' Yeshua was driving the boat forward with powerful strokes of the paddle from the stern.

'Cynan will buy us time,' she said firmly. She paused for a moment, raising her hand. He stopped, watching her narrow shoulders in the moonlight as the dugout drifted slowly and silently along the channel nosing in amongst some tall reeds as it lost momentum. Nearby an owl screeched. She turned towards the sound. Neither of them spoke. Only the water dripping from their paddles into the black water broke the silence. Yeshua didn't take his eyes off her. She like all her race understood the speech of the birds. The owl had told her something. He caught sight of the white flash of its wings as it flew on silent feathers past them and disappeared behind a stand of willow on a low island to the north.

363

Mora slumped over the paddle and he heard a faint sob. He leaned forward and put his hand on her shoulder. 'What did it say?'

'He's not coming.' She straightened and stared ahead of them up the narrow channel between the reeds. 'We have to go on alone.' She didn't turn and he couldn't see her face. 'We must put as much distance as we can between ourselves and Ynys yr Afalon before it grows light.'

'Flavius is following?' he asked softly.

She nodded. 'We can escape him. We are ahead.'

'And Cynan?'

'Cynan bought us time.' She forced a smile as she glanced up at the moon but he didn't see it. He already knew what must have happened. He heard her sniff, saw her brush her hand across her eyes, then she gripped the paddle again. The force of her first stroke slewed the dugout round and ran them back into the reeds. 'Sorry.' Her voice trembled slightly.

'Mora.' He put his hands on her shoulders and tightened his fingers. 'I am so sorry.'

'He will wait for me in the land of the ever young.' She dug her paddle in again, and pulled straight this time. 'We mustn't let him have died in vain. I have to get you away.'

'My father will reward him in heaven.' His voice was unsteady. 'You foretold this, Mora. You saw how many people will die for me. How can I bear it?'

This time when she stopped paddling she turned round and looked at him. Her face was intensely sad, her cheeks wet with tears. 'You have to bear it. It is your destiny,' she whispered. 'But the people who die for you will be ever blessed.'

He nodded silently.

'You are strong, Yeshua. Stronger than anyone I know,' she said. She managed a smile. 'You will be able to fulfil the prophecies. If your father is a god he will give you the strength.'

He nodded again. 'You are right. Sometimes I feel so weak. I pray that this burden might be given to someone else.'

She shook her head. 'This is what you were born for, my dearest. Now, let us get you back to your kinsman and allow him to take you home.'

They paddled all night and at dawn, as a skein of wild geese flew low overhead, sending their wild triumphant cries echoing across the sleeping countryside they pulled in under the shelter of some willow trees on the banks of the shallow winding river. They slept curled head to toe in the bottom of the dugout and when a herd of small fenland cattle wandered near them to drink at the river neither stirred. When they woke they resumed paddling, following the river as it merged with a larger swifter river which finally turned north towards the sea.

'How far do you think?' Yeshua rubbed his blistered hands on the cloth of his robe.

She shrugged. 'I have never come this far by water. The sky tells me we are close. It reflects the sea.' She gave an exhausted smile.

There were splashes of mud on her face and he leaned forward and wiped them off tenderly with a roughened forefinger. 'We should stop to find food.'

She shook her head. 'Not till we get there. Once you are on the ship you will be safe.'

'You think he is still following us?' He glanced behind them. She nodded. She could feel him; he had hired men to row him after them. To ride would take too long with the ground flooded as it was. He would be gaining on them all the time. She gave a rueful smile. This wonderful man with her was so special, so intuitive, so well educated and so holy and yet he could not read the signs. He could not hear the warnings the birds and animals brought them; he could not see the whipped white waves of the sea echoed in the storm-wracked clouds, he did not listen when the waters beneath their paddles murmured of the boat that followed them.

He was watching her and she saw with a pang of longing the affection in his gaze. 'You think I don't see enough of what is round me?' he said gently.

She felt the colour rise in her cheeks. 'You sometimes see too much.'

'But not the danger. I don't read the signs as you do.'

She smiled. 'Though you read my every thought.'

'I am learning.' The boat had drifted against the bank. Cautiously, not wanting to tip them up, he stood up and jumped ashore. After a moment she followed him. 'This is what I came to study with the druids for,' he went on. 'To understand their ways; to listen to their philosophies. This is why I have travelled so far, to the

365

north and the south and the east, and here to the west. To understand the different peoples of the world. To see why they worship
the gods they do and to understand how I can bring them to my
father.' Beside them an otter slid soundlessly into the water and
set out away from the bank, its nose leaving a V of ripples in the
water. He followed her gaze and smiled indulgently. 'So, what
does that gentleman say? "Hurry. There is a boat behind us,".'

She nodded wistfully. 'That is exactly what he says.'

'And you think it is Flavius?'

She nodded again. 'He is gaining on us fast. I suspect he has
several men to paddle him in a larger boat than ours.' She paused,
staring round. Now that they were on the bank she saw how open
the countryside was here once they were beyond the reedbeds.
'When he appears around the bend in the river we will have
nowhere to hide.'

'So what should we do?'

'Leave the water and cut across the land.'

He frowned. 'Are you sure?'

'It will take longer, but it will be safer. He knows where you
are going. He is going to try and cut you off so you can't reach
your uncle's ships.'

He nodded thoughtfully.

'The next time we see signs of boats along the bank, signs of
where people have been fishing perhaps, or traps or decoys, we'll
pull the boat up there and leave it. One dugout looks much like
another. He won't know if it is ours. Then we will strike off to
the north on foot. We can't be far from the coast now. It will be
much easier to outwit him once we are in open country.'

'You are a resourceful guide, my Mora,' he said with a smile.

She blushed again. 'My part in your story is to see you safely
out of the Summerlands.'

'Your part in my story,' he repeated softly. 'Is that how you see
it?' He studied her face thoughtfully. This time she met his gaze
and held it. After a moment he put out his arms and drew her
to him, holding her close. She nestled against his chest, feeling
the strong beat of his heart.

'I could come with you, Yeshua,' she whispered. 'Back to your
own country.' Rising on her toes she kissed him gently on the
lips.

For a moment he held her tightly, his eyes closed, lost in the beauty of this woman who had attracted him as no other, then gently he pushed her away. 'That is not part of my story, my little love,' he said softly.

She nodded. She had always known that she would lose him. She smiled bravely and turned back to the boat to hide the sudden rush of stupid tears. 'Come, a few more miles, then we will strike out across the woods. We might even reach Axiom by dark.'

Even as she said the words she knew they were not going to get there. The sky in the west was slowly growing prematurely dark. Flashes of lightning were lighting the horizon and the wind was rising. Flavius was drawing ever closer. The gods of the storm – or Yeshua's angel guardians – were going to have to help them now, otherwise they were lost. She could feel it in the tension in the air. She could see it the way the birds were flying fast and close to the ground away from the sea. She could sense it as they climbed once more into their boat, in the way the waters stirred uneasily beneath the hollowed oak of the hull and this time she could see that he felt it as well.

He grinned at her and unexpectedly she noticed excitement in his eyes. 'I shall see if I have learned properly how to command a storm and still the waves,' he said.

She nodded as she picked up her paddle. 'You have the power to do anything you wish,' she said quietly. He didn't hear her. Beside them the willow whips of a pollard tree had begun to thresh and flail in front of the wind. It masked the sound of paddles in the water as a large four-man canoe shot round a distant bend in the river and drew swiftly towards them.

'The police will be here in ten minutes.' Ben walked back into his study, his face grey with fatigue.

Greg was putting his mobile back in his pocket. 'I have just spoken to David. He is coming down himself. Someone is going to drive him tonight. He'll be here in a few hours.'

Ben nodded. He reached for the phone on his desk. 'I'll call Cal and Mat and let them know what's happening. Do you think we should go over there?'

'The trouble is we don't know where he is keeping her.' Greg frowned. 'My guess is she isn't somewhere we would think of.'

He shook his head. 'He doesn't know the area as far as I know.' He sighed. 'If only we had managed to follow him!'

'He would have lost us as soon as he reached the main road,' Ben put in sadly. 'He could have her anywhere. An old warehouse, an industrial estate round Wells or Glastonbury, somewhere in the hills, out on the levels. Even further away.'

The two men slumped into the chairs by the fire. Within minutes they heard the siren of a police car in the distance.

Mat was gasping as he caught up with the dogs, clasping his side as a stitch bit through under his ribs. The old barn was dark and silent, but the dogs were barking ecstatically and seconds after he arrived he heard her voice. 'Thiz? Pym? Is that you? Fetch help, dogs, please.'

'Abi?' Mat groped his way towards the great barn doors. 'Abi is that you? Are you OK?'

'Mat! Thank God!' He heard the desperation in her voice. 'Kier locked me in!'

'OK. Wait while I see how to get you out of there.'

'The door is round the side.' She sounded husky. She must have been shouting for hours he realised as he made his way around the stone wall, following the dimming beam of his torch until he found the door. Swearing in frustration as he pushed it, he shone the torch around the frame and then she heard an exclamation of anger as he rattled the padlock. Then his voice came close to the door again. 'Hold on. This is all pretty rotten. I'll see if I can find something to lever it off with.' For agonising moments she could only listen as she heard rattling and scraping and banging and then at last the splintering of wood. Moments later the door scraped open with a theatrical squeak.

'Mat!' Abi fell into his arms. Tears were pouring down her face. 'Thank God! I thought I would be there forever.'

'Are you all right?' The dogs shot in past them and raced over to the corner where Abi had been sitting. Abi smiled weakly. 'I think they are going to eat my supplies. Good luck to them. They've earned it. Oh Mat, how did you find me?'

'Kier told us he had locked you up somewhere. The man is insane. Greg and Ben went rushing back to confront him. We've been searching for hours, but in the end it was Pym and Thiz. They heard something. It must have been you shouting.'

'Or the CD. That was how he lured me here. I heard monks singing, the sound was drifting across on the wind. I thought it was ghosts.' She gave a wan smile.

'And of course you had to come.' He shook his head. 'You idiot! My God, I'd have run in the opposite direction if I'd heard that! You're just too damn brave for your own good! Come on, we must get you home. There are people searching for you up and down the county.'

'Thank you, Mat. I don't think I could have borne another minute in here.' She was still clinging to his hand. 'In spite of my prayers, I was so afraid. Afraid of Kier, and, yes, afraid of,' she shrugged, 'the ghosts.'

He nodded. 'I know the feeling. I'm just so glad I felt I had to go on looking. I couldn't just wait at home.'

'You and the dogs.' She smiled. 'They've gone awfully quiet. Where are they?' She turned back towards the darkness of the barn.

'Justin?' Cal's voice seemed to come from very far away. 'Justin? Ben just rang. Kier told them he has poisoned Abi's food.' Her voice broke into a sob. 'He's disappeared. They think he might be on his way back here.'

Justin stopped drumming. He felt the echoes fall away, the pictures faded. He stood up slowly and looked round. Even in the dark he could see the tears of worry and exhaustion running down Cal's face. He pulled her to him gently and held her close. 'Abi's not dead, Cal. I would have sensed her out there. Whatever has happened, she is still OK.'

'How can you be sure?' She pulled away sharply.

'I just can. You have to believe me.' He glanced round. 'Which isn't to say we are not very exposed here if that man is around. Is Mat back?'

She shook her head miserably.

'Then let's get you back into the house and I will go and look for him.' He tucked his drum into his bag and slung it onto his shoulder. The past could wait.

They made their way back to the house and into the kitchen

369

where she made her way wearily to the fireplace and stooped to throw on some logs. No Mat and no dogs. The house felt empty and cold. Then behind them the door opened.

Cal's face turned from misery to incredulous joy. 'Mat! Abi! Oh God, are you all right?'

'We're fine.' Mat ushered Abi in. The dogs followed them. 'He'd locked her in the old barn down on Parkin's Field.'

'And you're OK?' Cal seized Abi's hands and looked at her hard. 'You didn't eat anything?'

'Eat?' Abi stared from Cal to Justin.

'Kier said he'd poisoned the food he'd left for you.'

Abi gasped. 'No. No, I didn't eat anything. He left me some food, but, I never got round to it.'

'The dogs wanted to,' Mat said, suddenly very sober. 'Luckily the food was all in a cold box.'

'The utter bastard,' Abi said faintly. 'How could he! I can't believe he would actually try and kill me.'

'And I don't suppose he did,' Mat said thoughtfully. 'It was probably all a bluff, but we can't afford to take risks. He is obviously so dangerously unstable there is no knowing what he might do next.'

'Justin!' Cal turned to her brother-in-law. 'Take Abi back to Wales. She'll be safe there. He would never find her. Leave us to deal with Kier. Ben and Greg have called the police and it is only a matter of time before they catch him, but until then let's get Abi right away from here.'

'No way!' Abi shook her head vehemently. 'I'm not going anywhere.'

'You know,' Justin said, 'it might make sense.'

'I said no! I have to know what's happening here.'

'And you will know. For the present day news there is the telephone,' Justin smiled gravely. 'And for the rest of the story, you can follow it to its end wherever you are. It doesn't matter. You don't have to be here.'

'But I do! This is where it happened. This is where Cynan and Rom died.'

'Rom?' Justin stood up. 'The boy in the orchard?' He stared at her thoughtfully. 'Cal is right. You would be safer away from here. Only for a day or two until Kier has been reined in.' He smiled at her gravely. 'He is distracting us all from what needs to be done,

370

Abi. Which is to bless the boy and Cynan and set their souls free. You must see it makes sense. You and I between us can work better away from here. Place is no more a tie than time. You must realise that by now.'

Abi returned his look. 'And we can find out what happened to Mora?'

Justin nodded. 'And we can help to put things right.'

'How?' she challenged. She held his gaze firmly.

'I will show you.' He gave a wry smile. 'There are many places our callings touch and overlap, Abi. We can gain strength in finding what they are.'

'In your cottage.'

'In my cottage would be a good place to start.' His grin broadened. 'If only because we know we won't be interrupted. I am going to step out into the orchard for a few minutes while you get ready. Just to bless it and promise we will return. Then we'll leave. OK?' He smiled.

Somehow she didn't have the strength to argue any more.

As he climbed out of the car Kier nervously scanned the lower slopes of the distant Tor, now wreathed in mist and almost invisible in the moonlight, and he shivered. Leaving the car in the lay-by, he climbed the fence and walked out across the levels, trying to keep his courage up as he found himself picking his way through a waist-high layer of damp white fog. The night was very quiet, the moon distant and hazy. He shivered, forcing himself to keep going as his terror mounted. He shouldn't have left her out here all alone. What if something had happened to her? It seemed an age before he saw the dark silhouette of the barn in the distance, though it couldn't have taken him more than twenty minutes to walk there. It appeared to be floating in a sea of mist. He stopped in his tracks, peering towards it down the torch beam. The door was open. He closed his eyes for a moment in fury and frustration, trying to rein in his emotions, then he moved cautiously onward. No, his eyes had not deceived him. The door was open and she had gone. He studied the splintered wood. Someone had found her, then. He walked in and stared round, then he went over to the corner where he had left her the blankets and food. She had unfolded the blankets. He could see the imprint of her body on the sleeping bag. The radio had been switched off and had fallen on its side. The food box still had its lid in place. He pulled it off and looked inside. The sandwiches and fruit and samosas he had left there were all untouched. He threw down the lid and turned to look for the Bible. It was where he had left it, unopened. But then of course she would not have been able to read it in the dark. He had pictured her spending the night in prayer. Only in the morning when the light had begun to filter through the roof and round the doors would she have been able to see well enough to read.

He wandered across the floor, his shoes echoing on the hollow boards and suddenly he stopped. A gaping hole opened at his feet where the rotten boards had fallen in. He saw a new gash in the wood where someone had pulled up some more of the flooring and then, in his torch beam he saw the horse's skull lying on the ground. For several seconds he stared at it, taking in the long cranium, the huge teeth, the deep eye sockets, seeing the shadows begin to shiver and dance as his hand started to shake.

The scream started low down in his belly. He could feel it rising and there was nothing he could do to stop it! Throwing down the torch he turned for the door and fled out into the night. 'Sorceress! Witch! Enchantress!' The words spun out under the clouds and were lost in the damp tendrils of mist lying across the levels. Behind him the torch rolled across the floor and came to rest with the beam shining onto a wall laced with spiders' webs.

20

In the orchard Justin stood beneath the apple boughs, facing the moon. He raised his arms in supplication and closed his eyes in prayer. 'Romanus and Cynan, sons of the fen, children, both, of this watery paradise, you died here to protect those you loved. For so long your souls have cried out for justice, but know here and now, that your part in this drama has been recognised, the story will be told. Abi and I will return to bless this orchard, to pray in the church on your island, Cynan, to set right the memories and to tell the world that you saved Yeshua so he could return to his destiny in the Holy Land.' He paused, listening. A breath of wind rustled the leaves around him and he opened his eyes. A stray moonbeam filtered through the crisp golden leaves on the ancient apple trees, turning them silver and he saw a huge clump of mistletoe shimmering above him in a crook of the gnarled branches. He smiled. It was a sign.

In twenty minutes Abi had grabbed a quick shower, thrown some things into an overnight bag, tucked her Serpent Stone in amongst them and climbed into the car beside Justin. Cal thrust a packet into her hands. 'Sandwiches. Guaranteed not poisoned. And here's a Thermos.' She leaned in and put a basket on the back seat. 'Phone us when you get there, OK?'

As the car swung out of the gates Justin and Abi both glanced up and down the road. There was no sign of any traffic. He grinned across at her. 'You'll be safe at Ty Mawr. Once the others have dealt with Kier and he is safely out of the way we'll come back and if there are any loose ends, which I doubt, then we'll follow up Mora's story? Deal?'

Abi smiled. 'Deal,' she said.

*   *   *

Kier flattened himself against the hedge as the car drove past him, heading towards Glastonbury, or possibly the bypass and then who knows where. He had watched Abi climb in, watched them throw her bag onto the back seat, seen Cal pass them a basket, seen Justin fold his tall frame into the driver's seat, his face illuminated for a moment by the light from the front door and he had felt a sob of despair rising in his throat.

'The police were less than helpful, as it turns out,' Ben was explaining to his brother. Cal had brought coffee and biscuits to the table as they sat there with Greg. 'Because we found Abi and she is safe they seemed to think the whole thing was some kind of "domestic".'

'It was the sight of two clergymen and the idea of a third who has gone gaga, and then the magic word bishop that finished them,' Greg said with a wry laugh. 'I can just imagine the story they will be telling back at the station.'

'You told them about the poison?'

Ben nodded. 'Of course we did. I don't think they believed us. They said would we bring the suspicious food items into the station tomorrow and they would send it for testing.'

Mat snorted. 'It sounds as though they were disappointed Abi wasn't dead.'

'It would have made a better case.' Ben shrugged. 'To do them justice there was all sorts kicking off last night apparently at some pub somewhere in town. Blood and gore and GBH. We heard it on their radios. They needed our story like a hole in the head. No body. No violence. No poisoned sandwiches that we could hand to them and a dippy vicar.'

'Or three.' Mat grinned.

'Perhaps it is better they are not involved,' Cal said thoughtfully. 'With David coming. He wouldn't welcome the publicity for the Church. Can you imagine if the press got hold of this? And Abi is safe with Justin.'

They sat in silence for several minutes, then Mat looked at his watch. 'I don't know about you folks, but I might go and get some shut eye. Ben and Greg, you could kip down in the spare rooms. We haven't any guests at the moment. David's chauffeur is going to bring him straight here when they arrive, so I suggest we get a bit of rest. Wherever Kier is, he can't get at Abi, that's the important thing, and there is nothing else we can usefully do for now. I'll make sure the place is locked up and we can reconvene for breakfast.'

In the garden Kier watched the lights go out one by one. He saw the figure of Mat through the windows checking the locks were in place in the conservatory, then again in another downstairs window, then the light there too went out and all was silent. He glanced up. The lights upstairs came on briefly, then they also went out one by one. They had gone to bed. He frowned, feeling a constriction round his chest. Had Abi cursed him as she lay in that barn? Had she invoked evil spirits to torment him? He murmured a silent prayer in the dark. Stupid to have lost his torch. He could barely see as he walked across the lawn away from the house. He wasn't sure where he was going. He couldn't actually remember where he had left the car. Somewhere on the edge of the road, pulled into a farm gate. He wandered past some shrubs, smelling the damp night-time scents of the garden and came up hard against something which cracked his shin. He let out a cry of pain and leaned forward to feel it. A bench. He sat down heavily and leaning back with a sigh, he saw ahead of him the silhouette of an arch against the sky. Then he heard a woman crying.

They had found Romanus and Cynan that evening and borne their bodies home on stretchers of animal skins. When Gaius returned it was to a scene of devastation. He stood looking down at his son, his face white with grief. Already the druids had come from the college and taken Cynan back with them to lie that night in his own cell under the oak trees and within sound of the rustling apple orchards on the edge of the mere.

Lydia came to watch beside her husband and together they stood in silence, hand in hand. 'Flavius did this,' he whispered at last. 'Did he kill Yeshua?'

'I don't know.'

'Joseph waited as long as he dared. He had to take the ships out of the channel and round into the sea before the storm came. He said Yeshua knew he couldn't wait any longer.'

She nodded dumbly.

'Fergus Mor told me Mora was with him.'

Tears were running down her face. She was no longer capable of speech. Behind them Sorcha came out of the house and gently put a shawl round Lydia's shoulders, then she went back inside to Petra whose inconsolable sobs echoed round the compound and out into the night.

Kier could hear their grief. He shuddered, hugging his arms around himself, staring out into the dark. Whatever had happened here was of such incomprehensible sadness that it had soaked into the soil of the garden. He could feel the tears welling up in his own eyes.

Behind him the house lay in darkness. How could they sleep when such awful things were happening so close at hand? He stared round wildly, dashing the tears off his cheeks. Someone had to stop this. But how? How could anyone put right something which had scarred the ground where it had happened so deeply that it still echoed two thousand years later?

He stared out at the arch. How did he know it was two thousand years? Abi, of course. She had told him. She had woken these echoes with her crystal ball and her witchcraft. Without her these memories would still be sleeping under the ground. He stood up, slightly unsteadily and walked forward to stand for a moment on the edge of the flowerbed where the stones of the villa lay in the dark. This had not been the house where the tragedy had taken place. Intuitively he knew that. Someone had built a house there in later times, but the boy's blood was still crying out for revenge. Revenge against who? He stood staring up at the sky. The mist had gone. The clouds had parted and he could see the stars. Was this how Abi felt? She had come to him for help and spiritual guidance to deal with all this weight of guilt and fear and vision under the auspices of the church and he had turned away from her. He had called her names and reviled her, distracted by his own emotions. He had failed her. Again and again he had failed her. He turned sharply and began to walk across the grass, not thinking where he was going, heading automatically for the orchard and beyond it the steep path which led in one direction down to the levels and beyond in the other to the track up towards

St Mary's. Instinctively he knew he would find succour there. And answers.

It was several seconds before Abi could work out where she was next morning. She lay still staring at the whitewashed walls of the tiny room, taking in the deep set window embrasure with cheerful gingham curtains, the small pine chest of drawers with a mirror, a candlestick and a vase of rosebuds. Her bag lay on the floor near her, still closed. She brought her attention to herself. She was still fully dressed except for her shoes, laying under the bedcover rather than in the bed properly. She raised herself onto an elbow as memory returned. She had fallen asleep in the car. They had arrived in the early hours with a thick white mist lying across the hillside and Justin had woken her, led the way indoors, showed her round the cottage and directed her to his spare room while she was still half-asleep. She remembered nothing more of their journey or of their arrival.

They had abandoned the canoe next to several others at a landing stage on the next bend of the river, leaping out and running for the cover of some trees. There was no-one around and they hid, waiting, as the larger boat grew closer.

'Is it him?' Mora whispered. She was pressed against the broad trunk of an ancient willow aware of Yeshua beside her, his arm protectively round her shoulders.

He put his finger to his lips. Wisps of mist were drifting ahead of them, coiling around the low hanging branches of ancient trees. Mora glanced across at him and he smiled reassuringly. They could hear the sound of the paddles now, pushing in unison against the sluggish brown water and the low murmur of voices as the boat sped down the centre of the river.

'He's there. In the middle of the boat,' Yeshua breathed. 'They never even glanced this way. My guess is he is heading for the port. He knows the ships will have to catch the tide. He knows that's where we're going.'

'But your kinsman will wait for you,' Mora said indignantly.

'Not if it means losing his cargoes.' Yeshua released her and they moved away from the tree. 'It was agreed. If I was not there seven days after the full moon he would leave without me. The equinoctial gales will be on us soon. The weather is deteriorating. He can't wait any longer.'

'Not one day!' Mora was distraught.

'He doesn't know we are only one day behind.' Yeshua shook his head.

'But there will be other ships.'

'I am sure there will, but Flavius will be searching every one.' He walked further into the alder scrub and sat down wearily on a fallen log.

'Then what shall we do? We can't go back.'

He caught her hand. 'You can go back, Mora, and you must. You do not have to come with me any further. I have asked more than enough of you and those you are close to.'

She shook her head. 'I am coming with you until I know you are safe.' She glanced back. 'We can pick up the boat again. Now we know Flavius is on his way north we can follow more slowly.' She couldn't believe Yeshua's kinsman would just leave without him.

But he had. As the river grew wider and they felt the pull of the tidal water become stronger they approached the port at last, wearily keeping an eye out for Flavius and his crew. But the river was deserted. As evening grew near the grey water had become increasingly choppy and unpleasant and when they at last pulled into the bank they staggered ashore with relief. Leaving Yeshua with the boat, Mora walked towards the township. A pedlar carrying a basket of wooden spoons and little carved toys which he had hoped to sell to the sailors, told her that the last of the traders had gone. The harbour was empty, and just as well, as they stood looking down at the mud-coloured waves lashing against the quay in the strong north-westerly gale which blew up the channel. She turned back and told Yeshua the news.

Taking pity on them when he saw their crestfallen faces the pedlar led them to a farmstead where he knew the family and they found themselves ushered into a small round house where they were at last out of the rain and wind.

A druid priestess and an itinerant healer were guests to be honoured, as was the pedlar himself. They were offered baked fish and mussels, flat malt bread and blackberries with honey. Then their host pulled out a bird-bone pipe and played for a while

378

as they sat near his fire. It wasn't until long after they had eaten that he laid down the pipe and looked at them. 'There is a Roman in Axiom, who is looking for you. He has let it be known he will pay a reward to anyone who hands you in.'

Mora let out a little cry of distress. Already she was scrambling to her feet. The man held out his hand. 'We do not betray those who have eaten under our roof, lady.' He shook his head. 'I didn't take to the man at all.'

Mora put her face in her hands. 'We have nothing to repay you with.' He shook his head again. 'If this young man is a healer, he can suggest something for my aching bones and have a look at my mother. That will be more than enough. Then as soon as the storm lets up and the tides are right, we will make an offering to the goddess Sabrina and I will take you across the estuary. Drop you off in Silurian territory. They don't hold with Romans over there.' He chuckled. 'The way I see it after that, you have two choices. You can make your way back east across country and cross back into Gaul, that way. There are often quiet days, whatever the season, when boats ply the Straights, so I've heard. Or you can winter with the Silures and leave in the spring when the traders return. Either way yon Roman will lose track of you. If you stay here or go back to Ynys yr Afalon he will find you.'

It was two in the morning when Kier finally got back to his hotel. He had to knock up the night porter to get in. He regained his room and sat for a while, exhausted, on the bed. He must have dozed off because the next time he glanced at his watch it was nearly five. Splashing his face with cold water he switched on the kettle, then he took his notebook out of his suitcase. He had reached a decision as he sat in the little church in the dark, listening to the owl in the churchyard outside. He was going to follow Abi. She had taken a bag so she was going to stay somewhere. Cal had passed them a basket. If it was food it implied a long journey or going somewhere that might not be ready for them. Justin's house. It was worth a gamble, and what other lead did he have? He thought hard. Where was it Justin lived? Surely one of the articles he had read online had mentioned a town? Ten minutes later, fortified by a cup of coffee mixed with two pots of disgusting milk substitute, he had the answer. Hay-on-Wye. Fifteen minutes after that with the help of his credit card and the fact that Justin Cavendish was not a common name he had the man's address. He smiled grimly. The click of a button and he could download a satellite picture and mapped instructions on how to find the cottage. He silently thanked his former curate – former but one – he corrected himself wryly. Almost the only useful attribute that the man had possessed was a sure grasp of computer skills. One day when Kier had bemoaned the fact that he had lost touch with an old college chum the young man had introduced him to the art of people-finding. Kier finished his second cup of coffee, then he stood up. Within half an hour he was washed, shaved, packed and ready to go downstairs to pay his bill. Outside the window, even here in the city, the mist had returned.

Justin was sitting at the table in the living room when Abi appeared at last. A fire was blazing in the grate and the room was full of the incense smell of the oak blocks from the basket. He glanced up with a grin. 'How are you feeling?'

'OK.' She sat down opposite him. 'Did all that really happen or was it a bad dream?' She ran her hands through her long hair, still damp from the shower. She had dug a pair of black jeans and a blue shirt out of her bag, with a cardigan slung over her shoulders.

'It all happened.' He reached across the table towards a jug and poured her a mug of black coffee. 'I'll make you some breakfast. Welcome to my world.' He gestured towards the windows. The mist was still thick and white, lapping against the glass.

She took a sip of coffee and felt the caffeine hit as a physical jolt. 'Have you heard anything from Woodley?'

He nodded. They are all there and still waiting for the bishop to arrive, I gather. No sign of Kier. Cal is cooking them all a huge breakfast which is what gave me the idea.' He pushed back his chair. 'You and I have work to do later, so food would be a good way of grounding us before we start.'

She scanned his face. 'Work?' It was slowly dawning on her that she was alone with this man, a druid priest, who was far too good-looking and attractive for her peace of mind, in the middle of God knows where, part of something which had all the makings of a first-rate melodrama, and they were discussing breakfast.

'Did you bring your magic stone?'

She nodded. 'It's in my bag.'

'Good. That will be where we start.'

While he was in the small kitchen – 'only space for one at a time in here, so you can't help,' – she stared round. It was a man's room, a scholar's room, lined with books. On the table in the window she could see a computer – so he probably did have e-mail – and a phone, papers, more books. But there were other things, interesting things. Crystals, a drum, jars of dried herbs, bunches of ditto, a jar of large feathers – buzzard at a guess. Were these the working tools of a druid in the twenty-first century? Apart from the desk and writing chair there was the large table at which she seated herself, and two deep armchairs near the fire. There was no TV that she could see, and there were no other doors. In the corner of the room a small winding stair led out of sight to the upper storey. That must be where his bedroom was. Her own room was off a passage on the opposite corner on the ground floor, in a converted outbuilding of some sort, as was the kitchen and the obviously newly built bathroom with to her relief, every modern convenience. She was conscious of the smell of bacon drifting through the door. Not a vegetarian then. She bent to throw on another log. She suddenly felt ridiculously happy.

'How long have you lived here?' she asked as they tucked into the bacon and eggs and toast.

'About five years.' He gazed round the room fondly. 'This is a magic house. I was incredibly lucky to be able to buy it. A young couple, Beth and Giles Campbell lived here, but they decided it was a bit remote once they started a family. Before that, a friend of mine, Meryn Jones was here for years. My guru and teacher.' He gave a mischievous grin. 'He lives in Scotland now, so I have in a sense inherited his hideout.'

'It feels very special.' She looked towards the window. 'Is there a view?' The mist was still all round them.

He laughed. 'The gods of the druids have given us protection today. We are on top of the world here. You can see, and be seen, for miles.' He paused. 'I am sorry. Does it make you uncomfortable if I talk about other gods? It is easy to forget you are a vicar.' So he too was aware of the irony of their situation.

It was her turn to laugh. 'It should, but somehow it doesn't. Everything that has been happening to me has opened my eyes to other beliefs in a way I hadn't expected. If Our Lord studied with the druids, why shouldn't I?'

He reached for the coffee jug. 'Why not indeed.' He looked at her attentively. 'So, would you like to talk about your stone?'

They were shaken awake at dawn. 'Come.' The man beckoned Yeshua and Mora out into the cold rain-washed world. 'The gods are with you. The tide and wind are right. I'll take you over now.'

Mora glanced at Yeshua and put her finger to her lips. 'Think of Sabrina as the guardian angel of the river,' she had whispered to him the night before. 'Your father god will help us – but so will she.' And so it proved. The wind had dropped and the waves of the night before had settled to a gentle swell.

The boat was bigger than the ones she was used to on the meres and fens of home, with a small stumpy mast and a sail of tanned deerskin. A pile of nets lay in the stern. The tide was rising, carrying them over the mudflats then out across the deep channel and towards the northern coast. She could see two small islands with their attendant clouds of birds, and beyond them the dark hills of the interior of the Silurian territory, rising misty and mysterious in the distance. Once the breeze caught the sail they were able to ship the oars and sit back, enjoying the sunlight on the glittering water, watching the gulls swoop and dive. Nearby a seal surfaced briefly and gazed at them with soulful eyes before vanishing again under the waves. There were no other boats near them; if Flavius was still on their tail he must be waiting at Axiom for them to appear. Mora turned to look behind them, but there was no sign of any ships emerging from the harbour mouth beyond the point.

Their host ran the boat ashore at last on a pebbly beach below low cliffs. In the distance they could see a farmstead, much like the one where they had spent the night. 'They will see you on your way,' he said. 'Good people even if they are from over the water.' He chuckled.

Yeshua threw his pack onto the beach, then he climbed over the side and stood for a moment in the shallow water, holding the edge of the boat. 'I want you to go back, Mora,' he said. 'This kind man has said he will take you and put you ashore somewhere safe.' She had already risen to her feet and for a moment she stood balancing as the boat moved gently up and down beneath her, its nose firmly wedged in the sand, the tide already threatening to lift it free. 'From now on I go alone,' he said firmly as he saw her hesitate. 'You must go back to the college, to your people and to Petra.'

'But I want to go with you!' She caught his wrist, feeling the warm blood pulsing under his skin. 'Please.'

He shook his head. 'We have already spoken about this. Your story is not my story, Mora, not now. Our ways have to part.' He put his hand out and touched her cheek with a gentle smile. 'There is something you must do for me, Mora. I want you to heal in my name. Go back to Petra. She is going to need you. Lay your hands on her and pray to my father.'

'But you have healed her already,' Mora protested. She was clinging to his hand.

Gently he freed himself. 'Go home, Mora. Now, as the tide turns. I have to leave. I will always remember you.'

She felt the tears well up in her eyes. 'Will you be safe?'

He nodded. 'You know I will. It is written by the prophets. I will go home to my people and I will take up the position that my father put me on Earth to fill. He turned to look up the beach. 'It appears I haven't finished my apprenticeship in the Isles of the West. I will make my way north as far as I can go and then I will cross over to the eastern coast and return to my home from there. Do not fear, Flavius will not catch up with me. Not yet. But you must take care, my Mora. I do not want you to fall into his clutches.' He put both his hands on the gunwale of the boat and began to push it round. The tide lifted it at once. 'Take care of her, my friend,' he said to their host. He leaned in and put his finger on Mora's lips. 'Do not look back. Fix your eyes on the south.' With a last hard push he sent the boat sliding into the deeper channel, then he turned and began to walk up the beach.

Abi looked up at Justin. There were tears on her face. 'She didn't go with him.'

He shook his head. 'It appears not.'

'So, where were they?'

Justin stood up and went over to his bookshelves. He brought out an old cloth-bound volume and then after staring at the shelf for several seconds, another. 'There are legends that after visiting Cornwall and various places in Somerset including of course Glastonbury and Priddy, Jesus crossed over into South Wales. Interestingly there is one strand that follows him in a fairly logical fashion doing exactly what he said, according to your Mora's story. If I remember right, he was supposed to have landed near Monknash and Llanilltud Fawr on the coast near or in the Vale of Glamorgan.' He was rifling through the pages. 'Then the stories say that he went on, probably by sea, landing here and there up the coast of Wales, maybe over to Ireland, then to Scotland where he is supposed to have gone to Mull, I think, and of course to the sacred isle of Iona and then across to Fortingall where there is an ancient yew tree which would have been already ancient when he was there.' He saw her look of incredulity and smiled. 'It is a wonderful skein of legend and myth, always involving the druids, and, who knows, with maybe a bit of history thrown in, all trying to explain why in many eyes Britain is – or was – such a sacred, special place.' He sat down at the table and reached for the other book. 'I used to pooh-pooh this sort of thing as utter waffle, but over the years I have become more open-minded. Social and political historians will talk about attempts to boost Britain's self-esteem and the need for a Protestant foundation ethic and such like, but, who knows?' He shrugged. 'And now here we have a window into what happened, via your stone.'

They both looked at it, nestling on Abi's lap as she sat in one of the chairs near the fire.

'The Serpent Stone.' She smiled.

'Is that what it's called?' He nodded thoughtfully. 'I wonder why. Of course, the ancient druids were sometimes known as adders, as perhaps you know. In Welsh, the *glain neidre*, the jewel of the snake, was a special talisman, known to have powerful magical properties. No-one really knows what they were like, so perhaps we are looking at one here.'

She raised an eyebrow. 'But how does it work? Does it create a hologram?' Picking it up she turned it over and over in her hands. 'If we knew that, wouldn't it give us some idea as to its –' She paused, searching for the right word.

'Authenticity?'

She smiled. 'If you like, yes. And its purpose. Why does it exist?'

'I think a hologram might be a good way of describing what happens. I don't know any more than you, to be honest. I do know that technically crystal can hold a memory. From the esoteric point of view we can say that looking into a crystal is an aid to looking into your own subconscious, just like looking into a bowl of water or a saucer of tea leaves.' He grinned. 'But crystal has an extra quality which can be scientifically measured. Quartz oscillates to a specific frequency which can be made to match the frequency of sound and of thought. So what is happening may not come from inside your head, it may be an actual physical phenomenon of some kind. I will dig out a book for you if you are interested. Crystals can be encoded and I think that is what has happened here.' He stood up and held out his hand. 'May I?'

She handed it to him and watched as he cupped it in his palm. 'All we need to do is ask it,' he said after a few seconds, shaking his head. 'And that is for you to do. I have my own theories about how this was done, and how it is user protected,' he grinned, 'but I think you will have to ask Mora. It may be that we are not permitted to know that particular secret.'

A ray of sunlight fell on it, lighting the prisms in the cloudy crystal core of the stone. Putting it down, he stood up. 'The mist has withdrawn. Come out for a moment and look round. You need to clear your head anyway before going back to the story.'

Following him out of the door she stood and stared. The cottage and its garden nestled in a nook on a low summit; on almost every side the ground fell away in stunning open views across the grassy mountainside, ridged and folded and sweeping. To the north, he showed her, they could see out across the Wye Valley to the Radnor Forest beyond; to east and west more hills, pools of mist still lying in some of the hollows. 'It is beautiful.' She turned round slowly, taking it all in.

He watched her, touched by the carefree expression on her face as she walked across to study his herb garden, Meryn's herb garden, lovingly tended and enlarged by Beth. The strain and pallor had gone and with it the hunted look in her eyes.

Behind them the track led across the soft, sheep-cropped turf between the cottage and the hill road above. Abi stared at it for a moment. Was that a movement up there? The glint of sun on windscreen? She stepped away from Justin, thoughtfully narrowing her gaze against the glare. Kier was no fool. He could well have worked out where she might have gone; the others wouldn't tell him, but it was probably possible to find his address somehow. She sighed.

Justin frowned. Something wasn't right. He could sense it. 'Shall we go back inside,' he said quietly. 'I want to study the stone, maybe test it further.'

She followed him in. With a quick look behind him he closed the door and slid the bolt. She bit her lip. 'You saw it too. There is someone out there, isn't there.'

He nodded. 'I think so. We won't take any chances. There are only two doors and they both have stout locks and bolts. We have nothing to fear.' He glanced at her. She didn't seem afraid at all. Was that her own serenity showing through or was it her confidence in his ability to keep them safe? He gave an inner chuckle. What he was about to do would probably freak out your average clergy person. He wondered how she would react. Probably calmly, he decided. He hoped.

He closed his eyes, went briefly inside his head and in seconds he had cast a protective shield around the house. The sun became hazy; a pall of mist drifted back up the valley. Opening his eyes, he gave her a sideways look and saw her raise an eyebrow. 'Druid magic?' she asked. She had noticed then! She didn't seem phased when he gave a nod.

'I'm sorry. I am sure Christianity has its own esoteric branches; probably no more than special prayer but maybe you need to know how to word it?' He grinned.

'I suppose we just pray. Perhaps I don't know the esoteric stuff.' She went to stand near the fire. 'This is all so strange. Jesus, my Jesus, is different now. I see him in a new way. I'm not sure what I'm supposed to believe any more. This man, who kissed Mora, and paddled in the sea, down there in the Bristol Channel, is my God.' It was strangely easy to talk to him about her faith. In some ways easier than to his brother.

'I don't have to tell you, there is a lot about Jesus and boats in the Bible. His disciples were fishermen.' Justin came over and piled logs onto the fire. 'He stilled the storms. Who knows, perhaps that was druid magic he had learned here.' He frowned as he straightened, listening. All they could hear was the crackle of the flames as they licked round the logs. He hastened across the room and pulled the curtains, hurrying between the windows until the room grew shady. Then he went over to the door and put his ear against it. Abi hadn't moved.

He gestured at the front door silently. There was someone there.

Abi knelt down in front of the fire and held out her hands to the flames. She watched as Justin waited by the door. She could picture Kier the other side listening just as they were listening. He would know someone was at home because the car was outside, so why hadn't he knocked?

She hugged her cardigan around her shoulders and watched as the flames climbed higher, illuminating the chimney. There was a loud crack as one of the logs split and she jumped. She turned and looked at Justin. He smiled at her and gestured at her to wait. Not long, he seemed to say. Just be patient.

'I know you're in there!' Kier's voice was suddenly very loud in the room. He had crouched down and spoken into the letterbox.

Justin didn't answer. He tiptoed across to the table and reached for one of the jars. Inside were several bundles of dried herbs bound up with wool. Taking one out, he brought it over to the fire and pushed it into the flames. He waited until it had caught, then he blew it out gently, leaving the herbs smoking. Abi saw the trail of fragrant blue smoke spiralling lazily round his head. He winked at her and went back to the door. Somehow he managed to lever the inner flap of the letter box open and he held the bundle near it and, pursing his lips, he blew smoke towards the aperture.

They both heard Kier cough. Justin smiled – he had obviously been very close – and blew again, gently, watching as the smouldering sticks in his hand glowed red. Abi climbed to her feet and stood with her back to the fire, watching. Any lurking fear had gone. They were safe here. Kier couldn't get into the house.

He coughed again, then there was silence. After several moments Justin went to the front window and cautiously lifted the corner of the curtain. He grinned. 'He's thinking about it,' he said softly. 'The smoke is working on him.' There was another silence. They waited. Then suddenly a loud bang on the door. 'I know what you're doing. You think that pagan smoke is going to drive me away. Well, you're wrong.' Kier's voice was harsh and panicky.

Abi and Justin exchanged glances. 'I'm going to hit you both with bell, book and candle!' There was another crash on the door. Then silence.

Justin peered out of the window again. 'He's going.' His voice seemed unnaturally loud after the long silence. 'Back up the track, although I fear we haven't seen the last of him.'

'You think he's going to come back.'

'Well, don't you?'

She hesitated before nodding. 'He won't leave us alone, will he.'

'I doubt it. But while we wait to see there are things we can do. I think you should pray for him, Abi. Pray that he sees how foolish he is being. Pray that he will leave you alone in future. Pray for his soul which is tortured and in pain.'

'You don't think I haven't done that already?' She spoke more sharply than she meant to. His magic seemed so powerful, and his concessions to prayer so patronising.

He raised his hands in surrender. 'Of course. I'm sorry.'

'What is that stuff you are burning? It doesn't smell like church incense.' She sat down, staring back into the fire. 'If it has special powers I would like to know what they are.' She softened the unintentional sharpness of her tone with a smile and a shrug.

'Smudge.' He came over and threw the remnants of the bundle into the fire. She smelled the sweetness of the herbs as it burned. 'Something modern druids have learned from the Native Americans. They use wild sage to bless and purify and our guess is that other cultures, including our own tradition, would have done the same. I have made my own bundles. The different coloured wools mean the dried herbs I have used are for different specific jobs. That one, with red wool is to dispel danger and calm the atmosphere.'

'And the savage beast.' Abi shook her head slowly. 'I am out of my depth here.'

'No, you are not. You are a priestess of your church. And a good one, if I read the signs right. The trouble is you are confused, and rightly so, by all that has happened to you. As soon as Kier has gone we can relax and get back to Mora. I think you will find your doubts will be resolved.'

'Even when my bishop hears I'm shacked up with a druid priest burning smudge in the Welsh mountains?'

There was a moment's pause. 'Shacked up,' he repeated. 'That sounds potentially interesting. I wonder what he'll think about that.' He smiled as Abi blushed and it was a moment before she turned away and reached for the crystal.

He laughed softly. 'Don't worry. You forget that the bishop in question has known me since I was born. He's a Somerset man. There must still be vestiges of magic in his soul.'

It took two days for Mora to make her way back to Ynys yr Afalon, partly by boat, hitching a ride with one traveller after another and then on an ox cart for the last part of the journey. She did not go at once to see Petra and her parents, instead waiting on the landing stage until one of the young druids saw her and responded to her wave by coming across for her in a dugout. She went at once to see her father.

He took her into his arms and held her for a long time. 'You know that Cynan is dead,' he said gently. She nodded, her face muffled in his robe, her tears falling anew at hearing the words spoken aloud. 'And with him, Romanus.'

She pulled away and looked at him. 'How could he do it?'

'Flavius?' Her father shrugged. 'He is a man driven by evil gods and by a vicious master.' He sighed. 'Yeshua is safe?'

She nodded once more.

He took her hand and led her over to the two intricately woven wicker chairs which stood near the fire. His attendants had left them alone and the interior of his house was lit only by the flames licking over the burning peats. Outside the rain had started to fall again. In the distance she could hear the sound of chanting.

He looked sternly at Mora. 'I have sworn our community to silence about Yeshua's story here. We do not wish to attract the attention of any more vindictive dictates from the Emperor. His reach, and that of Herod Antipas appears to be as long as it is deadly. The Emperor bears no love of druids as it is. It is not our desire to bring his wrath down on the Pretannic Isles. Because Julius Caesar abandoned his attempt to conquer these shores does not mean the Romans might not be moved to try again.'

In the cottage Justin shook his head. 'What an irony,' he whispered. 'That the end of the druids came not through the hostility of Rome, in the end, but through Christianity itself.'

389

Abi, her hands clasped around the Serpent Stone, did not hear him.

'Cynan and Romanus have gone to the land of the ever young,' Mora's father said gently, 'but they have gone with Yeshua's blessing to the feet of his god. You know of course, that that young man was wise far beyond his years,' he went on. 'He came here to learn, but also he came to teach. You and I and all who have known him have been blessed by his presence in so many ways.'

She nodded, trying to hold back her tears.

'This island is a sacred place; now it is thrice blessed.' He smiled sadly. 'He won't come back here, Mora, not in his lifetime, but one day his spirit will visit us and we will feel that he is near again. I have seen the future here. It is tied up inextricably with Yeshua and his teachings. His uncle will return again and again, as he has always returned, but one day he will come here to settle and with him he will bring some special sign.' He reached across for her hand again. 'You will still be here, my daughter. You will see this for yourself.'

Mora stared at him. 'Did Yeshua tell you this?'

He shrugged. 'Not in so many words. But he and I talked many times. He told me that you too saw his destiny. One day you will serve his god, Mora.'

She shook her head. 'I love my own gods; the goddess.'

'We talked of the goddess. In his land she is called Sophia which means wisdom.' He stood up stiffly. 'Go now and rest and pray. Tomorrow you must go to see Lydia and her daughter. Take them the comfort of Yeshua's words. And remember,' he raised his hand and touched her hair for a moment, 'all this for now must remain our secret. Flavius is still in this country. He still harbours hatred for his brother in his heart and when he finds that his quarry has eluded him my guess is that he will return to try to wreak vengeance on everyone who has outwitted him.'

21

'The most ancient of the Christian churches were built on sites that were already sacred,' Ben said thoughtfully as they sat with their guests eating a late breakfast at Woodley. 'As we know Pope Gregory sent instructions to Augustine to reconsecrate pagan temples for Christian use.' He looked up at the others. 'Our St Mary's is one of those, and so, of course almost certainly, is the abbey in Glastonbury unless they were already dedicated to Christ by the Celtic church.'

The bishop leaned forward and helped himself to more home-made marmalade. 'I think we would all agree on that.'

'Sometimes,' Ben glanced at him cautiously, 'I have always suspected, there is a residue left of their previous incumbents.'

Greg nodded. 'I can substantiate that. I have dealt with sites where ancient pagan shadows remain. It is often the case where there have been problems with the church. The cleansing and maintenance of prayer space is something that ancient priests were taught as part of their training, but since the Reformation a lot of important knowledge has been lost. Sometimes just praying is not enough.'

'Incense?' the bishop said.

'Indeed,' Greg said. 'Not just a pretty smell. And also of course the efficacy of spiritual cleansing depends so much on the pray-er.'

'And if the pray-er,' the bishop echoed Greg's emphasis, pleased with the phrase, 'is not up to scratch for some reason, he can cause more harm than good.'

Greg sighed. 'I fear so,' he replied. 'There is so much to think about. I don't like to think of previous gods and goddesses as devils.'

The bishop looked at him enquiringly, a piece of toast halfway to his mouth. 'We are a missionary church, Greg,' he said reprovingly.

'Christ himself insisted on that. It is one of the commandments. "Thou shalt have no other gods but me".'

'Which isn't to say that the other gods didn't, and don't, exist,' Greg retorted quietly. 'In this day and age we would not dare speak out against a Hindu god. So why do we still get away with turning our old gods, Herne the Hunter, or Pan into the devil?'

'Originally, because he was so real,' Ben put in thoughtfully. 'Talking to people round here, where there are more pagans per square inch than in your average town, I would say I have quite a good angle on what they worship and why. They want a god or gods who is or are approachable. Not someone accessed through an intermediary and kept at arm's length. The gods they worship are far more like what we would call angels. Guardian angels; nature angels, perhaps. Devas, they call them, borrowing the name from the Hindu pantheon; spirits in charge of the elements and of trees and flowers. I find the idea delightful. And I don't find it anti-Christian. God and Christ himself acknowledge the reality of angels.'

'Good point.' The bishop nodded. He sighed. 'It is so very easy to understand the position of the young, especially young women, in resenting the inflexible patriarchy of our church. I had hoped we were taking steps to change, to be less puritan, less authoritarian, but people like Kier do not make that easy.' He sighed again. 'Well. First things first. Before anything else, we must call off the police and make sure this is not logged as an attempted murder or anything like that. Next we have to find Kier and I have to persuade him to come back with me to Cambridge. Then we, or more likely you, Greg, have to perform some kind of exorcism, I fear, to sort out this ancient bloodshed and its awful repercussions down the centuries and after that we have to decide what to do about Abi's visions of Christ. They can't be made public. You do all realise that?'

'Why not?' Cal felt it was time to stand up for the female sex, and say something.

'Why not?' The bishop looked at her askance. 'Come on, Cal!'

'You have proof that Jesus existed; that he came to Britain, that all the legends are true and Britain is a special holy place, and you say why!'

'Proof?' Mat said with a wry smile. 'I think David's point is that we don't have that, Cal. Not by a long way. And even if we did, think Lourdes; think mobs; think fundamentalists; think tourist junk. Think Abi being lynched.'

'And that is just for starters,' Ben put in. 'David is right, Cal. It can't happen. It mustn't happen.'

'And how are you going to stop Kier telling the world, as a way of justifying himself, that his curate went insane and started having visions?' she said furiously.

'One might say that so did a lot of the saints, of course,' Greg said.

'We won't let him say those things, Cal,' David said, ignoring the comment from his deliverance minister. 'We have to make sure he doesn't. And we will. Now, have you heard from Abi this morning? They did get there safely I assume?'

'Abi and the druid priest?' Cal was suddenly really angry. 'Yes, they got there safely. You don't actually believe anything, do you? It's all for show. Keep the status quo and keep everyone calm. Don't scare the horses!'

Mat got up and went round to stand behind her chair. He put his hands on her shoulders. 'Calm down, my love. We are trying to do some damage limitation, that's all.'

'What about the food that Kier left in the barn?' Greg asked suddenly. It seemed wise to change the subject. 'Has anyone been down there to collect it? Supposing someone finds it and eats it in the mean time?'

'He didn't poison it,' Ben said thoughtfully. 'I am prepared to bet on it. Well, no, perhaps not on someone's life; it would be wise to confirm it one way or the other. I wonder if we can have it tested somewhere without the police finding out.'

David nodded. 'It would help us judge his state of mind to know the truth. I'll ask Donald to see to it.' Donald, the bishop's chaplain, had been the overnight driver. He was at present upstairs asleep.

When the phone rang it was Mat who answered. He turned back to the table. 'That was Justin,' he said. 'Kier has followed them to Ty Mawr.'

'Don't let him see you!' Justin turned away from the phone as Abi peered through the curtains. Kier had returned with his car and parked outside the cottage right in front of the door. He was sitting at the wheel, his arms folded, staring straight ahead through the windscreen.

'Your smudging didn't work, then.' She walked back to the fire.

He smiled. 'I think it did as far as it went. After all it stopped him sending malign thoughts through the letterbox.'

She acknowledged the comment with a wry grin. 'Is the bishop coming to get him?'

He nodded. 'Though it's a long way to come on the off chance that he will stay here.' He paused. 'Shall we ask him in?'

'You're insane!'

'No. Druids are negotiators. We like to discuss things. And in any case there are two of us and only one of him. Come on, Abi. You are a Christian. You should be turning the other cheek.'

'I am not a very good Christian.' She felt like the sulky child again. She didn't need this. She wanted the door to stay locked; for someone to take Kier away and the sun to come out so she could sit outside in Justin's beautiful little garden, looking at the view and feeling safe.

Justin was watching her with wry amusement. He could see the conflict going on inside her. 'Abi, there is a car on its way with no less than four clergymen in it, one of them a bishop. Don't you think we owe it to them to keep the culprit on the scene?'

She turned to look at him. 'You just want to see if you can sort him before they get here!'

He smiled broadly. 'That thought had occurred to me. But in fact this is a problem for Kier's colleagues. I don't understand the technicalities of Church of England dogma. I would like to try and put the case for open-mindedness and free thinking though.'

She took a deep breath. 'All right.'

'Really?'

She nodded.

'OK.' He turned towards the door. 'First, go and hide your Serpent Stone. The sight of it would probably send him right over the top. I'd hate to think of him snatching it and chucking it off a cliff or something. Tuck it under the bed or somewhere.'

He waited for her to disappear down the passage towards her bedroom, then he slid back the bolt and pulled open the door.

*   *   *

Abi sat on the bed for a moment, holding the stone in her hands, reluctant to go back and face him. Was this the right thing to do? She stared down into the grey surface of the stone. 'What happened next, Mora?' She touched the crystal lightly.

She hadn't meant it to happen. Not now. Not with Kier so close, but she could see Flavius approaching his brother's house. Her stomach clenched with apprehension. 'Be careful.' The words of her whisper went unheard in the roar of the wind across the mere.

Flavius stood in the doorway looking down at Petra as she knelt by the fire feeding twigs under the pot of water. She glanced up and screamed.

He gave her a chilly smile. 'There is no point in screaming, niece. There is no one to hear.'

'What do you mean?' She stumbled to her feet, her eyes darting into the shadows. There were no servants in the house, no slaves, no farm workers. They were all out in the fields, or the woods, or fishing on the mere. Her mother and father had gone across to Afalon to speak to Mora's father. She had told them of her dream, to study with Mora; to become a druidess, to fulfil her brother's ambition for him and they had agreed. Now it was for them to see if the college would accept her.

She clenched her fists in the folds of her gown and stared at him defiantly. 'Yeshua isn't here. He has gone. You will never lay hands on him.'

He held her gaze. She was a pretty girl, now she was standing upright, with clear skin and bright eyes, albeit swollen and red from weeping. 'I will find him, never fear. If I have to follow him to the end of my days, I will find him.' He folded his arms. 'He cured your agues and your crippled bones, I hear.' There was a sneer in his voice. 'But did his healing last? Can you still skip around the fire, and dance for your supper?'

She straightened her shoulders. 'I am well now. As well as you are.' She looked him in the eye. 'A testament to what Yeshua did. I will tell the whole world what he did for me, and everyone else around here. He was a good man.' She paused. 'Not like you. My father will never forgive you for what you did to Romanus.' To her own surprise she had stopped being afraid of him.

Flavius smiled coldly. 'What did I do to Romanus?' The smile vanished as he waited for her to answer.

'You killed him! You know you did.'

'And you can prove that, can you?'

She hesitated.

'I thought not. I don't think anyone will ever know who killed the boy. Perhaps it was the druid. Perhaps they killed each other. Perhaps they killed themselves. It is the Roman way when life becomes insupportable.'

She shook her head. 'Cynan would never kill anyone. Nor would Rom.' There were tears in her eyes. 'It was you.'

He turned away towards the door. 'Nonsense! Be very careful of the accusations you throw around, young lady. They could get you into all kinds of trouble. I should if I were you be more worried about the fact that your pain is already returning, and your fever is building again and you are beginning to realise just how much of a fraud your friend Yeshua was.' Turning to look at her over his shoulder he fixed her with an icy stare. 'It will happen so quickly you will wonder why you ever thought you were cured.' Again the hard cruel smile as he gave silent thanks to the seeress, all those years ago in Rome for her curses, which he had never forgotten.

'No!' Petra burst into sobs. She was looking down at her hands. Already they seemed to be swelling again, her fingers bending into claws, and slowly she was aware of the dull ache starting in her wrists and ankles.

He smiled again. 'So, are you going to attest that the man was a fraud?'

'No.' She shook her head, tears pouring down her face. 'No. He was a good kind man; a great healer.'

Flavius sneered. 'You stupid girl. Don't you see, I was offering you a chance to live!'

She shook her head again. 'No, you weren't. You wanted me to lie.' She was still standing facing him, her face white with pain.

He shrugged. 'So be it. You will go to join your brother.' His short sword reflected the small flames licking up from the logs onto the softly glowing metal of the cauldron over the fire.

Her final terrified scream was lost in the hiss of steam as he tipped the cauldron over and lunged towards her.

*   *   *

'No!' Abi's whisper was a whimper of pain. 'No, oh no, how could you?' She put down the stone. How long had she been sitting here? She glanced at her watch, trying to shake off the horror of what she had seen. Standing up she seized a T-shirt from her bag, wrapped up the stone and tucked it under the far corner of the mattress. It seemed a bit obvious, but then she wasn't planning on Kier getting anywhere near her bedroom. She went to the door and listened. Nothing. Was he already inside? Had Justin offered him a coffee or a drink or something? Opening the door she tiptoed up the short passage, listening. There was no sound of voices from the living room.

Kier and Justin were standing in front of the fire, about four feet apart, awkwardly, both looking into the body of the room, not talking. She took a deep breath and stepped towards them. She tried to make herself smile, but her face refused to comply and she felt herself staring at Kier showing nothing but hostility in every atom of her body. Coming to a standstill on the far side of the central table, she looked from one man to the other. She said nothing.

Justin grinned at her and she saw a flash of mischief in his eyes. 'I have offered our guest some coffee or tea or a drink, but he has declined.'

She shrugged. 'His loss.'

Justin scanned her face for a moment, then he turned to Kier. 'In which case, my friend, perhaps it would be as well to discuss the reason for your visit with as little preamble as possible.' He paused.

For a long moment there were no sounds in the room but the cracking of logs in the fire and outside the lonely yelping of a buzzard riding the thermals high above the hills.

'I want Abi to come back with me,' Kier said at last. He cleared his throat uncomfortably.

'No.' Abi's response was so quick it made Kier step back. He looked surprised and for a moment almost frightened at the force of the one word.

'But this man is a pagan,' he said after a minute, sounding more hurt than angry.

'This man is a gentleman,' she said softly, and then paused, astonished at her own choice of words. 'He would never imprison me, or hurt me or make vicious unfounded accusations against me.'

'He's not a Christian, Abi.'

'Do Christians behave the way you have behaved, Kier?' she retorted.

He was still staring at her, but suddenly he turned away. He slumped into the chair by the fire and put his head in his hands. 'I'm sorry I frightened you. I didn't mean to. I left everything for you to make you comfortable. I wanted to keep you safe.'

'So safe you put wolfs bane in my sandwiches?' Her voice rose an octave.

He looked up and slowly shook his head. 'I didn't put anything in your sandwiches. I said that to make them realise how desperate I was. I would never hurt you, Abi. Never. I swear it.'

'The police are testing all the food you left with Abi,' Justin put in at last.

Kier looked shocked. 'The police?'

'Of course the police. You kidnapped and falsely imprisoned her and you were threatening murder.'

'Sweet Jesus!' Kier rubbed his face with his palms. Abi could hear the rasp on his unshaven cheeks. 'I don't know what's happened to me. I wanted to save your soul, Abi. I could see the danger. I could see the evil spirits spinning round you. They were everywhere in that house. In the church. Back in Cambridge. One day, suddenly, you were surrounded by whirling lights and voices. You didn't seem to see them.' He looked up and to her horror Abi saw tears in his eyes. 'I responded the only way I knew how. To try and surround you with Jesus' love and protection, to try somehow to protect you myself. I did it all wrong.' He dropped his face back into his hands, and she saw the tears trickling between his fingers.

Justin frowned. 'Can you see these spirits round her now, Kier,' he said gently.

Abi froze. She felt a cold breath circle round her as she stood staring at them. She leaned forward, her hands on the table, feeling the warmth and solidity of the old wood beneath her fingers, waiting in silence for his answer. Kier looked up and stared at her. Then he nodded.

'Describe them.' Justin walked over to his desk and produced his jar of smudge bundles. He scrabbled amongst the litter of pens and other oddments on the desk for a box of matches and lit the bunch of herbs, waving them gently until the flame died to be replaced by a wisp of blue smoke. He laid them in a dish and brought it back to the table, standing it in front of Abi.

'I can see a young girl. Her hands are all strange. She is holding them out, twisted, like claws –'

'No!' Abi almost screamed.

Justin looked at her sternly. 'Let him talk, Abi.'

'But –'

'We can deal with the situation in a minute. I need to know what Kier can see.'

'She is trying to protect herself from a man. He has a knife in his hand. A large knife. A sword. He is threatening her with it.' The tears were pouring down Kier's face now. 'He is going to kill her.'

As Abi opened her mouth to cry out again Justin stopped her with a sharp gesture of his hand. 'What is he saying?'

'The healing didn't work. The healing was a sham. Admit it. Yeshua is a sham!' Kier was shaking violently.

'And what is the girl doing?'

'She is terrified. She is trying to get out of his reach, dodging behind the fire. There is smoke and steam everywhere. There is a cooking pot lying on its side in the fire. She is screaming for her mother.' His whole face had collapsed. A string of spittle dripped from his lips. He wiped his face angrily with the back of his hand. 'Why is this here? Why can I see it and you can't? This all belongs to that house in Woodley. You have to stop it!'

'Do you know who Yeshua is, Kier?' Justin said. 'Listen to me, Kier. Can you hear me? Who is Yeshua?'

'I don't know!' Kier shook his head. He squeezed his eyes closed.

'He is a healer, Kier. A good man, from Galilee.'

Kier swallowed his sobs and stared at Justin, his mouth open. 'Galilee?'

'Galilee, Kier.' Suddenly the room was totally quiet.

'Jesus?' Kier whispered.

'Yes, Kier. Jesus. Jesus healed this child, then this man, this Roman, who wanted Jesus dead on the orders of Herod Antipas, decided to wreak his revenge on this little family who had sought safety on the edge of the Summer Country in faraway Britain.' Justin turned to Abi. 'Fetch the Serpent Stone.'

Abi didn't argue. She was trembling all over as she went back to her bedroom and extricated the stone. She brought it back into the living room and set it down on the table. A wisp of fragrant blue smoke lazily drifted over it, curling in the air and dissipating up near the ceiling below the beams.

Kier stared at it. He began to rock backwards and forwards, moaning quietly.

'You, Kier, have probably got more natural psychic ability than Abi and me put together,' Justin said. 'This sensitivity of yours has been suppressed and ignored and probably fought so strenuously that it has brought you to the brink of a nervous breakdown. You have to understand, that it is part of who you are. It is a god-given talent, not something evil, and it is something that you can use in complete assurance that it is compatible with your Christian faith. You are in the wrong job, Kier. You should be doing what the bishop's friend Greg is doing. Working to overcome darkness and bring in the Christ light. You have targeted the wrong person in Abi. She has acted as a catalyst. This stone is an age-old tool. Someone has told it this story; someone has encoded the horror and fear and evil of what happened at Woodley inside the crystal in this stone, and that someone wanted the story to be known one day perhaps in the hope that terrible wrongs could thereby be righted.'

Kier looked up at Justin, his face blank with misery and exhaustion. 'You believe this?'

'I know it.'

'And Abi is safe?'

'Abi is a strong woman, Kier. She is safe. She too has seen what you have seen, and been made unhappy by it, but between you, between the three of us, we can fight this evil. We can try and put some light back into the darkness.'

'We can't save that child's life retrospectively.'

'We don't know she died at his hand, Kier. To find that out we have to ask the crystal.' He paused. 'On the other hand,' he shook his head, 'perhaps we shouldn't ask the crystal, because maybe the act of watching what happened will mean that it did happen.'

There was a long pause.

Kier sat up. He groped in the pocket of his trousers and produced a handkerchief to wipe his face. He shook his head. 'I don't understand.'

Abi was frowning. She had been watching Kier's face intently.

Now she turned her gaze to Justin. 'Are we talking Schrödinger's Cat here?'

Justin shrugged. 'Something along those lines. We are actually talking about a fascinating phenomenon which is not unconnected with some very real magical formulae about which I don't know very much. I'm wondering whether the druids were adepts in a way we don't understand.'

'Mora?' Abi asked.

'Mora, or her father or the healer she trained with. Perhaps all of them.'

'And how does all this fit into the story of –' Kier hesitated. 'Jesus.'

'That is something we three have to unravel. Our villain is obviously the Roman with his sword at the little girl's throat, the Roman with the mission to kill Jesus before he went back to Galilee. Our victims are the children. Romanus and Petra.'

'And poor Cynan,' Abi put in.

'And poor Cynan. But it is Romanus who screams for revenge. His soul which is anchored to the earth by despair and hatred and disappointment and fear.'

'But the others –' Abi put in.

'The others are part of your story too.' He paced up and down the room a couple of times. 'But it is Romanus who is the source of all this energy.' He threw himself down in the chair opposite Kier. 'And Mora is our key. She wants to communicate with you, Abi. She has done so successfully and she has the tools.'

'And she thinks we can help?'

He nodded thoughtfully. 'She thinks we can help and she wants us to know the story.'

'Of Jesus.' Abi glanced at Kier.

'Of Jesus,' Justin agreed.

Kier said nothing. He sat back in the chair and closed his eyes wearily. He was slowly shaking his head from side to side.

'So what do we do?' Abi asked at last. Her voice was husky. She looked down at the crystal. The smoke from the smudge was still curling round it, as though seeking it out, testing, licking the cold crystal surfaces.

Justin nodded. 'We work together.' He glanced over his shoulder at the man in the chair by the fire. Kier's eyes remained closed.

'What about the car full of clergymen and bishops?' she whispered.

Justin smiled. 'Back up with knobs on. Ben will be up for it and so I suppose will Greg as that is his job. What about your bishop?'

Abi shook her head slowly. 'I have no idea. He's a nice man, that's all I can say. Of course, he was born in Priddy.'

'Oh well, if he was born in Priddy!' Justin laughed out loud. The sound seemed to percolate through to Kier's brain. He opened his eyes. 'You think this is funny?'

'No, not funny. Very serious,' Justin replied after a moment. 'This is something world shaking, Kier. We are going to try and influence the course of history. We have to see to it that Petra is or was saved. We cannot allow that anything else happened.'

'The space time continuum as they call it in sci fi books,' Abi added dryly. 'That kind of thing usually results in the end of the world.'

'Not with Jesus on your side it doesn't,' Justin said.

'Were you ever a Christian?' Kier asked suddenly. He sat up and leaned forward, staring at the fire.

'I was baptised.' Justin nodded. 'I gave up subscribing when I came face to face with some of Christianity's greater inanities. Chiefly their bloodthirstiness. That had nothing to do with the Jesus of my bedtime stories.'

'Or the Jesus of Mora's crystal,' Abi put in sadly.

Kier slumped back into his chair. 'And I didn't do anything to dispel your disillusion, did I,' he said almost to himself. They weren't sure who he was addressing. Perhaps both of them.

'Are the spirits and energies still weaving around Abi?' Justin asked after a moment.

Kier looked up, startled as Abi froze. He stared at her for a moment, then shook his head. 'I can't see anything.'

'No. Neither can I.' Justin looked at Abi and smiled. 'Don't look so shocked. Nothing has changed. You can cope with whatever is there. You can, both of you, cope.' He hesitated, then he walked over and put his arm round Abi's shoulders. 'What say we all have some soothing herb tea while we wait for reinforcements. Once they arrive we will summon the powers of darkness and see whether we can sort this whole mess out.'

'You make it sound so simple, but you still haven't said how,' Abi said with some asperity.

He shrugged. 'We'll play it by ear.'

She gave him a quizzical smile. 'And Kier?' she added softly.

'Kier is no longer a problem.' The husky voice came from the chair near the fire. 'I give up. I can't fight this. I am so sorry, Abi.'

The bishop's black Volvo rolled up to park alongside Kier's Audi at about midday. The four clergymen, all in mufti, climbed out stiffly and stared round at the view of the hills and the valley and beyond to the distant mountains, lost now in a haze, then as one they turned towards the cottage.

Cal had sighed with relief when they left after breakfast. At last they had the house to themselves again. She wandered back into the kitchen and began to collect the plates for the dishwasher. She was standing at the sink, rinsing the last of the glasses by hand when the dogs began to bark. Mat had been glancing at the headlines in the paper. He put it down on the table and looked up enquiringly. 'You don't think they've come back? I didn't hear a car.'

She shrugged. 'I'll go and see.' As she reached for a towel and began to dry her hands there was a sound at the back door.

Cal turned and looked at it. 'Did you hear that? Is there someone there?' She put down the towel and moved towards it.

'Cal, don't open it!' Mat's voice was suddenly anxious. 'Look.'

She turned to see him pointing at the dogs. They were huddling together, their tails clamped between their legs in uncharacteristic terror, the hair on the back of their necks on end. Side by side they backed away from the door, their eyes fixed on the knob which slowly began to turn.

Mat shot forward and slammed the bolt across. 'Who is it?' he shouted. There was no reply. He glanced at Cal. 'Come away from the window. Are all the other doors locked?'

She tried to think clearly. 'I think so. I don't know.' She could feel herself beginning to shiver. 'It's not Kier,' she whispered. 'He couldn't have got back here so quickly.'

He shook his head. The dogs were cowering now behind the settle and the silence in the kitchen was intense.

Mat tiptoed towards the table and Cal saw him pick up the bread knife. She felt her stomach turn over with fear. The earlier mist over the levels had returned and spread silently up through the gardens to encircle the house. Thick and white, it was drifting eerily past the windows. She resisted the urge to go and draw the curtains against it, backing away towards Mat. 'What's happening?'

His knuckles whitened on the knife and she saw him gesture towards the back door in sudden fear. Slowly it was opening. Wisps of clammy fog drifted in, weaving round the kitchen, then they saw the figure. A man stood, outlined in the doorframe, looking round. He was tall, square-shouldered, bare-headed, but otherwise dressed in the military uniform of the Roman army. They could see the breastplate, the epaulettes, the sinewy arms, the short leather skirt, the thonged boots. In his right hand he carried a broad-bladed short sword. Cal felt herself freeze. She couldn't look away. His eyes were dark and hard. They bored into her own and she knew she couldn't run; she couldn't move. Her heart was thudding dangerously. She couldn't breathe.

His face was hard, the angle of his cheekbones harsh, his nose aquiline, his mouth set in a thin merciless line. 'Lydia.' Somehow she heard his voice, though his lips didn't move. Oh God! He was going to kill her. He thought she was someone else.

'Mat?' Her voice came out thin and reedy, a whisper. Where was he? He had been standing near her with the bread knife. 'Mat? Help me.'

Mora was sitting miserably by herself in her small house, her eyes closed. Her father was right. She must speak to no-one, tell no-one what had occurred here, replenish her energies and her healing skills and then and only then go out once more to visit the sick, this time alone. She sighed unhappily. She was missing him more than she could have believed possible. Both of them. Yeshua and Cynan, the two men she had loved. Cynan, who was dead, who had died to save her. She pictured his face, remembered the touch of his hand, the promises they had made in the past of unswerving devotion before Yeshua had come. She had still loved Cynan and she knew he had still loved her. Had she betrayed him? Yeshua's influence had been so strong, his personality so overwhelming, her attraction to him so powerful, had she forgotten her first love, her loyalty to a man who was prepared to die for her and for Yeshua?

404

Hugging her knees she stared down into the flames. Before anything else she ought to go and see Petra. Yeshua had told her Petra still needed her. Petra, who was now healed. Petra who should be running about and dancing and laughing in the autumn sunlight, making up for the lost years of childhood. Petra who would one day, if her wish was granted, come to study here on the island with Mora. Her parents were probably still here somewhere, talking to Mora's father about it, but she knew already he would welcome Petra with open arms to the community.

Standing up she went to the doorway, looking down the hill towards the landing stage where two or three canoes lay tied to a post on the still, reedy waters of the mere. She could paddle over to the mainland now and walk up to the house. Why not.

Automatically she threw her herb bag into the bottom of the boat. She smiled ruefully. Petra should have no need now of her potions and ointments. Thank God!

She paused, letting the canoe drift gently into a patch of sedge. Thank God. She had grown used to Yeshua's god being the only god. She glanced behind her up at the Tor. The entrance to the otherworld, the kingdom of Gwyn ap Nudd was there somewhere near the great Menhir. She had grown up with him; now she was full of doubt. Was he just a helper of the one great god, an angel who held the keys of the underworld or a god in his own right, powerful and all seeing? She smiled sadly. She would never know. Yeshua, her Yeshua would one day return to Afalon, but in spirit not in body. She had always known that. Just as she had always known that he was returning home to face certain death. She felt a warm tear run down her cheek as nearby with a steady beat of its enormous wings a single white swan angled in over the water and came to land on the glassy surface near her. Picking up the paddle she began to head once more out into the still water.

The homestead was silent. She let herself in through the gate in the palisade and stared round, surprised. She had never known the place to be unattended. There was always someone around if not in the house then in the sheds and barns, or Sorcha's house – a member of the family, a servant. Slaves. Farm workers. Peat cutters. She peered in at the door of the main house. The fire was out. The huge central room was deserted and shadowy. She frowned. Where was everyone? She shivered. She knew the death of Romanus had hit the entire household harder than anyone could ever imagine.

The fact that almost certainly the boy had been killed by his own uncle was a blow few parents could recover from; it was almost as hard for the men and women who had known him since he was born. Her own loss, of the brave and patient Cynan was only made tolerable by the fact that the young man had been there with Romanus; neither of them had died alone.

She ducked inside and looked round the large room. She could see Lydia's favourite shawl, lying across the back of the oak settle. And Petra's gaming board, the game she had so often played with her brother. Mora blinked back her tears. 'Hello?' She glanced towards the sleeping quarters. The curtains had been looped back, the screens left open. The bowls and plates on the sideboard were washed and clean. The fire was out. There were no dogs running round the yard outside. Nothing. The place felt dead.

'Petra?' She turned back to the doorway. 'Is there anyone there?' And then she saw it. The huddled figure lying against the wall.

'No!' Abi was holding the stone in her hands, the tears running down her cheeks. 'Please, don't make me go on.'

'I think you have to, Abi,' Justin said firmly. He was sitting across the table from her. He reached out and clasped his hands over hers.

She glanced round the room, aware of the men seated around her, all silent, all watching. Only Kier was looking away, staring down into the fire, his hands twisting together on his lap.

'Try, Abi. Just a bit more,' Justin went on. 'We're nearly there. Please. You and Mora. Two priestesses, two women who heal in Jesus' name.'

She looked round pleadingly. They were all waiting, engrossed in the story, totally involved in their different ways with what she was telling them. She looked back into the crystal.

'The house is full of shadows. She could be wrong. It could just be a bundle of rags,' she went on, her voice shaking. 'There is nothing to see with; no flaming torches, no candles or lamps, no firelight and it is a dark corner. She creeps closer, her heart hammering in her chest, bile rising in her throat.' She paused and took a deep shuddering breath.

*   *   *

406

'Petra?' The voice was Mora's now. Echoing strangely round the room, disembodied. Ghostly. 'Petra darling, is that you?'

Mora took another step towards the bundle. 'Petra? Speak to me.'

'Petra is speaking to no-one ever again!' The harsh male voice behind her made her cry out in fear as she spun round. 'Why, if it isn't the druid healer.' Flavius sounded surprised. 'Yeshua's little helper! The one, so I hear, who whisked him out from under my nose.'

'You can't have killed Petra.' Mora's voice was husky, barely audible. 'No! Why?'

'Why? Because she was a witness of his healing powers, that's why. She was cured. But not very well, as it turned out. Before she died her hands were turning back to claws!' He gave a short harsh laugh. 'She was so suggestible, that child, so malleable!'

She gave a cry of horror. 'How can you be so evil?'

'Easily. It is in my nature.' He stared at her, his face devoid of expression.

Mora's mouth had gone dry. She felt her stomach clench with fear. He was going to kill her as well. Her gaze slipped down a fraction and she saw there was indeed a sword in his hand, half hidden in the fold of his tunic. The blade glinted in a stray ray of light from the doorway. She could see the dried smears on it which must be blood.

'Why are you so afraid of Yeshua?' she asked softly, somehow finding the courage to speak now she knew she had nothing to lose. He was going to kill her anyway. 'Why is your Emperor so afraid of him that you have to slaughter all his friends and hide all signs of his passing?'

He gave an infinitesimal shrug. 'I do not question my orders. I obey them.'

'And this is what makes your Empire so strong? Mindless obedience?' She was playing for time, she didn't know why. Who would come? No-one knew she was here. 'But of course it is.' A thought struck her and she felt her blood freeze. Had Lydia and Gaius returned to find him waiting for them? She met his gaze and held it. 'And Lydia and Gaius?' she whispered. 'Have you killed them too? And Sorcha and the rest?'

He smirked. 'Most of them ran away, but not Gaius. Fool that he is. He walked in here, calling for his daughter. Happy!' He gave a snort of derision. 'He really thought I would not kill him because I was his brother! All these years and he had failed to realise that I was put on Earth to kill him. There was no room for two of us in my mother's womb, and not enough air for us both to breathe when we were born. Only now, at last, am I free of him!'

She shuddered at the sheer venom in his voice. 'And Lydia?' she asked bleakly. Her fear for herself seemed to have retreated onto some distant unregistered plane.

'Lydia spurned me.' His face darkened and for a moment she thought he was going to spit on the ground.

'So, you have killed them all.' She paused, unable to speak. When at last she could find the words they were barely audible. 'But at least they are free and together. They will not be afraid of you ever again.' She was biting back her tears.

Behind him she caught sight of a shadow in the doorway. He must have heard something for she saw him raise the sword. He stepped sideways out of the light, then he spun on his feet and when he lunged with his sword, it was towards her.

'No!' Abi looked up. The others, still seated round the table, were watching her in horror. 'I can't bear to watch.' Tears were running down her face.

Standing up, Justin came to her and put a reassuring hand on her shoulder. She sniffed, groping in her pocket for a tissue. Waves of exhaustion were sweeping over her. 'Just five more minutes, Abi. Go back. See what happened.'

'No!' Kier stood up. 'You can't go on with this.'

'Sit down, Kieran.' David Paxman barely raised his voice but Kier subsided at once. 'I think we need to know this. Whatever is happening here, it feels very real to me. We must let it run its course. Please, Abi, only a few more minutes.'

She reached out for the stone. Her hands were shaking and her eyes tired as she peered at it. What had happened to Mora? Taking a deep breath she focused again on the cloudy, crazed surface of the crystal.

Whose was the shadow in the doorway?

22

'Cal?' Athena put her head in through the open back door and looked round. 'Are you there?'

Cal was sitting in the chair by the unlit fire, staring down at the floor.

'What's happened?' Athena took in the scene as she came in, threw her bag down on the table and ran across to Cal, dropping on her knees beside her and taking her cold hands in her own.

Cal looked up blindly. 'I am so frightened.'

'Why?'

'He came. The Roman. He stood in the doorway and looked round as though he was hunting for someone. Then he came in. He had a sword. He said he had killed them all, Athena. He killed his family out there in the garden. The children, the dogs,' her voice broke, 'his own twin brother. All of them.'

'But he didn't hurt you or Mat.' Athena gripped her wrists tightly.

Cal shook her head.

'So, where is Mat?'

She shrugged. 'He was here. He went out after him.'

'Sweet goddess!' Athena stood up and put her arm round Cal's shoulder. 'Tell me what happened. Exactly.'

'He came in and he raised the sword.' Tears started trickling down her cheeks 'I was screaming for Mat.'

'Where was he?'

'He was here. Right beside me. He picked up the bread knife from the table there. He raised it up and stabbed at Flavius.' She paused and took a deep breath. 'He brought the knife down and . . .'

'And?'

'And,' she paused and took a deep shuddering breath, 'and there was nothing there. Flavius wasn't there any more. He vanished.'

She swallowed hard. 'We couldn't move. We couldn't breathe. For a moment it was as though everything – time itself – had been suspended, then slowly everything went back the way it was. It was just Mat and me in here. No-one else. Nothing. The dogs came out from under the chair and they started to bark.' She gave a watery smile. 'Hackles up. They went ballistic. Mat said he thought that meant we were safe. The kitchen door hadn't really opened. It was still bolted.'

For a moment they sat in silence then at last Athena spoke, her voice little more than a whisper. 'If he killed all of the family out there, Cal, who is he hunting? Why did he come in here?'

Cal refocused on Athena's face. She shook her head. 'I don't know.

'Are you sure he killed Lydia? Didn't he love her?'

Cal shrugged.

'What about Mora, the druid priestess? Wasn't she the one who Abi has been contacting through her stone?'

Cal nodded. 'Oh God, Athena, you think he was looking for Abi?'

'Where is she?'

Cal swallowed hard. 'She's gone with Justin. To Ty Mawr.'

'That's sensible. She'll be safe with him.'

'Will she?' Cal threw herself down in a chair and clasped her hands on the table in front of her. They were still shaking.

Athena nodded. 'She will. She has to be.' She reached for the kettle and plugged it in, glancing at the door. 'Where are the dogs now? Did they go with Mat?'

'I suppose so.' Cal gave a wan smile. 'Don't open the door!' she called as Athena turned towards it.

'He's gone, Cal. Your Roman has gone,' Athena said. She sounded, she realised, a lot braver than she felt. 'After all, I didn't see him when I came in. I'm going to call Mat. He can't have gone far.'

He hadn't. He reappeared almost at once, his face white, the bread knife still clutched in his hand. 'I wish Ben was here,' he said, throwing it down. He had bolted the door behind him again. 'I wish everyone was here!'

'He's gone for now,' Cal said at last. She didn't point out that a bolted door had not kept Flavius out. 'The dogs will know if he comes back before we see him.'

410

'And if he does?'

'Perhaps by then the others will be back. At least he knows now that Abi isn't here.'

'But why should he be after Abi?' Athena put in.

'Because Abi has the stone? Because Abi can tell the story? Because she can tell the world what a shit he is?'

'And you don't think he will follow her and the stone to Wales?'

'If he does, at least she isn't there on her own,' Cal said after a minute. 'The others must have got there by now. They are all there. Kier followed them. They rang and told us he was outside the cottage. Ben went after them with the bishop and the bishop's chaplain and another man called Greg who's an exorcist.'

Athena stared at her. For a moment her face registered horror then slowly the corners of her mouth started to twitch. 'You are telling me that, what, three vicars and a bishop are on their way to Justin's house? Our Justin. Druid Justin?'

Cal nodded. After a moment she started shakily to smile as well. 'I would like to be a fly on the wall, wouldn't you?'

Athena nodded. 'Indeed I would,' she said slowly.

'Give it to me.' Kier had risen from his chair and moved stiffly towards the table. He reached out for the crystal. 'I'm going to help her.'

'No!' David Paxman stood up and reached across the table to intercept his outstretched hand but he was too late. Kier picked up the Serpent Stone and turning back to his chair by the fire, subsided once more, clutching the stone between his hands. There was silence in the room.

Abi turned to Justin in appeal but he shook his head and put his finger to his lips, watching Kier's face. Ben had risen to his feet anxiously, but Greg put out his hand and pulled him down into his chair. 'Wait,' he whispered. 'See what happens.'

Mora was clutching her side. She could feel the hot blood welling up between her fingers, cooling, turning sticky. In front of her Flavius had stepped back towards the empty fire pit, moving quietly, on his toes, his eyes fixed on the doorway where the shadow of the man hovered, just out of view, the silhouette

411

thrown, strangely distorted by the sunlight outside onto the wall.

'In the name of Jesus Christ, come out!' The disembodied voice echoed strangely in the shadows of the house.

Mora shrank back. The silhouette had straightened. The shadow figure outstretched a hand and she could see the shape of a cross thrown slantwise across the wall. He was holding something. Was it a reversed dagger? Crossed sticks?

Flavius shifted the grip on his blade and moved, light as a cat on his feet to the far side of the fire from where he could see out of the doorway. She saw his face tense, his concentration absolute as he looked from side to side. For a moment he hesitated and she saw a flicker of puzzlement as he crept closer. 'Who is there?' She heard him mutter the words as she slipped lower onto the ground. Her strength was going, her mouth dry. She could only watch as he moved again. He had reached the door and carefully, back to the wall, he peered outside. 'Nothing!' She heard the sneer in the words. 'A dream.' He moved outside, out of the shadows and she saw the light fall across his face. Then, 'Who are you?'

Again the voice, further away this time. 'Jesus Christ is here. He will save these women. He loved them.'

Mora could hear the blood pounding in her ears. She was struggling for breath. 'Yeshua,' she murmured. 'Save Petra. Save me. I can't do it alone without you.' She could see the shadow growing larger. There was someone out there.

'Who in Hades are you?' Flavius' voice rang out, sharp with fear, then she heard him scream.

As she subsided into unconsciousness she heard quick light footsteps running towards her and Lydia's voice, gentle in her head. 'Hold on Mora. I am here, my dear. Hold on.'

'Kier?' The silence in the room had lasted for several long seconds before Ben rose to his feet again. 'Are you all right?'

Kier had fallen back in his chair. The stone had rolled from his hands onto the floor, falling onto the hearth rug where it lay inert, the crystal faces gently reflecting the flicker of the flames from the fire. Ben moved towards him and took his arm, shaking him gently. 'Kier?'

Greg stood up. He walked over and stood for a moment looking down at him with a frown, then he reached out and put his hand to Kier's throat, pressing his two forefingers below the jaw. 'His pulse is steady.'

'Thank God!' Ben glanced up at him. 'For a moment, I thought the worst . . .'

'That was his voice we heard. With Flavius and Mora. There. In the past,' Greg said thoughtfully. 'It was. Wasn't it? I'm not imagining it?'

Both men turned towards Justin. He stood up. He moved over to Kier and took his wrist, also testing the pulse. 'That is amazing,' he said quietly. 'You are right. We heard his voice from the past. He is a walker between the worlds. A natural shaman.' The other men looked at him sharply, but to Abi's surprise no-one said anything.

It was several seconds before the bishop rose to his feet and moved over to join the other men looking down at Kier. 'We shouldn't have allowed him to do this. Will he be all right?'

Justin nodded. 'He should be.' He looked troubled. 'In theory he should sleep it off and wake naturally after a time, only . . .' He paused and put his hand on Kier's forehead.

'Only?' Bishop David prompted after a moment.

'He is untrained.'

'Meaning what?'

'Meaning that he could get lost; not know how to return, am I right?' Greg looked across at Justin.

Justin chewed his lip for a moment. 'He used the crystal as a signpost, or an access point, but then he dropped it.'

'Then give it back to him!' Abi elbowed her way passed the bishop's chaplain who seemed to be incapable of movement as he sat beside her, and pushing between the men, she scooped the crystal off the floor and put it between Kier's hands, trying to fold his fingers around it. They were inert. The ball rolled off his lap again.

She stood back in horror. 'Go after him!' She looked across at Justin. 'You can, can't you?'

Justin nodded doubtfully.

'Well then?'

'It's not that easy, Abi.'

'Of course it is. You have to.' Instinctively she had put her hands over Kier's. She could feel the healing warmth flowing out of her. Closing her eyes, she pictured Yeshua. 'Help me help

413

him,' she breathed silently. For a few seconds there was silence in the room then Greg reached forward and put his hand on her shoulder.

'Leave it for now,' he said. 'I think Justin's first idea was the best one, to let him sleep it off. With luck he will wake naturally and remember only that he has had a dream of the past. You, take the crystal again, Abi. We need to know what has happened.'

Abi hesitated. She was looking down at her hands. Justin stood up and came over to her. 'You have the gift of healing Abi,' he said quietly. 'I sensed it. But this is not the right time. Kier has something to do, or somewhere to go. Over there, in the past.'

She met his eyes doubtfully, then quietly she nodded and turned away.

Bishop David shook his head. 'I don't believe any of this!'

'Of course you do.' Greg managed a quick grin. 'Come on. You're known for your broad-mindedness. Let us pray together, then Abi can look and see what has happened to Mora.' He paused and looked at them thoughtfully. 'And Kier.'

When Mora woke she was in her own bed. Her father was sitting on a stool at her side holding her hand in his. He saw her eyelids flicker and he leaned forward with a gentle smile. 'At last. You have slept for a long time, my Mora.'

She moved uncomfortably and felt a tight restriction round her middle.

He nodded slowly. 'Addedomaros has been looking after you. He has strapped your ribs and stitched the wound. You lost a lot of blood but you are on the mend.'

'And Lydia?'

'She is all right. She is staying here on Ynys yr Afalon. She has been helping us.' His eyes sought hers. 'There is nothing left for her on the mainland.'

Mora closed her eyes, feeling hot tears slipping out onto her cheeks. 'Petra?' There was a long silence.

'Petra sleeps,' he said at last. 'Between life and death. We have tended her wounds and Addedomaros has dripped life-sustaining drinks between her lips, but her spirit has fled.'

'But she is still alive?' Mora struggled to sit up.

He shrugged. 'She still breathes. Addedomaros says –'

But Mora was not listening. Somehow she managed to swing her legs over the side of the bed. 'Take me to her.'

'You're not strong enough.'

'I am. I am strong enough. I know how to help her.'

Her father carried her. Petra was in a small cubicle near Addedomaros' own room. Lydia was sitting with her in the flickering light of two beeswax candles. The whole room smelled of honey.

Setting Mora gently on her feet Fergus Mor stepped back in the shadows as she stood for a moment, looking down at the unconscious figure in the bed. For several moments she didn't move then painfully she sat down on the edge of the bed. Smiling sadly at Lydia who was seated on a stool at the far side, she reached for Petra's hand. It was soft and supple but very cold.

'Petra?' she whispered. 'Petra, can you hear me?'

There was no movement in the girl's face. It was as still as carved stone.

'Petra. I am going to make you better.' Mora laid her hand on the cold forehead. 'I want you to wake up.' She hesitated, glancing up at Lydia, then at her father, her eyes for a moment full of doubt.

'Do it!' Abi whispered. 'Do it, Mora. Heal her in Jesus' name.'

She saw Mora turn and look back at Petra again. Had she heard her? Abi wasn't sure. The hut was full of shadows as the candle flames danced.

'Petra!' Mora's voice was stronger now. 'In Yeshua's name you are healed!'

There was a long pause. Lydia, Mora and her father were gazing at the child's face. The whole world seemed to hold its breath. A sigh of wind from the doorway flattened the candle flames for an instant and, as they watched, Petra opened her eyes.

It was later, when Petra was once more asleep, this time in Lydia's hut where she had been given a bed of her own after she had eaten and drunk for the first time in days, Mora went back to her father's house.

He looked at her as she settled on her stool. 'In Yeshua's name?' he repeated gently.

She nodded. 'He is the greatest healer I have ever seen.'

Fergus Mor stared down into the fire. 'I do believe he is,' he said at last.

There was another long silence, then for the first time she remembered to ask. 'What happened to Flavius?'

'He disappeared.' She heard the harsh note in her father's voice.

'He escaped unhurt?'

'We don't know.'

'And the man who was outside?'

Her father did not reply and she gave him a glance from under her eyelashes. 'I saw him. Or at least, his shadow.'

'As did Lydia. He too has gone. There was no trace of him. The whole area has been searched, but both men have vanished. There were no footprints. No clues. No trace at all save this one thing.' With a sigh her father heaved himself to his feet and walked across to the table. He picked up something and brought it back to her. It was a silver cross on a broken chain.

Dry-mouthed, Abi stood up and went back to Kier's side. Reaching under his jacket she pulled his shirt open. 'He wears that cross all the time –' She broke off, staring down at his throat. 'Nothing,' she whispered. 'It's gone.'

Greg moved over to her side. He pointed to Kier's neck. 'See that mark? And here, a raw tear in his skin, as though something has been pulled off.'

Abi looked up and they held each other's gaze. 'The cross is still there, in the past,' she whispered. She threw a pleading look back at Justin who was still seated at the table. 'Help him,' she whispered.

Justin rose to his feet. He came over and stood looking down at Kier's face then he reached for the man's hand, his eyes full of compassion. 'I will try and go after him,' he said after a moment.

'No!' Bishop David's voice was firm. 'We don't know what has happened or what is happening, but I do not want to risk anyone else's safety.'

Justin narrowed his eyes. 'Thank you for your concern, but this is my job.'

'And mine is the welfare of my clergy.'

'Then let me help him. He is lost in another world. He doesn't know where he is or how to return. He doesn't know the byways between the worlds.'

'And you do?' Bishop David fixed him with a steely look.

Justin nodded. 'I have been trained to do this, David.'

The bishop opened his mouth to retort and changed his mind. He shook his head. 'I am uncomfortable with all this. You are a pagan –'

'And I am dealing with pagan times and with pagan people and with pagan concepts.' Justin paused. 'These people were the friends of Jesus Christ. They risked everything for him. Your colleague has gone into the past in Jesus' name.'

'And he saved Mora and Petra,' Abi put in.

'With your help.' Justin turned back to her. 'That was the moment when history was at a point of balance. Without your prompting Mora might not have used Yeshua's name. In her father's presence she might have felt too inhibited.'

Abi shook her head. 'Rubbish. Mora was a strong woman.'

'Stronger with you beside her.' He winked, then he turned back to Kier. 'This part of the action belongs to me.'

Abi nodded. She laid her hand on the bishop's sleeve. 'We owe him this. We can't abandon him,' she said firmly. 'What if he dies?'

'I don't think he will die,' Greg put in doubtfully, 'At least . . .' He paused. 'You would be risking your life or at the least your sanity.' He had been staring thoughtfully at Justin. 'I know shamans do this in many cultures, but even so.'

Justin gave a wry smile. 'They do it in our culture too. Now please, let's not waste any more time. Can I suggest you all go out and leave me to get on with it. I find the overlay of scepticism in this room rather overwhelming. Why not go down to Hay for a few hours. Buy some books, drink coffee, walk by the River Wye, go to St Mary's and pray. I will ring someone's mobile when I have finished and call you back.'

Abi didn't go with them. She watched the car drive away from the doorway then turned back inside. 'Do you want me to go out too?' She had refused to accompany the men, but she wasn't sure Justin wanted her there. Behind them Kier lay back in the chair by the fire, eyes closed, unmoving. Justin shook his head. 'I don't want you to go. It depends. Can you sit in a corner in here and pray for me without interfering?'

'You want my prayers?' She scanned his face, searching for signs of mockery. He stepped towards her and put his hands on her arms, drawing her close. 'Yes, Abi. I want your prayers. I want

417

you to cover my back; to watch over me. To hold me in your heart and surround me with prayer. Because I don't worship in your church doesn't mean I don't believe in prayer. My faith is too complicated to discuss now.' He grinned suddenly, his boyish face lighting with mischief. 'Suffice to say, I was brought up a Christian. I respect Christian values and your prayers are as good as anyone's.' He leaned forward and kissed her forehead.

She pulled away. His touch had sent a bolt of electricity through her. She closed her eyes and tried to turn aside, aware of the blush creeping across her face. Not now. Don't fall in love with the man now! She had been fighting it for so long, surely she could fend off her feelings while poor Kier was in such peril. Justin was studying her, a quizzical smile playing round his mouth. She suspected he could read her every thought as gently he released her. 'Come and sit over here, on the far side of the table. You are going to watch me do things which will shock your puritan little soul.' He grinned again. 'They are just techniques. They work. They are ancient shortcuts into the other world. They are methods which the original Christians in this country would probably have known and utilised. Don't be afraid whatever I say or do, or whatever Kier says or does and do not move. Do not interfere. Do not touch either of us. If we fall asleep or seem to lose consciousness do not panic. Just go out for a walk and let us sleep. Understand?'

Abi nodded. She sat down obediently. 'But I am allowed to pray.'

He smiled. 'Quietly!'

'Quietly.'

'OK. Go for it.'

She put her hands together on the table in front of her, palm to palm, fingertip to fingertip and closed her eyes.

He followed the soft beat of the drum into the shadows, the Serpent Stone before him on the table. In the quiet room the smoke rose from the burning sage, to which he had added a grain or two of frankincense, dried mugwort and vervain, trailing up towards the ceiling. In his chair Kier hadn't moved. Abi's eyes were closed, but her lips moved in silent prayer; he could feel her calm strength.

His fingers stroked the taut deerskin of the drum, the call

418

growing softer, more persuasive. This was something he did rarely. Whatever he had said to the others, the way of the shaman was Meryn's calling, not his. He was a scholar, not a traveller of the ways, but Meryn wasn't here and Abi had asked him.

He could sense the atmosphere clearing and he stared round, trying to make out what he was seeing. There had been no rush, no swoop through time, just a gentle drift into the darkness. Then he heard it, the soft lap of water, the sibilant murmur of the wind in the reeds. He moved forward and felt the mist of cold rain on his face; under his feet the ground was soft and muddy. All was dark save for a small light in the distance. It flickered in the wind, beckoning him on.

Slowly he moved another few paces forward. He could see the outline of the house now, the doorway, the lamp on the floor just inside, out of draught. The place appeared deserted. He crept on, his eyes narrowed against the cold rain, aware that somewhere the slow drumbeat had stopped. He could no longer smell the burning herbs or sense Abi's presence near him. He was alone.

At first he hadn't seen the woman sitting by the fire, swathed in a dark cloak. He hadn't realised the fire was lit, albeit sunk to embers, barely warm. He stood looking at her, then he stepped forward, wondering if she would be able to see him. Her face was thin, weary, patrician, the long nose, the high cheekbones betraying her Roman origins, her face aged beyond its years with sorrow.

'Lydia?' He spoke very softly, not wanting to scare her.

She looked up and he saw the despair and lack of hope in her face. 'Who is it?'

She couldn't see him then, although she had heard him call her name.

'I am a friend, come from far away to try and help you.

'How can you help? Gaius wanted us all to go when Flavius came. He knew the danger. It was me who insisted on staying. It is all my fault.' She showed no interest in locating the source of his voice, turning back to stare into the fire. A stray breath of wind fanned the embers for a moment and the charred, cold end of a branch caught, flaring suddenly, throwing highlights on her face. She had once been very beautiful but her face was ravaged by grief.

'A man came here to try and help. I think he was the one who chased Flavius away.' Justin moved closer but she still didn't look round. 'The man with the cross. I have come to try and find him.'

419

'The man with the cross? When he spoke the words, Jesus Christ, my child's hands were whole again. Her hands were perfect, her face serene. She was smiling.' Tears spilled over again. 'He followed Flavius. He said he would not return until Flavius was dead.' She sounded distant. Uninterested.

'Do you know where they went?'

She shrugged. 'Flavius said he was going back to Judea. He said he would wait for Yeshua there. He killed my son and my husband, he all but destroyed my daughter then he laughed in my face. I wanted to kill him but I'm not strong enough. I was never strong enough.' She sighed. 'Then the man with the cross came. He knew Yeshua. He knew what had happened.' She inclined her face slightly as though looking towards him. 'They are long gone.'

'You still have Mora,' Justin said gently. 'She will be another daughter to you.'

Lydia nodded sadly. 'And Mora's child.'

'She's expecting a baby?' Justin was shocked into speaking loudly and he saw her jerk backwards, fear in her eyes. 'I'm sorry. I didn't know,' he said more quietly. He was searching his memory to try and fill in the story Abi had told him. 'Cynan's child?'

Lydia nodded slowly. 'Or Yeshua's. It matters not. It will be loved and cherished in the sanctuary of Ynys yr Afalon.'

Justin stood in silence for a moment, then he nodded. 'Indeed it will,' he said quietly. He took a step backwards towards the doorway, then another.

She heard him. 'You are leaving me?'

He nodded. 'I have to try and find my friend.'

She raised her head and for the first time stared straight at him. 'I doubt if you will find him.'

He felt his stomach tighten. 'Why?'

'He doesn't mean to be found. That was why he took off the cross and threw it down. He said without it he would be free to travel anywhere. Without it no-one would find him.'

23

'He's still in a coma.' Abi looked at Athena hopelessly. It was four days later and Kier had been transferred from Hereford Hospital back to Addenbrookes, in Cambridge. 'I wanted to go with him but they said there was no point. Bishop David said I should stay here with Cal and Mat. He says I have more thinking to do!' She gave a wry smile. 'David has even been to see my father. I sense there might have been a small rapprochement.'

Athena grinned. 'And what about Justin? Before you left, did he tell you any more of what happened when he did his shamanic thing?'

She shrugged. 'Not much more than before. Just that he has spoken to Lydia. She told him that Kier had followed Flavius to Judea and didn't want to be found. He said there was no point in him trying. Kier had thrown off his cross as a symbol of his intention. Now it is up to the medics to try and bring him back.' She shook her head miserably. 'He might die, Athena, and it's all my fault.'

'And how do you work that out?' They were sitting on the stools in Athena's kitchen, watching rain streaming down the window. Before them were two mugs of coffee and two large Danish pastries, courtesy of Bella who had come in to do an extra morning at the shop so that Abi and Athena could talk.

Abi continued. 'He followed me. He lost control of his psyche because of me.'

'Rubbish. He knew what he was doing, and he lost control of his psyche, as you put it, long ago, from what I hear.'

'You reckon?' Abi looked astonished. 'No, you're wrong. He just hadn't a clue what he was doing. Not a clue!'

'Where is Justin now?' Athena had taken a large bite of Danish and licked the icing off her lips.

'He drove me back to Woodley, then he went home to Wales.'
Abi couldn't quite hide the bleakness in her voice.

'To do what exactly?'

'I don't know. He just said he had to get back.'

Athena studied her companion's face for a moment and
suppressed a knowing smile. So Justin had made another conquest.
'Did he take your crystal?'

Abi shook her head. 'I've got it at the house in my suitcase.
I'm not sure I want to see it any more. The story is told.' She
frowned anxiously. 'You think Justin's going to go after Kier again,
don't you.'

Athena shrugged. 'I wouldn't put it past him.' She looked up
at Abi. 'You must realise he's not the type to give up. He will do
his best for Kier and for those others in the past.' There was a
short silence, as she sipped her coffee, then she glanced up at Abi
again. 'Have you ever heard,' she began cautiously, 'of people
going into what is called a persistent vegetative state?'

Abi nodded.

'And do they think that is what has happened to Kier?'

Abi shrugged. 'They haven't used that term.'

'Well, say it is something like that. You called it a coma. Have
you ever wondered where people's souls have gone while they
lie there?'

'No. You are not trying to tell me that they have gone off into
another world?'

'Why not? It seems perfectly possible to me. There is nothing
physically wrong with Kier, is there. You told me he was breathing
unaided and his heart seems to be working and the brain scan
showed nothing abnormal.'

Abi was silent for a moment, lost in thought. 'You agree with
Justin that he's gone after Flavius and to look for Yeshua. To see
for himself,' she said at last.

Athena took another bite of her pastry. 'In his shoes, I'd go.'

'In his shoes?'

'He's messed up. He's got this amazing power and he is terrified of it. He has lost you – not that he ever had you, of course,'
she added hastily after a glance at Abi's face. 'He has lost his job,
maybe his faith, his home if he's kicked out of the parish and he
has the chance to go adventuring, to slay dragons for the lady
Lydia, and perhaps to meet Jesus face to face.'

'You're saying,' Abi glanced up and gave a watery smile, 'that he's got, what did you call it, "Avalonitis"?'

'Precisely!' Athena leaned across and pushed Abi's plate towards her. 'Eat! Otherwise I shall be tempted to finish it for you and that would be very greedy!'

Mora had not appeared. He had searched for her on several occasions and at last conceded that this was women's magic. But Flavius and Kier, they were men. He should be able to find them. Had Kier caught up with Flavius? And if he had what had happened? Abandoning his latest attempt at travelling in search of them he gazed at the fire, conscious suddenly of the sound of rain against the window and of how remote his house was. Normally he revelled in being alone but today he was terribly aware of the miles of empty mountains and the high moors around him, the black, racing clouds, the brooks, the *nentydd*, turning to torrents as they hurtled down the steep hillsides, the sheer immensity of the coming darkness. Slowly he pushed himself out of the chair and went over to the log basket. A couple of nice dry blocks sent sparks rocketing up the chimney. He went back to his computer and glanced at the screen. Another e-mail from Greg; the two men had been trying to find common ground in their quest to help Kier. Justin's confidences had not as yet extended as far as sharing too many details of his journeying with him, but Abi was another matter. He looked at the phone. His thoughts kept going back to her. He hadn't mentioned Mora's pregnancy to her, nor Lydia's speculation as to the father of the baby. Would she understand? He knew why she was reluctant to look into her Serpent Stone again – she had seen too much terror and bloodshed – but in her shoes he would want to know everything.

It had been hard to part from her, but he could see she had more than enough to deal with without him irritating her further. Did he irritate her? He had thought so. Now he wasn't sure. One moment he thought she liked him and the next . . . He wasn't even sure where she was. She had murmured at one point that she might go straight back to Cambridge to see if her father was all right, though Ben had frowned and shaken his head and said, 'Not yet'. So she was presumably still at Woodley. Waiting. He stared thoughtfully into the flames. Perhaps it was time for an attempt to consolidate brotherly reconciliation. And before that, perhaps, one more journey into the past in the hope of finding Flavius.

Abi had unwrapped the stone and was looking at it a little quizzically. Outside it was dark; the rain had not stopped for three days. Already the levels were flooding. Downstairs in the kitchen Mat and Cal were sitting by the fire with their cocoa and the dogs but she had pleaded exhaustion and come upstairs to bed. Her thoughts kept turning to Justin. He had been disappointed in her determination not to go on with her quest, she could see that, but just for the moment she hadn't been able to face it any more. She was prepared to leave it to him. Until now. Until, realising that if she wanted to see him again she would have to come out of her seclusion and face the unravelling of the story. Taking a deep breath, she picked up the stone and stared into its face.

'So, Mora. Where did you get this thing?' she said out loud. 'Who gave it to you? Who showed you how to use it?'

'Sorcha?' Mora looked up at the figure in the doorway with an incredulous smile of joy. 'I thought you were dead!'

Sorcha came into the house and, at Mora's gesture of welcome, sat down near the fire. She shook her head sadly. 'I should be. I should have stayed. I loved them as though they were my own, but when he killed Gaius, stabbed him in cold blood in front of lady Lydia, I fled.' Tears gathered in her eyes.

'You couldn't have saved him, Sorcha.'

Sorcha shook her head. 'He chose a time when there was no-one there. The men were in the fields or hunting or down to the eel traps. He murdered his own brother with a knife in his chest.' Her voice was husky with pain. 'The lady Lydia is still crazed with grief.' Lydia and Petra were living now in a house in the small settlement of Glaston at the far end of Ynys yr Afalon. It was too soon, Fergos Mor had said, for Petra to decide if she still wanted to train as a druid. He wanted mother and child to have time to recover, to reclaim their lives. 'Lydia's punishment, Flavius told her, was to live, while Gaius died. To remember forever what had happened.'

'Punishment!' Mora echoed. 'For what did he think she needed punishing?'

'She chose his brother.' Sorcha shrugged. 'I have come to ask you to tell the gods what he did. To tell them of the injustice. To tell them of the evil and to ask them to punish him in his turn.' Her face flushed with anger. 'I want his name to echo down the centuries with the story of his betrayal.'

Mora gave a wry smile. 'God,' she hesitated, 'the gods, will know already, Sorcha. They know everything. But my father has told me to tell no-one. He feels we should keep all this to ourselves. For the sake of Yeshua.'

Sorcha shook her head stubbornly. 'No! That is what Flavius wants. He tried to kill Petra so that no-one would know what an amazing healer Yeshua was. If we keep Yeshua's name secret we are doing exactly what Flavius wants.'

'But I can't defy my father,' Mora said anxiously.

Sorcha stared at her. 'Write it down then.'

Mora shook her head. 'You know that is not our way. Everything must be committed to memory.'

'And so, one day, if something happens to this place, all this will be forgotten?' Sorcha stared down at the fire for a moment then she looked up. 'I saw Yeshua. I watched as he healed Petra. He is a great man. Someone so special.' She clasped her hands to her heart. 'And yet in a hundred, a thousand years, people will know nothing of his visit to this land. That's wrong. He chose us. He chose you. He chose the druids to live with and study with from all the people in the world.' She shook her head. 'You cannot allow him to be forgotten, Mora.' She hesitated. 'My aunt lives near the great caverns in the hills. There are stones there which can hold memories. They have been used from ancient times as talismans and sacred tools.'

Mora nodded. 'My father has one,' she said quietly. 'They are as you say objects of great power.'

'If you come with me to my aunt's we will find you one and you can tell it your story. You would not be disobeying your father, but you would be preserving the memory of everything that happened here.' Sorcha smiled. She held out her hand. 'Please. So that one day someone will know the truth.'

* * *

425

'So, that was it,' Abi addressed the crystal in her hand. 'You came from Wookey Hole or Cheddar Caves. Somewhere up there they found a seam of natural crystal in the limestone, and people knew exactly what its properties were.' She gave a shaky laugh. 'You're not even a magic Atlantean stone from deep within the Tor! It wasn't magic at all. They had invented the precursor to the crystal set; the CD; the mobile and two thousand years ago they were calling it an ancient art!' She glanced at the table where her mobile lay amongst the clutter of books. At last she had an excuse to ring him.

He came the next day. They agreed to meet in Glastonbury and Abi chose the coffee shop with the green sofa. 'Of course, as we discussed, there is huge controversy about what exactly a druid's egg was.' Justin was sitting at the table, turning the Serpent Stone over in his hands. He smiled to himself. He was still surprised how much he had missed her and how natural it felt to have her there with him again. They were comfortable together. 'I think this is one. I did wonder if it could have referred to some kind of natural crystal. There are so many theories about it – the main being that it was some kind of whelk egg case! But I can't help thinking this sort of thing is more likely.'

'It would be something of immense power; something to keep very secret, so no-one was supposed to know what they were,' Abi put in. 'Fergus obviously had one, as well. Perhaps the druids used them to store their secrets and if someone finds one, one day, all their hidden teachings will come to light.' She glanced at him. 'I spoke to Bishop David this morning. There is no change in Kier. He is stable and doesn't need a life support machine or anything.'

Justin nodded his head slowly. 'I have made enquiries.' He glanced at her. 'Over there, where he has gone.' He was silent for a moment. 'I have reason to believe he would not want to be called back, even if we could. He will return in his own time, be that a week or a month or twenty years.'

She stared at him in horror. 'And there's nothing you can do?'

'It is his choice, Abi.' He took a deep breath. 'Would you deprive him of the chance to meet Jesus?'

She chewed her lip for a moment. 'I just feel so guilty, as though somehow his unhappiness and panic and unpredictability were my fault.'

'They weren't.' He reached forward and laid his hand over hers. She was going to snatch hers away, then she changed her mind and left it there. For a moment they were silent, then he moved his hand and casually reached for his cup. 'I want to go back to Woodley,' he said at last. 'See if I can't make things up with Mat and there is something we need to do there.'

She glanced at him enquiringly.

'The orchard. I've talked to Greg about it. Romanus needs to be set free. Greg agrees you should do it with me.'

'Me?' She scanned his face thoughtfully and he nodded. 'Prayer. Incense. Druid and Christian together. Let the poor boy go.'

'With Cynan?'

'You think Cynan is still there too?'

She shrugged. 'He felt responsible. Besides Woodley was his special place. Or at least, St Mary's island was.'

He nodded. 'You and I would make a good team, Abi.'

For a moment she froze. She didn't know where to look. He saw her embarrassment and smiled. 'In a spiritual sense, of course. Ghostbusters to the gentry.'

'And to the church?'

'If you say so.'

The orchard was wet and windy, yellow leaves whirling in the air. Mat and Cal had watched them walk across the lawn from the kitchen window then they had turned back to the fire. The meeting with Mat had been fine if a little restrained. The two men had shaken hands and Cal, with a little more colour in her cheeks than was normal had smiled and hugged them both.

Justin took his drum out of his shoulder bag and then a candle holder and a small incense burner. 'I expect wind and rain in my job. More often than not I need several matches.' He grinned at her. 'Say and do whatever you feel is right, Abi. There are no rules for this kind of occasion.'

She reached into her pocket and drew out the Serpent Stone. 'I went up and fetched it before we came out here. I thought it might help to contact them.' She was aware of the rustle and hiss of leaves around them. She watched as, sheltering the flame with the flap of his jacket, he lit the little charcoal block under the incense and sprinkled on a few grains of resin from a small jar.

The blue trail of smoke was whipped away from them. She could smell nothing. As her hand went to the little cross around her neck she closed her eyes.

Romanus was tall for his age and thin, a good-looking boy with brown eyes and a gentle intelligent face. She could see the streaks of blood down his cheek, the worse, more terrible stains on his tunic. Cynan had the druidic tonsure, he was taller, more solid, a sadness in his eyes as though he had always known what his own terrible fate would be. 'Flavius.' She heard the name as a hiss of rain, a rhythm in the gentle drumbeat. 'Flavius must not be allowed to continue his persecution. He must be stopped.'

She stared round. The apple trees were gone. Instead she was standing in an olive grove. She could smell warm earth and fragrant sunshine. Flavius was standing alone with his back to her. Beyond him she could see the red terracotta tiles of a roof and somehow she knew it was his father's house. He had returned home. As he swung to face her she saw the haunted eyes, the face grey with exhaustion and she knew what he was going to do even before he drew the short sword. He held it up. Had his father guessed what he had done? Was the guilt of the blood of his own brother and his brother's son too much to bear? He was hesitating. He was thinking of his duty to his Emperor. His knuckles whitened round the sword hilt as he lowered it, the blade flashing in the warm Etruscan sun. His doubt was going. She saw his jaw grow firm, his eyes hard.

'Do it,' Abi whispered. 'The voice of thy brother's blood crieth from the ground!'

She saw his eyes widen as he looked round. The olive leaves rustled in the wind and small dust eddies rose and spun around his sandaled feet.

'Who's there?' he called. The sword was raised again now, pointing towards her although she didn't think he could see her. Then she realised he could. He was remembering the days of his youth when he had consulted a sibyl near the Temple of the Vestals in Rome and bought charms to win Lydia and then curses when they didn't work. When he had gone to ask for his money back she had spitefully told him that she had seen in her scrying bowl his doom in a woman's eyes, the eyes which were now gazing at him from a different time and place.

'Lydia?' he called. His voice was harsh with terror.

Abi felt herself take a step forward and she saw his face freeze. 'Mora?'

'Do it!' She wasn't sure if she had spoken or if the voice was someone else's, but the words seemed to come from her. 'The voice of thy brother's blood is crying out for revenge.'

He gave a sob. 'No!'

'Do it!'

Behind him she saw a man's figure through the trees. Flavius turned and saw it too. 'Father!' It was a broken whisper and in it Abi knew his father had discovered what he had done to his brother. 'I'm sorry.'

His movement was almost too quick to follow. He reversed the sword, gripped the hilt in both hands, and drove it with every last ounce of strength he possessed into his own stomach. For a moment he stood, his face wiped of expression, his eyes huge and glassy, then he fell forward onto the blade.

The wind had grown stronger. She could feel the rain, cold, on her face. The drumming had stopped and slowly she realised that Justin had taken her in his arms. 'I killed him,' she whispered. 'I killed him.'

He shook his head. 'He killed himself.'

'You saw?' She stared at him. She had begun to shiver violently.

'I saw. It may have been your destiny to push him to do the decent thing, but if you hadn't, then it would have been his own father.' Justin released her for a moment, pulled off his jacket and wrapped it round her shoulders then he put his arm round her again. 'Look.' He pointed off into the trees.

In the distance she saw Romanus and Cynan standing side by side. The older man put his arm round the younger in a gesture mirroring their own. He raised his other hand in acknowledgement. Then they were gone.

'They are at rest,' Justin said quietly.

'I can't believe I did it,' she whispered. 'I urged a man to kill himself.'

'You did what had to be done.' Justin steered her back towards the garden. 'You must not feel guilty. This was your destiny. Ask Ben. Or Greg. Or your bishop. You were the instrument of fate. There was unfinished business to be done and only you could sort

429

it out. You have acted as a very special catalyst in all of this, Abi. You are a healer and a priest. You, of all the women who have owned that stone have been able to resolve the anguish of this story and you were brought here to this house to do it. It can't have been coincidence that you were brought here.'

'By a bishop from Priddy.' She gave a watery smile.

He stopped again and released her. 'Flavius thought you were Mora.'

'I don't know why. I don't look like her. Do I?' She glanced up at him.

'Ah.' He hesitated, then he said, 'Do you know how your mother originally came to have the Serpent Stone?'

She nodded. 'I told you. It was handed down through the family, daughter to daughter.'

'For how long?'

She gave him a wry smile. 'For two thousand years? You really believe that? I wonder how many generations that is.'

He gave a small shake of his head. 'We must assume, I think, that Mora's child was a girl.'

She looked at him in astonishment and he nodded. 'I think you probably are her direct descendant. She was pregnant at the end.'

'With Cynan's child?' She glanced back at the orchard.

He saw the intense anxiety in her eyes as she turned back to him. Slowly he put his arm round her again. 'Who else's would it have been?'

Epilogue

Kieran smiled at the woman he was sitting next to. She had shared her food with him and passed over a skin containing asses' milk. They had been listening with crowds of other people to Jesus as he stood on the hillside, in the shade of the ancient olive trees. It had been months since Kier had left Britain. He had followed Flavius, making his long weary way to Rome, where Flavius had called in to see his parents, staying but a few days before resuming his journey across the Empire towards Galilee. At some point Flavius had doubled back and Kier had heard rumours that he had begun to retrace his steps towards his father's house. He didn't follow him. Somehow now, it didn't matter.

Jesus had been talking for a long time and he was tired. Kier could see the weariness on his face, but also the gentleness as people queued to approach him, to ask for his blessing. 'Are you going up to speak to him?' The woman glanced across at him. She had brought her daughter, a child of about five who had a twisted leg. 'Come with us. Help me carry her.'

They waited in line for a long time, but at last they shuffled closer until they were standing before him. Kier saw him smile at the woman, and put his hand on the child's head. 'She will be well. Put her down. Let her walk. Your child is very pretty.'

Kier realised suddenly that Jesus was looking at him; he assumed he was the girl's father. 'No. She's not mine.' He was so overawed he was stammering. 'I've come from far away to see you. From Britain. Avalon.'

He saw Jesus' eyes narrow in puzzlement. For a moment he hadn't recognised the name. 'Ynys yr Afalon,' he repeated at last and he smiled. 'You come from the druids. From Mora?'

Kieran hesitated, then he nodded.

'Bless you.' Jesus raised his hand and touched Kieran lightly on the shoulder. Behind him people were pushing closer, trying to attract his attention. For a few long seconds Kier held his gaze, then Jesus smiled again. 'Time to go home, Kier,' he said softly, 'there are people waiting for you.' Then he turned away and was swallowed in the crowd.

Author's Note

I first heard about the coming of Jesus to Somerset from my father who was at prep school in Weston-super-Mare. He remembers it being talked about and accepted as part of the history of the West Country. The story always intrigued me, but I never quite came to grips with it until I got to know Glastonbury

Through the last two millennia, probably for its entire existence, Glastonbury, by whatever name, has enchanted and captivated everyone who has been there and I was no exception. There is something very special about this place and I hope I have managed to convey something of that specialness and magic in this book. The town's two greatest claims to fame are its association with King Arthur and the story of Jesus. (And, of course, a succeeding chapter about the return of Joseph after Jesus' crucifixion). There has been almost too much information to use for research. I could have read for months and still not reached the end. The main books I have used I have listed in the bibliography on my website and of course I have used my own experiences and notes and photos and the information which has been so generously passed on by the many people I have spoken to while researching this story. One could study and dream in this fabulous landscape forever.

I would never have got to know Glastonbury and explored it so thoroughly without the help of my uncle Tony Rose and his wife, Daphne. Daphne, who has lived there for twenty-seven years, has been a mine of information and introduced me to so many people who have given their unstinting help. Foremost amongst these were Tim Hopkinson-Ball, an authority on the history of the town, and especially the abbey, (and who was noble enough on one occasion to climb the Tor with me) and Willa Sleath, a former Guardian and Trustee of the Chalice Well. I am also grateful to Frances Howard-Gordon who gave me a copy of her book, *Glastonbury Maker of Myths* and talked about the vibes!

The legend of Jesus and Joseph in the West Country captivates even those it doesn't convince. To write about it and put it into a Church of England frame has proved a little daunting, but I would like to thank the various members of the church who have given me their advice and opinions (and yes, even one bishop). None of them had actually read the novel but I hope they find they can enjoy it. I found myself inclined within the text to write long treatises on church history and the Anglican hierarchy, most of which I then cut out! Any mistakes and idiosyncrasies are very much my own and for them I apologise. One person I would single out however for his help on the problems and vicissitudes of being a curate and on Jesus in a druid and pagan context is Mark Townsend who was very generous with his advice.

Once more I would like to thank my wonderful team at HarperCollins, who together with Susan Opie and Lucy Ferguson have done wonders yet again with the manuscript, and Alice Moss who arranges all the publicity. And thank you as ever to my wonderful agent Carole Blake who somehow makes it all possible and to AJ who thought of the title!

For further notes and information please see my website: www.barbara-erskine.com.

Chronology

Pontius Pilate Roman Governor of Judea AD 26–36

Emperors: Augustus 27BC-AD14
           Tiberius AD14–37

BC

c4   Jesus born (Strange to think the entire BC/AD system of dates was based on a miscalculation of the date of Jesus' birth by a 6th-century monk called Dionysius Exiguus or Dennis the Little, who is credited with inventing the Anno Domini system)

        Massacre of Innocents

AD

c28   Baptism of Jesus by John the Baptist

c30   Crucifixion

c63   Joseph of Arimathea supposedly returned to Glastonbury with the Chalice and the cruets containing Christ's blood and sweat and set up a church there based on 12 donated hides of land

Chronology of the story

BC

22/21	Flavius and Gaius born
15	Lydia born

AD

2	Gaius and Lydia married
6	Gaius and Lydia to Damascus
8	Flavius arrives in Caesarea
10	Petronilla born
12	Gaius takes his family to Britannia
13	Family moves to Glastonbury
13	Romanus born
25–26	Jesus in Glastonbury